# DESCENT

# ALSO BY J LJACKOLA

## FANTASY ROMANCE

**Unbound Prophecy Universe**

**Unbound Prophecy**

*Ascension*

*Descent*

*Surfacing*

*Submerged*

*Riven*

*Adrift*

**Unbound Kingdom**

*Severed Kingdom,*

*Cursed Kingdom*

*Prophesied Kingdom*

*Unbound Kingdom (the trilogy omnibus)*

**Unbound Prophecy Prequels**

*Orlaina*

---

**Wicked Hues Series**

*The Forgotten Hues of Skye*

*The Coveted Hues of Skye*

*The Shattered Shades of Crimson*

*The Impossible Shades of Crimson*

*The Endless Shadows of Pete*

---

**Wicked and Fated Universe**

**Wicked Gods**

*Trial of the Gods*

*Tournament of the Gods*

**Wicked Warlocks**

*Curse of the Broken Prince*

*Fate of the Broken Queen*

**Wicked Shadows**

*Mark of the Shadow*

*Touch of the Torch*

FAIRYTALE INSPIRED

**Wicked and Twisted Tales**

*Of Candy and Betrayal*

*Of Petals and Lies*

*Of Giants and Betrayal*

MAFIA ROMANCE

**Wicked Cravings**

*Obsessive Cravings*

*Forbidden Cravings*

*Hostile Cravings*

*Unhinged Cravings*

# DESCENT

UNBOUND PROPHECY
BOOK TWO

## JL JACKOLA

tivshe

Library of Congress Control Number 2020902714

Paperback ISBN 978-1-960784-18-6

Electronic ISBN 978-1-954175-54-9

Fourth Edition

Distributed by Tivshe Publishing

Printed in the United States of America

Cover design by Dark Queen Designs

Map design by C. A. Jackola

Visit www.jljackola.com

# AUTHOR'S NOTE

Thank you for continuing to read the Unbound Prophecy series. Descent continues Violissa and Snow's journey and while it is still tame compared to my more recent books, Descent begins the step down the darker parts of the prophecy's path. You will see instances of nonconsensual touching, suggestions of sexual assault, and more episodes of violence as Tynan falls further under the influence of the Darkness.

None of this behavior comes from Sinow who remains faithful to and protective of Violissa.

J. L.

*To my parents for enriching my imagination,*
*my husband for encouraging it,*
*and my children for setting it free.*

SACRI
TENEBRON
BANISHED REALM
SACRI

GROVES
CIRILLIA

# PART ONE
# RESTLESSNESS

# CHAPTER I

Keary approached the door with apprehension. He knocked cautiously, unsure of the reaction it would trigger, but silence was his only answer. He had been dreading this moment, but he had no choice. Someone needed to bring Sinow back from the edge, and he was the best one to do it. Even if it risked Sinow's wrath. He drew a breath and braced himself before knocking a second time.

The sound of his knuckles against the wood echoed through the corridor. It seemed an eternity before he heard the growled "Go away" through the still-closed door. He had expected the response and so paid it no mind. He'd only knocked out of respect. Opening the door, he entered the room, taking a moment to let his eyes adjust to the darkness within. The sconces in the hallway emitted only enough light to cover the room's entryway. Blackness engulfed him as he moved forward and closed the door behind him with a flick of his hand.

"Leave me, Keary. I said to go away, and I meant it."

"I heard what you said, but I'm ignoring you," Keary replied curtly.

He continued his path across the room, remembering it well

enough to know the way to the windows. With a flip of his hand, he threw the long window hangings aside to let what remained of the pre-evening light flood the room.

Since the day the spell had torn Violissa from them, the days had grown shorter. The Councils had noticed it a few years after the incident, and since then, they'd calculated that about two hours of daylight had vanished. No one had an explanation for it except that perhaps the Fates were punishing them for Sinow's errors, as if losing Violissa wasn't punishment enough.

Hidden in his quarters to drown his misery and guilt, Sinow had no knowledge of the phenomenon, which was why Keary was there. Chosen by the Councils to face their king, Keary was ready to wake Sinow and ensure he opened his eyes to the threat that faced their world.

Once he let the light into the room, his king's ire eclipsed him. Keary disregarded it and turned to face Sinow, arms folded across his chest.

Little remained of the man he'd known, and the defeat he saw in his king saddened him. Circles hollowed out Sinow's eyes. His hair was unkempt and matted, his shoulders rounded. The fire that had once consumed him was nowhere to be found. In its place remained the insanity that marred his noble line. Only this time, that insanity was self-driven by a sense of defeat and hopelessness.

"When was the last time you shaved, Sinow? Or bathed, for that matter?"

Sinow glared at him, the intensity of those black eyes the only sign that hope remained.

"What do you want, Keary?"

Keary studied him, taking in the long ebony hair and full growth of beard upon his face, and sighed. The man who sat in the chair before him was no longer the man he had known. This man was a shell of what Sinow had once been. How had it come to this?

"You know why I'm here, Sinow."

"Then you may as well leave."

"No, it's time you came to terms with it."

The black in his king's eyes darkened slightly, challenging him, but Keary did not back down. He couldn't. Too much was at stake.

"She's gone, Sinow. It's been two hundred years, and neither you nor we have found a way to bring her back."

"Tread lightly, Keary," Sinow snarled.

"I won't. You need to face the facts. Hiding in this room will not bring her back. For Fates' sake, Sinow, we worried about the intensity of your search for her when we first lost her, but at least then you had some life in you. Now you've sequestered yourself in your room, refusing to rule, refusing to come out. It's like you've given up on life and are contemplating giving yourself to the Fates..." He trailed off as he realized that was exactly it.

Left speechless, he gaped at Sinow. What had come of his king? This man, whom he'd called friend, who had once ruled their kingdom with power and terror, was nothing more than a broken remnant of what he had once been. A man whom he'd watched wither away.

"Are you truly mad, Sinow?"

Sinow put his head in his hands and replied, "I can't live without her, Keary. You've no idea how empty I am."

"Ha, you did fine for hundreds of years before you met her."

"Yes, but I could always sense her. I always knew she was there waiting for me. Now—"

"Now only the Fates know where she is, Sinow, and they're not talking. Now, you have two kingdoms to rule and people who are wondering where their king is. Councils are not rulers for a reason, Sinow. We need you to come back to us. Our world has changed since that day." He gestured toward the window. "Our days have grown shorter. The cycle of our very existence is out of balance, and it is affecting our world. The Councils need your leadership, and the people need a king." He considered his words before he added, "Violissa wouldn't want you locked away in here."

"You have no idea what she would want."

Ebony eyes bore into him, their intensity unnerving to anyone but Keary, who would not cower to them.

"Nor do you, but I know she would want her people cared for and ruled properly, neither of which you have been doing. It's time to come to terms with the fact that you've lost her."

"Go away, Keary, before I force you out."

Keary sighed. At least if he made Sinow use his powers to punish him, he'd know his king was truly still in there somewhere.

"Leave it to the Fates, Sinow. Maybe they're bringing her back. Maybe they just need time."

Perhaps a little dose of optimism would motivate him. Keary wasn't confident it would do anything, but one could always hope. Keary crossed the room and stopped to look back one last time at his old friend before he closed the door behind him, unable to look at his defeated king any longer.

# CHAPTER 2

The door closed softly, but Sinow did not see it. Instead, he sat staring at the floor as he frequently did for hours on end. Light from the windows streamed in, and he raised his eyes to it, squinting at the brightness. It had been years since he had looked beyond the interior of his room. Years longer since he had walked in the sun. The well of anguish was too great, and if he contemplated letting anything remotely pleasant back into his life, the Darkness would surface and drag him under.

He leaned back in his chair, thinking over what Keary had said. Two centuries. It seemed impossible that so much time had passed since he had last seen Violissa. Since the day that had changed everything and left him raw and bleeding. Unable to heal the wound in his chest that never seemed to scab. He ran his hands through his hair as he recalled the first day that he'd locked himself away. Given up, not on Violissa but on ruling. On living.

Cyric had come to him, weariness mirrored on his face, and told him they'd run out of ideas. There was nothing left to try, no book left untouched, no spell left untapped. They were giving up, leaving it to the Fates, just as Keary had said moments ago.

Sinow had lost his temper, destroyed the room in his anger and stormed off to be alone, which was where he'd been since. The Councils didn't know the pain that had eviscerated him when he'd lost her. The expansive void that remained. How his soul had ripped in half, leaving an emptiness he could never replenish. There was no rational reason for the sensation, for him to be so devastated, but he was, and no matter how he tried to eradicate it, there was no escaping it.

Keary was right. He'd lived without her for centuries before they'd met, but there had always been a constant knowledge that she was out there. The deep, unrelenting desire for her had not erupted until the day they had met in the grove, but he had always sensed her waiting for him.

That day had been the tipping point, and the need had only grown from there. After their time in the Dream Realm, it had deepened until there wasn't a minute, an hour, a day when he didn't long for her. She was like a craving he couldn't satisfy, and only with his ascension had that need numbed, buried under his Dark powers but still there, brought back to the surface every time she was near.

If the Darkness still had him in its clutches, then the loss would be easier to bear, but it didn't. She had brought him out from under it that day, balancing the powers in him, and now there was no escape from the constant agony that came from knowing she was beyond his reach. By releasing his true self, she had cursed him to experience the never-ending loss of being without her.

Where the Dream Realm had given him a taste of her, an inkling of what they could be together, their kiss that last day had given him a mirror into her soul, into her true emotions for him. It had been a complete relinquishment of herself to him, unlike what he'd experienced in the Dream Realm. There the Fates had deceived them, feeding their desires only on a physical level.

But the kiss she had given freely with no interference from the Fates, and to this day, he could still feel her lips on his, taste her skin, her mouth. It had filled him like nothing in life ever had, and he desperately longed to experience it again, to have her back in his arms so he could hold on to her for eternity. He hadn't realized how much he needed her, how much he loved her until that day, and now she was gone, had been gone for so long. Too long.

Worry strangled him. Questions pummeled him. The unknown of what had happened to her and where the spell had sent her terrified him. There were no answers to tell him if she was safe, if she was trying to find her way home. He didn't know if she even remembered who she was or who he was. The thought gutted him, but not as deeply as knowing she was powerless. That someone or something could hurt her, and he could do nothing to stop it from happening. The endless tide of questions and worries had weighed on him until he was nearly out of his mind.

As if to torture himself, he had replayed the memories of that day repeatedly in his head. Recalling the confusion in her eyes, the doubt that poured from her. Doubt about him and his emotions for her, and Tynan had fed that doubt.

Sinow squeezed his hands into tight fists at the thought of his brother. He preferred not to let those thoughts in. Preferred to think of Tynan as dead rather than banished. Perhaps he had died, giving himself over to the Fates after so many centuries. It would be no loss, save for the fact that Sinow had not had the satisfaction of sending him back to the Fates.

He wiped his hand over his face, thinking as he often did, that Violissa had taken that doubt with her to wherever she was and likely still carried it with her. He couldn't erase the surprise on her face, the question in her voice, the accusation she had spoken. That he had tricked her. That his kiss had been false.

Sinow ran his hand through his hair, noticing how long and unkempt it had become. Resting his head in his hands, he continued to think about what Keary had said. The Councils were giving up, but he could never give up the hope of finding her. She was out there, and he would find her, explain what had really happened, and bring her home. That connection they had, the fated binding, told him she was alive.

He couldn't detect her presence as he had throughout their lives, but something deep within him still sensed her spirit. Every so often, he would lose the connection, and pain would tear through his chest, but just as quickly as it vanished, it would return, as swift as the beat of his heart. He'd worked tirelessly trying to draw on that connection. Tried repeatedly after he had locked himself away, but nothing worked. Eventually, he was content to simply sit and close his eyes, letting that small sense of her overtake him. That was how Keary had found him today.

He lifted his head and looked out the window, where Keary had drawn the blinds back. He squinted as his eyes adjusted to what remained of the sun as it completed its descent, giving way to the moons. Was Keary right? Were they really losing daylight? The power of their world had been out of balance for so long that perhaps they had adjusted to it. After Tynan had bound Violissa's power, the shift in balance had been immediate. It remained after her disappearance, and as the years went by, it had worsened.

Bound to their queen's power, her Council's power was slowly weakening. Her magic had fed their own, and without it, theirs would continue to weaken. The world needed a balance of Light and Dark. He'd learned that when he was young, his father often reaffirming it as they had drawn closer to the day he was to meet Violissa. He had never fully realized just what those words had meant until now. The world was leaning too much to the Dark, and if the days were truly getting shorter, then that balance was being disrupted on a deeper level than any of them had imagined. The Fates only knew what would happen next.

"The Fates only know," he mumbled, standing up and stretching. "They know everything and see everything."

Slowly, he lowered his arms from the stretch and straightened his back. Change overcame him physically as realization dawned on him. He stood taller, his aura strengthening, his power swirling around him.

He looked up and said, "And you've known all along. You know, don't you? All this time, and we've been looking in the wrong places." The knowledge of what he needed to do became apparent.

Moving across the room to a dresser that held a basin and mirror, he looked at his reflection and laughed. "No wonder they're concerned. They probably think I've lost it like Grandfather."

He conjured some water into the basin and splashed his face. It was time to clean up and be a king again. He had negotiating to do, and he was ready to rescue his queen.

# CHAPTER 3

*K*eary!

Keary jumped as Sinow's voice barked in his head. It had been so long since his king had used enaigne he had almost forgotten how it sounded.

*Now!*

*This is different*, he thought as he shifted back to Sinow's chambers. Expecting to find his king still sitting in the chair, his eyes went wide to see Sinow up and pacing the floor.

"My liege?" he asked hesitantly, afraid of the response he'd get. He took in the now shaven face and the tamed, shortened hair. In the brief time he'd been gone, Sinow had made a complete reversal. He again looked like the king he had once been. Seeing the formidable figure standing before him should have made him happy, but instead, Keary worried about the reason for the sudden turnaround. The words he'd spoken to Sinow had not been that inspiring.

"I'm going to find her," Sinow stated, his words terse.

"I thought that was what we've been trying to do for the last two centuries," Keary replied, hoping his tone didn't sound too condescending.

"We have been, but in all the wrong ways. The spells, the books, the potions, the search for cracks in our world that might lead to another world. It's all been wrong. I am the one who needs to find her. The Fates know exactly where she is, and they are going to lead me to her."

Keary gaped at Sinow, trying to find the right response. "You've truly gone mad, haven't you?"

When Sinow didn't answer him, he continued. "You can't be serious."

"Dead serious, Keary. The Fates know where she is, and they're going to send me there."

This was unbelievable. Sinow had gone over the edge, and now Keary needed to bring him back to reality. To think he actually believed he could summon the Fates.

"Ha!" he blurted, unable to contain his reaction. "You can't just call for the Fates and expect them to answer, Sinow. Regardless of whether you're king, they won't do your bidding."

"I don't expect them to do my bidding, Keary. Don't be ridiculous. But I will ask them to send me after her, no matter the cost."

Keary looked at him, concern blatant on his face. "And what if the cost is everything?"

"Then they'll get everything."

Alarmed, Keary responded, "Everything? Is she worth everything, Sinow?"

Sinow looked at him for a long time, and Keary wondered if he was contemplating what to say. After an elongated silence, Keary said, "Sinow, answer me. Is she worth it?"

"You know the answer, Keary. You know what will happen if she never returns. This isn't just about me."

"That's not what it sounds like, Sinow. You're willing to risk leaving your people, her people, our world without a ruler, to go after her?"

"The risk is the same whether I do or don't, and you know that."

Keary stopped, his creased eyes slowly turning darker with the heaviness of the situation. He knew; they all did. It was the unspoken fact to which no one wanted to put a voice. If she never returned, there would be no heir to either throne. The Light line would end, as would the Dark. There was a constant to the life of every king. For each king, there was only one woman destined to bear the king a child. One mate, one child.

There were other women, of course. Dark kings were notorious for their sexual needs, but those women would never marry the king. It was rare enough for a woman to survive a night with a Dark king. Dark power had a way of escaping during those times, and the damage was irreversible.

Only the king's mate would have the strength to carry a child of power. Kings recognized their mates on sight—they carried a distinct aura only the king could recognize. But that day carried mixed emotions. Although the mate would bear the next heir, every mate died in childbirth. While heirs weren't born with active powers, magic still formed in the womb. The sheer force of the magic within the child's core was enough to kill the mother.

If lucky, her heart would wear out from the strain and simply stop. Mothers of Light children received that gentle death. The Fates dealt a crueler hand to those who bore Dark heirs. Sinow's mother's death was so violent the king had removed the entire wing of the castle to purge the memory from his head. Of course, Sinow had been unique; no other child had been born with powers like he had been. Only Violissa. Any mother of a Dark heir died cruelly, but Sinow's mother had suffered the worst.

As Violissa was Sinow's mate, there would be no other. There never had been for him. Different from his predecessors, he had desired only Violissa and so had never taken another. She was the Fates' choice for him, and whatever power bound them kept Sinow from even considering another woman. Even if he forced himself to take another, which Keary doubted he could, there would never be a child. With Violissa gone, their chance of an heir for either throne was gone.

Not only did Sinow's sanity depend on getting Violissa back, but the fate of their world depended on it. Without the ruling powers, the Councils' powers would fade, balance would turn to chaos, and their world would fall apart.

Looking over at the still open window, knowing the shortened day would end sooner than it had the day before, it was clear the chaos had already begun.

"What do you plan to do?" he asked Sinow.

"Violissa is the only one with whom the Fates have spoken." Keary noticed the slight cringe when Sinow spoke her name. "I'll go somewhere that bears her essence, somewhere that only belonged to her, hoping if I surround myself in it, I can then draw on what remains of her to call them."

"You're going to her castle," stated Keary.

"Yes, but only to her room. The essence of her Council contaminates the rest of her castle. Her room, however..." He paused, and Keary saw the pain reflected in his eyes as a memory took hold. His eyes were distant for a moment, then he looked down briefly and continued, "Her room was hers alone and so holds no other essence but what remains of her."

Keary waited a moment to speak, uncertain what to say. Sinow sounded like a madman; there was no possible way he could think this would work. But the hope he was clinging to was enough for Keary to disregard the insanity of the idea and let him go. If it didn't work, however, would it leave Sinow in worse shape? He didn't have an answer, but he said a quick prayer to the Fates that they would help his king. They needed this to work, no matter how insane the prospect of it was.

"What do you need from me?" he asked Sinow.

"I need you to inform the Council. There's no need to tell the entire Light Council, but those who are here should know. If this works, then you can tell the others. They'll be concerned when they notice the shift in power."

"Do you truly think it will work, Sinow?"

"I must believe it will, Keary. It's all I have left to hold on to."

Keary nodded. "Good luck, my friend." He extended his arm and grasped his king's in the familiar way of their people. Sinow grasped his back, acknowledging with a nod.

Backing away, Sinow said, "Goodbye, Keary."

In a blink, he was gone with his shift. Nothing but the slight stir of air remained. Keary looked to the sky and said another quick prayer, then quietly left the room, unaware it would be the last time he'd ever see it.

# CHAPTER 4

Sinow shifted quietly into Violissa's room. He didn't worry about her Council. Even if they sensed his presence, he knew they'd leave him be. The two realms had been at peace since the day of her disappearance. He had released them from the Banished Realm the day Tynan had cast them there and forged an alliance with them that had grown deeper as the search for Violissa lengthened.

With them, he'd ruled Cirillia, leaning on them to understand the differences between their two lands. He ruled fairly and considered Violissa in any decision involving her realm, not wanting to disturb the natural ways of her people. The disruption her disappearance had caused was hard enough on them.

He'd stayed out of Cirillia and ruled from a distance, knowing his presence would strike unnecessary fear in them. Raised to fear their king and his Darkbearers, the people of Tenebron understood that way of life, but there was no need to rule Cirillia the same way. The Light Council assured him their people lived a life of peace and unbelievable innocence. So, he had kept his distance and ruled from afar, letting the Lightbearers be his voice.

As so, he had not set foot in Violissa's castle. The thought of entering it brought the reality of her disappearance to a point with which he had not been comfortable. Keeping himself away from anything that had to do with her, anything that remotely reminded him of her, had made it easier to bear. Now, as he stood in her room, the longing surfaced. The same unending desire to have her back had held him hostage since she'd disappeared. Scraping his hands through his hair, he pushed the emotions aside, and with their quieting, contemplated the madness of what he was attempting. To think the Fates would listen to his call. Better yet, listen to his demands. Rubbing his temples, he thought just maybe he had lost his mind again.

*Well, I'm here. There's no turning back now.*

With a sigh, he glanced around the room. Reminders of Violissa surrounded him. The last time he'd been here was the night that had started his descent into this never-ending nightmare. He breathed in the scent of lilac that still clung to the air even after all these centuries. His pulse quickened at the smell. Eyes closed, he pictured her, something he had avoided doing because it only led to an ache that pounded through his body like strikes of a hammer.

Bracing himself against the wall, he opened his eyes again and forced himself to walk through the room. He had ordered it to remain untouched, and her Council had obliged, leaving it there to sit, frozen in time as if waiting for her return. Shafts of light from the full moons spilled through the drawn curtains, illuminating the specks of dust that danced in the air as he moved. He ran his hand across the vanity, which held a silver-backed brush, long golden strands of hair spreading from its teeth. Her hair.

He picked one up gently, closing his hands in a tight grip around it, as if doing so would bring her back. A chair sat near the window, and Sinow imagined her curled up in it, book in hand. He couldn't stop the smile that tugged at his lips. At the opening of a long closet lay a lilac dress, crumpled where she must have slipped out of it, likely too distracted with the war to pick it up. A layer of dirt still clung to the hem.

He walked back toward the bed, thoughts of the last time he'd seen her in it running through his mind, but this time, no smile pulled at his mouth. The memory of what the situation had forced him to give up that night resurfaced, marring any chance of fond memories.

"You linger too long in memories, Dark Child," he heard a woman say behind him.

There was no need to turn to know she was a Fate, likely the same who had visited Violissa.

"We know what you seek. Tell us why we should oblige your wish," a male voice added.

So, he had drawn the attention of two Fates. Turning to face them, he hoped it was not an ill omen.

Sinow regarded the two, both of whom had taken mortal form. The woman, with long silver hair, straight as a mare's mane, had the green eyes of the Elvin. There was no question the man was of Sinow's bloodline. Dark power swirled around him, his black eyes speaking of an ageless knowledge that belied his status as a Fate.

Out of respect, Sinow bowed, then stood tall and strong, before he answered, "Because I need her."

The man stepped forward, anger seething in his eyes. "But you lost her. The two of you foolishly disregarded all we offered, and you lost her. Just because you now realize the error of your ways is no reason for us to change the course you have set for yourselves."

"This is not the course we chose. Tynan made that decision, and it was Tynan who brought us to this point."

"Blaming Tynan for your mistakes does not solve the problem, Sinow," said the woman, her voice like a soft breeze. "Violissa took the first step from your destiny, and you let her. Both too scared to trust the path ahead. Now you ask for our help, ask that we change the path your actions rewrote for you."

Sinow ran his hand across his face in frustration. Everything they said was true. He could refute none of it. He and Violissa had left the door open for Tynan's treason, and he had taken that opening and widened it while they had played games with the prophecy.

Exhaling, he looked between the two Fates. "Violissa and I are both to blame for our situation. You are correct, and if I could go back and undo it all, I would in a heartbeat." The words were vulnerable, and he detested any show of weakness, but this was not the time for pride. "But that is beyond even your power, so I ask that you let me bring her back. I need her, and our world needs her. Our world is out of balance. I feel it deep in my core, and that balance is shifting every day. Even the sun and moons reflect it. The days have shortened, you know that."

Pity sat in the eyes of the female Fate, and as much as it rubbed against the Darkness in him, he did not turn from it. Everything was riding on convincing the Fates to help him. If they chose not to, he didn't know what he would do.

She opened her mouth to speak, but the male Fate spoke first.

"You are bold, child." He stood taller, arms crossed over his chest, eyes daring Sinow to fight back. It took all his force, but Sinow kept himself in check, knowing if he crossed them, he would never receive the help he sought.

"You think we don't know these things? There is no question the balance has tilted to the Dark, and that tilt worsens with each passing century. Have you not noticed her Lightbearers grow weaker?" His tone carried an edge now, and Sinow fisted his hands to avoid reacting. "No, of course you haven't. Instead, you lock yourself away from the gifts we've given, from the world you rule, pitying your situation and mourning what you let slip from your fingers. The balance shifts because their queen is gone. The Dark slowly fills the void and will continue until this world lives in total Darkness."

Sinow's power pulsed with the rise of his anger, and the Fate glared at him as if daring him to use it. He clamped it down, knowing it would only destroy his chances if he let it slip free.

"Then you have even more reason to send me after her. I can bring her home and restore the balance. Send me to find her and let me make this right."

The Fates looked at each other for a prolonged time, and he thought maybe they were speaking in enaigne. Silently debating what to do with him. The thudding of his heart with each second that passed seemed to echo through the quiet room.

Turning her attention back to him, the female said, "We will send you."

The sigh of relief that escaped him was almost too loud, and he chastised himself for reacting prematurely. There was bound to be some price they would demand of him. A price he would pay, no matter how steep.

"He needs to be punished. They both do. I warned you we could not give him this so easily," the man said through clenched teeth. His Dark power seeped around him, and Sinow braced himself, knowing this Fate was the one who held his future in his hands. Who would determine the payment for the woman's kindness.

"We have punished them enough. All of us decided that."

"Not all. I do not agree that their punishment has warranted our interference. I thought I made it clear I would not agree to this unless there were conditions."

The female let out an exasperated exhale, then gave him a slight nod.

Sinow wasn't certain they expected to give him this much insight into their world. These were the Fates, the deities of their world, with the power to take his magic and his life in less time than it would take him to blink. Just standing here with them was a blessing, but to hear them discuss his fate and Violissa's, their role in punishing them for not following the prophecy was awe-inducing.

He waited as the female responded, contemplating her appearance. No record existed of the Fates or what they looked like. There was only speculation claiming there were Fates who followed the Light ways and had created the Cirillians and those who followed the Dark ways and created Tenebron. But there was no mention of a female in their histories.

She pursed her lips, her emerald eyes growing darker. Those eyes reminded him so much of Violissa's that it hurt. Eyes she had inherited from her mother. The Elvin princess. Which led him to question whether this Fate was Elvin.

His thoughts stalled when she replied to the male Fate, "You and your brothers made it very clear. That does not mean I agree."

"You don't need to agree. Now explain his punishment so we can return."

She bristled, and Sinow wondered at the dynamic between these two. There was a story there that drove his curiosity, but one he would never be privy to.

Turning back to him, she said, "We will send you after her, but it will not be easy."

Hope bloomed, a swelling sensation filling his chest. "I'll face any challenge you give me. Just tell me how to find her. Is she in another realm?" Sinow asked hastily.

"You may regret that to which you have just agreed," she said, her eyes growing sad. "She is in another world, far from ours and not within our reach."

"Another world?"

"Another world within a different universe. There are others like us who created their own worlds with their own rules. Not all of our kind were as generous as we were to our people."

"Get on with it, Orlaina," the male snapped.

She shot him a look, her irises turning a deep sage. Sinow made note of the name he had not heard before.

"She is in the human realm. It is a place very different from ours. One ruled by a being who does not trust his people with magic as we do. His world is a place where no magic exists and, as so, you will be beyond our powers. I have bargained access for you, but it will be brief, and it is all he will allow."

His hope rose, and he folded his arms over his chest to stay the nervous excitement that coursed through him. "That should be enough. All I need to do is find her, and I can bring her home."

She shook her head, and his confidence faltered. "She is powerless in this world. Mortal yet immortal. She lives and dies as a mortal of their world, living life after life. The spell has taken advantage of her weakness and woven its way into her mind, warping it. She has no memory of who she is or was. No memory of you. It will not be as easy as you think."

"Enough, Orlaina." Curt and hard, the male interrupted her. "Here are your conditions. We will send you to this world and tie your lifeline to hers. You will be mortal just as she is—dying when she dies, reborn when she is reborn." Sinow's excitement shriveled, replaced with a sense of dread. "Your memories taken just as hers are. We can give you one chance every lifetime during which you will both meet. That is all the magic permitted."

It was enough. As long as he could find her, their fated bond would ensure she returned with him. The dread faded, and an urgency took over.

He wanted the Fate to stop talking so he could find her, but he continued, "Your memories will return once you have both awakened, and you will have three days from that time to convince her to return with you. If you fail, she will be gone from your grasp until the next life cycle. You will not find her, and she will not remember."

It wouldn't matter, because he would only need that one chance to rescue her. "I don't understand why that would be a problem. She will return with me the moment she realizes who I am and who she is. I agree, now send me."

The Fate tipped his head, studying him. His black eyes held knowledge that should have warned Sinow of what was to come next. "You do not wish to hear the other conditions, Dark child?"

"I wish to find her and bring her home so we can set things right. Time is slipping as we stand here."

A grin so twisted that Sinow almost stepped back shadowed the Fate's features. "You should not be so hasty when I have not told you the true price you risk. You have until her thousandth year in that world to return with her. If you fail, you lose everything."

His stomach sank, hope faltering. "Everything?"

"Your throne, your power, your immortality. All of it forfeited." There was a sense of glee in the Fate's words that further stressed the horror coursing through Sinow.

Swallowing back the instinct that told him to walk away, to find another way to bring her home, he considered the offer. He had known they would bargain, known he would need to give them something in return, had told Keary he would willingly give up everything. Now that the words hung in the air, the weight of the choice seemed heavier than he had anticipated. Could he live without his power, without his throne? Live a mortal life?

He closed his eyes and thought about Violissa. Shared time in the meeting grove and in the Dream Realm. Her scent, her touch, the taste of her skin. The smile that lit her eyes to a brilliant green. The voice that danced in his ears and opened his heart. He had loved her long before his awareness of the emotion, long before he had ever seen her. And he knew he would give it all up for even a moment to hold her in his arms again, experience the softness of her lips, and smell the scent of lilac that sat so delicately on her skin.

He opened his eyes and answered, "Yes. All of it for her."

"Then so be it," the male Fate answered. He moved closer to Sinow, closing the distance between them. The power that emanated from him coursed over Sinow's skin. "I will warn you, the path you chose will not be an easy one. I hope you have it in you to survive else you have doomed this world. But I suppose you did that when you deviated from the path." He glanced back at Orlaina. "That was to be expected, though."

He vanished, leaving Sinow alone with her. The emerald orbs were dimmer now, holding a melancholy that permeated the air.

Sinow's eyes lingered on her. The similarity to Violissa was powerful, causing an ache in his chest. The wisp of silver locks that swept over her cheek did so just the way Violissa's would. He could almost feel Violissa's soft curls under his fingers. The memory was a strong one, stealing his breath, and he struggled not to show any emotion. The Fate smiled a sad, knowing smile.

"Your heart aches for her. We bound you to her, and only now do you understand the depth of that connection. Two souls entwined, and no distance can ease the need you have for one another." She walked over to him, and her hand moved to lie on his chest, just over his heart.

"Dark child, that you would risk everything to find her does not surprise me. Your every breath is as one with hers, and so it shall be in the other world. Know that the deal you have made is one you may come to regret. For all our sakes, I do hope it will not be."

He smiled and grabbed her hand, a bold move considering she could strike him down in an instant, even given all his powers. Thankfully, she did not move. "I will bring her back, and together, we will make things right. We will follow the path you have written for us without hesitation this time."

"You may come to regret saying that as well, for the path my brothers have set for you will be the hardest test you've faced. Stay true to your quest and do not give up on her, no matter what she may do. Now, close your eyes and clear your mind. May my blessing follow you to your new world. Good luck, Sinow."

With her last words, the weight of her hand lightened, and the surrounding air stirred. Light at first, then so powerful it pushed against him, trapping the air in his lungs. He struggled to open his eyes, but they remained closed. There was no fighting the force that had him in its clutches. The air grew so heavy it seemed to weigh him down like a wet cloak. Just as he thought he might scream from the intense pressure that encased him, it lifted. Weightless, he floated. He tried to open his eyes, but they remained closed. Drifting, he braced himself, unsure what to expect next.

A jerk to his body at his midsection had him doubling over. A whirring sound filled his ears, so loud it sent searing streaks of pain through them. He bit down to contain his scream when everything ceased. The noise, the sensations, all awareness faded until there was nothing.

---

THE BOY LOOKED AROUND. He stood alone in a field but didn't know how he had gotten there. Hands running along the tall stalks of wheat that surrounded him, he tried to determine why he was there. He needed to find something. No, someone. Her. That's all he could remember. He drew his hand through his hair. Memories evaded him. Only a void greeted him when he tried to recall anything. He couldn't even place who he was. All he knew was that this place was foreign to him.

Glancing around the field, he tried again to remember why he was standing there. Finding something. What was it he had remembered just a moment ago about finding something? Try as he might, he couldn't remember.

He began walking, not sure what direction to go but driven by the need to move forward. The Fates only knew if he was right. Fates? Where had that term come from? It didn't seem right for where he was standing. Walking through the field of tall wheat, he saw a farmhouse in the distance. Was this where he belonged? He didn't know, but something was driving him toward it.

"You there! Boy! What are you doing in my field?"

An old man stood behind a plow to his left. The ancient mare strapped to it was panting from the strain. The boy could tell the poor thing had seen its last days.

"I asked you a question. What are you doing here, boy?" The old man was trying to look authoritative, but his age and the shake of his hand gave away his fear.

The boy looked around again. There was nothing within miles of the farm. Was this why the man was so frightened, or was there something else?

"I don't know," he stated.

"You don't know what you're doing in my field?" the man asked.

"No. I don't know what I'm doing here or how I got here."

The man's stiff posture relaxed, but his tone still contained an edge. "You're a far cry from town, boy. Did you hit your head and lose your way? What's your name?"

"I'm not sure," he paused. He could sense his name. It was right there in the corner of his mind, but he couldn't quite reach it. "S...S...Si..." he gave up, defeated.

"Simon?" the man guessed.

"Maybe," he answered with a shrug.

"Well, Simon it is then. Where's your family, Simon?"

He thought about it. Family? He knew what a family was, understood the concept, but did not know if he had one.

"I don't know. I don't remember a family."

The man brought his arm up and wiped the sweat from his brow with it. "Well, do you at least know where you're going?"

He had known a moment before. Remembered that there had been a destination, a reason he was wandering this field, but the memory had fled. He looked around the field and shrugged. "I guess I'm heading here."

The man looked at him oddly. "Here? You were coming to my farm?"

"I truly don't know, sir, but it seems like a good place to be right now."

Giving his horse a pat, the old man walked over to him and looked him up and down. "So, you've no friends, no family, no place you call home, and no memory if you do?"

He nodded.

A glance back at his mare, then toward the dilapidated farmhouse. "Simon, my horse is tired, and so am I. My back is old as is hers, and our legs don't hold up to the strain of work like they used to. My home is old as well and in need of a pair of strong young arms to help her keep us warm and dry. My wife is barren, so we have no children to help us with the work. If you're as strong as you look, you can stay on with us as long as you prove useful."

"I think I'd like to do that, sir," he said, contentment washing over him. He walked over to the mare and laid his hand on her back.

"Yes, this is where I need to be," he said absently, knowing in his heart that whatever he had been searching for, he would find here.

# CHAPTER 5

A perpetual state of banishment hung over Tynan. An empty existence without his power. An eternity of nothing but the innate power that sat in his core. A weak imitation of what his true magic could do. It sufficed for now. Gave him just enough ability to make food, water, and shelter. To survive the endless length of days and nights that had passed before he'd come across an oasis. A town founded by two mortals his father had banished millennia before his birth. Centuries of inbreeding had led to a fully functional village with plenty of mortals to enslave and use. And that's exactly what he'd done with the little magic left after his brother had stripped him of it.

That day was one he had thought of repeatedly as he'd walked the miles of deserted land, carrying the book he had hidden in his robes as a failsafe. The book had spoken to him as he wandered, whispering the words of the spells until he'd memorized each one as if they had always been a part of his essence. Spells he would one day wield when his wait was over.

Patience was a gift he had honed through the centuries of plotting against Sinow, and it made the meaningless passing of time in the Banished Realm tolerable. As did the mortal females he continued to use, satisfying his needs with the ones who survived his brutality until their bodies could no longer take it.

The woman below him whimpered, but he paid her no heed, binding her with his magic and readying to have her body bring him the only pleasure he had in this worthless realm. The air turned, a heat building in it, and he lifted his head and sat back on his knees. The woman squirmed, trying to move away from him, but he took no notice as he rose from the bed and snapped her neck with a simple turn of his fingers in the air.

Power. So much power that he opened his arms and welcomed the burning of it as it soaked into him. His power had returned, but with it, a power unlike anything he'd held. It washed over him, coursing through his veins, and rushing through his core.

Movement in his periphery caused his hand to go out. He squeezed it, not bothering to look at the second woman as she collapsed to the ground, her heart turned to ashes. She mattered no more than the one in the bed. None of this mattered. It was only a place he had chosen to rest until the day he could return to Tenebron. A day like today.

He continued his path to where he had stored the book, sweeping the stones aside and revealing its worn leather cover. It pulsed almost as if it were breathing. Using his power, he lifted the book into his hands, feeling the life inside. The cover flew open, the pages fluttering as a black haze spread from it. The spells. He recognized the words in the fog before him, sensed the stirring of acknowledgment deep within him.

The knowledge of every one of those spells as they settled into his being and burrowed themselves into him. Every spell he'd repeated for the last two hundred years flowed through him. Their magic stretched into his veins, turning his eyes blacker than an endless night. They danced with his power, and understanding settled over him.

He threw his head back and let out a maniacal laugh that crashed against the walls of the dwelling.

"Oh, big brother, what have you done?" He released another volley of laughter because he knew exactly what that love-struck moron had done, exactly what Tynan had been waiting for him to do. Sinow had found a way to reach Violissa and left his precious kingdom unprotected.

He closed the book and shrank it down, tucking it into the cloak that now draped him. Rolling his neck and cracking knuckles, he set his power free. The walls of the dwelling crumbled, and he stepped through the wreckage and into the village.

Fear clouded the air, his Darkness surging in reaction. Mortals ran, but dark tendrils of power swept from Tynan. They struck all who stood in their path. Fire erupted from his fingers and lit the building across from him with flames. With a sweeping arc of his hand, they spread from dwelling to dwelling until they engulfed the entire village. The flames rose high in the sky, fueled by his power. Strolling through the village, he killed the remaining villagers, no longer needing them and wanting no survivors.

Shadowed in madness, Tynan walked through the flames, casting his soulless eyes to the northeast, saying, "A new reign has begun, and it will be the most terrifying one yet," before shifting to claim the heritage that had once been his brother's and now belonged to him.

# CHAPTER 6

Your pacing will do nothing but wear a hole in the stone beneath your feet, Keary," Kanine said as he rubbed his eyes.

Keary studied the eldest of the Council, seeing the weariness in the tilt of his shoulders.

"I can't sit still, Kanine. I have a dreadful sense that this will not turn out well." He stopped and looked out the window. Dusk was just beginning to settle in, and the pink flush of the descending sun cast an ominous red glow across the land. Something nagged at him. "I should have stopped him. There must be another way."

It was Daneele who answered. Several of the Lightbearers had convened when Keary had sent word of Sinow's plan. "Keary, we went through everything. He knew that as well as we did. This was his last resort, and I pray to the Fates they listened to his plea. We need Violissa back. All of us need her." Daneele stood and stretched, then turned back to Keary. "The hardest part will be waiting for them to return."

"If they even sent him. I haven't..."

Magic rippled against his skin, halting his words.

"Did you feel that?" he asked Kanine, assuming it was something with his Dark magic.

Cyric answered instead, "I sensed it. The power is in balance again. Sinow's plan must have worked. They sent him after her and answered our prayers." There was such hope in his words that Keary hated to shatter it.

"Don't be so quick to assume that, Cyric," Keary said. He rubbed his arms at the absence of his king's power. There was an emptiness there that seemed unnatural, like a hollowness that needed filling. "We don't know where they are, and we don't know how long—" His magic twisted and writhed. Pain tore through him, an unrecognizable presence clawing for entry and peeling back his defenses. He doubled over, clutching his stomach, the essence so vile he thought he might be sick. It plunged into his core, staking its claim and demanding he recognize it as it filled the space where Sinow's presence had once been.

"Keary?" Daneele asked, coming closer, his brows knitted with worry. "Kanine?"

Kanine was on his knees, hands braced on the floor. He looked up at Daneele and said, "Run."

"What?" Daneele and Cyric passed a look between each other.

"It's Tynan," Keary said, his voice scraping across his throat, the words coming out between pants. "He's infecting us."

"But Tynan is in the Banished Realm," Cyric said, taking a step closer. "His powers are bound."

Keary shook his head, dropping to his knees as nausea rolled through him. "No, they *were* bound." His voice broke, his power bucking at the violation to his body and his code. Tynan was murdering innocents, and every ounce of pleasure he was taking from it passed through Keary. "Tynan has king's blood running through him. If there is no other reigning king in our world—"

"His binding has come undone, and he inherits the throne," Kanine muttered between gasps of air. "Only one person can move between the borders of the Banished Realm: the King of Tenebron."

Cyric and Daneele blanched, Cyric grasping Daneele's arm to steady himself. "This cannot be. Sinow would never have allowed this."

"Sinow would not have known, just as we did not until now," Keary said, struggling to catch his breath as Tynan's reach insinuated itself even deeper. "You need to go. He will be here soon."

"Something unnatural contaminates his power," said Kanine. Keary recognized the same essence, one his magic wanted to eject from his body but could not because it belonged to the man who was now king. "I've never experienced anything this vile. He's worse than his grandfather ever was," Kanine continued, lifting his head to look at Cyric and Daneele. "Go quickly. Protect your people as best you can. We will be subject to his will, required to do his bidding as our king. No matter how heinous his commands." He peered over at Keary. "It takes an unbelievable amount of strength to resist a king's call."

That statement had been for Keary only, a pronouncement from a man who had once defied the most terrible king in their history. The only one who knew what faced them.

"Run," he told Cyric and Daneele as he held Kanine's gaze.

"The Fates be with you," Daneele said before they shifted.

He prayed they took the warnings to heart. Cyric would, but would the rest of the Lightbearers? He didn't have time to ponder it as Tynan shifted to the courtyard with a thunderous landing. The ground bellowed from the impact, and the castle shook around him. How had he come to have so much power without an ascension? There was no explanation Keary could find. It went beyond anything they knew about king's blood. A shiver slithered down his spine and within seconds, the side of the keep tore from its bearings. In its place stood Tynan.

"Hello, boys, miss me?"

Dread encapsulated Keary. Tynan's eyes were wild, with no

brown to be found in the irises. Only the black of a Dark King under the thrall of his power. His hair was shaggy and down to his shoulders, his features more hardened so that his face no longer looked thin and carved. He resembled Sinow more now, but with madness eclipsing the softer features Sinow bore.

"What have you done, Tynan?" Kanine asked, his voice calmer than Keary had expected.

"I don't think that's the question you need to ask right now, Kanine," Tynan bit back as he walked across the room, black cape stirring the dust from the demolished wall, feet crunching the debris below. "The question is, what has my brother done?"

Tynan turned and faced them. Tendrils of ebony seeped from under his cape. The Dark power left a faint red tone in the visible aura around him, seeping into those tendrils almost like something tainted his magic. Frantic eyes held something unrecognizable, a madness that infected the surrounding air.

A Dark King was to be feared, but a Dark King who had succumbed to the madness of his power was to be avoided at all costs. Once beyond that line of sanity, there would be no going back, no longer any morality to his actions. Nothing but violence and blood would satisfy his lust. Keary had heard the stories of the few mad kings in their history, but stories did nothing to prepare him for what he saw in Tynan. Kanine was right. The power that came from him was fouler than Sinow's had ever been when the Darkness had him in its clutches. Even to a Darkbearer, Tynan was terrifying.

Because a Darkbearer under the control of a king who no longer honored his code, who was so lost to his powers that he no longer cared for the laws of their land, had no choice but to follow his king's commands, no matter how they went against that code to protect their people and kingdom.

"He finally went after her, didn't he?" Tynan continued. "It took him long enough, but my patience paid off. With Sinow gone, do you know what that makes me?" He paused, but Keary knew what he wanted them to say, and neither he nor Kanine would give him the satisfaction. "That makes me king!"

Keary looked over at Kanine. He was the only one who had ever been under the control of a mad king. The Darkness had Tynan in its hold and had warped whatever part of him had remained when Sinow had banished him centuries before.

Where Keary expected to see fear in Kanine, he found only defiance. Kanine had once told him that those who had turned their loyalty from Sinow's grandfather to his father, Drostan, had noticed a pull from that control. Their new loyalty allowed them to defy their king in small ways that had laid the ground for Sinow's birth. Keary suspected that had been the reason Kanine had never spoken the truth of Violissa's heritage. It had been his way of fighting back, the one thing he could do in a time when things had seemed hopeless.

Keary had no loyalty to Tynan, and he knew no others on the Council would. His loyalty lay with Sinow as it always had, but the reach of Tynan's king's blood called the Darkbearers to answer it. From what Kanine had told him, there was a way to deny that call, a way to remain loyal to his true king.

With that thought, the taint of Tynan's power ebbed from Keary's soul. He would defy Tynan with every breath and protect the realms until his true king returned, even if it killed him to do it.

# CHAPTER 7

A haze of dirt clung to the window, but Sinow could still see Violissa through it. Fingers touching the glass, he longed to go to her. He had hovered there all night, waiting and watching as the last minutes went by. There was no avoiding them, no freezing time and stopping the inevitable that came with them.

His hair pulled as he ran his hands through it in frustration. Doing nothing was killing him, but it was useless to do anything else. He had sworn to himself that he would not act as he had in the past, that he would do nothing this time but watch. In past lives, he had banged at the door to get to her or chased her down as she fled. In some lives, others had dragged him from her as he fought with what little strength he had left to reach her. Never had he given up, even knowing the consequences. This life, however, he would not fight. In this life, he would only observe what happened when he did nothing.

He wanted to curse the Fates for their trickery, but he couldn't blame them completely. They had warned him, but he'd been too impatient, too young and headstrong to stop and listen. The true extent of what they had offered, he did not realize until it was too late. The spell that had sent Violissa to this world had burrowed into her mind, warping her memories and changing them.

The outcome was the same in every life. With no memory, yet driven by the prophecy, they would meet and fall for one another. Violet and Simon—their names in this world. Names that followed them through every life. The only consistency other than the void that sat in his chest when she turned from him each time.

As Violet and Simon, with no memories to guide them, only the magic of the Fates, there was no way to avoid their instant attraction to one another. No way to slow the need that drove their moods. No escaping the pull of the prophecy, even in this world of no magic. The Fates had woven it too deeply through them to avoid the instant love. The power of their bond was too great to stop. Caught up in it, they would make love, their all-consuming need for one another too intense to deny their desires, their mortal forms too weak to abstain.

Upon waking, their memories would return, but mistrust and doubt layered Violissa's. Warped by the Darkness of the spell Tynan had cast, she would only see what the spell wanted her to see. Only see the terror of the war on her people, the Darkness in Sinow's soul during that time. Only see Sinow casting the spell at her and her Council. No memory remained of any pleasant moments in their history, even the brief few they'd had. No memory of their kiss.

The spell manipulated her memories, distorting them, erasing any knowledge that she had ever loved him. If it was there, it lay buried so deep that she couldn't find it. What frustrated Sinow even more was that she had no knowledge of going through this with him in so many lifetimes. It was as if she started with a blank slate upon recognizing him, and only he knew the pain of losing her life after life.

Three days. Three days had seemed an eternity when he'd closed his eyes that day in her castle, but now he understood how short they truly were. With a mind riddled with gaps and twisted by the spell, those three days were like mere seconds.

So there he sat, not wanting to watch the inevitable but needing to see how it happened when he wasn't fighting with every scrap of energy to make her remember. To sit and simply observe her.

Perched in a window seat across from where he hid, she looked radiant. Sunlight poured through the window, outlining her silhouette, creating an angelic shine to her golden locks. She had her knees drawn to her chest, and tears ran down her cheeks. He wanted to wipe those tears away, but if he showed himself, she would just run as she had each time before.

Sinow wondered if memories of the final moments in their world had caused those tears. He had no way of knowing, but he couldn't assume the tears were for him.

His stomach lurched when the clock hit its first strike of noon, signaling the end of the third day. Gripping the windowsill, his tension grew with each strike. He kept his eyes locked on her, taking in every feature and preserving it before fate ripped her from him once again. Hands planted on the window, he remained a silent observer. All the while, pain lashed at his heart so violently he thought he might pass out. On the last stroke, Violissa lifted her head and looked directly at him. Recognition sat in her emerald irises along with a longing he hadn't seen in centuries.

"Sinow?" she mouthed, but her form faded like dust cast from the sunlight and into the shadows. Leaving only sparkles of gold where she had been. The room followed, disappearing bit by bit until even the house no longer existed. Left standing in an empty field, it appeared as though she had never been there.

His three days were up, and the Fates had moved her somewhere out of his reach, where she would remain hidden from him for the rest of this lifetime. They would wipe her memories again, a blessing he supposed, while they would leave his intact so that he would bear the pain of his loss for the years to come.

Inhaling the slight scent of lilac in the air, he closed his eyes and prayed her life would be short this time. It was selfish, he knew, but he didn't think he could stand another long life of yearning for her. Searching every inch of this world and never finding her. Living with the knowledge of what had been and all he had lost.

# CHAPTER 8

Keary waited at the tree line, masked in the shadows of the forest. With his eyes darting around, he tapped his fingers on his leg to calm his nerves.

*Come on.*

If Tynan found out, there would be no choice but to go into hiding. Tynan already mistrusted him, suspecting Keary's loyalty was to Sinow and that he had severed the control Tynan had over him. Too distracted with his vengeance, Tynan didn't realize his dominion over the Darkbearers had slipped, their loyalty to Sinow stronger than Tynan's call of king's blood. Without the full power of an ascension behind him, the connection had been weak to begin with. At first, it had been strong enough to force them into actions they regretted, but that hold had further weakened. Now they used illusion and mistruths to make it seem they were under his influence and doing his bidding.

Once Tynan had claimed the throne and the kingdom, he had turned his attention to Cirillia. Keary and the other Darkbearers had fought him as much as they could, but they were bound by their obedience to their king, and Tynan was now their king. As much as they tried to defy him, they suffered with every step.

The Lightbearers were already weak from Violissa's absence, and as was common knowledge, they were not fighters. Tynan tore through Cirillia, burning villages, decimating towns, until he finally came to Violissa's castle, demolishing it in one sweep so that all that remained were piles of rubble.

The Lightbearers were trying to save as many people as they could. They used magic to conceal them, moved entire villages into the forests for cover, and tried to thwart him every step of the way. With Tynan's attention set on destruction, Keary and a few of the other Council had been trying to help the Light Council when they could, which was why he was standing here now. Kanine had come up with a plan but needed the help of the Light Council to bring it to fruition.

Daneele shifted in with Cyric, and Keary breathed a sigh of relief. He had sent the message hoping they would receive it, but there had been no way of knowing if it would reach them. Seeing them here was affirmation that it had.

Keary pulled his hood down and greeted them. Weariness sat in their features—heavy eyes, dark circles, strained expressions. Since Tynan had taken the throne, life had been difficult for everyone, but especially the Light Council. They had been fighting for the lives of their people, and it had been a long, arduous battle, one which the Darkbearers could only assist under cover of night or risk Tynan turning on their own people.

"Keary, what news have you?" Cyric asked.

"Kanine has an idea. He thinks we can hide your people and ours. Protect them from Tynan."

"That's what we've been trying to do, to no avail," Daneele said, his tone belying his frustration.

"I know, Daneele. We're doing all we can, but..."

The call of king's blood was so hard to explain to anyone other than a Darkbearer. No one would understand the loss of autonomy they experienced under Tynan's control. King's blood was the connection between the king and his Council, and it was unbreakable. It embedded the code their king lived by into his Council and forced their allegiance, no matter if they believed in that king's ways. They had no choice. The Fates tied their will to the king's the moment they called them to service.

Sinow and his father had followed the true code of a Dark king—to protect his people, to serve justice, to punish those who threatened harm to their kingdom or people—and never forced their Darkbearers to do anything against their will. They respected their Council, and their Council remained loyal.

Tynan, like his grandfather and others in his line before them, took their will away, which stirred discontent. But fighting back was a slow process, almost impossible because it meant rebelling against a force that bound them to their king. That binding ensured their king could sense any doubt or hesitation, any thoughts of rebellion.

"It's difficult to explain, but please believe we are doing all we can. Now, I have little time, so I'll get right to the point. Kanine thinks we can use the Banished Realm. Offer it as a place for those who want to be free of Tynan's tyranny."

Cyric's eyes widened. "The Banished Realm? That's on Tenebron's westernmost border, Keary. How will we ever shepherd people that far?"

"We will shift them. We can work out the details, but for now he needs to know if you remember the spell the Elvin gave your Council when they formed the boundary between Cirillia and Tenebron. The one that hid the Lost Realm."

Cyric huffed, a sound that seemed odd coming from a Lightbearer. "That was millennia ago, Keary."

"I know, I know. He thinks it can fortify the Banished Realm and make it a haven for those who want to escape Tynan. He believes we can manipulate the spell to fit what we need and to keep Tynan out."

Cyric's eyes drifted away as he contemplated what Keary had

told him. The long pause had Keary shifting on his feet. This was a desperate idea, but these were desperate times.

When Cyric's focus returned, he pressed his lips together before saying, "Tell me everything Kanine told you."

Keary's sigh of relief was strained. There were still too many obstacles, too many things that could go wrong for him to relax. But there was hope, and with that hope in mind, he began to talk.

# CHAPTER 9

Daneele watched as the boundary flickered with color. The black mist of Dark magic collided with the blue haze of Light magic as he continued to pour his power into it. The chaos was clear only to the Council positioned strategically around the magical boundary that separated the Banished Realm from the rest of their world.

*That should be enough. Pull back*, he heard Cyric say in enaigne.

He lowered his hands, stopping the flow of power, then yelled over to Kanine, "Pull back," knowing the Dark Council hadn't heard the command.

Kanine did so and must have sent the message through enaigne to the rest of his Council. The boundary soaked in the chaotic flurry of the two opposing powers. Flickering in shades of blue and black, a twisted blend of enemy powers trying to meld into one force.

They were taking a colossal risk, but Tynan had left them with no other choice. With Sinow's absence, the situation had deteriorated quickly. Tynan was a force no one had expected. His strength and power were on par with Sinow's, and none of them understood where it had come from. But Tynan's power was corrupt and vile, tainted worse than even his grandfather's had been.

He had been quick to go after the Lightbearers, who had tried their best to protect their people. But they were no match for Tynan. Tynan had learned quickly that their powers were fading, a fact that he used to his advantage. Not long after Violissa's disappearance, the magic had lessened. Barely noticeable at first, now it was like an animal had burrowed its way into Daneele's core and carved out pieces of him.

The only consolation was that Tynan's hold over the Darkbearers was weak. It had been from the beginning. One by one, they had turned their forced allegiance until now they stood fighting side by side with the Light Council in one last attempt to protect as many mortals as they could, both Tenebron and Cirillian alike.

Since the day Keary had told them of Kanine's plan, they had been sneaking people out of Cirillia and into the Banished Realm, hoping they could protect them from Tynan. By combining their power in the spell Cyric had remembered from the days of the last king, they were attempting to seal the realm from Tynan. It had taken some work, but they had manipulated the spell to allow those with good intentions and those who needed help to enter the realm. Tynan would have no way in, but for those who entered for protection, there was no way back out.

This made it impossible for the Darkbearers to help the refugees inside the Banished Realm. They would stay and fight Tynan as they had been, beyond his sight and avoiding discovery. The Lightbearers would divide their forces, leaving half to help the refugees establish their new homes and half to remain in Cirillia to guide people to the Banished Realm. They wouldn't be able to save everyone but would help who they could, heal who they could heal, and bury those who needed to be buried. All while staying out of Tynan's sight.

Daneele watched as the Light and Dark powers continued to

fight one another until the resistance gave way and the magic combined, creating a dark purple haze that coated the sky, touching down to the ground in a domelike fashion. It flickered there, the magic settling into the original boundary before it vanished. All that remained was a subtle glimmer of magic that would go unnoticed to the untrained eye.

Daneele looked over at Kanine. "Is it done?"

"I believe so. We need to scatter before Tynan comes. Go, help the refugees while your brothers and mine gather more."

"Good luck," he told Kanine.

"May the Fates be with us all." He shifted, leaving Daneele to enter the boundary and begin his new life in hiding, caring for their people until Sinow brought his queen home.

Magic cascaded over his skin as the boundary granted him access into the Banished Realm. Only two of the Lightbearers had entered the realm with the refugees. Until today, when Daneele, Cyric, and Anwell would join. He glanced around, seeing the village across from him. It would eventually spread far beyond and into the realm as more people came to seek sanctuary from Tynan's rule.

The ground bellowed as though something large had dropped on it. Tynan. They had kept him distracted while they worked, but it seemed their activity had finally caught his attention. He would see the magic they had imbued on the realm and strike back.

A bead of sweat trickled down Daneele's face, and his pulse pounded in anticipation. The years of fighting had worn him down, as it had all of them. He missed the old ways and missed his queen.

At first, they had tried not to think about the loss, had instead preoccupied their minds with the search for her to keep from grieving her. After Sinow left, the fight against Tynan had further delayed the grief. Sinow had believed she was still alive, trapped somewhere, but Daneele had doubted him until the day Sinow vanished. That day had reignited hope in him that Violissa would one day return. He still had faith in the prophecy, still had faith that Sinow and Violissa would fulfill their destinies.

Daneele watched the boundary quiver as Tynan attacked it repeatedly, sending a prayer of thanks to the Fates when it didn't cave. He couldn't see Tynan, but he heard a roar of frustration. The quivering increased, and he suspected Tynan was furiously hitting it with everything he had, but the Fates were with them. The barrier remained intact.

They were safe for now.

# CHAPTER 10

Sinow watched as they dragged Violissa to the pyre. She struggled to break free, but it was impossible. The four large men held her too tightly. He could feel the bruises their hands were leaving on her skin. Not that it mattered; she'd be dead within the hour.

Part of him wanted to save her, wished he had even a small amount of his power just to punish them for daring to even think of touching her. He wanted to rip apart the coarse binds that held his wrists and crash through the wooden cage that held him. His need to do so tore through him as he watched their angry faces.

Words like witch and devil's whore were being hurled along with the stones that pelted her skin. The impact bruised his skin as each one hit its mark—his body the mirror to her pain. All this because the boy in the front was jealous that she'd chosen Sinow when he'd wanted her all this time. Of course she had; she had no choice. Prophecy and the Fates ruled their destinies, and this was their chance meeting in this life. Not even one day had passed since their memories had awoken.

There was another part of him that wanted to just let it happen, to not worry about the useless struggle to save her. He only had two more days to convince her he truly loved her. So many lifetimes now, and he had yet to succeed. The Fates had warned him, telling him the spell would manipulate her memories, but he had been too foolish to heed their warning. Until it was too late.

No matter how hard he tried, he couldn't get her to see what had truly happened. She hated him every time she woke. It was getting tiring, and he dreaded every long life that followed. Years of searching for her only to come up empty-handed. He should just give up and wait for the cycle to start again. He'd be reborn and have another attempt to convince her.

This punishment the Fates had given him was worse than anything he could have imagined. The incessant longing for her went unfulfilled, leaving him with a constant hunger for her.

If he let them kill her, the clock would reset, and they would both be reborn again. That would be the easiest way, but he wouldn't let that happen. He would fight them until his last breath. It wasn't in him to stand back and watch them murder an innocent, especially when it was Violissa. She was his, and he would keep fighting for her, just as he had, life after life, no matter how much heartache it caused him in the end.

The flames rose around her feet. It was amazing she hadn't screamed out in pain yet. She was a queen to the very last. Heat scalded his skin as if he were burning with her, her pain in death always his. Unable to stand by any longer, he threw himself against the cage, hoping he could somehow undo the binds and break the bars before it was too late.

"Violissa!" he screamed to her. She turned a tear-stained face to him, all defiance gone from it. His skin burned, the pain growing as hers did. He could endure the pain, but he knew she couldn't. She held her head back and let out a blood-curdling scream as the flames wrapped their way around her body. Her screams gutted him but strengthened his resolve, and despite the pain that ripped through him, he slammed the wooden cage, breaking through before they could stop him.

"Violissa!" He choked as the smoke filled his lungs, just as it did hers. He barreled through the stunned crowd, wrists still bound, as her screams died. Weakness overtook him when the fire became too much for her body. He collapsed, wheezing, his body wracked with pain. He tried looking for her in the flames one last time, but his eyes grew too heavy. Taking one last spasming breath, he closed them on this life, ready to start the next.

# CHAPTER 11

Daneele sat on the bench listening to Maggie talk about the weaving she'd done to perfect the piece of clothing she held in front of her. He was half-listening, half-scolding himself. What was he doing? She was barely a girl, only just turned twenty. He needed to get up and stop this charade, but something kept pulling him back to her. He looked at her as she talked, her hands gesturing animatedly with the excitement of what she was sharing. Her auburn hair ran long and loose down her back, as was typical of their women. Her blue eyes sparkled with life he hadn't known since they had lost Violissa. She made him happy, reminding him of the queen he missed. Her energy was infectious; her smile contagious.

He rubbed his head.

*Get up, you fool, and move to another part of the realm.*

He knew what was happening, and he was struggling to fight against it. He was the Keeper, the closest to his queen, the last person she should ever doubt. Yet, here he sat, his vow to her in question. His sacred vow as a Lightbearer—never to love another, never to let temptation rule him, never to lie with a woman. Celibacy was sacred to both Councils, and none had ever challenged that norm. In fact, the thoughts in his head should not have even existed. The power he held desensitized him to the needs of the flesh. That power, however, had weakened substantially. After too many centuries without Violissa here, it had lessened more than he wanted to admit. Was that the reason these thoughts were in his head? The reason for his attraction to Maggie? Fates, he was thousands of years older than she.

He'd been hollow since Violissa's disappearance. All of them had been. The love they had for their queen was special. It ran deep, and without her there, the loss was undeniable.

Maggie smiled at him. "Are you listening to me?"

"Yes, it's quite fascinating," he replied, returning her smile.

"You are not a good liar, sir. You haven't heard a word I've said. What is it that's going through your head, then?"

*That I love you and I shouldn't,* he wanted to say to her, but he bit his tongue. Love was something only reserved for his queen, and yet here he was, sharing it with someone else. He was a traitor, a vow breaker, and a coward to let his guard down and allow those emotions to form.

"Daneele?" she asked softly. She brought her hands down to her lap and quietly looked at him. He was about to respond when he sensed something was wrong. He looked away, absently putting his hand on hers before pushing himself up. Taking a few steps from the bench, he sent his power out to determine what it was.

"Daneele?" she asked, worry heavy in her voice. "Is everything all right?"

Looking up at the now constantly dark sky, he saw the change. The black of night had turned a deep shade of crimson. A crash across from him turned his attention. Keary was lying on the ground, painfully pushing himself up after shifting into the realm.

"Keary!" he yelled, moving toward him.

Pain ripped through him, stopping him mid-stride.

Keary looked up at him. "It's over, Daneele. Tynan has us. The fight is over."

"Daneele, your skin," he heard Maggie say. He glanced down at his hands, which were glowing, a bright blue aura building from them. He looked toward the edge of the realm. The blue was drifting from him toward the border. It covered his entire body, slowly pulling away from him.

Meeting Keary's eyes, the acknowledgement passed between them. A deep black mist was coming from Keary's body, drifting in the same direction. Power. Something was stealing their power. Keary stiffened, then dug his hands into the ground as the aura around him grew. A scream erupted from him just as a shredding sensation drove through Daneele's core. The pain was so massive, he doubled over, collapsing to the ground as his power fled from him.

Somewhere, he registered Maggie's scream, accompanied by others in the village. A Council dropped from the sky, his power barely enough to shift him into the realm. Another landed to the right of Daneele. But so much pain tore through him all he could do was lie on the ground as it eviscerated him. He stared at the blood-red sky, unable to move, barely able to breathe, and prayed to the Fates that they would end this torture soon. The only answer to his prayer was the hazing over of his eyes into unconsciousness.

---

DANEELE OPENED his eyes and regretted doing so immediately. He stared at the ceiling, reaching for what was no longer there. An emptiness he hadn't had since the day Violissa left was all that answered him. Having his powers bound by Tynan had been excruciating, but this had been so much worse, like someone had gutted him with razor-sharp claws and left him hollow. At least when Tynan had bound him, his powers had still been in him, unusable and locked away in his core, but still present. Now, there was nothing but an emptiness that demanded to be filled. He was like a thirsty man who couldn't catch the falling water with his mouth.

Something soft rested on his arm, and he looked over to see Maggie sitting on the side of the bed. Her face bore shadows of sleeplessness and worry lines that should not have been present. She gave him a sad smile, opening her mouth to speak the words he was not ready to hear yet. The acknowledgment that they had lost their only advantage over Tynan. He raised his hand to stop her, shaking his head but unable to make words form.

Pushing himself up, he looked around to see that someone had moved him to his home. He rose from the bed, stabilizing himself as a wave of unsteadiness passed through him. Maggie stood, her blue eyes creased, but he walked past her, letting his fingers absently drift over her hand as he did.

There were a few others in the front room, mortals who had been leaders in the village. No one dared speak; they all awaited his next move. With hesitant steps, he moved past them, out into the openness of the night. The sky had changed to black again, no red remaining to remind him of what had happened. Not that he needed another reminder, the gaping void in his core was enough. He spied Keary sitting with Brom on the bench where he'd last sat with Maggie.

Sitting down with them, he remained quiet. None of them spoke, the silence stifling. They remained in that agonizing quiet, pondering the loss they now bore, wondering how to live a life without the tools to help their people.

"Did everyone make it here?" he eventually asked, his voice like a heavy weight in the stillness.

"A few stayed behind," Keary answered. "They couldn't make it past Tynan and thought it was better to stay to continue saving who they could. They won't last long. If they're able to escape Tynan's notice, they can't do much without their magic."

"They can try, and when they've exhausted all means, they will find their way back to us," he said.

Brom flexed his hand in and out as if doing so would spark even the slightest magic. Daneele knew their pain; it was a bond that only they would share. Only the Councils could understand what had truly happened. To comprehend the impact on their lives and on the lives of the mortals they had sworn to protect. He looked up at the sky, likening the expansive emptiness to what he now carried inside of him. The twinkle of a dim star caught his eye, then another, and another, until the sky had filled with stars.

"They are lighting for us," Keary said. The stars held the spirits of past Light and Darkbearers who had opted to spend their eternity watching over the world once they had served their purpose. "Sending us a sign." He looked at Daneele, giving him a reassuring nod. "We'll make it through this. They have faith. Now we need to as well. Even without our powers, we are still Council to the king and queen. We are symbols of the rule of this land, and as so, we need to continue to act like it. Tynan can take away our magic, but he cannot take our true power. He can never take our faith. Faith in the way of the Fates and faith that our king and queen will return."

Other Council had made their way over to them. He presumed they had shifted here from the other areas of the Banished Realm and from outside of it before their powers were completely gone so that they could take strength from each other. Only a few were missing, those who remained trapped outside the realm. Those before Daneele stood straighter, their pride returning with Keary's words.

"Gentlemen, Keary's right. We must have faith to instill that faith in our people," Daneele said. "Lead the way Violissa and Sinow would want us to lead, power or no power. We are Lightbearers and Darkbearers at heart, chosen by the Fates. Never must we forget that."

Daneele rose from the bench, Brom and Keary following. They stood tall and clasped their hands to their hearts.

"Let us lead our people, just as we have in the past."

Kanine gestured for him to look behind them. Turning around, he saw the people crowded together, waiting for the Councils to guide them. They kneeled before the Councils, a sign that nothing had changed in their eyes. Even without power, they would remain under their advisement and protection. Daneele turned his sight back to the sky and nodded toward the stars, sending a prayer of thanks and another prayer to the Fates to bring Violissa and Sinow home soon.

# CHAPTER 12

Tynan walked through the castle halls, enjoying the way the servants scattered to avoid him. They had feared him before, but that fear had morphed into terror. He flexed his muscles, power coursing through them. He had leeched every ounce of magic from their world, including that of both the Light and Dark Councils.

Those fools had thought they were smart, thought they had tricked him. Hiding mortals in the Banished Realm. It was a novel idea, one for which he gave them due credit, but they had made a mistake in thinking he wouldn't notice.

At first it simply irritated him, then it had amused him. He had let them go, let them play their games. He didn't care if they sneaked people through that blasted realm border. The game of cat and mouse was one he played to perfection.

He had watched as the Dark Council betrayed him one by one, knowing he could have simply punished them. But what was the fun in that? He didn't need them anyway. If anything, they had made it easier for him, rounded all of those mortals up in one place. No need to chase them down, although he did love the sport in it.

He'd finally grown tired of the game and played one of his cards. One spell. And what a spell it had been. Unsuspected and powerful. Tynan had held onto it for the longest time, waiting for just the right moment, understanding that it was a unique spell, meant for a single use. Those spells were unheard of now, but ancient history had record of a few instances. This spell, one he had discovered hidden deep in the book, was a beauty that needed to be used only as a last resort. He was certain the limited use had been a fail-safe, so the wielder wouldn't take advantage of it. He was just as certain the Fates had never imagined how he would use it.

His hands rubbed together vigorously as he thought about the rush he'd experienced in that moment. Within minutes, he had stolen every ounce of magic in the land and, in doing so, he had absorbed all the Dark power he had taken. Not a single drop remained except his, leaving his strength unmatched. He doubted even his brother could come close to defeating him.

He had waited centuries for just the right moment, waiting for them to grow comfortable, enjoying the constant fighting, until today when he had grown tired of the game and invoked the spell. The rush it had given him when he watched the flow of magic seeping from the Banished Realm was well worth the wait.

Now, with no one left to stop him, he had set his sights on getting through that damned boundary. Having tried to break through many times, he had yet to succeed. With the magic taken from the land, he was certain it would leave the barrier weak.

He looked to the southwest, toward the final realm he had yet to conquer.

*Time to take the rest of what is due to me*, he thought, shifting toward the Banished Realm.

The rustle of leaves peacefully settled back to the ground after his shift, a contradiction to the havoc and destruction he intended to cause.

# CHAPTER 13

Daneele paced, trying to focus his thoughts, those conflicted beasts that insisted on bombarding his mind constantly these days. How had this happened? No, how had he let this happen? That was the real question. It had been nearly thirty years since Tynan had stolen their power. It seemed like just yesterday. Since then, the remainder of both Councils had made their way into the Banished Realm. They had discussed the event in depth, perplexed as to how Tynan had done it. No one had the ability to take power. It wasn't possible, yet he had.

Not only had taken it from the Councils, but he had leeched the magic from everything. The light had faded completely from their world. Only a brief few minutes of sunlight graced them each day now. The land lacked its luster, the green of the grass now a muted gray. Plants had wilted so that they could barely grow enough food for their people. What they managed to harvest was bland and tasteless. Even the air differed from what it had been before.

Tynan had bled the magic from their world and taken it for himself, something no one understood, yet here they were, three decades later, living as any mortal men might. Uncertainty remained as to whether their immortality was still present. Each had begun to age slowly, at first not noticeably enough for their people to see, but with time, the changes had accelerated so that they now looked and felt as though their age was catching up to them.

Since that day, Tynan had increased his attacks on the barrier, determined to break through to the Banished Realm. Much to their surprise, he had yet to succeed. Something in the combination of their spell and power had sealed it from any attempt to break through, no matter how formidable the attack.

Daneele realized he had worn a path from his pacing, growing restless with the wait. Inevitably, he turned back to his internal debate. Without his queen here to punish him, he punished himself regularly. Would she have punished him if she were here? The others thought the Fates had a hand, but he wasn't convinced. Instead, he allowed only disappointment in himself.

He had been strong enough to push away the temptation when he'd had his gifts, but with them gone, he had become weak like mortal men. He wasn't the only one. A few of the Darkbearers had fallen prey to the needs of mortality. He, however, was the only one who had fallen in love. The only one who had given in to it, the only one who was too feeble to stop his heart. And so, here he waited.

*Fool*, he cursed himself.

He'd fallen for Maggie when she was young, a mere twenty to his long life, but he had kept it to himself, keeping her at a distance until there was no stopping the inevitable.

As the years went by, his emotions had grown too strong, and he had given in. She filled the hole left by his queen and the loss of his powers. There was no denying it, and with time and the slow advance of years, he decided it was worth risking the ire of his queen...if she ever returned.

Violissa had been gone so long he wondered if it even mattered anymore, and with that thought in mind, he had asked Maggie to marry him. The others didn't judge him. Rather, they supported the decision, knowing he'd been wrestling with it for so many years. Maggie was getting older. They all knew she wouldn't marry anyone, letting any other chances for love fall by the wayside. Although she was still young, considering mortals could sometimes live almost two centuries, she was in her late forties and getting past the age when other men would take her hand. He knew she was waiting for him, hoping one day for the impossible. And so, he became not the first to break his vow—Mackay had beaten him to that with a woman from a neighboring village—but the first to love, the first to marry, and now, the first to conceive.

Keary slapped him on the back, interrupting his train of thought. "If you walk this path any more, Daneele, you'll dig yourself right into Cirillia. Stay calm, she'll be fine."

"Does it always take this long, Keary?" he asked.

"Now how would I know, brother? You're the only one who's had the audacity to produce a child. Maybe your punishment is the wait!" His laugh was boisterous.

Daneele inhaled sharply as Cyric emerged from the small cabin and rushed toward them with a huge smile. "Congratulations, Daneele. You've got yourself a baby girl."

Daneele could never have imagined how those words would change their lives in the most unexpected of ways.

# CHAPTER 14

The sound of the heart monitor beeped a steady rhythm behind his bed as Sinow listened to the nurses talk. The one closest to him, and now taking his pulse, was new. He thought it may have been her second day, but now the days all ran together, so it was difficult to say.

"So, what's his story?" she whispered to the other nurse. Julie, thought her name was but didn't care enough to remember.

"Not much to tell, really. No family, no friends, nothing even here in his apartment to tell anything about him. He must have a lot of money, though. The rent in this area is outrageous."

"If there's no one, then who pays for us?"

"Some attorney's office handles all his money and writes the checks to the agency. That's about all I know."

A hand brushed his hair from his face. "Shame, even at this age, he's quite handsome. I bet he was a looker when he was young. Maybe his wife died?"

"No, there was no wife. He never married. But I think there was a woman once." There was silence for a moment, while he guessed the new girl was questioning this information with a look.

"What? I did some digging around and got a few tidbits." She paused, then whispered, "Sometimes he mutters her name in his sleep. Vi is all he says, over and over."

He stopped listening and let his mind wander. For a few minutes, he was back in Tenebron, the cool air running through his hair, the sound of the horses in the stables braying as they sensed his power draw near, the banter of his Council like music to his ears. Then she was there, her long golden curls flowing with the breeze, eyes sparkling like gems in the sunlight. He reached his hand up to catch the one loose curl she could never seem to tame.

But as suddenly as she'd been in front of him, she was gone. The world crashed around him, and he was alone in the dark again. He cursed his weakness. These human minds were as fragile as their bodies. He fought against the disease that ravaged his brain and, in turn, the body in which he was trapped. There were times when he could pull himself from the delusions that plagued his mind. He imagined it was a blessing Violissa did not have her memories, which were still bound by the Fates, leaving her to believe she was human, while Sinow knew this was just a shell for who he really was. Those memories of home were the only ones the disease could not touch. They remained ingrained deep in his consciousness, too far for the human illness to reach.

An ache built in his chest at the thought of Violissa in pain. His pain was a mirror of hers, just as his death would always be. But without knowledge of who she truly was, all she had was the ravaging of her mind to define her. This lifetime had been the longest one she'd had. The dementia began about five years earlier, just after his eightieth birthday. As the disease had cleaved its way into his mind, then his body, Sinow had waited for Violissa to die. Only then would they start over. But it hadn't happened. The years had crept by painfully slow. He didn't know if the Fates were being cruel or if the spell she still carried had cursed her to live this longer life. He had no answer, but he knew he didn't want to think about the other possibility.

Once separated, he never knew what happened to her for the remains of her life. No matter how he searched the world, he never found her again. And in every lifetime, he had searched relentlessly. Selfishly, he liked to think she lived a solitary life, never giving another man what was rightfully his. He didn't care that it was selfish and even unrealistic. Violissa was his. She had always been and to think of her with another man left him too blind with jealousy to consider. But the possibility existed, no matter how he convinced himself otherwise. She had no memory of him, no idea who he was or what they meant to each other. The thoughts plagued him through the countless years of every life, but especially this one.

He couldn't stop the thoughts as they crept in, invading his mind. What if she had married, had children, grandchildren, even great-grandchildren? What if she was clinging to this life for someone?

He heard the heart monitor pick up its beat as the questions made his blood boil, even in this state. To calm himself, he cleared his mind. It did no good to dwell on it. Although he had remained chaste for her, the thought of even considering another woman causing the bile to rise in his throat, that didn't mean she had the same reaction. He had realized long ago that this was the burden the Fates had given him.

His mind pulled away again, but this time there was a noticeable difference. Weakness washed through his body, every organ slowing in response. Violissa's time was drawing near, as was his. His breathing slowed as his heart struggled with one last effort. The tug came, a pull deep inside of him that he experienced each time he and Violissa died.

As he drifted closer to his last sleep in this life, he waited for the single thought that passed each time he died. His heart beat its last beat when he sensed it. For a moment, their souls touched, and in that space in time, her awareness of him woke. A brushing of her mind against his. Her soul stretching to reach him while his last breath exited his body. Warmth and emotion. Recognition and fear until death drew her away from him.

This was why he kept fighting.

This was why he suffered each life, suffered every rejection she gave, suffered the longing, the need, the regret. That last moment when their souls touched was all he needed to fill him through another life of need and relentless agony.

*Sinow*, her voice called as the Fates dragged her away one more time.

*Vi*, he sent out to her, their souls separating completely. A wave of her love for him rushed through him as it did each time. He soaked it in, letting it wash over the ethereal form he was in, letting it soak into every space there was until the darkness over-took him and it was time to start over again.

# CHAPTER 15

Keary woke with a start. He'd been dreaming of the old times again. He wiped his eyes as if to wipe away the memory of how life had once been. The rolling green of Tenebron's hills, the stony cliffs that defined the end of their land from Cirillia, the power that had once filled his veins. Each memory stung, reminding him of the losses they had endured since the day Sinow had disappeared from their lives.

He sat up on the edge of the bed, stretching his arms to wake the muscles that seemed to ache more every day. He wondered if the aging would continue for eternity or if he would die like a mortal. The thought was a strange one, one he had not had since he was a child, well before the Fates had marked him as a Darkbearer. How had it come to this? He still wasn't sure how it had all happened. It had been so fast.

Over half a century later, Keary still remembered the gut-wrenching pain of that day in every part of him, as if someone had punched a hole in his body and torn all the vital parts from him. They had lost everything: their powers, the land, the kingdoms. Although if truth be told, they had lost it long before that day—

when Sinow had left to find Violissa. The day he had lost his king was the day Keary had lost everything.

He shook his head to clear the memories. It wouldn't do for the people to see him this way. The Councils were powerless, but the people still looked upon them as the leaders. They were still immortals even if they were aging. He laughed at the thought of an immortal aging, then looked at his wrinkled hand and ran it through his graying hair. He was the youngest, and as so, time had been easier on him. Cyric and Kanine, as the eldest, had not fared so well. They looked as though they were withering away, fragile as the pages of an ancient book might be. Their wrinkles were deep crevices in their faces, and the gray had long turned to white in their hair.

Keary wondered how much longer they would hold on, but then he knew both men had fought to bring the prophecy to fruition, and as so, they would fight the ravages of time to see their rulers return.

With an effort, Keary pushed himself up from the bed and walked toward the door of his home. It lacked the grandeur of his former home, but then again, everything about him lacked the grandeur to which he had been accustomed. He pulled the door open and stepped out into a crowd forming in the center of town. The sun would rise in the next few minutes, and no one missed the precious event.

When Tynan had taken the magic from their world, the shortening of the days had accelerated. Without Light magic, there was no longer the balance that kept it raised for so many hours. Each century that had passed since Violissa's disappearance had brought shorter days until now there were only mere minutes to enjoy the warmth of the sun on one's skin.

"Keary," Anwell greeted him as he walked.

"Anwell." He nodded in respect. "Another day ahead of us. Any chance it will be any different from the last thousand?"

"Doubtful." Anwell grunted. "Until our king and queen find

their way back, I suspect we're stuck in this endless cycle. The fading sun is the only thing that tells me the days are different."

Cyric and Daneele greeted them as they came to the building they had designated as their meeting hall when they had first arrived. To maintain order, the Councils had spread themselves throughout the Banished Realm to oversee the different villages that had grown over the years. They would meet every three moons to discuss matters of the realm. Since they no longer had the power of enaigne to communicate over the distance, they relied on those meetings as their way to discuss important issues arising throughout the realm. Today would be the first day of their meetings, and both Councils had gathered.

As Keary stood talking to the other men, something caught his eye from the tree line, a shimmer he hadn't noticed before. Noting an intense draw toward it, he stepped away from the others.

"Keary?" Daneele called as he spied Keary moving away.

He didn't answer but continued his path. The light flickered again, deep in the trees, and he followed, thinking he needed to hurry, or he would lose the last few minutes of daylight.

When he reached the tree line, he stopped short, hearing the others behind him.

"Any reason you're ignoring us, Keary?" Kanine called. Keary pointed to where the green sparkled with the last of the sun's peak. Within the trees stood a woman with shimmering green eyes. If he hadn't known better, he would have thought her to be Violissa, but he knew better. Her long hair hung straight down her back in an almost translucent way, her body holding the same quality. She moved her hand to beckon him on.

"What?" Kanine asked, looking to where Keary had indicated.

"You don't see her?"

"See who?" Kanine's brows knitted. "Are you all right today, Keary?"

Keary shrugged and said, "I'll be right back," leaving Kanine behind.

As he drew closer, Keary knew there was no mistaking his thoughts that this was one of the Fates. Power streamed from her, lighting her emerald eyes with an iridescent glow. She stood tall and proud, those green irises layered with lifetimes of knowledge. He dropped to his knees in respect as she moved toward him, her feet making no sound on the fallen leaves below them. Around him, there was silence, not a single noise to be heard save the sound of his breathing.

"The children have lost their way," she said, her voice sounding like the rain as it softly rolls down the leaves of a tree, almost musical in the way it left her mouth. "They need your help." She lifted his chin, those emerald orbs almost too brilliant to look upon. "Without you, our world will cease to exist."

"Without me?" he asked, not understanding why he had suddenly become of such importance. "Don't you mean without them?"

She had said children, but he knew she was speaking of Sinow and Violissa. Something had gone wrong. He'd known it deep in his core but refused to acknowledge the thought, even with each passing century. She nodded, then gestured to him to stand before she continued to speak, walking gracefully through the trees. He followed, intent on hearing what she had to say.

"The Dark child has been unable to break the spell. It has wound itself deeper around Violissa's memories with every passing life. The Dark intent of it has thwarted every attempt he has made." She halted and turned to face him. "We had suspected this would be so, but never did we imagine the true scale of its wrath." A tear slipped from her eye, and an ache built in his chest at the sight. He did not know what she was talking about, but he offered himself anyway. She was one of the Fates. What could be so terrible as to make a Fate cry? Whatever the cause, they needed help, and Keary needed his king back. He would do as they asked, regardless of the cost.

"What is it you need from me?"

She lifted her head and gave him a slight smile, the forest behind her shimmering in the final touch of sunlight, or maybe it was she who had caused the shimmering. He would ask himself that question over the years and never quite know the answer.

"The spell that Tynan struck Violissa with mutated when Sinow cast his own spell to protect her. It has become a curse, weaving itself through her memories, clouding them, changing them, darkening them so that she sees nothing but the terrible moments in their history. Even those moments of hope, it has marred so now all that remains is her pain and sorrow at the loss of her Council and the betrayal she thinks Sinow has done to her. We have no power where they are and thus no ability to help her see the truth. We had hoped Sinow would break through, but even he cannot. This is his final lifetime. If he fails, all hope is lost."

"What will happen to them if he fails?" Keary was afraid to ask, but knew he needed the force of what he suspected was the answer to drive him.

"If he fails, he will return to our world. He gave up everything to find her, and so he will return with nothing. He will be just as any ordinary man, powerless and mortal."

"Tynan will kill him. Sinow does not know what has happened since he left."

She nodded in agreement as the words fell from his mouth. Words that horrified him, the emptiness they left like a ravine he didn't think he could surmount if that future came to be.

"Violissa will remain in the world where the spell cast her," she continued, her statement not easing his apprehension. "She will continue to live her life over and over for eternity, with no memory of her true self, no memory of our world, and no memory of Sinow. She will go through each life as she has for centuries, oblivious but for the anguish of those losses, particularly that of the man she loves, that tears through her heart every beat it takes."

Her sage eyes held a depth of sadness that was almost palpable.

"What do you need me to do?"

"The one who rules their world will allow us one last chance to save them. We will send you to his world, to the same time that now holds Sinow. You will be the same age as he is in that world, but your memories will remain intact. You must take someone with you to shadow Violissa's life. The two have not met in this lifeline, so there is still hope that you can help him break the spell."

Keary was having trouble comprehending what the Fate was saying. That Sinow was on his last attempt, that he would lose everything if he failed. And somehow, Keary and another were supposed to help in a feat that had so far remained insurmountable to his king.

"Am I to bring one of her Council with me?" he asked, tucking his trembling hands under his arms.

"No, you will bring the child of Daneele, Paige. She is the only one who can grow close enough to Violissa while you build trust with Sinow." Build trust with the man who had once been his friend, a man he had grown up with and knew better than anyone else. It made no sense. She must have read the confusion. "Sinow does not know who he is, nor does Violissa. In their minds, they are Simon and Violet. Two mortals living mortal lives and unaware of who they once were. And they will remain ignorant until the time when they wake. This is why it is imperative that Paige be with Violissa when that happens."

"Paige?" He pinched the bridge of his nose. "But she never knew Violissa. She's the last person I would take." He stopped as power stirred in the surrounding air.

*Stupid to question a Fate*, he thought.

"Sorry, my lady. I will take Paige."

The Fate walked toward him and held her hand out over his. A heaviness filled his palm, and he opened it, seeing a large gem. She moved her other hand in a wave, and a long chain weaved its way through the top of it. The gem shimmered, then darkened until it looked like nothing more than a plain muted green stone. He glanced at her as even more questions mounted.

"It is imperative that you and Paige not reveal your identities to Sinow and Violissa. They will not know you until they wake. Your journey to them will separate you, but you must do all in your power to find each other. There are ways in their world that will make this easy, and you will learn them quickly. When the time comes, you must keep Sinow and Violissa apart as often as possible. They are not to consummate their relationship until the right moment."

The confusion grew. "What? I thought you needed them together."

"No. Once they cross that line, they awaken, and Violissa keeps him at a distance. If this happens in this lifetime, there will be no more chances. You and Paige are being sent to keep them together but apart. Their love must grow in their mortal form, as it did when they lived as immortals. Without that seed, there is no hope of breaking through the spell. We've watched his failure for too many lifetimes. You and Paige will keep their lust for one another at bay at all costs."

He wanted to laugh at the absurdity. He had to keep his king from bedding Violissa, or their world faced an unfathomable doom. How was he to explain this to the Councils? He ran a hand over his chin and sighed as she continued.

"Once they have pronounced their love for one another as their true selves, a portal will open, leading you all back to our world. But Tynan has more power than we anticipated."

Keary tilted his head, studying her as he contemplated her statement. Anticipated was an odd word to use, unless they had known this would happen. He wanted to question her about it, but she continued before he could.

"When we created the portal in our bargain with Sinow, the return portal established on the meeting grounds that bind Tenebron and Cirillia. Their profession of love will summon the portal in the other world and here. Tynan will sense it and lie in wait the moment he does. He is intent on destroying his brother.

That will be the moment he needs to succeed." There was something in her eyes, a flutter of emotion that darkened them. "Use the stone, and a second portal will appear in this realm to bring you home. Tynan's focus will remain on the false portal, and their return will remain unhindered. But know this, it is Violissa and Sinow who must use the stone to open the portal. Only when they combine their powers will the alternate portal appear. No one is to step in before they do so."

He dropped his eyes to the stone, marveling at how deceiving it looked. Dull and small, with no sign of the immense power it held.

"When you are ready for your journey, give the gem to the girl. Her touch will trigger the portal for your departure. She must then safeguard it until it is time to return to this world. It must remain with her until Violissa is awake and ready to use it. Only Violissa will understand what she and Sinow will need to make it work."

Keary lifted his gaze back to the Fate, but she was gone, a faint glimmer of light all that remained. He rubbed his hand across his face and closed his eyes at the task she had set before him. How was he to convince the Councils he hadn't lost his mind, and how was he to convince Daneele to send Paige? The Fates had chosen him; whether it was a blessing or a curse, he hadn't decided. They had sent Sinow to save Violissa, and he had yet to succeed. If he couldn't do it, then how were Keary and Paige to do so? His king had been gone for almost a thousand years. No one talked about the time that had passed. No one wanted to admit that they'd lost their rulers. No one wanted to face the consequences of what that meant, the futility it gave to their struggle if it were true.

Keary closed his hand around the gem. This was a sign that hope remained. The Fate had confirmed that both Sinow and Violissa were still alive. That in itself was a blessing. Inhaling, he turned back toward where he had left the others, praying the Fates would give him the strength to fulfill the task they'd placed on his shoulders.

"I AM NOT TO GO ALONE." Keary said.

The others had listened without interruption, no one doubting his words, no one questioning him. He had shown them the stone when he returned, physical proof of his interaction with the Fate. The light of hope had grown in their eyes as he'd told them about his visit with the female Fate. But he had left this last detail to the end, not wanting to break the news to Daneele that the Fates wanted Paige to accompany him, although he suspected Daneele knew. They had always thought she had been born for a purpose.

"Paige is to go with me."

He looked at the man who had become his friend over the long years. Daneele lowered his head momentarily and closed his eyes. When he looked back up, his emotions masked, the face of the Lightbearer looked back at him. As Keary had suspected, Daneele had known his daughter would be the one to accompany him. As the only child of a Council, she was unique. While a few of the others had strayed from celibacy—the burden of living without their powers increasing the needs that only overcame mortal men—none had fallen in love and none had borne a child. Only Daneele. Some suggested Paige was part of the Fates' plan to bring their world back in balance, but as she had no powers and Daneele's immortality had not passed down to her, there was no way to substantiate that theory.

"I will fetch her. Give me time to tell her mother first," Daneele replied. Although he was hiding his emotions, Keary could still hear the defeat in his voice. "When do they plan to send you both?"

"As soon as you bring her to me."

Daneele nodded, and Keary saw the momentary sadness overtake his features before he covered it and walked away. Keary couldn't imagine what he was going through. First, he had lost his queen, and now this. And from the hollow space that remained in his own chest, Keary knew all too well the pain Daneele experienced daily from the loss of his queen. Not a moment went by when the weight of Sinow's absence didn't burrow deeper in him.

"I hear we're going on an adventure," Paige said excitedly as she ran toward them a short while later.

Keary shook his head; the girl never ceased to amaze him with her enthusiasm. She was the perfect example of what he'd previously imagined a Cirillian to be. Annoyingly positive, constantly smiling, overbearingly helpful. She was like the irritating little sister he'd never had.

When she'd been born, both Councils had taken her in as one of their family. There was never any question about it. It had just naturally happened. Since she was mortal, they'd all become protective of her every move, something that would have bothered him, but she took in stride. As she'd aged, and the village boys had found an interest in her, they'd learned quickly that they had to go through not only Daneele, but all the Council before they'd even get to talk to her. It had seemed a good thing when she was younger, but now that she was eighteen, and the boys had become men, they'd grown fearful of the Lightbearer's daughter. Keary wasn't sure if being born so had been a blessing or a curse for her.

Paige flipped her auburn hair back and smiled up at them, blue eyes brimming with excitement. "Are we really going to bring them back? Am I truly going to meet the Light queen?"

Keary laughed. "Always ready to jump into action, eh, Paige? I don't think you'll be as eager to go when you learn the rest of the situation."

He paused and looked up at the others.

"The time in their world mirrors ours. We are being sent to their current lifelines, and the Fates will separate us as soon as we are there. I may not be close to you, Paige. In fact, it may be years before we meet again. The Fates said there are ways of communicating in their world that are faster than ours. When we arrive, we will need to find out what those are as soon as possible." She nodded in understanding.

"I'll be with Violissa?" she asked, her voice rising a pitch.

"Yes, and I will be with Sinow." He looked up at the empty sky, now devoid of light. The sun had set from its brief rise and now the moons were waiting in the balance to start their ascent. Until then, the sky would remain a black abyss. "We must go." He took the necklace the Fate had made to hold the stone and draped it around Paige's neck. "You are to keep this safe and let nothing happen to it."

"I have to hold it? Shouldn't you be the one? You're the Darkbearer." She suddenly seemed very young to him. Of course, she was when compared to his two thousand years.

"No, you need to be the keeper of it. Just like your father is Keeper for Violissa and Cirillia, you are now a Keeper. This is your role, not mine."

She drew in a big breath, her eyes growing brighter as she admired the stone. "So, what do we do now?"

"We say our goodbyes, and you touch the stone so we can bring our king and queen home."

# CHAPTER 16

A ripple of power washed over Tynan's skin. He stopped and closed his eyes, homing in on the source. The Banished Realm. The thorn in his thigh. What were they up to now? Somehow, a spell had been cast, but was unlike any power he knew. It had a unique signature, neither Light nor Dark. Keeping his eyes closed, he reached out for the power, searching for the source. It couldn't be any of the Council. He had taken their magic decades ago.

His eyes darkened. The Fates. The Fates were stepping in finally. His lips curled in a snarl. So, they wanted to change his plans. He had expected them to step in centuries ago, but they had remained silent, letting him ravage the land, slaughtering and violating as he went. He rolled his neck, letting the power flow from him. They were in for a fight if they thought they could stop him. He was here to stay, and today, he was planning to change the game. Nothing they did would stand in his way.

He had been trying to get behind the barrier and into the Banished Realm since the day he cast the spell to rid the land of magic. The barrier should have been breached by now, but no matter how he tried, he couldn't get through it. The protection spells upon it were too strong, a mix of Light and Dark magic combined to oppose his own. It frustrated him to no end, but he had a plan.

Bending down, he studied the ground below him. He was in the Sacred Groves, or what remained of them. In a fit of rage, he had demolished them, ripping every tree from its roots, burning every strand of grass, leaving nothing but a charred wasteland. There had been something about that grove he'd never liked. It had reeked of Light magic even after he had taken the last of the magic from the lands.

The only good that had ever come from this part of their world was the entranceway to the Lost Realm, in which he'd found the book, his prize possession, now locked away safely in his castle. He had no need to carry it with him anymore. His time in banishment had cemented every word to his memory, and when his power had returned, the spells came to life in him. They were his, and with them came immeasurable power. Enough power to destroy even his brother.

No need for that, though. His brother was lost somewhere. Lost with Violissa in a world far from his. There was no way they would ever return now. It had been far too long.

Centuries had passed since the day Sinow had left him the throne. Fool. He had everything, and he gave it up for what? For some whore of a Cirillian who probably didn't know the first thing about pleasing a man. They deserved each other, and both deserved an eternity of suffering. He absently rubbed the cheek where Violissa had slapped him that day in the meeting grove. Licking his lips, he thought about what it would be like to have forced her down and stolen her virginity. The image of her writhing under him caused a reaction he hadn't expected.

Standing, he adjusted himself and tried to clear the thought from his head. He had no desire for that yellow-haired wench, so the thought of her should not have elicited a reaction in his body. Rolling his neck to release the tension that had set in, he briefly wondered if he only wanted her now because she was the one thing of Sinow's he had yet to take. His hands clenched in and out as he pondered that thought.

A drop of sweat rolled down his forehead. His heart raced as he imagined taking her in front of Sinow and watching his torment as he stole the only thing his brother truly held sacred. Too bad she was lost out there. That would have been the most satisfying thing he had done yet.

He looked around at the remnants of the grove.

*Concentrate, Tynan. Why did you come here?*

Ah, the ooze. Kneeling down next to the black puddle of slime that had emerged, he remembered hearing about it from Sinow. It had appeared in Violissa's castle and on the land in the Sacred Groves right after Tynan had stolen the book from the Lost Realm. He glanced around the land before him. There were spots of the stuff in various places around him, thick and black as it oozed from the ground. There was a connection to the creature that had appeared on Violissa's land.

He searched his brain, trying to recall the name of the thing until it came to him. Torathar. A tie between the ooze and the Torathar existed, and the Dark power in him told him there was also a connection to him.

He reached his hand out toward it, and it called to his power, moving slightly, condensing and yet growing at the same time. The closer he came, the more it seemed to pull up toward his palm, reaching for it.

He watched as a puddle close to this one moved, combining with the first. Then another did the same, all the smaller puddles slowly heeding the call of his magic. He let a sliver of his power drift toward the spot, which had grown in size. It reached up and coiled around the stream of power, climbing higher as he stood. The mass grew, feeding on the Dark magic, pulsing and expanding. All the smaller puddles had now merged into this one. He halted his pulse of power and pulled his hand back, stepping away from the mass.

It didn't return to the ground. Instead, it continued to shift, spiraling around the space where his magic had been, climbing higher and higher. The pulsing increased as it continued to feed on the essence of magic that remained.

Curious, he sent an even larger stream of power toward it. The black form froze, then slowly widened until it was like a wall in front of him. Long and thin, it stretched itself across the expanse of the empty grove. He sucked in his breath as he realized the enormity of what he had just created.

After contemplating it, he decided to test what other abilities the substance had. Raising his other hand, he called on all of his power and poured it into the black wall. It soaked the magic in, expanding in depth until Tynan stopped. Standing back, he watched as it collapsed into itself, then grew to an enormous height that towered over him until it shifted its shape, rounding and shrinking slightly.

Craning his neck to watch it, he saw something akin to a face take shape, although the result was monstrous. Like something out of a child's nightmare. As thick arms spread from the mass with hands that contained only four trunk-like fingers, he appreciated the terror this creature would evoke. Looking down at him, the newly formed beast bellowed out a cry that would have left any mortal running in horror, but not Tynan. He stared the beast down, sending his enaigne out to see if it would hear him.

*You are my creation, and you will obey me*, he told it. *I have the power to keep you alive, to feed you. Your will is mine.*

In answer, it shook from top to bottom. Tynan wasn't sure if that was an acknowledgment or a denial. He waited patiently, then realized the beast was tearing itself in two. Tynan walked around to witness the sight. It had split its back half off, and that half was now taking shape to match its maker. Another piece pulled away from the original and formed a third creature. Tynan sent his power out to all three and watched them expand in size. He wasn't certain he could control one beast, let alone three.

*You will obey and stop reproducing until I command you to.*

It turned toward him, as did the other two. His pulse raced as he waited, but no more emerged.

*Bow to me, for I am your master.*

They stared down at him. He didn't move, showing no fear. His breath released when they tipped their heads in unison and squatted down on their huge legs before bowing their heads in deference to him.

A slight sigh of relief escaped Tynan. As a plan formed in his head, a devious grin crept over his face. He had his weapons. He would crush the Councils and all those mortals they had stolen from him. Not even the Fates could keep these creatures from tearing through the barrier and letting him lay claim to the last piece of land in their world. Nothing would stand in his way now.

# CHAPTER 17

As Paige touched the stone, the air rushed from her lungs, and everything faded. She was conscious but barely, plummeting through a tunnel that seemed to never end. The force from behind kept the air knocked from her, and she was like a fish out of water, opening and closing her mouth in a desperate need to catch a breath.

Just as she thought she would die, everything went black, the air had flooded back to her, and she fell weightlessly. The sensation lasted for countless minutes that may have been mere seconds, but she was too terrified to know the difference. With a sudden shock to her feet, she teetered slightly before the sensation of ground under her feet took hold.

She waited for more, but when nothing came, she opened her eyes. The darkness had given way to daylight. She blinked her eyes several times, adjusting to the sunlight. The sun was full in the sky, and she couldn't help but smile at the sight. Their sun barely peeked above the horizon, lasting mere minutes, but the sun in this world shone full with all its might. It was glorious, and she wanted to stand there and soak it into her skin, but she needed to focus. She could stare at the sun in their world once they had the king and queen back. Once they restored the balance, she could wonder at the sun for the rest of her life.

She searched for Keary, but he was nowhere around. He'd warned her the Fates would separate them, but she hadn't realized just how scared that would make her until she was truly alone. Alone was something she had never been. Constantly surrounded by her parents and the Councils, she rarely had moments to herself. They kept her shielded as if she were breakable, and she supposed with their long lives, to them, she was.

Putting her hands on her hips, she studied her surroundings, knowing it would do no good to look for Keary. He wouldn't be there, no matter how hard she searched. These new surroundings were foreign to her. Nothing looked like home. There were structures in the near distance, but she wasn't sure what they were. She thought they might be houses, but they were much bigger than the small wooden home she and her parents lived in. They looked to be made of some sort of stone she had never seen. And there were so many of them, it was almost as overwhelming as knowing she was in another world. Away from her family. Fear skirted the façade of strength she'd worn, and she shoved it aside, knowing it had no place there.

A stone path led through the houses and ran in different directions, including where she stood. It seemed to go on forever, and she thought she'd never seen a stone that long, so there was no way it could be stone. She kneeled down and put her hand on the rough white surface. Then, just as suddenly, she pulled her hand back. She gasped, her eyes fixed on a hand that was hers but was not hers at the same time. Moving her hand back out, then pulling it back in, then back out again, she continued to stare at it, her eyes growing wider each time. What kept appearing was not her hand.

She stood and looked down at her feet. No, those were definitely not her feet. But when she picked up her foot and shook it, the other foot did the same thing.

*Oh no. This can't be.*

Keary's words came back to her. They would be in the same place in life as Violissa and Sinow were in currently. She hadn't asked what age that would be. It had never occurred to her that she would be anything different from the eighteen years she was in their world. She'd been wrong.

She looked down again at the small hands and picked up the small girl's skirt. Everything was tiny. Tiny hands, tiny feet, tiny shoes, tiny clothes. Her heart raced, tiny thuds resounding in her ears.

Violissa wasn't a woman in this world. She was a child. Paige swallowed her fear. This was her duty, no matter how frightening or altering. Her job was to find her queen. Calming her erratic breathing, she heard children laughing, and turned her head in the direction, knowing instinctively that was where she needed to go.

Feet taking her closer, she clutched her hands to her sides to keep them from shaking. A group of girls and boys were running around, some playing tag, some kicking around what appeared to be a ball, though it was unlike any they had in their world. Black and white squares decorated it.

More children were moving back and forth on a contraption that intrigued her. They appeared to be flying, their legs kicking high into the sky as they clung to thick silver vines. She stood mesmerized by their movement until she heard a small voice. A girl of about eight years stood before her, golden curls spilling from the braids that tried to bind them, her emerald eyes sparkling in the sunlight.

"Hi, I'm Violet," she said to Paige in the most beautiful voice Paige had ever heard. There was no mistaking who this girl was.

Violissa.

# PART TWO
# SLEEP

# CHAPTER 18

Violet stared at the ceiling. She tried to focus on the small lilacs painted across it. Sometimes, just that small focus would push the nausea and dizziness away. They had come on strong and quick this time, forcing her to lie down to avoid crashing to the floor. She took a deep breath and slowly sat up on the edge of the bed. She needed to get moving. Paige was downstairs waiting, and she'd be calling up again at any moment.

Right on cue, she heard, "Come on, Violet, time's-a-ticking!"

Violet smiled. Paige had been her best friend since she'd stumbled onto the playground when they were eight. Violet's great aunt had taken her in when no one could find her parents, and they'd been inseparable since. Paige understood her like no one else. A car crash had killed Violet's parents when she was just a toddler, and she had lived with her great aunt since that day. Violet had taken Paige under her wing just as her great-aunt had done, and now they were as close as sisters.

She pushed herself up, and after waiting a moment to make sure the nausea had passed, she stood, grabbing her shirt and pulling it over her sports bra. She walked over to the mirror that stood in the corner. It was rare that she used it. She didn't bother worrying about her looks, didn't wear makeup or spend hours fooling with her hair. In fact, she used the mirror so infrequently she had to peel a layer of piled clothes from it to access it.

When she managed to uncover it, her green eyes stared back at her. They were currently a rich green, reflecting her mood. Her eyes were always changing, and those close to her could read her emotions just by their shade of green. She pulled her long blonde hair up and threaded a hair tie around it. One curl sprung loose and brushed her cheek. She rolled her eyes. There was no use in trying to force it back. It had a mind of its own. She had always thought it was waiting for someone to wrap his finger around.

Violet brought the heel of her palm to her head as another wave of nausea hit. Wave was the word she used to describe it because that was what people understood, but it wasn't quite the right word. It was more like a tug deep within her core, a pull to something or someone.

She lowered her hand and looked back at the mirror, chewing her bottom lip. She'd had the sensation all her life, but it was getting stronger, as if in anticipation of something. The tug went hand in hand with the emotions that would wash over her. A notion that this wasn't right, that this wasn't where she was supposed to be. An urgent nagging that she had lost something, or someone. Him.

She knew it sounded ridiculous, but he was out there. It sounded like a fairy tale when she said it out loud, but she knew with every fiber of her being that her soul mate was just beyond her reach, and that all of this was tied to him.

Even in her dreams, he was present. There was never much left to remember when she woke, but those dark, almost black eyes that seemed to see into her soul stayed with her. She had been waiting for him, had waited all her life, and knew she would continue to wait. There was no other, and there would be no other for her. She had no desire for anyone else, to the frustration of every man in town.

"Violet!" Paige called for her again. She could hear the impatience in her friend's voice and knew she needed to stop daydreaming. Grabbing her phone and earbuds, she ran out of the room and down the stairs.

"Why are you in such a hurry for me to beat you again, Paige?" she asked as she reached the bottom step.

Paige put her hands on her hips. "One of these days, I'm going to win fair and square," she said. "And today is that day."

Violet laughed and hugged her friend. "If thinking so makes you happy, then keep thinking it." She opened the front door and stood on the porch, stretching her not quite awake muscles.

She and Paige ran a few days a week and always made it competitive. They would race to the outer edge of the park that sat in the center of town, splitting off to see who arrived first. Violet won most times, but she slowed her pace every so often to let Paige take bragging rights. Looking up at the cloudless sky, she thought this would be a good day to win.

"Come on, slowpoke," Paige joked as she jogged down the porch stairs. "I don't want you stretching too much. Those long legs of yours need to be slow today so I can kick your ass. It's my turn to win." She stuck her tongue out at Violet and jogged away.

Violet shook her head and laughed. So, that was how it was going to be today. As she ran to catch up with Paige, she realized her headache had disappeared. Maybe it would be a good day after all.

# CHAPTER 19

Mountains kissed the sky, setting a backdrop to the quaint town Simon had only heard of through Keary's stories. The quiet hustle of small-town life hummed as he walked toward the park. With storefronts that looked like someone had taken them from a painting and the college tucked in a few streets up, it looked like the ideal place to settle down and raise a family. Not the kind of place he would have settled since the New York penthouse apartment he rarely stayed in was as close to settling down as he came. But it fit Keary and reminded Simon of the town where he and Keary had grown up back in Ireland.

When Keary had first approached him about being a silent partner in his bar, Simon had questioned just why he would want to open it here. He would have given Keary as much money as he wanted for a bar, so why not open it somewhere more populated?

But now, as he drew closer to the tranquil park, he could appreciate Keary's insistence on setting up shop here. And Keary had been here enough years for Simon to know he wasn't going anywhere. Simon, on the other hand, traveled constantly. He couldn't seem to stay in one place long. A compulsion drove him to keep moving, always searching. It sounded ridiculous, but he searched every face, turned at every voice, always looking for the one thing that had eluded him his entire life. The woman from his dreams.

He had dreamed of her so many times for as far back as he could remember that he'd memorized the pieces of her that stayed with him. The dreams never showed all of her, offering only glimpses, but they were enough to sense a tie to her. A knowledge rooted deep within him that told him she was out there. Almost like his soul was bound to hers and only she could free it.

A streak of golden hair, a glint of green that sparkled like cats' eyes, lips lush and parted. And he would wake with an ache so intense that he had to catch his breath. A hint of lilac would linger in the air until it faded, only to return the next dream.

Lately, the dreams had become more frequent, and with them, the need to keep moving. A constant sense that the search was ending. He hoped it would soon; there was an emptiness to him he could never seem to fill. No matter how much he traveled and no matter how successful he became, it remained, and he suspected nothing would ease it until he found her.

Passing the last of the shops, he found himself in front of the park. Most of it was open land with paths winding along the sides that stood shaded by the overlooking tree line. A large opening cut through the middle, branching out into another section of the park. He assumed what was beyond the trees led to more park, but the trees blocked his view. There was something peaceful about it, something that called to him. He'd never been much of a nature person, but he appreciated its beauty.

Drawn to find out where the tree line led, he took the path to the left and began walking. Checking his watch absently, he saw he had plenty of time before Keary expected him. With sleep escaping him yet again the night before, he'd left the city much earlier than he and Keary had discussed. Always the businessman, he figured it would give him time to take in the town and see if his investment had been a wise one. So far, the numbers hadn't been impressive, but with the college nearby it provided a crowd during the school term, and the locals seemed loyal to Keary.

This had been Keary's dream since they'd been young. Even before they had moved to the States, he had talked about opening an Irish pub like their uncle owned. Even if the venture had failed, Simon would have kept Keary open. There was no way he was going to let his best friend fail in his lifelong dream.

Simon continued on the path but soon veered off to move closer to the wooded area, an unexplainable pull drawing him there. A trail jutted out ahead of him, and he noticed it cut across the field and ran straight through the park over to the other side. A running trail, perhaps. He noticed the tug again, but once he reached the area where the trail cut out of the woods and into the park, it disappeared.

Turning, he looked across the park. The path he'd been on had ended a short while back and twisted over toward the other side of the park, leaving this open space near the end of the trees as a kind of quiet retreat removed from the main open area. The running trail was worn only lightly, so he imagined it wasn't a popular route. Whoever ran this trail preferred to be in the natural setting and not the constructed version. He stood contemplating the trail when the light step of feet caused him to turn, but not quickly enough. The force of a body slammed into him, setting him slightly off balance. Catching himself before he fell, he looked over to see what had hit him. An apology formed, but as the words came out, the wind rushed from his chest.

The world around him fell away, and he knew his search was over.

# CHAPTER 20

As the wind brushed over her skin, Violet picked up her pace. She was on her usual path through the woods and could see the empty park just through the tree line, a slight morning mist still coating the grass with dew. The fresh air rushed over her skin, and she wondered if this was how the ancient people had experienced nature, long before the time of cell phones and cars. Long ago, when running was a necessity for survival. A world she thought she would have been happy in.

She ran her fingers along the bark of the trees as she gently leaped over a fallen branch. Just before breaking from the forest into the open grass, she looked down at her phone to change songs. Her peace shattered when she slammed into something hard, the impact sending her tumbling to the ground. Stunned, she lay there, trying to get her bearings until a voice came from behind her.

"I'm so sorry. Are you all right?"

The voice cascaded up her spine and danced in her ears. Time seemed to slow, and the world spun like it did every time she had an episode. She took a breath and slowly turned onto her back, pushing herself up on her elbows. That breath froze in her throat, and her heart stopped as she looked upon the source of the voice. For what seemed an eternity, his rich chocolate eyes drew her into their spell.

*But they aren't quite brown, more black than brown*, she thought as the air kicked back into her lungs.

When she finally blinked, she saw the eyes belonged to the most gorgeous man she'd ever laid eyes upon. He wasn't a pretty boy handsome, but rather had a rugged, broody essence to him. A solid square jaw, lips that turned upward to a gorgeous grin, thick black lashes that outlined his dark eyes. This was the face of someone with confidence and power.

She could have lain there and stared at his intense beauty all day and, as it was, no matter how hard she tried, she couldn't pull her eyes from his. Her mind registered the thick black hair that crowned his head, short but with just enough length that it left the tips of his bangs shyly touching his forehead where the hair fell. Long enough to run her fingers through. She wanted to chastise herself for the thought but was too struck by his presence to do so.

He was tall, his shadow spilling down across her, blocking the sun that shone above. As he reached his hand down to help her up, she forced her eyes from his, only then registering the thick, muscular chest that showed slightly beneath his T-shirt and the strength of his hand as it grasped hers. A current ran through her when their skin touched, causing her to peek up at his eyes once more.

Again, the wind fled from her, and her chest squeezed beneath her shirt. This man had rendered her helpless. She couldn't move, could barely breathe, and no matter what the rational side of her mind screamed, she wanted nothing more than to fall into this man's arms and give her entire being to him, mind, body, and soul for all of eternity.

She was standing now, so much closer than she ever would to a stranger. But he wasn't a stranger. She registered that knowledge somewhere in her consciousness. That acknowledgement sounded odd, but she recognized his touch and his presence as if she had always known him. Knew this was the man for whom she had waited, the man she had dreamed of every night since she could remember. She didn't know how she knew that, but she did, and as she inhaled deeply, her chest heaving from the pain of it, she could see by his reaction that he had the same thought.

*Say something!* she screamed to herself, wondering momentarily why he too seemed so speechless.

She wanted to kick herself for not being able to draw her eyes from his, or pull her hand away, or even mutter one word. Every instinct that made her a strong female presence in her everyday life seemed to have fled, leaving her wanting only for him to take her in his arms and keep her safe. It was a thought she'd never had, one that went against everything she'd ever believed about herself.

Forcing herself out of her trance, she tried to say something but only managed to come up with a quiet, "You're not from around here."

She wanted to crawl under a rock and die. Was that seriously all she could muster? Thankfully, he didn't laugh or ridicule her. Instead, he smiled. A beautiful, reassuring smile that, if given the wrong circumstance, she thought might just be a little terrifying. Thankfully, this was not the case, and it warmed her soul.

"You're quite observant," he replied, his smile broadening. Heat rose in her cheeks. "I'm visiting," he paused and ran his hand through his hair, "but I'm thinking it might turn into a longer visit than I expected."

Her knees weakened as he brought his hand down to her stray curl and slowly wrapped it around his finger, as though he'd done it a hundred times before. And deep within her, she registered acceptance that the strand of hair that had annoyed her for years had been there for him all along.

He was closer now, their bodies moving nearer so that only a sliver of space separated them.

"Simon?" she replied. "You're Simon Black, Keary's friend."

She'd heard about him ever since Keary had moved to town, but she'd never seen a picture. "I'm Violet." She would have gone on with the adrenaline rush that had surged through her when he'd woven his finger through her hair, but he interrupted.

"Vi." The name was barely a whisper.

Oh, how she hated that nickname coming from anyone else's mouth, but from him, it sounded perfect, as if she'd reserved it for him all these years. She tried to read what he was thinking from his expression, but his eyes kept drawing her back.

The world seemed to fall away, leaving only the two of them. Time stopped as he breached the distance between them. He tilted her face toward his, and she gave him unspoken permission, letting her mouth part just slightly. They were so close that his lips hovered just above hers, barely touching hers until she lifted slightly on her toes and finished the movement for him.

With that kiss, everything else faded. There was only him, and the currents that soared like streams of electricity through her body. She ached for more, pushing herself against his chest as his tongue greedily sought hers out. Tingles encapsulated her nerves, pulsing through her veins, and imprisoning her senses. Far within her, the ache that had sat in her core for as long as she could remember faded, replaced with a hunger that tore through her.

His hand loosened her hair from its tie, his fingers freeing the strands and threading through them as his other hand slipped down her body and encased her hip. She moaned, her body primed and ready for him to claim. Hands sliding below his shirt, she ran them over his firm muscles and around his back. He squeezed her hip, bringing her body closer, and she could feel his need for her as it pressed against her. A shiver tickled its way over her skin as his hand encompassed the back of her neck like a statement of ownership.

Lost in a bevy of sensations, her body awakened by his touches and craving more, she let reality fall away and escaped further into the ecstasy of his touch.

# CHAPTER 21

Resting on her knees to catch her breath, Paige glanced around, wondering where Violet was. They had raced this path for years, and it was rare that Paige won. The only time she did, Violet arrived within seconds, and Paige was certain she had let her win. Violet thought she was sneaky, but Paige knew the truth.

She wiped the sweat from her forehead with her arm and paced. It had been twenty years since she had met Violet on the playground in Ireland. Twenty long years of waiting and anticipating what was on the brink of happening today. She shook her hands out to free herself from the nerves, but it didn't help. Within hours Simon would be there, and the clock would start ticking. She had no idea what would happen when they met. If she and Keary could stop the inevitable.

She had called Violet her friend for so long it would be difficult to see her as anything else. But it would all change when she woke, and Paige would have to refer to Violet as her queen, as Violissa. It still seemed strange to call her a friend. To call her Violet knowing who she really was. To hear Keary call the Dark King Simon rather than Sinow.

She tucked her hands under her arms to quiet them. Terror had gripped her since Keary had told her of Simon's intention to visit. So many questions swirled in her mind. Most about what would happen when Violissa's memories returned. Her father had always told her the queen had been kind, but Paige wasn't so sure if that was the truth.

Her father and the rest of the Council had raised her on stories of the king and queen. The wonders of Violissa and the love she had for her people had encompassed most of those stories. But some were darker.

Elvin blood that ran through Violissa's veins, and the Council had always credited that part of her heritage for the more volatile moments in their queen's history. And those moments had always involved King Sinow.

Paige rubbed her arms at the chill that crept up her spine. Sinow terrified her, but what made this all so much more unsettling was the idea that the spell had warped Violissa's memories. Twisting them and burying the truth so far beneath it, she couldn't free herself enough to see the truth of their past and the love they had for each other. If the king couldn't get through to her when she woke, Paige didn't know how she possibly could. Worse was what her queen would think once she discovered Paige had been lying to her for the past twenty years. She didn't think forgiveness would be simple.

Paige stopped pacing and hit her palm on her forehead.

"Stop it, Paige," she muttered.

She needed to concentrate, and she needed to figure out where Violissa—Violet—had disappeared to.

Paige trotted through the tree line down the path Violet would have run, hoping she hadn't hurt herself. When she broke through the trees, she stopped short, nearly tripping over her feet. There across the green was Violet, but this was definitely not how Paige had expected to find her. She was standing very close to a tall, solidly built man. So close he might have been whispering in her ear. She didn't recognize him and moved closer, only to discover they weren't talking. They were kissing. And that man wasn't just any man. This was the Dark King.

Goosebumps traveled down her arms as she observed Sinow for the first time. He had to be the most beautiful man she'd ever seen in an extremely terrifying way. She had the instinct to bow down and avert her eyes before she remembered she wasn't home. He had no power here.

Drawing closer, she experienced a tingle on her skin, almost like the magic of the prophecy permeated the air. The two were locked in a passionate kiss, their hands traveling everywhere as if they had been lovers for years. So, this was the prophecy at work. The attraction was so strong that they were all over each other, and Paige figured they couldn't have been together for more than a few minutes.

She fumbled for her phone and caught it as it nearly slipped out of her now very sweaty hand. She hit Keary's phone number.

After what seemed an eternity, he picked up. "Yeah, what's up, Paige?"

There were times when Paige thought Keary had forgotten who he really was. The way humans talked and acted came too easily to him, and she worried what would happen when they returned home...if they returned home.

"He's here," she blurted, panic straining her voice.

"Slow down. Who's here?"

"Who do you think is here?" She rolled her eyes and envisioned reaching through the phone to shake him. "Sinow is here and Violet, I mean Violissa, is with him. Not just with him, but all over him. They look like they're about to tear each other's clothes off."

She heard shuffling, like he might have dropped the phone, before he said, "Wait. Sinow is there, at your house?" His voice had climbed a pitch.

"No, at the park," she replied, rubbing her shaking hand on her temple. "Violissa and I were running, and we got separated. I guess they must have run into each other. What in the Fates am I going to do, Keary?"

He inhaled a little too loudly before saying, "You're going to calm down and get a hold of yourself. We knew this was going to happen."

"Did we?" she squealed, hating how irrational she sounded. "I don't remember hearing anything about them being lip-locked within seconds of meeting each other."

"I warned you. The Fate told me they couldn't control themselves because of the prophecy."

She realized she was wearing a small divot in the grass with her pacing and stopped herself.

"Is this how they were at home?"

"There were complications at home." She could hear his frustration through the phone. "It will take a few minutes for me to get to you. Where are you, by the way?"

With a sigh, she tucked her trembling hand under her arm and said, "We're at the park, on the field side with the open green. Opposite the lakeside."

"Damn, then it will definitely take me a few minutes. You need to stop them. It's imperative that you separate them before it's too late."

She started pacing again and ran her hand along her hairline.

"How in the world am I going to do that?"

"Remember who you are, Paige. You are the daughter of a Lightbearer. Use your head and think of something fast."

She stared at the phone. He had hung up on her and was probably bolting out of the door to meet her there. Until then, it was up to her to do something before the pair were too far gone. She didn't know what would happen if she left them, but she guessed it wouldn't be PG-rated.

"Ugh, damned prophecy," she pouted as she stormed across the green to intervene.

Their bodies linked, they didn't notice her approach. Paige

swallowed, feeling like a voyeur as they continued to make out, their clothes in disarray and starting to come off. She cleared her throat, hoping even the slightest distraction would break their trance, but it didn't.

"Um, Violet?" She balled her hands in frustration and moved closer. Part of her wanted to stop and simply stare at the king. This man was beyond perfect. Good Fates he was gorgeous. It fit that with Violissa's beauty, he would look that good, but did the Fates really need to go this far with their rulers? It was a little too unbelievable. She shook her head to clear it and hoped no one had noticed her moment of voyeurism.

"Violet, I know you like to find things to distract you so I can win the race, but this is well beyond anything I would have expected," she said loud enough that anyone in the vicinity should have heard.

That did it. The two stopped kissing and quickly stepped away from each other, hands falling to their sides, shirts dropping back to their original positions. She let out a sigh a bit too soon as their eyes met again, and they started moving close to one another. It was like a magnetic pull forcing their bodies together.

"Oh, for Pete's sake!" she declared. She moved in to separate them, only noticing the growl from Sinow after she'd stuck her hand between them. The sound caused the hair on her neck to rise, and she prayed he wouldn't become feral on her. She absently wondered if that could happen.

"Hi, I don't believe we've met. I'm Paige, your kissing companion's roommate and best friend."

His eyes went wide—eyes that were so dark they almost looked black—and he backed away, running his hand through his hair. The move was definitely the way to melt the heart of every woman within a hundred miles, and Paige tried not to swoon, knowing this man held the power to kill her locked away inside of him. As he straightened his spine, bringing himself to his full height and towering over her, her knees shook. Fear slithered through her, causing her breath to seize. She looked up into the eyes of the legendary Dark King, and her knees almost went out on her. If she were home and he at full power, she'd be dead by now.

The Councils had trained everyone in the old ways. The one rule that had struck fear the most was that no one looked a Darkbearer in the eye without permission, or else they would be driven to madness as punishment. That punishment was the least horrific. To even dare approach the king or, even more boldly, to look him in the eyes without permission, meant instant death. The man now meeting Paige's gaze and extending his hand out to take hers, contained the power to instantly take her life. The thought of that much power stole her ability to think, and she held back the urge to run in terror.

*He's just a man here. He's just a man here.* She repeated the mantra in her head to give her strength as she shook his hand.

"Simon," he said, his voice a rich baritone.

"Simon? Like in Keary's friend Simon?" she asked, pulling her hand away quickly and pretending she didn't already know the answer to that question.

"Yes," Violet cooed. "Simon."

Paige turned to her friend, rolled her eyes, and kicked her playfully. "You didn't tell me you had a boyfriend," she teased.

Blush swept up Violet's cheeks. It irked Paige that it seemed to make Violet that much more appealing. Was there no end to it?

Simon chuckled behind her, and she forced herself to turn back around to look at him. He was gazing at Violet, his dark eyes shimmering.

"I can't say I normally greet people with that much enthusiasm," he said to her, looking right past Paige like she wasn't even there.

Violet laughed, the sound like tiny bells on a spring day, and Simon seemed to melt.

"Nor do I. Perhaps it's a greeting in certain countries?"

Paige was about to answer that in no country did people kiss like that upon meeting, but Simon spoke first.

"Doubtful, but it's one I don't regret."

The blush grew closer to crimson, and Violet somehow became even more attractive. Paige was about to scream in frustration when she heard Keary's voice.

"Damn, did you get a little off the beaten path there?" Keary yelled as he jogged across the open field.

Paige watched Simon turn and greet his friend. He walked forward and embraced him in a hug.

Slapping his arm and laughing, he replied, "Just a little." He glanced back at Violet. "But it was completely worth it."

This was the first time Paige had seen the two men together, and the resemblance was so that they could have been brothers. Sinow had about two inches on Keary, and his build was slightly bigger, but otherwise, they looked so alike it was uncanny. Is this what all the Dark Council looked like before Sinow had left? She couldn't picture the old men who had helped raise her like this, but then, she'd never pictured Keary, who now looked thirty years younger, that way. Imagining her father that way seemed a ridiculous notion, but then, if this was truly what the Dark and Light Council had lost when Sinow had left, they had lost more than Paige had imagined.

She'd been with Keary in her life as a human for so long now that she sometimes forgot he was a Darkbearer. Seeing him standing with the Dark King brought her back to reality. Sinow was a massive presence, and she could only imagine him with power. He must have been terrifying. It made her curious to know if he was anything like his brother.

Her father had told her the story, but she always wondered if he had softened it some to protect her or maybe protect the myth that Violissa and Sinow had become. Their story and the possibility of their return had given their people hope throughout the centuries of Tynan's reign. If Sinow were anything like his brother, that hope could shatter and turn to fear and desolation.

Paige had never seen Tynan. She'd been born well after their people's escape, but she had to imagine he looked similar to Sinow. The thought of both at what she envisioned their full power sent a shiver up her spine.

Looking at Sinow and Keary together made her suddenly doubt herself and her place with them. These people had a history together, a past that defined them, one that had defined their world. They held power she could only imagine was greater than anything this human world could fathom. She wasn't any part of this. She didn't have any power and wasn't immortal. In all honesty, she didn't even know the three of them. As Simon and Keary turned to face Violet, Paige suddenly felt incredibly small and inconsequential. Fear choked her again, and she wanted more than anything to be home again.

# CHAPTER 22

The overwhelming need to strangle Violet's friend hammered at Simon. Violent and intense, it was difficult to simmer. A rumble had risen from his chest, coming out in a noise he'd never made. One that sounded distinctly like a growl. He had stepped away, putting distance between the women and him, worried by the sound.

Desire coursed through him, urging him to get back to Violet. To erase the distance that now separated them and forget the others were with them. He couldn't tear his eyes from her. She was stunning. Her hair golden in the sun, her eyes shimmering just as they did in his dreams. There was no doubt she was the one, and the certainty cemented itself in his gut. The draw to her was undeniable. It almost seemed like a tether existed between them, tightening the closer he came to her, straining for their bodies to connect. Kissing her had been easy, expected as if his body would wither and die if he didn't. And so when she'd taken the step, rising on her toes so that their mouths met, he hadn't considered they were standing in the park. If her friend hadn't interrupted, he knew without a doubt he would not have stopped. He would have made love to Violet with no hesitation.

That thought had him struggling for a rational explanation. He ran his hand through his hair, catching her eyes and losing himself again. That undeniable need hit him, gripping itself around his insides and controlling his mind and body. He wanted to kiss her again, wanted to touch her, to hold her, and he would have done so but for their audience.

"You getting bigger?" Keary asked, punching Simon's arm.

It had been too long since he'd seen his friend, and they both knew it. Too many years and miles had come between them, yet being with him again was like returning home.

"Not in the least. You just haven't bothered to come visit me in so long you've forgotten how much bigger I am than you."

Once the words left his mouth, he knew he'd set himself up for a well-deserved comeback, and Keary didn't miss a beat.

"You know the road goes two ways, right? You must since you found your way here today. What happened all the rest of the years?"

"Touché," Simon replied, putting his hands up in surrender.

Keary was right. He'd had no excuse. Years had gone by since Keary last visited him in New York, and Simon always seemed to have a reason for not visiting Keary on his turf. He was always too busy to make the trip. Whenever the idea even crossed his mind or whenever Keary brought it up, something would require his attention. It had never failed until now. This time, the stars had aligned, and there he stood.

Keary slapped him on the back as a forgiving gesture.

"I see you've met Violet and Paige," he said, changing the subject.

Simon turned toward Violet again, wondering if this time he could keep his hands to himself. It was hard. He was so drawn to her, as if his survival rested on having her in his arms.

He steadied himself and said, "If I'd known what you were hiding up here, I would have come a long time ago."

Violet smiled, her cheeks taking on a blush that only enhanced her beauty.

"You can't be serious," Keary responded. Simon pulled his gaze from Violet, his brows furrowing. "How long have I been telling you about the beautiful woman who would be perfect for you? And how many times have I tried to persuade you to come meet her?"

The air fled his lungs. All this time, she'd been here, and all this time, he'd avoided coming here. He ran his hand across his face. He considered slapping himself in the head but held back, reluctant to look like a fool.

"This is the beautiful blonde?" He looked back over at Violet. "Vi is the one you've been nagging me about all this time?" She gave him a quirky look at the word 'nagging'. "Sorry," he responded instinctively, giving her a grin.

"She doesn't like that nickname," Paige burst out.

"It's okay, Paige," Violet said, putting her hand up to stop Paige.

"But you hate it when people call you that."

He cringed as regret stabbed him, hating that he had called her something she didn't like, but Vi just seemed right when it came out. She didn't quite seem like a Violet. There was something about it that didn't fit her.

"I know, Paige, but I kind of like it when he says it. I like the way it sounds, like I've been saving it for him."

Paige opened her mouth to retort back, but Simon noticed Keary shake his head slightly and mouth something to her that he couldn't make out. She held her tongue, and Simon wondered what the exchange had been about. It was curious the way the two kept looking at each other, like they knew something. He caught Violet's eyes again, and the thought slipped away.

"As I was saying, Vi and I bumped into each other, more or less."

"Ran your mouths into each other is more like it," Paige muttered.

She had a mouth on her, and he had a suspicion his aggravation would be constant around her.

"Paige!" Violet exclaimed before he could.

"It's true, Violet," she said, crossing her arms. "I'm not sure what else you would call it."

Simon really wanted this conversation to end and for Paige and Keary to leave so he could go back to kissing Violet. He rubbed his cheek, trying to fathom what he was thinking. Shifting his stance, he scraped his hand through his hair again. The situation was out of control. He was out of control, and he needed to get a grip. From the pursing of Violet's lips, he could see she was just as flustered. An urge to push the others out of the way and drag his teeth over her bottom lip filled his mind. As if the same yearning was raging through her, those emerald irises flicked to his, growing large as her lips parted. He gripped his hands tightly and pulled his gaze from hers, noticing the tight ball she had her hands in.

Whatever was happening between them, it was mutual, and that had his heart pounding almost too loudly. The sharp inhale she took when his gaze lifted back to her was the same she took each time their eyes met. It reached into a place deep within his being that recognized that reaction. Almost like he had seen it before, experienced the thrill in his pulse at hearing the drag of breath and the stuttering of her heart. Creasing his brows, he wondered at the last thought, not knowing how he recognized that her heart had stuttered but understanding that it had.

Violet chewed on her bottom lip, something that only made her even more desirable.

A throat clearing from Keary interrupted his thoughts. "I hope you two are through staring at each other because I'm a little uncomfortable watching this interaction. Should I get you a hotel room?"

Violet's blush deepened as Keary elbowed Simon.

"Not yet," he replied, still unable to take his eyes from hers.

"All right then, we'll save that for later. Violet, you and Paige need to finish your run, and Simon, you need to come with me. We've got some catching up to do, buddy."

Simon tore his eyes from Violet and looked at Keary. He didn't seem the least bit surprised by the idea of his kissing her, something that should have warranted some reaction considering how long Keary had known him. Paige's eager response left him with no time to ponder the reaction.

"That's right," she blurted. "I won the race this time, Violet, but since someone distracted you..." She made a gesture of quotation marks that caused Violet to smile. She had a beautiful smile, and her eyes shone a bright emerald that seemed to radiate, reminding him of stars rising in the endless black of night. Paige continued, breaking his trance, "...I'm suspicious that you let me win again. We've got to finish the race so I can beat you fair and square."

Simon bent down to pick up Violet's phone, which was still where it had landed after their earlier collision. Violet went down at the same time. Currents sparked along his spine when her hand brushed his. Their eyes met, leaving him spellbound once again. Time stopped, and all that seemed to exist was the two of them. He didn't know how long they stayed like that, but the distinctly loud clearing of Keary's throat woke him.

The phone was still in his hand as they both came up, awkwardly bumping heads. Violet laughed, a sound he could only imagine came from fae creatures. It was like music to him, cascading down to the very depths of his soul, claiming it as its own. She rubbed the spot on her head where they had bumped and smiled at him, and his heart nearly leaped out of his chest to get to hers.

"That's quite a number you did on your phone, Violet." Paige said, breaking the hold that was over him. He looked down at the phone in his hand. The screen had a large crack running through most of it.

"That is pretty bad," he said. "I'll buy you a new one."

"What? That's nonsense," she responded. Pressing the home button, she pointed to the screen as it lit up. "See, it still works."

He smiled when he saw that her home screen was a field of violets.

"You're getting a new phone. It's my fault you dropped it. I wasn't looking where I was going."

"And I was changing songs on my playlist. We're both guilty," she answered.

"Let him get you the phone, Violet. No matter how hard you fight it, he's going to get it anyway. Just give up," Keary interjected.

She bit her lip, then smiled. "Okay. But it really is fine." Her hand was still resting on the phone while he held it, their fingers touching. He didn't want to let go, worried the second he pulled away from her, he might lose her.

"Come on, Simon, we've got some catching up to do," Keary said.

He was ready to go. Simon knew this but still couldn't pull himself away from her. Something deep down screamed for him to stay, some primal protective instinct he couldn't understand. He knew that no matter how hard he tried, he wouldn't be able to walk away from her on his own. As it turned out, he didn't have to. Violet closed her eyes, breaking the connection. The air whooshed back into his chest as she gently pulled the phone and her hand from his. She opened her eyes again, the emerald in them warming his soul.

"Come on, Violet," Paige said, backing away from them in a slow jog. "You know if I beat you, I'll never let you live it down."

"She's right," Violet said as she hesitantly backed away from him. She pulled her hair back up and put her earbuds in, then flashed him another amazing smile. "The last time she won, she told everyone in town. It's all I heard for a month." She paused, her eyes sparkling in the sunlight. "Simon, I hope we'll see each other soon." She had walked far enough that the magnetic pull holding him prisoner faded slightly. In its place was an emptiness he couldn't explain.

"Goodbye, Vi. I'm sure we will."

She turned to catch up with Paige.

"No goodbyes for me, Violet?" Keary teased.

"Goodbye, Keary," she shouted over her shoulder with a laugh as she jogged toward Paige.

Simon watched her, the uncomfortable sensation in his chest growing with every stride her long legs took.

"Come on, I'll show you around," Keary said, wrapping his arm around Simon's shoulder. "You'll live without her for a few hours at least." Simon shrugged his arm off and punched his friend in the bicep. "You're getting weak in your old age."

He took a step, then stopped, needing to keep the connection with Violet for just a little longer. On impulse, he turned around, calling after her. She halted her steps and turned back to him as he jogged over to her.

"I didn't realize I'd see you that soon," she said when he reached her. She really hadn't gone too far, and he suspected she could run much faster than she had.

"What are you doing tonight?" he asked on impulse.

Her eyes twinkled with amusement. "Are you asking me out?"

"Of course I am," he answered sheepishly, combing his fingers through his hair.

"Well, it just so happens I have a date tonight." His heart sank, and he hoped she didn't see the disappointment on his face. "With Paige." He resisted the urge to slap himself for overreacting so fast. "The college orchestra is having a special show at our local theater. I volunteer there, so I need to attend." She paused, chewing her lip. "If you don't mind sharing me with Paige, you could come with us."

"Yes," he said, wincing at his quick response. What the hell was wrong with him? He needed to get a grip on his reaction to her. He was completely out of control. "That would be nice. I'm sure it will be great."

"Well, it's no New York Philharmonic, like I'm sure you're used to seeing, but they do an impressive job."

He chuckled. "Believe it or not, I've never been to one of their shows. In fact, I've never been to a show in the city."

She lifted her eyebrow in disbelief. "Not even Broadway?"

With a headshake, he shrugged.

"How can you live in New York City and not have been to a Broadway show?"

"Easily. I've never had the right person to take with me."

She bit her bottom lip as a pink hue colored her cheeks again.

"Then a date it is," Keary said from behind him.

Irritation slipped through Simon at the thought of Keary encroaching on their moment, but he shook it off.

"A date," he said to Violet. "What time should I pick you up?"

"Why don't we do dinner before the show?" Keary interjected.

Simon swung around and gave him a dirty look.

"What? Paige will need a date, so she's not a third wheel."

"That sounds like a plan," Paige answered. He hadn't noticed her sneak up on them either, and his annoyance was mounting.

"Dinner and a show it is then," Violet said. "Paige and I will meet you there. What were you thinking, Keary? Kasey's?"

"That'll do. Let's say five?" Keary answered.

Violet looked back at Simon and smiled. "Five o'clock it is."

"Then it's settled. Keary, Paige, give us a minute," Simon said, narrowing his eyes at Keary. He wanted Violet to himself for another minute before he had to let her go.

Paige made a sound as if to resist, but Simon noticed Keary motion for her to back away. He studied his friend, who looked away as soon as he caught Simon's gaze. They were acting suspiciously, but for the life of him, he couldn't fathom why.

Paige walked away, and Keary moved back, putting his hands up in surrender.

"Are they always so clingy?" asked Simon in a joking tone, although part of him was serious. He didn't expect the answer she gave him.

"Annoyingly so. You'll get used to it." She stepped closer to him. "Five seems so far away."

He lifted his finger to catch her wandering curl and gave her a sideways grin. "It does, doesn't it?"

She was so close that her heartbeat was prominent where her chest met his. Her face tilted toward him, and before he knew it, his lips had met hers again. He took in the sweetness, the warmth of her mouth and the softness of her skin. His hand dropped the curl and moved to cup her chin, his other hand gathering around her waist. He didn't know if he'd ever be able to pull himself away. There was a need in him that screamed to not let her go. That need roared as the kiss deepened. But there was something else there now, a subtle notion that if he didn't let her go, he'd lose her completely. He didn't know what to make of it, but even with the intense need he had for her, that sensation was enough to make him pause. He dragged his lips from hers, hating to stop but heeding that instinct. Her irises had shifted to a sage hue, and concern lined them for just a moment before they shimmered to a vibrant green. It was captivating and left him speechless.

Hand still wrapped around the nape of her neck, he remained enraptured until she reached her hand up to bring it down, and said, "Tonight?"

"Yes, tonight," he replied.

She brought both hands up to his face and kissed him again. Not a needy kiss, but a giving kiss. One filled with her desire for him but also with the emotion that was currently flooding his body. With hesitation, she drew back and dropped her hands before taking a deep breath. Giving him one more smile, she turned and ran toward Paige. As she approached the tree line, she looked back, gave him a small wave, and disappeared into the trees.

Simon stood there, unable to move, his mind reeling. Every emotion assaulted him at once. Everything in him wanted to run after her, but he knew he couldn't. He'd have to wait until tonight. Longing tore through him, followed by a rush of excitement. He'd found her. All this time, she'd been here, waiting for him, and he'd finally found her.

"Come on, lover boy," Keary called. Simon forced himself to stop staring at the trees. His friend was standing with arms crossed, a smug look on his face.

"Is that the 'I told you so look'?" Simon asked him.

"Oh yeah, you're never going to hear the end of this from me."

As they walked out of the park, he couldn't help but glance back to see if Violet was watching him.

"Where did you park your car?" Keary asked.

Simon gave him a sideways look. "You're not going to say anything else about what just happened?"

"Of course I am. I'm just trying to figure out where to start."

Simon shrugged. "Up the street in front of a coffee shop."

"Wait, that was your car I ran past? The fancy Mercedes? That's a sweet car. I think I should ask for a raise if that's what you're driving around now."

Simon let him ramble on while he turned the words through his head.

"You ran here?"

"What?" Keary asked, distracted from his car obsession.

"You said you ran past the car. Why were you running?"

Keary seemed a little taken aback, his response delayed.

"Oh...well...someone mentioned there was a stranger wandering around town, and I figured you'd gotten lost."

Simon scrunched his eyes, appraising his friend as they reached his car.

"Small town," Keary said with a shrug, avoiding his eyes while running his hand along the car's roof.

Simon let it go and got into the car.

"I can't believe you really just stood in the middle of a park and made out with a complete stranger," Keary said. "What were you thinking?"

"I wasn't," Simon answered, annoyed at the sudden change in conversation. "I just went with it. And she's not a stranger."

"Really? Have you known her long? I don't think thirty minutes counts as long."

He rested his head on the steering wheel. "You know what I mean, Keary." Frustration tainted his words and strained his muscles.

"Just because I know her doesn't mean you do, Simon."

Without lifting his head, he made a quick move and punched Keary in the rib cage.

"Ouch! All right, all right."

"I know her, Keary. I've known her all my life. She's the one." He picked his head up and leaned back into the seat.

Keary was quiet. Simon didn't have to say anymore. Keary would know exactly what he meant. He understood. Understood that after years of fending girls off with excuses, taking the dates that wanted to go with Simon but went out with him instead, sticking up for Simon when they were young and the other kids didn't understand, helping through the disastrous day when they were eleven and Jenny O'Shea cornered him on the playground. Instead of walking away with the kiss she'd wanted, she ran away crying with Simon's vomit soaked through her smock dress. Keary understood the power of what Simon had said, just as he understood the significance of Simon kissing Violet today. That's why when Simon opened his eyes again and looked at the friend he'd known for twenty years, Keary gave him a coy grin.

Rubbing the side where Simon's punch had landed, he said,

"So, the girl of your dreams was here this whole time?" He chuckled. "Okay, I really have to say it at least once. I told you so."

Simon laughed. "Just once, or I'll punch you again."

"What are you going to do?"

He ran his hand through his hair and thought about Violet. "I don't know. Is it too soon to ask her to marry me?"

Keary looked at him as though he were mad. "Just a little."

"Well, that was the more gentlemanly of the things I'd like to do." His mind wandered to the touch of her skin, the taste of her lips.

"Geez, lover boy. Just drive for now."

He shook his head to clear the thoughts. He needed to get a handle on those thoughts, on his emotions, and, especially, on his body. Control dominated his life, and within the span of an hour, he had been more out of control than he'd ever been. He gripped the steering wheel as a rampant need to jump out of the car and run after Violet overcame him. He knew exactly what would happen if he did that, and this time, he wouldn't stop.

"You going to pull away from the curb sometime soon, or am I stuck here watching you fantasize about Violet a little longer? If so, I'm going to run in and get some coffee."

"Shut up, Keary," he returned, thankful for the redirection and the reminder that it would be best if he just cleared his mind and drove.

# CHAPTER 23

Simon eyed Keary when they pulled in front of the building. "Why didn't we just walk?" he asked. They had driven down the street only a few blocks.

"You don't like walking, remember?" Keary replied as he got out of the car.

"I don't? Since when? I live in New York City, Keary. I do a lot of walking."

By then, Keary had shut the door and walked away, leaving him to talk to himself. He shook his head and got out to follow him.

"What do you think?" Keary asked, looking at the building in front of him. Keary's baby. When he'd asked Simon to fund the bar, Simon hadn't hesitated. He had the money and knew Keary would use it wisely. Standing there, he could see it had been a wise decision. Positioned toward the end of the main street, the bar was past most of the shops, but not all of them.

Based on what Keary had told him about the locals who frequented the bar and the college kids from the local college who hit it during the school year, he'd been worried about its appearance. Surprisingly, he found it to be the opposite of what he had expected. The look was classy, black trimmed with four square windows lining the front. A stylish sign ran across the top announcing the name of the bar as Keary's Irish Pub, understated yet still sophisticated.

"I'm impressed, Keary. You could find this in New York or Boston. It's not what I expected. It's better." Keary's brown eyes brightened with pride. Slapping him on the back, Simon continued, "Let's see what it looks like inside."

Inside was even better. Simon ran his hand along the bar top and took it all in. Spacious but cozy, the room housed about ten tables, a small stage, and a bar wrapped in a square toward the back of the space. Mugs hung above it, and green vinyl topped stools surrounded it.

"Damn, Keary, it looks just like Uncle Pat's."

"That was my intent."

He should have known. Keary had told him he had intended to base the bar on their uncle's back home in Ireland. Really, it was Simon's uncle. He and his wife had taken Simon in after his parents had died when he was a toddler. When Keary came wandering into his life with no family to be found, nor any memory of one, they had taken him in as well. The two had grown up together since the age of eight and were more like brothers. His uncle had owned the town's pub, with his aunt caring for the adjacent rooms they ran as an inn. Spending so much time there had sparked Keary's interest in owning his own pub one day. He had a fascination with different ales and was always in search of new ones.

"You really did it," Simon said, walking around. "Well, you did it. I paid for it."

"Couldn't resist, could you?" Keary joked.

"No more than you could resist the 'I told you so' earlier," he replied with a laugh.

"Holy shit, you must be Simon," he heard a voice say behind them.

Turning, he found an overly buff guy with sandy hair and dim blue eyes, followed by a girl with short black hair and clothes that were too tight to leave her unnoticed. A few small tattoos graced her arms, and one peeked from her slightly exposed chest. It would have been a sexy look to most men, but Simon wasn't most men. She was about Simon's age, maybe a few years younger. From the disheveled look they both had about them, he wondered if they'd been doing more than stocking supplies in the back from where they'd emerged.

"Do I want to ask what you two were doing back there?" Keary asked.

The girl gave him a flirty smile and a wink before saying, "Just stocking, boss."

"I'm sure you were," Keary replied, crossing his arms.

"Chelsea?" Simon asked Keary. He knew Keary had a taste for women who were a little on the wild side and that he'd had a fling with his bartender. She fit the bill for his type.

"That's me," she answered.

The man came over, extending his large hand.

"I'm Chad," he said, shaking Simon's hand and staring awkwardly at him. It was a reaction he often received when people first met him. He always brushed it off. There was something empowering about how intimidating people found him.

"Why are you even here, Chad? I told Chelsea to come in early, but I don't remember saying anything to you," Keary said, tilting his head.

"I needed help with some things," Chelsea answered.

"I'm sure you did."

She gave him a coy smile, then looked back at Simon. "Is there something they put in the water over in that town you two are from?"

Simon scrunched his brows, not understanding the question.

"They don't make guys like you here," she explained. "Keary, you didn't tell me he was even better looking than you."

She walked over to Simon and laid a hand on his bicep. He tried not to recoil like he wanted to, instead giving her a scowl that she ignored. His stomach turned as it always did, and the bile rose in his throat. Violet was the only one who didn't trigger that reaction in him. He took her hand and removed it from his arm, enjoying the shiver of fear that ran through her when she met his eyes.

"The serious kind, huh? If you want to loosen up and have a little fun later, I get off at midnight."

"Chelsea," Keary scolded as Simon grimaced.

"What? It's worth a try. He looks like a sexier version of you, so if he's anything like you in bed, it's worth asking," she said, winking at him.

Keary shifted his feet and cleared his throat, which had Simon throwing a glance at him. Keary was the most relaxed man he knew, a trait that offset Simon's intensity, but he suddenly seemed very uncomfortable. He doubted it was from the woman's advances, since Keary was the biggest flirt he knew.

"He's taken," Keary answered, causing Simon to raise a brow. "Now get back to work."

"Damn, why are all the good ones always taken?" she muttered as she walked away.

Chad followed, peering back at Simon. His irritation shadowed his eyes, and Simon sighed. The last thing he was interested in was this guy's girl.

"So, Simon, who's the lucky girl? Did you bring her with you?" Chelsea asked, hopping over the bar and acting like the previous interaction had never happened.

Keary chuckled, his stance relaxing as he headed toward the bar. "Violet."

"Keary," Simon warned, ignoring the need to punch him. He'd always been very private about his life, preferring to keep people guessing. When people asked if he was seeing someone, he would change the subject. Even though there never was a someone, he didn't think it was anyone's business.

"Welcome to small-town life. It's worse here than it ever was back home," Keary replied, sitting at the bar.

"That's funny. We have a Violet here in town," Chad said, pulling chairs down from the tables.

"Wait," Chelsea said, "you don't mean our Violet, do you?"

Keary grinned. Chelsea grabbed her phone and looked down at it while Chad stood gaping.

"Our Violet?" Chad said. "The 'no one touches me,' Violet? I thought that text was a joke, Chelse."

"Me, too."

"What text?" Simon asked, his head hurting.

She flipped her phone around to show a long text chain in a group chat. "Well, first I got a text from Tara, who said she'd been out walking Knuckles. That's her new puppy. Cute as—"

"The point?" he interrupted.

She reeled back before she lowered the phone and continued. "She said that Violet was in the park kissing a stranger. Then, a few minutes later, Kasey added to the chat that she had seen her going hot and heavy with that same guy."

Simon rubbed his face. This was one reason he had moved to the city. He preferred the anonymity it provided. No one was in his business, and he stayed out of theirs.

"There was a group chat?" he groaned.

"Word travels fast around here, and everybody knows everybody."

"You were the guy?" Chad asked, his eyes like saucers.

"No shit, Sherlock," Chelsea retorted for him. "Chad, you're pretty and all, but sometimes, you're lacking in the intelligence area."

Simon put his head down on the bar.

"You made out with Violet?" Chelsea asked. "Do you have any idea how many guys have tried to get a piece of her and failed?

Have you been dating her all this time? I mean, you've only been here a few hours, right?"

"Ha, maybe we all got her so turned on over the years that she finally broke and let loose on him," Chad said.

A protective instinct tore through Simon, tinged with a streak of jealousy. He wanted to pound Chad's head into the wall until it was a bloody pulp. He shook his head, trying to get the thought out of his mind.

"Clearly, Chad, because you and the others here in town are so hot compared to him. I'm sure she was just settling since she didn't pick you. Keep trying to convince yourself, Chad," Chelsea snapped.

"Chad, make yourself useful and set the room up," Keary said, wiping his eyes.

"Now, where were we?" asked Chelsea, grabbing two mugs from the hanging rack.

"About to walk out of here," Simon grumbled.

She filled the mugs with beer and placed them in front of Simon and Keary.

"Drink and talk."

"It's a little early for drinking, isn't it?" he asked, watching her pour a shot for herself and one for Chad.

She took the shot, then wiped her mouth on the back of her hand. "Not on a day like today. So, you and Violet?"

"Do we really need to have this discussion? Keary, don't we have numbers to review?"

"You might as well get used to it," Chelsea said. "Think of me as practice for the rest of the town. This place talks, and it's already talking. The men in this town covet Violet. She's refused to date anyone her entire life, and when the men in town finally gave up, they raised her to a saint-like level. Very hard to live up to. In fact, I hated her throughout high school until I finally gave up, too. She's just too nice to hate. Now, they all protect her. Every man in this town would step in front of a truck if it meant she was safe. I'd like to get that kind of devotion from just one man." Distracted, she wiped the bar top for the tenth time.

He thought about what she'd said. Had Violet really never dated anyone? His heart leaped at the thought of what that meant. She was his and only his. The memory of her lips on his came back to him. Her fingers running up his back. No, it couldn't be. No one kissed that well without experience. Not that he would know. He'd never been with anyone. Had never had any interest in anyone before now. Jealousy shot through him at the idea of her being with someone else.

"Hello? Man, he's got it bad, Keary," Chelsea said, bringing him back to reality.

He took a sip of his beer.

"When they fall, they fall hard, Chelse, and this one," Keary shoved Simon playfully, "this one got hit hardest."

"Shut up, Keary."

Keary laughed and changed the subject, chatting about this and that with them. Simon paid little attention. His mind kept wandering back to Violet, no matter how hard he tried not to think about her.

People filtered in as the day went by, and Keary introduced them. Simon lost their names within seconds. Bored with the inquisition about his feelings for Violet, he was finally able to get Keary to take him into the office for a business conversation, hoping numbers would help him concentrate. They didn't.

The day dragged, thoughts of Violet consuming him through the numbers, the earnings, supplies, operating costs. What usually focused him did nothing for him today. Finally, having had enough, he asked Keary to take him to his place.

Following a tour of the main street, which he'd pretty much seen earlier that morning and only left him looking for Violet around every corner, they made it to Keary's apartment.

"You know you're not staying with me, right?" Keary asked as they stepped through the building door.

"Of course, I am. Just like old times."

"Oh, no. I love you, buddy, but you are not waking me up at two in the morning when you can't sleep every night."

"It won't be too bad," he said, stepping into the elevator. "It's only for a few nights. You put an elevator in? I'm impressed once again."

Keary had brought up the idea of renovating the old building and updating it to accommodate four apartments. Again, Simon had handed over the money to fund the project. He trusted Keary with his life, so there was no hesitation in giving him money.

"It added an extra updated touch."

The elevator opened onto the second floor, where two more apartments stood.

"You really think you're only staying a few days?" Keary asked, his tone teasing.

Violet's face flashed before him. "Good point."

"Well, it's a good thing I think ahead. Knowing the girl of your dreams was here, I saved one apartment for you. Mine's across the hall."

"You left an apartment unrented for the last six months?"

"Yup. Just had it cleaned and furnished for you. Thanks for the bonus, by the way."

Simon glared at him. "You know, the deal was to pay the money back, not to keep borrowing."

"Don't worry. The tenants downstairs cover enough and my rent—"

"Goes to your paycheck?"

Keary didn't answer, instead, he opened the door and walked in.

"Just say thanks, and we'll move on," he said jokingly. "You've got plenty; you'll never miss the few months that it sat here. Anyway, you'll need somewhere to stay while you obsess about Violet."

"Hmm." He looked around. The apartment was large, with

one bedroom and an open living space that blended with the kitchen. An island counter, the sides stained black under the marble countertop, divided the two areas. A set of sliding glass doors led to a small deck where wooden chairs sat with a view that overlooked the town. "This will work."

They hung out the rest of the afternoon, catching up on what they'd missed since the last time they saw each other. Time sped as the fun of being with Keary again took over. He'd never realized just how much he'd missed his friend until they were back together, and then it was like they'd never been apart.

As five o'clock approached, his pulse quickened in anticipation of seeing Violet again. Nerves ran through the pit of his stomach, and he felt like a schoolboy. He didn't like being so out of control, but he didn't care. All he wanted was to be close to her again. He watched the minutes pass and waited for his agony to end.

# CHAPTER 24

Violet stood just beyond the tree cover, watching Simon until he finally walked away with Keary. He looked back a few times, her heart racing each time he did. She wanted to run to him, to kiss him, to have his skin against hers again, the strength of him beneath her fingers. Head resting on the bark of the tree she'd been leaning on, she closed her eyes as the sensations flooded back to her.

He was here. She'd thought maybe, just maybe, she was crazy all this time. It had been so long, and she had turned down so many men, believing he was out there and that she would know him when he found her. That he would recognize her. And he had. The years of patience and devotion to a man she had never met, who to others was imaginary, had paid off.

The further away he walked, the less the magnetic pull controlled her. The need for him still echoed through her, currents pulsing like electric shots that warned her he was too far from her, but at least she could breathe again. When he was too far to see, Violet forced herself to walk away. On the other side of the trees, Paige paced with her arms crossed over her chest, her reflection following her movement in the lake beside her.

"Violet," she exclaimed when Violet came toward her.

"I guess you won?"

"Seriously, Violet. Oh my God, you were making out with him. What were you thinking?"

Violet twirled around before dropping onto the grass. Looking up at the clouds, she stretched her arms out, relishing the coolness of the grass against her skin.

"I wasn't. There was no thinking. I didn't have to think about it, Paige. I would have given myself to him right there if you hadn't interrupted." The power of what she had said hit her, and she knew it to be true. Butterflies frolicked in her stomach. She had wanted him, would have let him have every inch of her body if there had been no disruption to their frenzied moves.

Paige sat down next to her. "Are you serious? Violet, he's a complete stranger."

She peeked over at Paige, expecting judgement in her blue eyes but finding none. Just curiosity. "He doesn't seem like a stranger to me. I've known him all my life, even if we've never met."

Paige crinkled her eyes before saying, "He's the one, isn't he?"

The fullness in her chest pressed for release, and she could only nod, her words lost to the emotion.

"You always said he was out there. You said you would know the instant you met him, and no one believed you."

"No one but you." She smiled at her best friend and grabbed her hand, pulling her backwards onto the grass next to her.

"It's him, Paige. It's really him. Every part of me knows it." She wrapped her arms around herself and laughed.

Paige turned toward her, resting her cheek on her hand. "Well, now what?"

"Would it look too desperate if I ran after them and asked him to make love to me?"

"Violet," Paige snapped, looking horrified.

"Okay, okay." She tried not to giggle, but with the rampant

fluttering of butterflies in her gut, she was finding it difficult not to. "Too much?"

Paige flopped onto her back, covered her eyes with her arm, and shook her head.

"Try to focus, Violet. We need to get going. You volunteered to cover Miranda's shift at the store today, remember?"

"Ugh. I did, didn't I?" How was she going to concentrate? Maybe it would be quiet today. She looked up at the clear sky and wondered what Simon was doing right now. Was he thinking about her? Warmth bloomed in her cheeks.

"Do I even want to know what you're thinking about?" Paige asked, nudging her in the ribs.

She nudged her back. "It wasn't anything dirty."

Her cheeks grew warmer, and she knew they had darkened to a deep pink.

"Sure it wasn't," Paige teased, standing up. "Although I don't blame you, Violet. He really is hot."

Violet looked up at her, noticing how Paige had said the words in a hushed tone like it was something she shouldn't say.

Rising, Violet chuckled. "He is, isn't he? I could spend hours running my hands along those muscles." The thought sent another rush of flutters through her stomach.

"Violet, what has gotten into you? You never even take a second glance at any guy, and Simon has you talking like you're in one of those romance novels in the bookshop. What would Aunt Emma say if she heard you?"

She didn't have an answer, thinking this really was like a scene from one of those books, as Paige grabbed her arm and led her away.

They walked home rather than running. Simon had Violet's mind too preoccupied to avoid some clumsy move that would surely send her toppling for the second time that day, and Paige didn't seem to care. They talked the entire way home, with Paige teasing her for most of it.

ALL HOPE of her shift at the store being slow shattered as news of her kissing episode in the park traveled through town. As she addressed question after question from nosy neighbors, she concluded it had been fortunate that she and Simon had stopped when they did. If they had lost complete control and had sex in the park, she couldn't imagine the reaction they would have received. She smiled to herself at the thought, noting the flush of her cheeks once again.

Finally free, she headed home through town, hoping to see Simon before their date, only to find he was nowhere to be found. Keary probably had his attention. She was sure they were hanging out, catching up somewhere. He probably hadn't even had time to think of her, and all she'd done was obsess over him.

When she arrived home, she showered and dressed, picking a lilac cap-sleeved shirt with a matching skirt. She'd bought the pair on a whim the previous summer but had not had the chance to wear them. The color was her favorite, and the skirt was the kind that fell gently to the top of her knees, swirling around her delicately when she moved.

"Wow, Violet, that looks great on you," Paige said when she got downstairs. "Since when do you dress up for something like this?"

"Since I have a reason to do so," she said, her smile so wide it made her cheeks ache. "Will you braid my hair, Paige? One of those fancy *Game of Thrones* braids?"

She and Paige had been obsessed with the show. Daenerys was her favorite character. She wondered what it would be like to have that kind of power and confidence. To walk through a room and have everyone stop to look, to have them all respect and listen like she did. Paige always looked at her like she was crazy when she explained why she admired the character so. "You really don't see what others see, do you?" Paige would ask each time.

"A Daenerys braid?" Paige asked. "Feeling sexy and confident today, are we?"

Violet's laugh came out easily. "Confident? Maybe. Sexy? Eh."

Paige rolled her eyes, then motioned for her to sit so she could start braiding. They sat in silence as Paige's fingers weaved their magic. Violet never had the patience for all the intricate weaving, but Paige did, and she was exceptional at it. As Paige's fingers worked, Violet picked at the hem of her skirt, absently wondering if Simon liked braids.

"Violet?" Paige interrupted her thoughts. "Can I ask you a question?"

"Sure."

"What was it like?" she asked. Her voice carried a strange, slightly reverent tone to it, as if she were asking about something sacred.

"What was what like?"

"When you saw him for the first time today. What was it like?"

In all the years she'd known Paige, not once had her friend questioned her insistence that there was someone out there, someone who needed to find her. It didn't surprise Violet that she believed her when she said Simon was the one.

Taking a moment to ponder the question, she thought back to the moment her eyes had met his. Warmth flooded her body, and she brought her fingers to her lips.

"Well," she started, "it was like everything stopped. The world just slipped away, leaving only the two of us." Fingers resting on her chest, she detected the thudding of her heart. "There was this sensation so far inside of me that it almost seemed like it touched my soul. A notion that everything was right, like the world had been upside down and suddenly corrected itself. I couldn't breathe, and when we touched..." She paused, catching her breath at the thought. "When we touched, it was like magic. Not the corny stuff you see on TV. This was deeper, older, real. Every part of me came to life, and for the first time, I was truly awake."

Paige had stopped weaving. "You're in love with him," she stated.

"That's ridiculous. I just met him." But even as she argued, she couldn't deny the impact of the word. Love wasn't something that happened in seconds. It took time to develop. There was no reason to even contemplate being in love with a man she had only met hours before. But he didn't seem like a stranger. Part of her recognized him like she had known him her entire life, and maybe beyond that. There was a certainty to that knowledge, something that made it seem she'd known him for lifetimes.

She brought her fingers back to her lip, remembering their kiss. She had sensed it from him, too, that knowledge of her. There was an intimacy there that only came from two people who had known each other for a very long time, who knew the intimate details of each other, the contours of their bodies, the weight of their lips pressing against each other, the rhythm of their heartbeats. And with that recognition, there had come a longing to reclaim it.

"Violet?" Paige asked, pulling her back to reality, her fingers weaving again.

"Yes," she answered, "yes, I suppose I am. I suppose I always have been. Does that sound mad?"

Paige finished braiding and stood up to inspect her work, not answering the question right away. She folded her arms across her chest.

"To any normal person, it does. But you are not normal. You are more special than you can even imagine. I have no doubt that you and Simon are fated to be with one another, and I don't think you've gone mad." She leaned down and kissed Violet on the forehead. "You are my best friend, Violet. I've known you long enough to understand that if you say Simon is your soulmate, then he is. Now, get your crazy ass up, and we'll do our nails. Might as well have you completely fancied up for your first date."

They spent the rest of the time doing each other's nails. Violet insisted on leaving her fingernails with only a coat of gloss. She wasn't really into anything that covered her natural features. Besides, she knew they'd just get chipped up in about fifteen minutes once she got to work the next morning. Digging in soil all day battled nail upkeep, so she never bothered. She wasn't normally in the shop like she had been earlier and knew she'd be back outside the next day.

When their nails had dried, she looked at the clock.

Paige caught her and teased, "You know, it's only about two minutes past the last time you looked."

"I know, I know. I can't help it. Why is it moving so slow? It's only four-thirty." She looked at Paige with a mischievous grin. "We could leave early, you know."

"Violet, it only takes fifteen minutes to get there."

"Please, Paige?" She put her hands together to feign begging.

"That's very unbecoming, Violet."

"Please?"

"Ugh, all right, all right. You win. We'll leave early."

She hopped up and hugged her friend, then ran to get her shoes on.

"Watch your toenails!" Paige yelled after her.

# CHAPTER 25

Violet! Don't you look just beautiful. Oh, honey," Violet's Aunt Emma said, greeting them as they walked down the tree-lined street. She descended her front steps and hugged Violet.

Returning the hug, Violet said, "Thank you, Auntie."

A boisterous, round woman who had never had children of her own, Emma had adopted Violet after the accident had taken her parents. Never married, she'd been ten years older than Violet's mother and had taken Violet in with welcome arms. When Violet found Paige, Emma hadn't hesitated to make her part of the family as well. Her heart was as large as her laugh, which filled the room.

Both Violet and Paige adored her. When they graduated from college, she had given them the house, moving three doors down to live with her best friend, Bessie, who was just as animated.

"Are you going on a date with your new man? I hear he's quite a looker."

Heat flared in Violet's cheeks as Paige laughed and answered for her.

"You've never seen anyone who looks like Simon, Aunt Emma."

"How did you know already?" Violet asked.

Her aunt put her hands on her hips. "Do you think anything happens in this town without me knowing? Although you may want to be a little more discreet next time, Violet. I hear you were all over each other in the park."

Violet rested her head on her palm.

"No taking that back, Violet," Paige said playfully.

"Will you be bringing him to the bar after tonight's concert?" Emma asked, spinning Violet around to look at her. "My God, you are beautiful, little elf."

Her aunt had nicknamed her 'little elf', saying an elf or a fairy must have snuck in and taken advantage of her mother because she looked like no one in the family.

"Yes, I suppose we'll be there. The plan was to celebrate after the show, so I imagine he'll come with us. It is partially his bar anyway, right?" Her insides knotted at the thought of spending the entire evening with him.

Paige rolled her eyes and elbowed her. "I'm sure that's the only reason he'll go."

Violet ignored her and kissed her aunt on the cheek, saying, "I'll see you at the show."

Paige gave Emma a quick kiss as well, and they were off again.

Her heart started racing the closer they came to the restaurant. She could barely contain her excitement at seeing him, and she didn't have long to wait. He was standing in front of the restaurant, slowly pacing, but stopped and froze when he saw her. Again, the world seemed to fall away, leaving only the two of them. Her breath caught in her throat as his eyes met hers. The way he looked at her made her feel like she was the most beautiful woman in the world. Normally, she would have been self-conscious of someone looking so intensely at her, taking in every inch of her, but she wasn't. Not with Simon. From him, it made her almost believe she was a queen.

Lust clouded his eyes the closer she came to him, and it almost seemed like he would devour her, something she would willingly let him do. When barely any space remained between them, her feet stopped, and she let his eyes entrance her. His fingers brushed her cheek before they encompassed the back of her neck. Electrical currents charged through her at his touch, and her lips parted in reaction, an exhale escaping her. Gently, he dragged her close and kissed her. Sensations buzzed through her body, bringing it to life, and as she rested her hand to rest on his chest, she understood completely that this man held her heart and soul for eternity. That she belonged to him and only him.

Recognition that they weren't alone forced its way into her consciousness, and she drew back. Their lips slowly separated, their eyes locking again. It was easier to stop this time, but the need for him still screamed within her, and from the tension in his jawline, she could see he'd had the same reluctance to stop the kiss.

Giving him a bashful smile, she said, "Hi again."

A return smile and a chuckle that spread across her skin like a warm blanket accompanied his response. "Hi there." Taking a step back from her, his eyes grazed over her, leaving her flesh heated in its wake. "You clean up well."

Her face warmed, and she resolved to get used to the sensation that seemed a constant around him. "As do you."

And he did. He looked even better than he had in the morning. Sexy was an understatement for this man. As he ran his hand through his hair, his eyes dropping, then meeting hers again, her chest leaped painfully. Moving her hand to her face, she discreetly checked to see if there was drool running down her chin.

The black dress shirt he wore was just tight enough to accentuate the muscles below. Sleeves rolled to reveal his chiseled forearms, left her to imagine the muscle that worked its way up the remainder of his arms. This man was like something out of a book, and she briefly entertained the notion that the Greek gods weren't as beautiful.

Even his pants were black, but the look suited him. In fact, she couldn't imagine him in any other color. Black almost seemed to make him a little dark, almost dangerous, and she blinked at the unexpected reaction to that thought.

A pulsing need overcame her, and she reached out and snagged his shirt. Standing on her toes—because even at her height of five-nine, he towered over her—she pulled his mouth to hers. His hand once again encompassed the nape of her neck while his other grabbed her waist and brought her flush against him. Every part of her came alive, and she didn't want to be without his touch or his kisses again. That sensation that all was right, that this was where she belonged, washed through her, and she clenched his shirt tighter.

"All right, you two," she heard Keary say behind them, his tone frantic. "If there was anyone in town who didn't already know about this, they do now. Plus, I don't think Kasey's going to be too happy with all the nose prints on the front of her restaurant."

Simon's smile formed on his lips, but the kiss continued until, with a hesitation she noted in his taut muscles, he parted his mouth from hers. His hand remained on her waist as he moved her to his side, and she smoothed out the material of his shirt where her hand had wrinkled it. She dropped her eyes to avoid Paige's uncomfortable stare.

"Geez, you two," Keary muttered. "I go in for two minutes to get a table, and you're at it already. Paige? No help here?"

"I...they..." she tried to explain, before giving up with a defeated shrug.

Simon glanced at Violet, his chestnut eyes searching hers. "She's seriously too beautiful not to kiss, Keary."

"I haven't kissed her, Simon, so I know it's possible to avoid," Keary retorted.

With a lopsided grin, he said, "Your loss, my friend."

"Get your asses in there before you get arrested for lewd behavior."

Simon's hand stayed on the small of her back as they walked into the restaurant. Taking the seat next to her, he pulled his chair as close as he could to her. Thighs brushing, fingers entangling, shoulders leaning, they couldn't stop touching each other. Subtle gestures that left Violet's stomach in a frenzied knot and the air constantly restricted in her lungs. When space came between them, he would shift his position so they were touching again, and she would sigh with relief because not having him that close left an unexplainable ache in her chest.

There were moments when Violet forgot Paige and Keary were there. Lost in all that Simon was, the rest of the world faded from existence until Keary would bring her back with a story, or Paige would share a memory from their childhood. She could have sat there all night, letting the timbre of his voice nest further into her being, soaking up his closeness, the scent of cloudy nights and cedar that tickled her nose, but time passed too quickly and before she was ready to have it end, it was time to leave for the concert.

As they walked toward the theater, Simon pulled Violet close to him and kissed her hair. It was a gentle act, one that had her peeking up at him to see the contentment on his face. She brought her hand up and touched his cheek. He'd been quiet since they left the restaurant, and she wondered what was going through his mind. It seemed an odd thought, considering she didn't know him well enough to understand his thoughts or to even read him.

"Why so quiet all the sudden?" she asked.

He glanced down, his eyes darkened by the evening sky. "Just thinking through something."

"Watch him, Violet, he overanalyzes things," Keary said, clearly not realizing she hadn't directed the question toward him.

"Uh oh," added Paige, "you two may not be perfect for each other, then. Violet's gonna drive you crazy."

"Why's that?" he asked, the corner of his mouth lifting as his eyes remained on Violet.

"Because I don't analyze anything," Violet replied. "As Paige likes to say, I'm the fly by the seat of my pants type."

"That's an understatement," Keary interjected.

"So, I like to go with my gut and prefer to rely on my instincts. There's nothing wrong with that."

"Mmm. Yeah, you're going to hate me then," Simon said, the brown in his eyes shimmering.

Shrugging, she replied, "We'll figure it out."

"See?" Paige joked.

Violet waved her off.

"What were you thinking about?" she asked Simon, bringing the conversation back to where it had started.

A smirk that left her knees weak formed before he said, "Given what you just told me, you'll think it's nothing."

"Try me," she challenged.

"Well, don't you think it's odd we were both born in Ireland, not far from each other, and both raised by aunts and an uncle in my case?"

"Coincidence," she answered.

Steps halting, he looked down at her. "I don't believe in coincidence."

The affirmation was so confident it made her doubt herself for a moment. She chewed her lip, conflicted by his piercing gaze.

"How and when did your parents die, Vi?"

A shudder ran through her, but it wasn't from fear, even if every instinct told her his intensity was something to fear. Instead, it was a jolt of hunger that clawed at her, an unsatiated need that bellowed from deep in her core. She inadvertently took a step back at the force of it.

"I'm sorry if that sounded insensitive," he murmured, reading her reaction wrong.

"You're fine. It was a long time ago. They died in a car accident when I was two. I don't even remember them."

Lines formed between his brow, his eyes darkening. "I don't remember my parents either, Vi, because my parents died in a car accident when I was two as well."

She went to step back, but he stopped her, taking her elbow. Confusion clouded her mind.

"How can that be?"

He didn't answer her, saying, "Still think it's coincidence?"

"Well, if you two are getting deep, it gets better," Keary blurted, something akin to panic tainting his words. A look passed between him and Paige, and from the dagger eyes Paige was shooting at him, Violet suspected she wanted Keary to stop talking. Yet another perplexing moment between the two. There had been a few since Violet had met Simon, and she couldn't figure out why it made her uncomfortable.

"How can it get any weirder than this?" Paige said, her voice a pitch higher than normal.

"So, it turns out you both share a birthday, too. Same day, same month, same year."

Violet's sight flew to Keary, her eyes going wide. The stuttering of her heartbeat made breathing difficult.

"You never thought to mention that before?" Simon asked, suspicion rife in his features.

"You didn't know each other before, and it seemed odd to just mention it out of the blue."

"We were born on the same day?" she asked, her attention turning back to Simon. The revelation seemed too impossible to be a coincidence when she considered the other similarities between them.

"Winter solstice," he mumbled. "Still think it's coincidence?"

"Not coincidence, fate. We were born on one of the most magical days of the year. The Fates had a hand." The words were out before she could think about them, falling from her mouth as if they were natural, familiar even.

"Fates?" he asked, his brows pinched.

"Fate. Fate had a hand in us." Chewing her bottom lip, she reconsidered her words. "That's too much, isn't it?" she asked, regretting what she'd implied.

His hand reached over, and he wrapped his fingers in her curl. "Keary, Paige, give us a moment."

There was a bit of grumbling from Keary before Paige pushed him away.

Simon stepped closer to Violet, his expression serious, and dipped his head down to touch her forehead.

"We kissed within seconds of meeting each other. I would have taken you right there in that field if Paige hadn't stopped us. I wanted to with an innate need I cannot explain and that I don't understand." The pounding in her chest was so loud he had to hear it. The confidence that oozed from him had her legs trembling, and she worried they would give out on her. "I would take you right now if it weren't completely inappropriate. Trust me, it has crossed my mind multiple times tonight, and I'm having an incredibly difficult time holding myself back even now. There is no doubt in my mind that some higher power is at work here, and never once have I doubted that my path would someday lead to you. So, no, that was not too much."

The hitch of her breath was the only movement her stunned body would allow. His words washed over her, lighting every nerve on fire. His lips crashed into hers, and she leaned into his hold as his arm around her waist drew her against him. Need curled its way into every cell of her body, and she moaned against his mouth, threading her fingers into his hair and deepening their kiss. Nothing else existed, and the memory of standing on the sidewalk with others to witness their passion slipped away with the clarity of Simon and what he did to her.

# CHAPTER 26

Violet had consumed Simon's thoughts all day. So by the time he saw her walking toward him, looking like a goddess with her hair braided, curls left to brush against her cheek, her eyes as brilliant as the most priceless emerald, it had taken all his strength not to carry her away and make love to her. He craved her like his lungs needed air, and sitting with her at dinner, unable to pull her into his arms, had driven him mad. Every opportunity that offered even the slightest chance of touching her, he took. He'd spent the evening soaking in the lilt of her voice, the sunshine in her smile, the softness of her skin and reveling in her presence.

Now she was in his arms, her lush lips in a heated kiss with his, her body against his, and he didn't think he would ever let her go again. Having her so close, kissing her and touching her was perfection. The world seemed in balance when she was near, where before it had been unstable. The emptiness that had been a dull throbbing his entire life no longer hounded him. He had opened himself to her, honestly revealing the battle he'd been waging since meeting her, and no matter how mad it sounded, she had continued to look at him with only affection.

Her hands pulled at his hair, pushing his mouth further into hers as their tongues danced. Heart thudding in an erratic rhythm that matched hers, he pushed at her shirt, caressing the delicate skin of her back. All awareness of where they were and who was watching fled, because only Violet existed when he was with her. But the moment didn't last, no matter how desperate he was to hold on to it.

"Whoa, whoa! Okay there, guys. There are children around, and you two are going at it for the world to see," Paige said, sounding slightly frantic, the sound piercing through the bliss that had enveloped Simon.

He released Violet, drawing his mouth away, and leaned his forehead against hers. She was tall, but even at her height, he had to stoop to reach her.

Violet placed her hands on his cheeks, her emerald orbs creased with worry before she stepped from his arms. The distance between them left the air fleeing his lungs, and he struggled to stay upright. Her hands were trembling, and she smoothed them over the lilac shirt that had nearly had him salivating when he'd seen her. It left a flash of her stomach showing where it ended, and if he followed the path of the buttons, he could see a peek of cleavage where it dipped at her neck. He swallowed, turning his eyes from her, and scraped his hands through his hair.

"I don't see any children, Paige," she said, her voice holding a sexy rasp.

"Well, they're around, and besides, can't you two contain yourselves for five minutes?"

*No, we can't,* he wanted to say, but he silenced his remark.

"Clearly not," Keary answered for them. "Look, people are filing into the theater. We'd better get moving if you want to go back and check on everything before the show starts, Violet."

Violet volunteered at the theater and wanted to run in the back to check on a few things before the concert began. She had told him she had played the piano in the orchestra when she was young and still volunteered her time to support them. Her hands seemed to be in everything, and he had marveled at how involved in the community she was.

He hated to part from her but knew it wouldn't be long before she was sitting beside him enjoying the concert. The hours apart from her earlier had been a struggle, and he hoped he could endure her absence. Rubbing his palm over his face, he questioned how he'd gone twenty-eight years without her, yet now he couldn't handle a few hours or even minutes.

"We wouldn't want you to be late, Vi," he said to her, brushing her curl back and detesting the ache that was already aggravating his chest.

"Hmm, no, I guess not," she replied in a defeated tone.

Keary ushered them forward, mumbling, "You two are a handful."

"Hey, you're the one who insisted on chaperoning us," he snapped back.

Violet chuckled. "Chaperones. That's exactly how you both have acted all night."

Paige and Keary exchanged another of those looks Simon had noticed before Paige laughed the comment off. "Whatever, Violet." It came out stiffer than funny. "Look, we're here. Now get inside, and we'll get the seats," she continued.

Violet brushed Simon's hand slightly as she walked away. "I won't be long."

He watched as she went through a side door to the building, that wretched feeling of loss hitting him once again.

Following Paige and Keary in, he admired the architecture of the building. Tucked in the center of town, the theater still had the old box office booth outside. The interior was red velvet, and worn red and gold carpeting sank below his feet. A small concession stand stood to their left, and pictures lined the wall to their right.

Two large doors opened into the theater itself, where he could see the rows of seats that led to the stage.

"Paige! Keary!" a woman exclaimed as they filed through the lobby area. There weren't many people here yet, not that he imagined there would be in such a small town.

"Violet's in the back?" the woman asked. She was older, in her sixties, with graying auburn hair. Her blue eyes looked him over. "And you brought the new beau." Her strong Irish accent belied her origins, the familiarity of it reminding him of home.

"Simon, this is our Aunt Emma," Paige said, introducing the woman.

"You are quite the looker," Emma said, taking his hand.

He tried not to recoil. Shaking hands had been a practice of tolerance he'd repeated until he grew comfortable enough to endure it. Touching anyone, especially women, had always been uncomfortable for him, and he avoided it at all costs. His business ventures were the only encounters where he indulged in necessary contact. Otherwise, he kept to himself...until Violet.

"Do they breed the men in your town with special drugs, Keary? You two could be brothers. If they had had men like you when I was growing up, I would not have remained single."

"Aunt Emma," Paige scolded as Keary laughed.

Simon wasn't sure what to say, so he stayed quiet. Violet's aunt, however, did not. She took his arm and gave him a tour of the theater.

"Is that Violet?" he asked, seeing a playbill on the wall of the lobby.

"Yes, that was the year they did *Les Mis*. She was wonderful."

"I remember that one," said Paige. "She made me do it with her. I hated acting. Being up on stage with all those people looking at me. I didn't mind the singing, but the acting. Blah."

"You two were great."

Simon tuned their banter out and looked closer at the picture.

Violet was young, just a teenager, but her beauty was evident even at that age. The picture was black and white, but even then, the sparkle of her eyes came through.

"Violet is the reason we're able to celebrate it," he caught their aunt saying.

"I'm sorry, celebrate what?"

"The hundredth anniversary of our little theater. Today is the exact day of the first show. That's why the orchestra is playing here tonight instead of up at the campus."

"That's impressive, but how is Violet involved?"

"We almost lost the theater. The owner was struggling to pay bills, and things were badly in need of repair. Violet loved this place, still does. Music is in her blood." She gave him a wink before continuing. "She inherited money when her parents died, not a lot, but enough. Since she had never used it, she donated most of it to help pay for renovations. With what she gave, they brought it back to its former glory. All she asked was that they add a pit for an orchestra."

"The plays here have live music?" he asked, trying to imagine such a small theater having an orchestra.

"She worked with the college, and the orchestra director at the time agreed to do the music for the shows during the school year. The new director, who went to school with her, continued the tradition when he took over."

"Word spread about how good the programs here were, and now there's never a show that isn't sold out," Paige continued with a touch of pride in her eyes. "People from all over the area come to see them. Tonight is special, though. Only the orchestra will perform, and the show is for locals only."

"Everyone is heading to the bar after the show to complete the celebration, so it's a win for us, too," Keary added with a wink.

They continued to talk while the patrons slowly filled the seats, but Simon's mind wandered. He couldn't get over the fact that

Violet had donated her inheritance to the theater. He was all for gifting to charity and was a regular contributor to different organizations, but he also had a sizeable income. Violet worked at a garden shop.

"Does she make that much money working at the shop?" he asked.

They looked at him as if he had two heads, and he scratched his temple, suddenly self-conscious.

"She doesn't work at the shop, Simon. She owns it," Paige explained. "Today she was just covering for a cashier."

He tried not to gape. "Wait, Violet owns the garden shop?"

"Yup, she won't tell you, but she's pretty in demand in the horticulture world."

"That's true. No one raises plants like Violet," Emma continued. "There's something magical about it. She has the most beautiful flowers, and her gardening skills are unmatched."

Keary gave him a goofy smile. "Buddy, Violet is to the garden world what you are to the corporate world."

Before he could reply, his phone vibrated with a text alert. Hoping it wasn't his assistant, he pulled his phone out and looked. It was Violet. They had exchanged numbers earlier.

*Free to escape the chaperones?*

He tried not to laugh as he waited for the next line she was typing.

*If so, meet me upstairs. Go back to the lobby, take a left, and follow the stairs.*

He answered with a short *Got it*, then put his phone back down. The three of them had moved on in the conversation and were chatting about some issue with a stop sign that sounded entirely too inane for his liking.

"Where's the bathroom?" he asked Keary.

Keary pointed the way, and Simon made his escape, his heart racing at the thought of being alone with Violet. He found her exactly where she said she would be, and she pulled him into a small, dark room.

"Prop room?" he asked, waiting for his eyes to adjust.

"More like an everything room," she replied. Even in the dim light, her eyes shimmered like sage stars.

"Good." He crossed the distance and pulled her close to him, loving how her heart raced against his chest. "Then we have a few minutes alone."

"Mmm, hmm," she mumbled as he slid his hand over her hip.

He'd been stronger through the evening, able to hold himself back easier, to accept just a kiss, to be content with simply having her close, but as she ran her hand up his chest, that instinctual need for her took over. It held him hostage, left him unable to fight, to maintain any inkling of control. Stepping her into the wall, he captured her mouth. A moan escaped her, only encouraging him. His hands ran the length of her body, taking in every curve. Scooping her leg up, he let his fingers drape over her thigh. She pulled at him, dragging her fingers through his hair and over his shoulders.

Heated and out of control, he grabbed the back of her neck with his other hand and twisted his fingers into her braided hair. When she pushed his shirt up, the contact lit the flames in him so that he didn't think he could halt them from devouring him. The only thing that could extinguish them was Violet.

The sleeve of her shirt fell, exposing the swell of her breasts, and he nearly salivated. He pushed his hands further up her skirt, skimming the lace trim of her panties as he dropped his mouth to the flesh above her neckline. Awareness crashed through him. An understanding that they didn't have a choice, that something powerful drove their actions, be it fate or not, and neither he nor Violet could stop what was happening. He lifted her, pressing his firmness against her and embracing the recklessness that went against his usual controlled demeanor.

But just as he slipped his fingers below her underwear, a force tore through him like a banshee screaming through the night. It coursed through him, loud and demanding, stealing his breath. He released her, and she stumbled to catch her footing, staring at him as he stepped out of her reach and tried to determine what the sensation had been. His heart hammered viciously as he ran both hands through his hair in confusion.

Remembering Violet, he looked back at her, still trying to regulate his body. He expected to see hurt reflected in her eyes at the way he'd dropped her and fled from her contact. But it wasn't there. She tipped her head, her brows drawn in confusion as she brought her arms around her stomach.

"What was that?" she breathed.

Worry nagged at him. She would hate him for what he'd just done. Would see it as a rejection when it hadn't been. He apologized, assuming her question was accusatory.

"I'm so sorry, Vi. I don't know what came over me."

She continued to stare at him and chewed her bottom lip. No accusation reflected in her eyes as her hand remained on her stomach.

"No, Simon. What was that sensation?"

Relief erased the tension from his muscles, and he took a step closer to her. "You felt something, too?"

She nodded, her brows knitting.

He didn't have an answer for her. Only that whatever it was, it had been strong enough to stop them both, strong enough to hurt him, leaving his insides shredded until he'd moved from her. From the way her arms clutched her stomach, he suspected it had done the same to her. An overbearing instinct to protect her overcame him, and he moved back to her, brushing the wayward strand from her eye and noting how she relaxed with his touch.

"I—" She didn't have time to continue as the door opened, and Keary walked in.

"There you are. What the hell? I've been looking all over for you two." His eyes volleyed between them, and it almost seemed like he wanted to scold them before the look on their faces stopped him.

"Are you both okay? Did something happen?"

Simon shot him a look. The way he had asked gave Simon the suspicion that Keary had expected something to happen to them.

"We're fine, Keary," Violet replied before he could say anything.

Slightly irritated and still confused by what they had just experienced, Simon said, "We needed a few minutes alone, Keary. So, let us have it."

Keary looked at his watch. "You've had plenty of time alone, and the concert is about to begin. Your aunt is wondering where you are, Violet, and Simon, she thinks you got lost somewhere. It's clear you took a wrong turn."

He stood with his arms crossed, his demeanor and tone annoying Simon.

"If you weren't my friend, I'd punch you right now, Keary."

"That's a lie. You'd punch me anyway. You just don't want to do it in front of Violet."

A flash of crimson tore through his vision, but Violet put a hand on his arm. The sensation cooled the fire in him, and he calmed.

"It's all right, Simon. He's right. We should get back." She kissed his cheek and took his hand to have him follow.

"I'll be right there, Vi. I just need a minute."

"Okay." She searched his eyes before saying, "I'll see you down there then."

Her hands rubbed her arms while she walked away, her sight on the floor like she was lost in thought.

Keary stood at the door, studying him.

"What are you doing, Keary?"

"I could ask you the same thing, Simon."

"It shouldn't concern you. We're two consenting adults."

Keary's expression morphed, and for the first time since Simon had met him, he saw fear in his friend's eyes.

"You can't have her tonight, Simon. You need to wait. If you wait, you'll have her for eternity. Don't take her tonight."

Not giving Simon a chance to reply, he turned and walked away.

Cryptic words that made no sense. Concern had layered the words, which only left Simon more confused. He'd known Keary a long time, and never had he seen him look so serious about anything. He turned back toward where he and Violet had been moments before, contemplating what had happened and pushing the cryptic warning aside. Whatever it had been, Violet had experienced it, too. Rubbing his temples, he tried to find meaning in any of it but came up empty.

"Simon, let's go," Keary called from down the stairs.

This wasn't the time to think about it. Leaving the room, he closed the door quietly behind him and followed Keary to their seats.

Violet looked up at him as he sat down, her smile revealing her happiness at his presence. She leaned in close to him as the orchestra came onto the stage. There was no shyness about her, only an insinuated claim he accepted, hoping she would do the same. A claim between them, a statement that would lead anyone to think they had been with each other for years and not mere hours.

Throughout the first half of the concert, she sat close to him, at times resting her head on him. Just as it had been in the restaurant, they constantly touched each other. When she seemed too far away, he would take her hand to bring her close again. There were small moves here and there, neither wanting to be apart from the other.

He paid little attention to the show. The music was pleasant, the musicians talented, but he could only focus on Violet. His ears listened, but his mind was elsewhere, and his other senses were on her. He took in the scent of lilac, the softness of her hands, and the feel of her thigh when he accidentally brushed it, the weight of her knees as they pushed against his leg when she tucked them under her. Heard her soft breathing, the sweetness of her laugh, the harmony of her hands when they clapped.

Throughout the concert, he snuck glances at her, wondering at her delight, at the golden light of her hair that shone even in the dark, the sparkle in her eye when she caught him looking at her. He couldn't help it; she mesmerized him. There was a need there that she had filled, one that had always been there and, for the first time in his life, he was whole. Without a shadow of a doubt, he knew she was the reason for it.

A short intermission provided Simon with time to steal Violet away, but he failed. Curious townspeople took up that time instead. He clung to her hand as she introduced many of them to him. Neighbors, school friends, even a goddaughter whom Violet seemed to adore.

Seeing her with the girl, his mind wandered to thoughts of her with their own children before he shook his head to clear the ridiculous thought away. It was too early to even contemplate such a thing. But when she picked up the little girl and rubbed noses with her, the thought became pervasive. He imagined a boy in her arms, with his ebony hair and her vibrant eyes, something telling him it would be a boy and not a girl. He watched her place the child down and spin her around, a sense of longing rocking him so hard that he swayed on his feet.

The lights flickered, signaling the time to return to their seats was near, and he let out a relieved exhale. Violet kissed the girl goodbye, then reached for Simon's hand. Her eyes sparkled, and he pulled her close, kissing her and not caring that everyone saw them.

"What was that for?" she asked, her smile lighting her eyes.

"Just seemed like it needed to be done."

"Well, I'm glad you did." She sat back down in her seat, tucking her feet under her again, and patted the seat next to her.

Taking it, he took her hand as she leaned in toward him, resting her head on his shoulder.

The second half of the concert was a repeat of the first for Simon. Too enraptured by Violet, he didn't take the time to appreciate the music. As the concert drew to an end, the director put down his baton and walked from his podium to the front of the stage. Someone ran out with a microphone and gave it to him.

"We're about to play the last number, so I want to take a minute to thank you all for coming tonight. We truly appreciate the full house for this special event. The theater is celebrating a hundred years of sharing the arts with a community that has embraced it more than I would have ever expected when I first moved here. When I stepped in as the orchestra director for the college, I was excited to discover the playhouse and the orchestra had such a strong partnership. It's rare to see a live orchestra backing players unless you're lucky enough to be somewhere like Broadway."

The crowd cheered, and he put a hand up to hold the applause. "When Violet and I were students at the college, we were in orchestra together. After a late practice one day, I realized I'd left something in the concert hall after the recital. When I made it back, everyone had left, but just as I was about to throw the lights on, I heard the piano and saw that Violet had stayed behind. That day was the first time I had the privilege of hearing a voice that has no description. I stood enraptured by it, and even when she finished the song and had left the building, I sat there in awe. Entranced by a siren's voice until the janitor found me and kicked me out."

He paused while the crowd laughed, and Simon glanced over at Violet, seeing the color in her cheeks that told him she didn't enjoy the attention.

"I never told her that. It's creepy to say you watched someone when they didn't know you were there. Sorry, Violet. But that day, I vowed that if I ever got the chance to direct an orchestra, I would make it my goal to pair that voice with the beauty of these instruments. Today is the first day I've ever had that chance."

"Oh no," Violet said, squirming in her seat. "Paige? What's he doing?"

"Shhh, just listen."

"To mark the special anniversary of this glorious theater, I'm going to call in a favor."

There was more laughter through the crowd and fierce clapping. Violet had put her head down in her hands.

"I'm going to kill you, Paige," she muttered.

"Don't blame me. I didn't agree to this. Keary did."

Violet shot her head up and gave Keary a deadly stare. Simon had no idea what was going on, but the look she gave Keary was priceless, and his lips tugged against the smile he was holding back.

"Violet. Please come join me on the stage."

"No, Tom. Not gonna happen," she mouthed, waving her hands to signal she didn't like the idea.

"Violet, it's for a special cause. These folks came for a concert. Remember, the ticket prices go for the benefit of this theater, the one you love so much. The least you could do is honor us with a song. Just one, I promise." He put his hands together to gesture a begging pose.

She shook her head defiantly, and Simon had another protective surge of adrenaline. He wanted to whisk her away to safety but didn't know how to make that happen. Curiosity kept him from shielding her from the attention. She'd said nothing about singing, and from the way this man had talked, her voice was good.

"Go on, Violet. They never ask, and it would make the event special," her aunt said, leaning over.

A chant began on the stage, then spread through the crowd. Her name resounded through the theater.

She looked over at Simon. "Sorry," she told him, looking completely mortified.

He leaned over, cupping his hand around her neck, and drew

her face to his. "Don't apologize. I could probably take most of them out to protect you, but I suspect even I'm outnumbered. If you want me to, I will."

Her lips lifted, lighting her eyes, and she shook her head.

"Then you'd better go before I change my mind and do it anyway. I can hold them back long enough for you to make a run for it," he teased, trying to ease her stress.

"Come on, Violet," Tom said from the stage. "Besides, you can't deny your new boyfriend the chance to hear that beautiful voice."

Crimson climbed in her cheeks.

"Boyfriend?" he said, liking the sound of it.

Giving him a shrug, she touched his cheek, saying, "That sounds right, doesn't it?"

"Definitely."

With an exaggerated sigh, she stood and lifted her hands in surrender.

A round of shouts and applause thundered through the theater as he and Keary stood to let her by. Her fingers brushed against his before she left the row, and that strange need to keep her by his side resurfaced. It was such an unexpected sensation, and he rolled his neck to fight it off. The further she moved from him, the more it grew, but the more that intense desire to touch her faded, replaced with a hollowness that engulfed him. He rubbed his chest to alleviate it, but it didn't help.

When Violet reached the front of the stage, she playfully elbowed the director before turning to the orchestra. Their laughter carried through the auditorium while she talked to them. After a few more seconds, Violet turned back toward the crowd. Tom placed the microphone in the stand and adjusted it to her height, and Simon fought the stir of envy at the smile she gave the man. A craving to have all her smiles to himself overcame him, and he swiped a hand through his hair, not comfortable with the possessive thought.

"Now that you've roped me into singing, what song did you pick for me?"

"Since you rarely grace us with a song, Violet, and when we do, it's usually very familiar songs from the Irish roots that make up this town, I'd like to hear you sing that song again. The one I heard that day. I haven't heard you sing it since then. Do you remember which one it was?"

She rubbed her arms like she was fending off a chill that had gone through her, then nodded. "That song, Tom? Really?"

"Yes. The students have been practicing, and we're ready when you are." He resumed his place at his podium before picking up his baton and peeking back at her to await her signal.

She shook her head, muttering, "You owe me for this," as she adjusted the microphone.

Inhaling, she glanced back at him and signaled for him to begin.

Tom moved his baton up, and the orchestra members picked up their instruments. The music began.

Simon recognized the song, but the name eluded him. He leaned forward in his seat and waited for her to sing, his breath caged until she opened her mouth. Her voice washed over him, claiming every piece of him she hadn't already claimed. It was delicate, like the sound of hummingbird wings on a summer day, mesmerizing him and holding him hostage to its power. Each word blanketed him like the soft caress of a lover, leaving a brand on his soul he knew would always belong to him. Powerful yet constrained, it resonated through the theater, pulling him into its hold, possessing him, owning him.

He couldn't take his eyes off her, and part of him wanted the song to never end, knowing the loss of her voice would wound him just the way being away from her did. When the song ended, silence remained. A spell had fallen over the crowd and over him. Only when her eyes met his through the rows of enthralled listeners did the air flee his lungs and the spell lift. Within seconds, the crowd erupted, standing with thunderous applause. Violet took a bow, then turned to the orchestra and clapped for them. Simon followed her moves until she walked offstage.

Too stunned to move, the echo of Violet's voice imprinted in his mind, Simon stared at the space where she had been. He was standing now with the rest of the crowd but had no recollection of how or when he'd gotten to his feet.

A warm hand covered his, and he jerked to awareness, fighting not to pull from the touch as he met her aunt's kind eyes. "Are you going to be all right, son?"

Keary moved closer to him. "I think he's speechless."

"Violet's voice will do that to you," she replied, giving his hand a pat before removing it.

"Simon, it's time to wake up. Everyone is leaving," Keary said jokingly, moving his hand back and forth in front of Simon's face. Simon smacked his hand away. A glance around him confirmed Keary was right. The people were indeed exiting the building.

"I'm fine," he said, finally finding his voice. He rubbed his hand over the back of his neck. "I just wasn't expecting that."

"I like to say the fairies blessed her with that voice," her aunt said. "It's enchanting."

Indeed, it was.

"Welcome to the club. It's like a siren call you can't resist," the man in front of them said. Jack, he thought he remembered Violet telling him. His wife smacked him on the back of the head.

"Ouch, woman, what was that for?" he asked, rubbing his head.

"We're so glad you're dating Violet," she said to Simon. Dating? Were they dating? It seemed like it, but really, they'd only just met today, so could it be called dating? "Now all these boys can stop dreaming about her and concentrate on their wives again."

"Still won't stop us," Jack said with a wink as they walked out of the row.

"That's okay, because now we can dream about him," his wife retorted, shutting her husband up quickly and clamping down the stir of envy that had re-emerged in Simon.

Keary chuckled, landing a hand on Simon's back. The thought of Jack or any other man in town dreaming about Violet was enough to cause his tension to return, and he didn't appreciate the sting of jealousy the man's words had caused. The emotion rooted deep within him and was one he had never experienced before.

"Come on," said Keary, "let's go out front and wait for Violet."

"I'll go grab her," Paige said. "She'll need rescuing. Tom's a talker."

She hurried off, fighting against the flow of the exiting crowd before either of them could respond.

"Has her voice always been so..." No word seemed worthy of what he'd just witnessed. "Ethereal?"

"Ever since I met her," Keary said over his shoulder as they joined the flow out of the theater. "She doesn't sing very often. Only once, maybe twice a year, do we ever get to hear her. She prefers to keep it private, and everyone in town respects that. If we know she's going to sing, it's town only, except for special occasions like this. And even this was only townspeople save for the orchestra and you."

Even with as social as Violet seemed, Simon could understand why she'd want to keep this part of her life private. A voice that unique would attract attention, and she didn't seem like the type of person who wanted that kind of attention. He could still sense the remnants of it on his skin, like it had left a mark on him. Rubbing his face, he tried to clear away the sensation, hating how out of control he once again was. There was a familiarity to her voice, one he couldn't pinpoint, but he couldn't shake the feeling of déjà vu.

"You still with me?" Keary asked, pulling him back to the present.

"Just lost in thought," he answered absently.

"You've got it bad, buddy." Keary shook his head. "Can't say I didn't try to tell you. Wait, can I mention that one more time, you know, how I told you so?" He had himself laughing so hard he could barely get the words out.

"Shut up, Keary, before I really do punch you this time," Simon answered playfully, before he sighed. "Yeah, I've got it bad."

"Got what bad?" Violet asked from behind him.

He grimaced, hoping she hadn't heard Keary's jeering. When he faced her, the wind rushed from him, and he had to steady himself. Every time he looked at her, the floor seemed to disappear from under his feet, and he was falling. Deeper and deeper.

"That strange addiction people get when you sing, Violet. You know, it's like a fever that overcomes them," Keary replied, covering for him.

Simon made a note to thank him later. He already felt like a weak fool around her. No need to appear any worse.

Taking his hand, she leaned up and kissed him. It was an act that was natural, like they'd been a couple for years.

"So, you're under my spell, huh?"

"Oh, brother," Paige muttered. "Let's go before they start making out again. I think I need a few shots first."

Violet nudged her. "You take all the fun out of things, Paige."

The walk to the bar was quiet, and he didn't dislike the silence. He kept his arm wrapped around her, and she leaned her head against him, occasionally looking up at him.

"I'm still here," he said. "I'm not going anywhere."

*Not without you by my side*, he thought, kissing her head.

When they reached the bar, Keary bought the first round, but Simon was more interested in talking with Violet than drinking. Thankfully, Keary and Paige gave them space, as did everyone else. The longer they talked, the more he thought he could never let her go again.

His lust for her had waned to a low hum he could ignore,

content to listen to her voice as she talked and just being in her presence. But as the night went on, it became a thrum he couldn't disregard. Forgetting everyone else, he stood and held out his hand. Without hesitation, she took it, and he led her past the bar, past Keary and Paige, who were deep in conversation, and down toward the office. The need to have her alone and to himself had become a force he didn't think he could contain any longer.

# CHAPTER 27

It was strange to see Sinow and Violissa together and even stranger for Keary to see them as mortals. He could only remember two instances where he had witnessed them together in their world. Strange to think that he'd spent all these years trying to bring them back together when they barely knew each other. He had spent more time with Violissa as Violet than Sinow had ever had with her, even through all of their mortal lives. As he watched them together and witnessed again the power of the prophecy, he couldn't help but be sad for them. They had been pawns of the Fates from the very beginning, and now the Fates had trapped them in this never-ending loop that neither could seem to escape. They had no choice. Their lives were not their own. They never had been. If they could finally break through this spell, it would all be worth it. Everything they had sacrificed.

He remembered how broken Sinow had become when he'd lost Violissa. That kind of pain didn't come from a spell, and it surely didn't come from lust. It only came from true love, a love that had matured after their initial meeting when it had only been the prophecy that had driven their desires. A love that he now realized was truly unbreakable. The prophecy wasn't a curse; it was a blessing that would inevitably improve their world, but at what cost?

He took another sip of his beer. He missed the strong taste of their ale from home. Drinking human beer was like drinking piss water. Even the strongest ale in this world was nothing compared to theirs at home. Still, it was all he had right now, so he swallowed the stuff to take the edge off. That was one advantage of this mortal body. Alcohol affected him now. The Dark magic he once held always burned the alcohol off before he experienced any of the pleasant side effects it gave him as a mortal. There was no getting drunk as an immortal, but as a mortal, he'd experienced the pleasure and the unintended hangovers on too many occasions.

Paige walked toward him. She'd been nervously moving around the room, socializing, but Keary had noticed how her eyes never left her queen.

"I don't think I can do this, Keary," she mumbled, taking the barstool next to him.

Her hands were shaking slightly as she rested them on the bar top. She looked small and mortal in that moment, vulnerable in a way he hoped he'd never be. What were the Fates thinking, sending her into this mess? She was an outsider, and he suspected she felt that way. As a child, she had always tried to assert herself in Council business, always wanted to be part of what her father was doing.

As an adult, she had this romanticized vision of what they had been like, of what their lives had been before Tynan had destroyed it all. In reality, she knew none of it. She had no idea who her father really was, who any of them were, least of all Violissa and Sinow. And here she was, caught in the middle of one of the most important moments in their history. The balance of their world hung on what was happening.

As a Darkbearer, he could grasp it, but as a mortal who had never witnessed magic in any form other than the pounding from

Tynan as he battered the shield that surrounded the Banished Realm, Paige was in over her head.

He put a reassuring hand over hers. "Take a deep breath, Paige. This is what we've waited for, what we've planned for all these years." He looked over to where Sinow and Violissa sat, both leaning in as close as they could to one another. "All we have to do is keep them apart long enough."

"Keep them apart?" Chelsea asked, replacing his now empty beer bottle with a new one. He groaned, hoping she hadn't heard too much. He hadn't even seen her there. "I thought you were all for this match? Why would you want to keep them apart? This is the first time Violet has let any man close to her, and damn, they look really cute together. I mean, really, do they make anyone as gorgeous as the two of them? I thought you were sexy, Keary, but him," she drew a breath and let out a whistle, "he is so hot it's painful. Pair him with Violet, who could put any model to shame, and you've got the best-looking couple this world has ever seen."

"Thanks for the compliment, Chelse. What am I, chopped liver?" Paige asked.

"Sorry, Paige. You're pretty and all, but these three? Come on, you must see it, too."

"You've no idea," Paige muttered.

"That's enough, Chelsea. Don't you have customers to serve?" Keary said, growing tired of the conversation.

She put her hands on her hips. "Chad has it covered. I want to know why you were so happy for Simon earlier, and now you suddenly want to keep him from Violet."

"I didn't say I want to keep him from her."

"That's not what it sounded like." She stopped and waited for him to speak. When he didn't, she continued, "Then what did you mean?"

"It's complicated."

He squeezed the bridge of his nose, wondering why he was even having this conversation. He needed to walk away and started to do so when Paige said, "They don't need to be apart, they just can't get too close, too fast."

"Damn it, Paige." Keary slammed his hand on the bar. "That's enough."

"Why? What happens if they move too fast?" Chelsea asked, laughing. "Do they explode? Does the world end?" She continued laughing until she noticed Paige's face. "Oh my God, what happens?"

"He dies, we lose her, we lose our world. We lose everything."

Keary looked at Paige, knowing his mouth was hanging open. "Paige, what are you thinking?" he barked.

"What? Why does it matter anyway? You said this is it, this is what we've been waiting for, right? In a few days or even hours, it will all be over, so what does it matter?"

He wanted to strangle her. All this time they'd kept it quiet, and here she was babbling away like a drunk woman. He looked down at her empty glass and contemplated how much she'd had to drink since they'd gotten there. He rubbed his head when he realized it was too much.

"Oh my God," Chelsea exclaimed. "I was right. All this time I was right."

"Calm down, Chelsea."

"No, I knew it. You guys are gods or something, aren't you? Trapped in human form. Just like in those movies."

Her voice was rising, and Keary glanced around before grabbing her wrist and pulling her roughly toward him.

"Chelsea," he growled. He saw the look of fear cross her face and welcomed the thrill of it. "You need to be quiet and calm down now. We are not gods. It's a complicated, long story, and this isn't the place or the time for it. All you need to know is that it is imperative that the two of them not consummate their relationship until they've had time to realize how much they love each other. Now, since you were too nosy to know when to stop asking questions, you're going to keep this quiet and help us."

He let her wrist go, and she drew it back to her chest, rubbing it. "I always knew you had a darker side." She gave him a sly smile. "Too bad you didn't let that come out while we were in bed together."

He cringed. This human body had made it all but impossible to keep his vow of celibacy that all Council, Dark or Light, upheld. Sinow would punish him when they returned, but he knew he wouldn't be the only one. Years without power to fill that need had left a few of them guilty of sins against the crown.

Chelsea had been a mistake, but a good one. He'd had her a few times before they concluded that their working relationship was better outside of the bedroom, although they'd both indulged a few times since then. Sometimes the long nights with too many drinks left him needing a release that his power would have filled.

He met her brown eyes that twinkled with humor. With her black hair and brown eyes, she would have been one of theirs in Tenebron if they were home. She would never have even been afforded the opportunity to meet his eyes, would have been punished for the mere attempt. But here, they all looked at him, never even imagining the sheer power he'd once held. The power he would hold again once his king returned to his throne with his queen.

"Uh, guys, I hate to interrupt your flirting, but where did they go?" Paige asked, breaking his thoughts.

Keary whipped his head over to where Simon and Violet had been. Their stools were empty.

He shot from his stool, scanning the bar. "Where did they go?"

"I don't know. I just looked up, and they were gone."

"Calm down and turn around. They're in your office. I saw them walk by." Chelsea pointed past them to the back of the bar where the hallway led to his office. He could see the light from below the door frame and breathed a sigh of relief. They hadn't left, so he still had some control.

Sitting back down, he grabbed his beer and took a deep drink to calm his nerves. How he hated these weak bodies, the emotions that triggered too unexpectedly.

Paige quirked a brow and asked, "Aren't you going in after them?"

It was a valid question. He had returned to his seat instead of running after them. As fearful as he'd been moments before, he was calm again. Sinow and Violissa had sat for the last two hours talking, occasionally interrupted by friends but mostly alone, and things had been fine. They would be fine.

"No, I'm not," he snapped.

"Wait, you just said they needed to stay apart. I would think leaving them alone would go against everything you just said," Chelsea piped up.

"I know I did. I think they'll be okay. They need a little time alone." Both looked at him like he was crazy. Maybe he was. He leaned closer to Paige. "Listen, when Tynan interrupted them when they first met, it seemed to do something. They could tolerate being near each other without ripping each other's clothes off after that day."

"But that was when they had their powers to help rein in their desires. Now they're powerless mortals," Paige said.

"Sinow once told me that the more time they spent together, the easier it was for them both. He said it was still incredibly hard to be near her and not touch her, but time seemed to lessen the instinctual piece of it they initially couldn't control. Let's give them a few minutes to test that out before we go barging in. Maybe it'll help get us to the end game sooner."

"Not that I know who this Sinow is, but what if it doesn't? What if you're wrong?" Chelsea asked.

"Then we're all doomed," he replied heavily. "Let's just pray I'm right, for all our sakes."

# CHAPTER 28

The muscles in Simon's back flexed beneath his shirt as he closed the office door, and Violissa imagined what they would feel like against her skin. That aggravating heat bloomed in her cheeks again, and she rubbed it away, trying to clear her mind before he turned but failing miserably. He gave her a sexy, lopsided grin that had her insides just as heated as her face.

"And what were you thinking about, Vi?" he asked, walking over to her.

She couldn't tear her eyes from his, sinking into their warmth and swimming in their depth. Eyes that she thought might be keen enough to see straight into her soul. His finger reached for her loose curl, and she leaned into his touch, placing her hand on his solid chest. Tilting her face to his, she scrunched the material of his shirt in her hand and dragged his lips to hers. It was a heated kiss, one that sank into her being and claimed her just as each of his kisses had. Each was a brand that laid ownership on her, one she would proudly accept because she wanted no other man to kiss her. No other would compare, and she thought just maybe having this one taken from her would leave her too devastated to survive.

Every part of her came alive again, and she welcomed it because before this she'd been asleep, like a princess locked in a tower waiting for her prince to wake her from the spell.

Simon's hand smoothed over her braid, and she suddenly wished she'd left her hair down so he could tangle his fingers in it. His other hand dropped to her waist and brought her body flush to his. Butterflies flapped in a torrent of flurry, tying her stomach into nervous knots. She'd dreamed of his touches for so long that finally experiencing them was ecstasy. His hand pushed at the bottom of her shirt, finding her skin, and flames blazed through her. She shivered in excitement, moving her fingers under his shirt, then across the muscles of his chest before bringing them up his back. He groaned, his kiss growing fiercer.

Their touches became more hurried, his hand skimming her waist, then moving to scoop her bottom. The move pressed her further into him, his desire for her evident in the firmness that now rested against her. This time, the butterflies rebelled, whipping their wings and leaving her wanting more. He pushed at the edge of her shirt, raising it higher and caressing her stomach before his fingers skimmed the edge of her bra.

A moan scraped its way from her throat, and his kisses became greedier. But just as she thought there would be no stopping them this time, a painful tug wrenched her stomach, as if something was trying to keep her from him. It came from nowhere and forced her to pull back from his lips. Brown eyes searched hers, and she clutched her stomach as his frown deepened. She tried to catch her breath, the remnants of that tug still sharp in her core. It was so similar to what she'd experienced at the theater.

Hands dropping from her, Simon scraped them through his thick hair and stepped away from her. His eyes questioned her.

"You felt it again, didn't you?" he asked.

She nodded.

"We need...we need to slow down, don't we?" she asked, still panting.

His hand rubbed across his mouth and chin in thought, then

he combed his fingers through his hair again. A wave of déjà vu passed through her, causing a chill to run up her spine as if she'd seen him do it countless times before.

"Wait," he mumbled, as if contemplating the power of the word. "We have to wait."

He peered up from the floor and met her eyes. In that look, she sensed the relentless yearning, the struggle this one small word had caused. It told her everything, and in that unspoken moment, she almost imagined they could talk to each other simply through their shared looks.

Violet walked over to him and rested her head on his chest. He leaned down and kissed her hair, wrapping his arms around her. Safe. That was the thought that ran through her when she was with him. She was safe, and he would keep her that way, protected from anything that might try to hurt her. He would keep her safe and even put his life before hers.

"I would wait an eternity for you," he said, his lips brushing her hair.

Again, an inkling of déjà vu ran through her, and she wanted to question it, but the door to the office flew open, and Chelsea stepped in. A rumbling growl came from Simon as his sight shot to the open door. The lethal look in his eyes had turned them closer to black, and his muscles went taut, like he was ready to attack.

Violet swallowed, not comprehending the mixed emotions his reaction caused in her. A blend of fear and desire. As Chelsea made some excuse for the interruption, Simon's rigid posture relaxed.

Muttering something about a special bottle of rum she'd ordered, Chelsea rummaged around in Keary's desk. Violet knew very well she didn't need anything. Keary and Paige had sent her. There was no doubt in her mind about that. Simon paced the room, his frustration rolling from him in waves.

"I'll let you two get back to whatever it was you were up to," she said, backing out of the room and closing the office door.

"She didn't leave with anything," Simon observed, scratching his head.

Violet laughed; he was right. Chelsea had left just as she had entered—empty handed.

"Our chaperones again?"

"I would bet money on it." Chestnut orbs searched hers. "What is it about us that makes them not want to leave us alone?"

"I don't know, but maybe it's a blessing considering what just happened."

He walked over to the couch against the far wall and sat, resting his head in his hands. The sense that she had seen him like that before flashed through her mind. She was getting a little annoyed by the constant déjà vu, but she had to admit it was better than the waves of nausea to which she had grown accustomed.

Simon lifted his head and searched her eyes again. Every time he did, her breath caught and her heart skipped.

"What do we do now?" he asked, the longing for her clear in his voice and in the strained lines on his face.

Her chest swelled, and she didn't know if either of them could go through with waiting like they'd been discussing. Holding themselves back for longer than a few minutes was challenging enough, although she found it easier the longer they spent together. She could meet his eyes without the overwhelming urge to tear his clothes off, but the impulse was still there, and a need for him still flared every second she was with him.

She walked over and sat down next to him. Curling a leg under her as she turned her body toward his, she inhaled his scent.

"We wait. We take it slow."

He took her hand and rubbed his fingers along hers. "How long have we known each other now?"

She laughed. "Twelve hours? Maybe? That sounds funny to say, considering where we are."

"Yes, it does," he answered, staring at her hand as his fingers traced her lifeline. "You know, Vi, I've never had this happen before."

"It's not something I'm used to either, Simon," she answered quietly.

"Really?" He drew his hand up to run his fingers through her wandering curl. "As beautiful as you are, I'd think you'd have men lined up to kiss you."

"Ha! You can't imagine how far from the truth that is."

She paused, slightly afraid to admit how wrong he was, knowing it would also confirm that he really was the one for her, the man she would marry, the man whose children she would bear. She feared admitting it would push him away or add pressure to an already complicated situation.

Doubt crossed her mind. There was a possibility that he would run from the weight of how serious this was. But there was also the chance he would stay and admit it was the same for him. This man, whom she'd known for less than a full day, whom she'd already gone farther with than any man before, might not understand the significance of what he was to her. There was only one way to know, and she sent a silent prayer that baring her soul to him wouldn't destroy what they were only just discovering.

# CHAPTER 29

Simon's attention fixed on Violet as she gnawed at her bottom lip. The habit only made her more alluring. She'd gone quiet suddenly, and he worried about what she was thinking. She seemed like she wanted to tell him something but was holding back, and he hoped he hadn't offended her with the comment about kissing. There was no way she hadn't been fighting the men in this town off. No way what he'd heard earlier about her could be true. She was the most attractive woman here, and to be truthful, she was the most beautiful creature he'd ever met. He didn't think there was anyone who could hold a candle to her.

Fear pummeled him as another thought occurred to him. She'd said she wasn't dating anyone, but maybe that hadn't been the truth. Envy that was becoming all too familiar slithered through him. No, it couldn't be that, or Keary would have told him. He wanted to believe she'd given him the truth.

Maybe it was something worse. Had she been serious with someone, even married to someone before she'd met him? This time the jealousy coiled around his chest. The thought of her with anyone else made him crazy. His fist tightened, and his heart rate increased, and somewhere deep within him, fire stirred, sending a need to hurt and punish clawing through him.

He didn't know what he was thinking. They weren't kids; they were both in their late twenties. There was no way she hadn't dated other men and, likely, slept with some. That sting of jealousy flared again at the thought. There was a need in him for her to be his and only his, as if he had claimed her. Deep down on an instinctual level, he knew it to be true. She was his, and he would kill any man who so much as tried to touch her. Or anyone who had already touched her. He blinked in reaction to the unhinged thought, one that was far too out of control for how he normally acted.

These were not the thoughts of a rational man. He cleared his head and waited for her to speak, hoping he could keep his uncontrollable, insecure thoughts at bay.

Violet looked down and picked at the seam of her skirt. A strange sense of familiarity swept through him, but he shook it off as he watched the skirt move slightly higher from her fidgeting, revealing more of her thigh. Lust rippled through him again.

*Focus, Simon*, he told himself. They had agreed to wait, so ripping her skirt off and taking her on this sofa wouldn't be the most gallant thing for him to do, no matter how much he wanted her.

"This is going to sound strange, and you'll either think I'm crazy or slightly neurotic, so I won't blame you if you run away." She peeked up at him, that loose curl sweeping across her eyebrow and landing over her eye.

Gently, he pushed it back with the rest of her hair. "There's nothing you could say that would make me run from you."

She smiled at him again and took a deep breath. "Please don't laugh."

He put his hand up. "Scout's honor."

"Were you even a Boy Scout?"

He chuckled. "No, but it was all I could think to say."

"Well, that's reassuring," she said, laughing along with him.

"Now, what's all this about, Vi?"

"Promise you won't laugh?"

"I promise, I promise."

She hesitated, chewing her bottom lip. She looked like she was searching for the right words before she blurted, "You're the first man I've ever kissed."

He reeled back, knowing his eyes had grown large.

"Seriously?" he asked before he could catch himself.

"You promised."

"I know, I know. I'm not laughing. I just find it a little unbelievable." A beautiful arc formed where her brow raised. "Go on, please."

She looked back down at the hem of her skirt, eyes locked on the string she'd loosened.

"I've never even been this close to a man before you. Even if I'd wanted to, I wouldn't have been able to."

"You've never wanted to before?" He knew it wasn't her point, but he couldn't help the swell of excitement at her admission.

"Well, no. But I don't think it would have mattered. I have this thing." She rubbed her nose with the back of her hand. "It's hard to explain, but basically, I get sick around guys. Paige calls it my man allergy."

This time a boisterous laugh fled him, and her eyes flashed to his, irritation clear in them. He hadn't been able to stop himself. It seemed impossible that she really got sick around other men.

"You promised," she said, rising from her spot next to him.

He grabbed her hand, pulling her back down. "No, stay and tell me the rest. Please, I wasn't laughing at you."

"Then what were you laughing at?"

"I'll tell you after you finish telling me."

"There's not much more to it," she stated flatly. Clearly, he'd bothered her by laughing, and that hadn't been his intention.

"How sick do you get? A stomach ache, nausea?" he asked, trying to get her to talk more.

"No, worse than that. I get violently ill. Back in high school, Paige and I got invited to a party. We ended up playing a game of spin the bottle. Patrick and his friends fixed it so that he would end up in the closet with me. He didn't like the 'no' I'd given him multiple times before that day. I guess he thought I'd change my mind being locked in the dark with him."

He didn't know why, but the thought made Simon's blood boil. It was that instinctual reaction that had only appeared when he'd met Violet—possessive and protective.

"He got a little more than he bargained for when I threw up all over him."

"You didn't?"

She nodded, an impish smile curving her lips. "I did. It was terrible. It went everywhere, and he was not happy about it. Unfortunately, he had a lot more sway with most of the school than I did, and he made the rest of the year miserable. Vomiting Violet stuck for months."

"Really?" His heart ached for her, and he wanted to find this guy and beat the crap out of him for hurting her.

She must have read his expression because she quickly followed up with, "Oh, it worked out. The following year, some boys from a rival school cornered me under the bleachers after a football game ended. Patrick and a few of the other guys saw it and messed them up pretty bad. I don't know why they did it, if it was one of those, if we can't have her, neither can you things or just a don't mess with one of our girls thing. From that day on, everything went back to the way it had been, only the guys became more protective. Everyone in town seems to look out for me and Paige. Patrick's daughter is even one of my goddaughters."

He shook his head at the thought of anyone trying to hurt her, forcing away the streaks of anger that shaded his vision.

"So, you have an allergy to men? Well, all men except me, it would seem?"

"It would appear so."

Of all the possibilities of what she was going to tell him, that had not been one. He pinched his brow, irritated at himself for how irrational he had been and stunned by her extraordinary confession.

"Why are you laughing? You said you wouldn't laugh, and here you are doing exactly that."

He reached for her hand again and pulled it into his lap.

"I'm not laughing at you, I swear. I'm laughing because I'm relieved. I know you won't believe this, but..." He paused, trying to figure out how to say it without sounding like he was making fun of her. "I have the same allergy."

"You're allergic to men?" she asked playfully.

"Huh? No." He shook his head and gave her a bashful smile that was out of character for him. "I'm allergic to women. Can't get near them without becoming nauseated. Keary calls it my female fright."

She tried to pull her hand back, hurt reflected in her eyes. "Are you making fun of me?"

"No, no," he reassured her, dragging her back to him. "I'm being serious. I really can't even think about being with a woman without the bile rising in my throat."

She gave him a look. "Do you think about that a lot?"

"Throwing up?"

"No, silly. Being with other women."

She was jealous, and he couldn't help but enjoy the moment. "You're cute." Her frown caused him to chuckle. "No, in fact, I never think about it. I never found anyone I wanted to think about before today."

Her emerald irises sparkled until they narrowed. "You can't be serious. You can't have the same issue I have. It's uncanny."

"I promise you I do. I would never lie to you."

Her sight flitted between his eyes, searching for any doubt, but he gave her none. He was telling her the truth. The thought of another woman had never even crossed his mind. Even if it had, he would have become sick. Somehow, his body knew she was the one and had saved him from any other. Saved him for her.

She leaned up and kissed him, bringing her hand up to his cheek. The touch was gentle and caused his heart to stutter. She brought her leg over him and straddled him as his tongue danced with hers and his hunger for her returned. He moved his hands to her hips, saying, "You're not making this easy on me, Vi."

"Maybe we don't have to wait," she breathed between kisses.

Her hands ran the length of his chest, shoving at his shirt. Maybe she was right; maybe he'd imagined that sensation. He wrapped his hand around her neck and crushed his lips to hers. Her hands were under his shirt, lifting it higher, and she tugged at it. A slight separation of their lips and she pulled it over his head before he forced her mouth back to his.

Her moves were confident, and she didn't appear to be someone who had never done this before. Then again, confidence guided him so that it seemed like he'd been touching her for years. The sensation of knowing her kisses and her body was almost too strong to ignore.

He smoothed his hand under her shirt, caressing her breast. The soft moan that escaped her only increased his yearning for her. He pulled the bottom of her shirt and lifted it over her head. Watching the rise of her breasts in the purple lace bra she wore below, he knew there was no way he could stop now. Her mouth was on his before the shirt fell from his hands and she ground down on his length, fueling the fire in him. Gripping her neck with one hand, he cupped her breast, feeling the reaction below her bra and rubbing his thumb over it. Her skirt no longer separated them, and she pressed down harder over him so that her warmth teased him.

A feral growl started low in his diaphragm and worked its way up, rumbling in his chest. There would be no stopping this time. He would have her. All of her. Dropping his hands to her hips, he gripped them tight, forcing her chest against his and his firmness further into her. Her hands grasped his shoulders as her hips moved in a motion that drove him mad. Only two layers of material separated them, but just as he reached up to tear her bra off, that sensation hit him again. This time, it was like a desperate scream rising from within him so forcefully that he couldn't help but push her away. She gasped, her eyes going wide.

Drawing in a ragged breath, she said, "You felt it again."

He shook his head, his entire body aching to return to where they'd been moments before. "Heard it again."

She lowered her head against his chest. "I don't know if I can wait," she whispered. "This hurts too much."

He leaned his head back and took a deep breath. He knew exactly what she meant. Lowering his head again, he tilted her face up and kissed her forehead before resting his forehead against hers and saying, "Neither do I, but...something wants us to wait and as strong as it is, I think we need to listen."

The defeat in her expression killed him. Draping his finger along the swell of her breast, he said, "You are so beautiful." The temptation was there, her body still straddling him and almost naked. But he stopped himself, knowing they needed to heed whatever that sensation was or something bad would happen. He remembered Keary's words at the theater. Eternity. She would be his for eternity if he could just be patient. "And I want you more than anything I've ever craved."

He traced the path of her curves, dropping his mouth to her neck and kissing it, relishing the sweet taste of her skin. Her head fell back as he lowered his lips, running his tongue over the edge of her bra.

"That's not helping," she purred.

He sucked her nipple through the material, dragging his teeth over it before releasing it. He peeked up and gave her a sly grin. "I can't help it. You're addictive. I may have to wait, but that doesn't mean I can't touch."

She opened her mouth to respond, but the sound of the door opening had both their heads turning toward it. He was quickly regretting not locking the damned door.

If Paige had come in to say something, she'd forgotten it the moment she saw Violet in his lap and the two of them with their shirts off. Her mouth hung open, and her cheeks turned bright red. Simon had an iota of pity for her until he reminded himself that she had barged in and interrupted them.

"I, uh," she stuttered. "Violet, what are you doing? How am I supposed..." She drifted off and, throwing her hands in the air, turned on her heel and slammed the door closed as she left.

Violet turned back to him and shrugged. "Chaperone one? How long do you think it will take for chaperone two to come in?"

Chuckling, he said, "I'd venture it won't be too long."

The moment was gone, and although he wanted to go back to where they'd left off, he took Paige's entrance as a sign. Tracing his hand down Violet's arms, he leaned over and picked up her shirt. "If I'm going to have any semblance of control, you need to put this back on. Otherwise, I can't make any promises."

She leaned over him to pick up his shirt, her chest pushing against his skin.

"You really are not helping here, Vi," he said, sliding his hand between them and caressing her breast.

"Neither are you, Simon. And you need to put this on if I'm to have any semblance of control."

She handed him his shirt, but he yanked her closer, his mouth crashing into hers as he stole one more kiss.

"Simon," she breathed, and the reaction in his body was instant. "We agreed."

Dropping his forehead, he said, "I know," before pushing her away and watching her put her shirt on. He lifted her from his lap and settled her next to him. Pulling his shirt on, he leaned on his knees and held his head in his hands.

"Who are we to each other?" she asked so softly he barely heard her.

"What do you mean?"

"Well, it's clear there are forces at work here beyond our knowledge."

"You mean like fate?" he asked, lifting his head to look at her. "Like you said earlier?"

She chewed her lip. "I guess so."

"So, you think we were fated to meet each other?"

"Maybe. Or maybe our fates are intertwined." She paused, chewing a little more on that lip. "How else do you explain us or that instant attraction we had?"

*Need was more like it,* he thought.

"This." She moved her hands between them. "How else do you explain our allergy to anyone of the other sex except us?" She used her fingers to make quotation marks as she spoke the word allergy.

She had a point. There was something between them that was inexplicable. Whether fate or destiny, he didn't know. He wasn't the kind of man who believed in those sorts of things, but as she rested her head against his, that unexplainable call rushed through him again. Perhaps she was right.

"Fate," he repeated.

"We need to wait," she said. "Whatever this is, call it fate if you will, but whatever it is, something is telling us to wait. We both feel it."

He took the loose curl and moved it from her eye. "Yes, and it's getting stronger."

"Simon? You don't think..." She paused, lifting her head. "No, that's crazy," she answered herself.

"What's crazy?"

"Well, I was thinking about our chaperones. You don't think they know about this, do you? I mean, that would be insane to think they know something and are trying to stop us from going too far. Right?"

He thought about the shared looks between Keary and Paige. The constant interruptions.

"No," he said with some hesitation, "it's just not possible."

She laughed. "You're right. It's just silly talk."

As if to prove her wrong, the office door swung open and in stepped Keary, arms crossed.

"Chaperone two arrives. Keary," Simon scoffed, his irritation fueling a need to leap from the couch and attack his friend. Keary's entrance certainly lent credence to Violissa's suggestion that he and Paige were trying to keep them separated. It made no rational sense, but he couldn't deny the suspicion their actions aroused.

"Simon, Violet," Keary addressed them in a parental tone that only further aggravated Simon. "Violet, you should get back out there. Whatever you two were doing when Paige walked in here has traumatized the poor thing."

"Then she should have knocked," Simon grumbled.

Violet laid a hand on his leg. "He's right, Simon. I should go back out. I'm sure people are missing us. Besides, Paige is a little attached at the hip to me, and she gets anxious when I'm away from her too long."

She pushed herself up from where she sat and smoothed her skirt down.

He watched her walk toward Keary, his eyes drawn to her movement, from the swaying of her hair to the subtle swing of her hips. The further she moved from him, the greater the sense of loss grew. She stopped in front of Keary, lifted on her toes, and kissed his cheek, saying, "Okay, Dad, I'm leaving."

Simon chuckled, but Keary only continued to stare him down. Violet glanced back at Simon, a look of longing crossing her eyes before she reluctantly turned and walked out of the room. With the closing of the door came a tearing sensation in his core, like something had ripped her from him. It was an endless void that threatened to devour him, and he lowered his head to his hands to fight the sensation.

"What are you doing, Simon?" Keary asked, and Simon detected the hint of pity in his tone.

"What does it look like I'm doing?" he snapped, lifting his head. "I'm spending time with the woman of my dreams. Is there something suddenly wrong with that?"

Keary sighed and unfolded his arms. "No, there's nothing wrong with that. But there is something wrong with how fast the two of you are moving."

"Excuse me, but I distinctly remember you moving that fast with quite a few girls back in college," he bit back, knowing he had Keary cornered. Keary stuttered slightly but recovered quicker than Simon expected. "That was different, and you know it. That was just fun, but you and Violet are different."

Simon stood. "You're being hypocritical, not to mention too authoritative. Since when did you become so patriarchal, interrupting every time Violet and I are alone, like you're her father and she's just a teenager?"

"I'm not being hypocritical." He rubbed his forehead. "And I'm not trying to treat either of you like children. You and Violet are perfect for each other. I know you're meant for each other. I've always known it, and you know it, too. You all but admitted it earlier."

"Then why doesn't that make it okay to move fast?" He heard the doubt in his voice as he said it, thinking of that unexpected sensation that kept returning.

"Because it doesn't. You need to slow down. If you rush this, you might lose her. I told you, just wait, be patient."

A moment of doubt crept into his mind. He hadn't thought of losing her before, only thought of having her. She'd only been his for a day, but the thought of not having her with him was overwhelming. He was drowning, trying to catch his breath as the waves spilled over his head.

"Simon?" Keary interrupted his thoughts.

He opened his eyes, only now realizing he'd closed them.

"I can't lose her," he whispered. He hated how weak he sounded and how it went against everything in his nature. He detested weakness.

Keary's eyes creased, the concern evident. "Then slow down."

"We are," he answered. "We agreed things were moving too fast. I don't know how to explain it, but there's this sensation that we need to slow down and take our time. It keeps returning, so we've agreed to heed it."

The divot between Keary's brow crinkled further. "That's what you were doing when Paige walked in on you?"

"Yes, it was. Look, Keary, whatever this is, you don't have to be concerned. We're figuring it out on our own. I don't know why you have this need to act like you're our father, but..." He stopped and thought about what Violet had said. "Is there something you're not telling me?"

Keary put his hands up. "I'm only looking out for the two of you. You're my best friend, and Violet, well...she's Violet. The last thing I want is for the two of you to not be together." But Keary hadn't answered the question.

Choosing not to push him on it, Simon replied, "Don't worry. We'll be fine."

Keary gave him the wise sage look he sometimes had that always made him seem like he was centuries old and not twenty-eight. "All right, let's go back out there. I'm sure Violet is waiting with bated breath for your return."

"I'll be out in a minute," he replied. "I need to calm down before I can be social again."

Keary gave him a knowing look. "Don't make her wait too long. She might get restless and come looking for you. I don't need the two of you to end up back in here again."

"Get out, Keary," Simon ordered, pointing to the door.

After Keary left, Simon found his way to the bathroom. He

leaned over the sink and splashed water on his face. He needed to get a hold of himself, but he couldn't. Being near Violet made every rational thought disappear. The world around them fell away, and it was as if nothing else existed. Now that she was no longer near him, he couldn't think straight.

Patting his face dry, he rested his hands on the sink and looked at himself. There was no rational way to think about the situation. Even the adage "love at first sight" didn't apply. If anything, it was too weak to describe what was happening to them. Love? Did he love her? A woman he'd only met that day? But she was so familiar. He had dreamed about her almost every night since he could remember. Seen the hints of her blonde hair, the shimmer of her emerald eyes. Every part of him screamed she was his, and his heart slammed viciously against his chest. Love was a word that encompassed so much with its meaning, yet it didn't seem strong enough to describe the emotions that were gripping him.

Maybe Violet was right. Maybe this was something bigger than them, something out of their control. He only wished he understood what it was and why it was happening.

He had no more time to ponder the situation. The bathroom door opened, and a man walked in. Simon had met so many people that he had trouble recalling the man's name.

He was about Simon's age, with sandy brown hair and the build of a football player. Simon vaguely remembered that he had gone to school with Violet. Brad, maybe? Giving him a polite nod, Simon headed toward the door, but the guy didn't move to let him by. Instead, he stood taller and crossed his arms over his chest. The stance was threatening, as was his expression.

Not one to be intimidated, Simon straightened to his full height, which left him staring down at Brad. He'd never been the type to start a fight, but he was strong enough to end one quickly. Men like this didn't frighten him. In fact, nothing frightened him. He stood a few inches taller, and even though Brad was built, Simon knew instinctively that he was stronger.

Not wanting him to think he had the upper hand, Simon confronted him. "May I help you with something?"

He didn't back down, instead taking a step closer to Simon. "Look, you seem like a nice guy, and Keary has vouched for you, but I still need to say this. Violet is special in this town. There isn't a person here who doesn't know her, and I'd venture to guess there's not one who doesn't love her." Shades of black streaked Simon's vision, but he restrained his urge to punch the man and let him continue. "All of us have had to deal with her rebuttals. We've had to settle for friendship, and after all these years, we've become extremely protective of her. Hell, I can't count how many times she turned me down, and she was a bridesmaid in my wedding."

Simon's fists curled. "Is that it?"

"No. Those of us who've had to deal with her rejections came to a...call it a group consensus that she needs to be protected. We watch out for her and keep her safe. For the first time since I've known her, she's interested in someone. I don't know if you're the one she's saved herself for all these years, but if you are, you need to be careful with her. I've seen the way she looks at you. What I wouldn't give to have a woman look at me that way. If I were any other man, I'd venture to say she's in love with you already, but I don't believe in that stuff."

As interesting as all of this was, Simon wanted desperately to get out so he could see Violet again.

"Look, I'm not sure what's going on either, but you don't have to worry about me. I'll protect her, just as any of you would."

He moved to leave again, but Brad put his hand out and landed it hard on Simon's chest. Simon raised his brow, his jaw tensing, all instincts set to attack him for touching him.

"You hurt her, and you'll have us to deal with. Do you understand?"

Simon bristled and moved the hand off his chest. "Don't touch me again or you'll need to learn how to live one-handed."

Taking another step closer so that he now towered over him, he said, "If I hurt her, you can stand in line because I'll have myself to deal with first."

Brad took a moment to consider his words. "Good, then we have an understanding." His demeanor changed, the threatening glare retreated, and he stepped away, saying, "Come on out. The guys want to get to know you."

Eyes blinking, they followed Brad's path to where he opened the door and stood waiting for Simon.

"I'll buy you a beer for putting up with me just then and not making me fight you."

With a snicker, Simon said, "It wouldn't have been much of a fight. And you know I own this bar, right? I don't need to pay for my drinks."

"Then you can buy us a round. You've been with Violet all night, and the rest of the guys are just as curious as I am. Let's go before they come looking for me, and you'll have to threaten them, too."

"I wasn't the one who started with the threats," he grumbled, following Brad out of the bathroom. He wasn't looking forward to talking to a bunch of men who he now knew had all been in love with Violet at some point and likely still were. Nor did he like the thought of being away from Violet's side. The only consolation was that Violet would be in his sight again.

# CHAPTER 30

The rest of the evening dragged for Simon, who was stuck talking to the locals in town. They peppered him with questions about the city, his business, about traveling and all the places he had been, all of which caused him to wonder if any of them had ever left this town. He doubted it. It seemed like the type of place where people stayed. He must have answered a million questions before the conversation turned to Violet. He listened to stories about her childhood and their school years with her, things she'd done. It amazed him how integral she was to every part of life here.

At one point, he even met the ass from Violet's closet story and his wife. He kept his temper in check and didn't deck the guy. They'd been kids, and Simon hadn't even known her then, so punishing him for something that happened that long ago didn't seem justified. The story about the closet came up, and everyone got a good laugh about her sudden stomach flu.

Simon looked over at Violet and caught her eye. He'd been glancing her way the entire time, wishing he could get back to her. She was only across the room from him, but it seemed like miles. The night was endless without her by his side.

When Keary rang the final round bell to announce it was closing time, Simon finally let out a relieved breath. Violet was over at the bar again, talking with Chelsea and Paige, who hadn't left her side all night, and he pondered how he would ever get her alone again. Maybe it was a good thing. They had agreed to keep it tame, but he truly didn't know if he had the strength.

As people filed out and said their goodbyes, he made his way over to her.

"Need help cleaning up?" Violet asked Keary as Simon came to stand next to her.

Being so close to her again refreshed him. She turned and gave him another smile, her eyes tired but still sparkling. There was a slightly different hue, a rich sage that drew him in.

"No, go home. You both look exhausted," Keary replied.

"I can walk them home," Simon said.

Keary quirked a brow. "Seriously? We live in the safest town in the country, and you're worried about them walking home alone?"

Simon wanted to punch him. He knew exactly why Simon wanted to walk them home. He was merely making this difficult.

Violet wrapped her hands around his arm and said to Keary, "It would be nice to have an escort."

Paige shrugged. "Fine with me. I don't mind being the third wheel for a little while." She started walking toward the door. "No making out the entire way home. That last image is still ingrained in my mind, and I can't unsee it. I'll be outside waiting."

Walking home with Paige wasn't ideal. She grated on his nerves, but he had no choice.

Keary pursed his lips before saying, "Fine, but can you find your way back to the apartment?"

"I have a pretty good sense of direction after all my time in the city. I'll be fine."

"Goodnight Chelsea. Night Keary," Violet said, taking Simon's hand and pulling him toward the door.

"Night, guys. Don't make Paige uncomfortable again. The

poor thing is still having flashbacks," Chelsea called, waving to them.

Apparently, Paige hadn't kept her mouth shut about what she'd seen them doing, which was nothing more than sitting and talking, albeit without shirts on.

The fresh air hit Simon squarely in the face when he exited the building, energizing and waking him. He probably should have stayed and helped Keary, but this was the better option, and having Violet with him made it the perfect one.

Paige walked ahead of them. "I'll just be up here if you need me, trying to envision anything other than your hands and mouths on each other."

"Smart ass," Violet replied, squeezing Simon's hand.

He pulled her closer to him and breathed in the lilac scent that still seemed to cling to her. It was odd that her perfume still smelled as fresh as when he'd met her for dinner. She laid her head against him as they walked. Dropping her hand, he wrapped his arm around her, thinking that he never wanted this moment to end.

"Is your house far?" he asked.

"Why? Are you trying to free yourself of me already?" she teased, her voice a light sound that tickled his ears.

"Quite the opposite. I was hoping we would have to walk a few miles."

"Too bad for you, then. Everything in this town is close," Paige said, clearly hearing everything they were saying. His dislike of her was increasing.

They walked in silence after that. Not that he minded the silence, and with Violet there was no discomfort in it. He took the time to appreciate the small things about her that he had missed in the crowded bar. From the softness of her skin beneath his hand to the gentle way her hair moved in the night breeze to the subtle rise and fall of her chest. Contented, he thought the moment was one he could exist in forever, but Paige stopped in front of a large country-style house, and he knew it had come to an end.

The house was exactly how he had pictured a place Violet would live. A long white wrap-around porch held two rocking chairs on one side and a porch swing on the other. The house itself, a deep shade of blue, was two stories, its window style revealing its age. Roses bordered the porch—shades of white, yellow, and pink—and spread the width of the house. Beds of violets wound their way up each side of the sidewalk that led to the porch steps.

Paige ran up the front steps and opened the door. "Goodnight, Simon," she said with a slight bow. His forehead crinkled. Had she really just bowed, or had that been his imagination? "Violet—"

"I know, don't be long, or you'll start flicking the porch light. Got it, Mom."

Paige gave her a nasty look, then ran inside, closing the door behind her. Violet's laugh floated on the breeze as she turned back to him. Eyes like bright gems twinkled with humor.

"She'll really do that, too. I would not put it past her."

"I don't doubt it," he answered. She smiled at him, and his heart jumped against his chest.

"So, Mr. Black, I would invite you in, but...I don't think that would be a good idea," she said playfully, resting her hand on his chest.

"Although that wouldn't be the worst idea, it's likely not the best, considering." He brushed her hair back from her face. She had freed it from her braids at some point in the night, and now it hung loose down her back. He pulled her rebellious curl toward him, wrapping his finger around it. He decided he preferred her hair to be loose. Something about it being down stirred a memory that he couldn't quite define.

She leaned up on her toes and kissed him passionately, as if kissing him that way would change their circumstance. If she didn't stop, it would work, and he would have to break their pact of waiting. He imagined picking her up and carrying her into the house, then laying her on her bed and making love to her the rest of the night. The image didn't help him, and he brought her flush against him.

Threading his fingers through her hair, he deepened their kiss, all the while hearing his conscience tell him to stop or he would lose control completely. As if she sensed this, she pulled herself away. She had grabbed his shirt so that it was now balled up in her fist, so she quickly let go and self-consciously smoothed out the wrinkles.

Taking her hand, he asked, "Tomorrow? Breakfast?" He didn't think he could wait much longer than that to see her again. As it stood now, he couldn't even imagine sleeping tonight.

She answered, "Tomorrow, yes. No, oh no. Not breakfast."

His heart dropped, and she must have seen it on his face. Angry with himself for the show of weakness, he quickly joked, "You have another date with the orchestra?"

She giggled. "No, not this time. I have a date with Paige. We have a job tomorrow."

"But you own the company. Don't you have people who work for you?" he asked.

"I have employees, but I'm really hands-on, and most of the jobs I work myself. Especially the important ones like this one."

"All day?" he asked.

She scrunched her mouth up in frustration. "Yes." Her eyes revealed the sadness that was gutting him. "I guess I'm going to have to change my policy and start delegating more, aren't I?"

"I think so. I suppose I have no choice but to be patient tomorrow."

Her fingers drifted over his jawline. "I'm sure Keary will keep you busy. And I've no plans in the evening."

He didn't know if he could go a whole day without seeing her. In fact, he didn't think he could make it through tonight, let alone the next day. But he had no choice. She'd had a life before he met her, and he couldn't simply ask her to give it all up just to be with him, no matter how badly he wanted her to.

Brushing the curl back from her eye again, the thought occurred to him that at some point, that conversation would arise. He would need to return home. It was inevitable. While he could work remotely, there were still meetings and places he would need to be. The company wouldn't run itself. But leaving her was not an option. There was no doubt in his mind that he couldn't live without her, knew it with certainty even at this early stage.

"Where did you go?" Violet asked, interrupting his thoughts.

He gave her a lazy smile. "Just thinking that tomorrow is going to be a very long day."

"Yes, it will," she replied, pulling his head down and kissing him again.

The light on the porch flicked off and on. Paige—the thorn in his side.

Lips hesitantly drawing from hers, he dropped his head. "Would it upset you if I ran up there and ripped the light out?"

"It might." She brought her hands up to each side of his face and looked up at him. "Patience, right?"

He nodded, not wanting to pull his eyes from hers. The fingers of her other hand traced his cheek to his jawline, then ran over his lips as if she were trying to imprint his face to memory. He kissed her fingers, her palm, her wrist. The urge to continue and devour her the rest of the way was one he fought.

The light flicked again, and he groaned.

"Goodnight, Simon," she breathed as her lips met his again.

He laced his hand through the hair at her neck and pulled her against him again. Every part of him bellowed not to let her go, but as her lips slowly separated from his, he knew he had no choice.

"Goodnight, Violet," he murmured.

She backed away slowly until his hand was free to drop from her waist. Hesitating, she looked as if she wanted to say something, then closed her mouth and smiled. There was no need to talk. It was as if they could speak to one another simply through their eyes. She spun and ran up the steps and across the porch. When she had the door open, she stepped through and turned back to him, raising her hand slightly with a gentle goodbye wave before she shut it.

At the closing of the door, a rush of loss washed over him, and his chest seized its movement. He almost wanted to crumple to the ground just to survive the onslaught of emotion. The sensation was indescribable, and he didn't understand it. Minutes passed as he stood there and stared at the door until he forced himself to move his feet and walk away. For the first time in his life, he didn't want to spend the night alone when alone was all he'd preferred before. Stuffing his hands in his pockets, he made his way back to his place, knowing it was going to be an extremely long night.

# CHAPTER 31

Paige leaned against her bedroom door. She'd avoided Violet when her friend had finally come into the house, running up to her room instead of staying and talking. Her legs were shaking so badly that she slid to the floor, folding her arms around them and tucking them into her chest. She was a wreck. Caught in the middle of something beyond her comprehension and her abilities. This was the stuff of magic and prophecy and the Fates. Not something for a mortal like her.

Seeing the prophecy in play was stunning. She'd thought the park was bad, but things had only worsened as the evening progressed. The two hadn't been able to keep their hands from each other. Keary had caught them at the theater, and she had caught them in the office. How did the Fates expect her to stop this?

She banged her head against the door. The day she'd left for this world, she'd been excited. Never had she imagined what she was getting into. Having to relive her life as a child in a world she didn't understand with a woman who was her queen but was now her best friend. The prospect of saving their world, of finding their rulers, had seemed like a blessing. But the closer she came to this moment, the more the nerves increased. And now here she was, but without the excitement and only fear.

Dropping her head to her knees, she stifled a frustrated scream. Every emotion had run its course through her this evening, and it had left her exhausted. She hadn't known what she was getting into all those years ago. This wasn't a game. This was serious. The power of the prophecy was far more than she'd expected. She'd envisioned it as some sort of fairytale, but this was no kid's movie. How wrong she'd been. The Fates had designed their prophecy, so there was no escaping its power. These people were under a force more powerful than she had ever imagined, one that terrified her because she didn't have any idea how to slow its course.

Rising, she rubbed her hand down her thighs to dry the clammy consistency her nerves had given them. She heard Violet's door close. This was her queen. The Light queen and her soulmate, the Dark king. Two people who had been myths because they'd been gone so long. Stories her parents had told her when she was little.

Pinching her brow, she fought the rush of homesickness that often hit her. She wanted to be home, back in the safety of her mother's arms. Wanted to hear her father's voice, see his warm smile again. She sat on her bed and rested her head in her hands. What if the Fates had chosen wrong? She wasn't her father, wasn't a leader, wasn't wise and knowing like he was. This was so far from who she was that she didn't know what to do.

She laid her head in her arms and cried, awash in a storm of doubt. A powerless mortal in over her head with no idea how to surface. Those thoughts would have angered her father, who had always told her how special she was, how she should be proud of who she was.

A memory stirred of leaving her world so many years ago with Keary.

*The small home where she'd grown up was all she'd known, just as the Banished Realm was. She looked over it one last time, taking in the glimpses of her parents and her life in the objects that filled the room. Her father's books on the table. Her mother's quilt on the chair by the hearth. This place was safety and security, just as her parents were, but she was leaving all of that behind. Following the path the Fates had now laid for her. The excitement of the news gave way to nerves, and she leaned on the chair, hearing her mother's soft sobs from her bedroom.*

*Her mother had feigned strength when she'd said goodbye to Paige, folding her in her arms and holding her tight. But Paige knew her mother would suffer, and she didn't know if she would recover from having her only child taken from her. A child who should never have been, from a marriage that should never have been.*

*Taking a long lungful of air, Paige turned her back on the cabin, stepping onto the porch and closing the door to the sounds of her mother's anguish. Wiping a tear away, she tucked her hands under her arms, hiding the trembling that now held them prisoner. She was leaving all she knew behind, and it suddenly didn't seem as much of an adventure as it had when her father had told her of it.*

*Her father was waiting for her at the bottom of the steps. He made no note of the tears that glazed her eyes or the way her legs shook with every step closer she came to him.*

*"Ready?" he had asked, understanding in his blue eyes.*

*"No." The word came out like a squeak, an admission that passed through her barriers without permission.*

*"Your mother will be fine, Paige. She's stronger than you think."*

*But that wasn't her concern. She knew of her mother's resilience, and with her father by her mother's side, she did not worry.*

*"I know," she said, sitting on a step and folding her legs closer to her.*

*Her father did not move from his spot, but concern showed in the creasing of his brow. "Then what has turned your excitement to doubt? You're questioning yourself, which is not like you."*

*His honesty stung in its truth.*

"I don't think I can do this, Father. I can't be the one the Fates chose. Keary must be mistaken."

Her father put a hand out, and she took it. He pulled her into his arms and smoothed her hair down, laying a kiss on her head.

"My dear child. Have I not always told you it is by the Fates' design that you are here?" He took her shoulders and pushed her a step back, looking intently into her eyes. "You are no ordinary woman. You are unique. The daughter of a Lightbearer. The only child ever born of a Council. The Fates do not make mistakes, my child. You are here for a reason. Perhaps it is for this reason, or perhaps this is only one of many. Whatever the Fates have planned for you, today is the day for you to step onto the path they have laid and embrace your destiny."

His words emboldened her, but doubt remained, peppering the recesses of her mind.

"But, Father, I have no power. I am not like Violissa or King Sinow. I am not like you or any of the Council. I am powerless."

His laugh had her scrunching her nose and frowning.

"Have I taught you nothing, Paige? Power does not define a person, nor did it define any of us in our past lives. My power has been stripped from me, but I am still the same man as I was the day Tynan stole it. My heart is still the same, my thoughts, my actions, my choices. They define me, not my power. They always have." He tucked a strand of her hair behind her ear. "Without that power, we are mortals just as you and your mother are. Mortals who make mistakes, choose wrong paths, mistrust their hearts." With his words, her courage slowly reformed. "If you strip away Sinow's power, you have a man who chose not to follow his heart and let Violissa make the choice for him. Take Violissa's power, and you have a woman who was too blind to trust her heart, too stubborn to trust the Fates, too rash to trust her Council, too naïve to trust the man who held her heart. Without power, they are simply people who made mistakes. It was not the power that defined them Paige, it was their emotions and *their actions. They were simply too blind to see that. Under it all, we are all the same."*

*They were words that defined a history she had not been part of but that had still shaped her. And those words opened her eyes to the possibility that she could take this path the Fates had laid for her and traverse it to the end.*

*She smiled at her father, hugging him one last time as his words continued to strengthen her resolve even as she stepped into the portal that took her away from everything she loved.*

And not once had she doubted her path until today.

Inhaling, Paige picked up her head. She could do this. She just needed to keep her father's words in mind. Violissa was just a person like anyone else. A woman who needed help, a woman suffering who couldn't find her way out of the darkness, and it was Paige's job to help where she could.

The Fates had asked for her. They had not chosen another mortal or a Council. They had chosen her. And she needed to have faith in their choice. There was one reason she was here, and no matter how challenging it seemed, it was her mission and Keary's to keep Violissa and Sinow apart as long as possible. She could wallow in self-pity later, but right now, she had a job to do. If it meant continuing to flick porch lights for days on end or walking into uncomfortable situations, then she would do it. Whatever it took to get her queen and king home. That was all that mattered.

# CHAPTER 32

Dreams of long, golden hair and sparkling green eyes encompassed Simon's sleep. Only this time, Violet's face was there, clear like it never had been. In his dream, she reached her hand out to him. The light purple gown she wore draped to the ground and floated in the breeze behind her. There was a glow about her. Magic stirred the air surrounding him. He understood its origins even when he had never touched magic in his life. The thought of why slid from his mind as quickly as it had entered.

Recognition in her eyes confirmed his suspicion that this wasn't new. That whatever lay between them was ancient and deep. The knowledge of each other cascaded through their gaze.

Behind Violet stood lush fields that reflected the green of her irises. A castle stood proud and massive against a forest that bordered it. He was familiar with it, had been here so many times in his dreams, but there was always the sense that even before that, he had known this place. Home. The word sank into his mind, and a longing took shape within him.

The air grew thick, the wind strengthened, Violet's hair blew back from her face with the sudden force, the beauty of the golden arch it created entrancing him. She glanced behind her, then turned back to him, fear etched on her face. Her hand reached out to him, and he saw the desperation in her eyes. Stretching his hand out to her, he found that no matter how he tried, he couldn't reach her. He struggled with all his might to save her.

Saving her, that's what he was doing. That's why he was here. The power of the thought resounded through him, and he pushed against the wind to reach her. It strengthened, sending his step faltering and pulling her away from him. A push and pull that left a gulf of space between them. One he questioned if he could surmount. A black mist formed behind her, and panic twisted her features. He wanted to take it from her. To take her into his arms and shield her from the terror that had hold of her.

She called his name. It wasn't his name to claim, yet it was. There was a difference in it, but deep inside, he recognized it as his.

*Sinow.*

The name weaved through him, forcing him to remember but no matter how he tried, he couldn't. The knowledge of it sat just beyond his reach.

Ebony encased the world behind her and rolled in waves toward her, slowly pulling her back. Her fear grew palpable, and he struggled more to reach her, but to no avail. The blackness coiled around her like rope, dragging her from him. There was a flicker of golden hair, then nothing but blackness. The world caved in around him, and he fell, still reaching for her even though she had long disappeared. He heard the echo of her scream as the void devoured him, only this time, the scream contained only one name: Sinow.

Simon shot up in bed. Adrenaline coursed through him, his heart pounded, and he heaved panting breaths. No longer was he in a fantasy world watching a magical ribbon of darkness drag Violet from him. He was back in the apartment Keary had set up for him. The world he'd just been in was gone, leaving him with a faint longing to go back.

Wiping his hand over his face, he attempted to remove the grogginess that settled on him each time he had one of these dreams. This had been the most vivid. Never had he seen Violet's face, had only caught glimpses of her hair or the glimmer of her eyes. He had the sense, as he had in the dream, that she wasn't Violet. That she was someone else who looked exactly like her. But that couldn't be. She had known him, called him by name.

No, not his name. What was it she had called him? The name escaped him as the memory of the dream slowly faded. Reaching over, he looked at the time on his phone. Three o'clock in the morning. There was no going back to sleep tonight. Throwing the sheets back, he climbed out of bed, ready to resume the normal start of his day. One that always began when the world was sleeping because the dreams refused to let him rest. Almost like they needed him awake so that he wouldn't miss whatever it was they were pointing him toward.

# CHAPTER 33

The dirt squished between Violet's fingers as she smoothed it around the plant. She breathed in the scent of soil and lavender before sitting back on her knees and staring at the plant. This was her favorite part of her work—having her hands in the dirt, her nails embedded with it, her senses heightened with its smell. While gardening usually offered an escape for her, today was not one of those days. Her focus was off, her mind on Simon, no matter how many times she scolded herself for it. His hands on her skin, his lips on hers, the strength of him against her. Even now, her mind drifted back to him. As much as she loved working, she couldn't distract herself from the sense of loss that had remained since their goodbye.

"Violet." Paige's voice interrupted her thoughts.

Flinching, she shaded her eyes with her hand to see Paige standing over her with her hands on her hips. Oblivious of her presence, she wondered just how long Paige had been standing over her and made a mental note to be more aware of her surroundings.

"Do you mean to tell me I've been working my ass off on the

side of the building, and all you've managed to accomplish is this?" Paige gestured her hand out to the few plants that rested in the soil.

Gnawing her bottom lip, Violet dropped her eyes, hearing Paige huff before she stooped next to her. Violet glanced back up, knowing she wasn't skilled enough to hide her guilt. Paige reached over and tucked Violet's wayward strand behind her ear.

"Tell me you haven't been daydreaming about him this entire time."

There was no sense in lying about it. "I can't help it, Paige. I even dreamed about him last night."

"That same dream you always have?" Paige was the only one who knew about the dreams she'd had since she was a child. The dreams were always the same: flickers of dark, nearly black eyes, a presence of strength. The man who was out there waiting for her to find him. And now he'd found her.

"No, this was different. I saw his face, not just his eyes, but his face. He stood across from me and, Paige, he was beautiful. Dark and powerful. There was an aura around him. Like magic. Tangible yet intangible. Power and strength." Brows furrowed, Paige continued to stare at her. "It's hard to explain, and I know I sound like I've lost my mind, but it was Simon. I know it was."

"You haven't lost your mind, but I wouldn't share that with anyone else, or they'll drag you off to the mental ward." A flicker of pity passed through her cerulean eyes before she gave Violet a smile and rose. "Get to work, or I'll call the local asylum before they do."

Violet threw a handful of dirt at Paige, who dodged it and ran back to the side of the building. She returned to planting, only then seeing how little she'd accomplished. No wonder Paige had been frustrated with her.

After a while, she found her rhythm and kept thoughts of Simon at bay. Until a shadow fell over her. Not bothering to look up, she snapped, "Go away, Paige. I'm not daydreaming."

"Should I be worried that you're daydreaming about another man, or is it safe to assume it's about me?"

Her eyes flew up, and she craned her neck to see Simon standing above her. Heat flared in her cheeks as she fumbled for words but found none. Giving up, she gave him a shrug and a bashful smile.

He lowered himself, and the air stuck in her lungs. He was too beautiful, and she struggled not to reach out and touch him. His black-brown eyes twinkled with amusement as he reached over and touched her flushed cheek.

"Having trouble concentrating today, Vi?" He was so confident, and it starkly contrasted her awkward response to his presence.

"Possibly. Am I the only one?"

"Can't say that you are," he replied with a gorgeous smirk that caused her heart to thud aggressively.

"Is that why you're here?" she asked, trying to keep her voice calm.

He studied her, his gaze so penetrating she almost lowered her eyes. "Maybe."

The answer was terse, and she had the notion he'd wanted to say more, but had held back. They stared at each other and, once again, everything beyond him disappeared. A spell enchanted her every time he was close.

She swallowed, asking, "How did you find me?"

They were on the campus at the school president's house, working on a project she'd recently taken.

"I'll always find you, Vi." Her inhale was sharp, the words so certain that she did not doubt he would travel to the ends of the world to find her if he ever lost her. Her wayward strand popped free from where Paige had tucked it, and he reached over and fingered it. "We stopped by your shop, and they said you and Paige were out here. And yes, I was growing a little restless. I thought maybe you'd like to take your lunch break with me."

His words caused her smile to spread, her cheeks pained from the size it had grown. Pushing herself from the ground, she tried brushing the soil off her hands by wiping them on her jeans, but only made herself look even dirtier than she already was. There was no way she didn't look a mess. She'd thrown her unwashed hair into a messy bun before they'd left, and from the many strands that now layered her neck and cheeks, she knew it hadn't held up well. She was sure dirt and sweat caked her skin. Simon confirmed that fact by bringing his finger up and wiping a dirt smudge off her cheek.

She wanted to crawl under a rock until he said, "You must be the only woman who can make dirt look sexy."

Her brow quirked. "You must be delirious because there's no way this," she gestured to herself, "looks sexy."

He dragged her to him and kissed her. "Sexiest thing I've seen since last night," he said against her lips before resuming the kiss. It was a kiss filled with yearning, like years had kept them separated instead of mere hours.

It was easier this time to break away from that kiss. Tension still sat within her, like an instinct that battled for her to continue it, but there was a sense of forever that had settled over her. Like this wouldn't disappear, that she wouldn't lose him if she stopped touching him. Knowledge that this was forever and if she was patient, he'd be by her side for lifetimes.

He brushed her hair back, and she gazed into his chocolate eyes, questioning why her mind had told her she would have him for lifetimes rather than just this life.

"What are you thinking, Vi?" he asked, laying a kiss on her temple.

"Just wondering how you snuck away from Keary," she replied, not wanting to reveal that she'd been contemplating an endless stream of lives in his arms and wishing that were the truth. That this would never end, even with death.

"I didn't," he answered. "He wouldn't leave my side. Did you really expect anything different? He's over talking to Paige."

Just as he said it, Paige and Keary came walking around the corner of the building.

"Of course," she said with a wink. "I should have known. So, I take it they're accompanying us on our lunch date?"

"I hear we're going out for lunch," Paige said, answering the question for her. "Although, Violet, I have to admit you didn't earn a lunch break." She pointed to the weak excuse for a landscaping job Violet had done.

"I can't argue, Paige, but in my defense, someone had my mind preoccupied," she answered, smiling at Simon. "Maybe some lunch will help me focus."

"I doubt it, but I'm starved," said Paige.

They walked down to the campus, stopped at a local food truck, and sat in the shade enjoying the food and each other's company. When they finished, Simon insisted on staying with Violet, sitting on the ground next to her and helping with her task.

"You really love this, don't you?" he asked as she placed another plant into the soil, smoothing the loose bits with her palm.

"I do. There's a peace to nature that has always existed for me. I don't know how to describe it, but it's like a gentleness, a calm that I don't get anywhere but when I'm outdoors surrounded by its beauty."

"What do you do in the winter?" he asked.

"There's natural beauty in winter as well. The quiet of the snow as it falls, the hush all around during and after the snowfall. The creak of the bare tree limbs in the wind, the sparkle of the icicles. Nature doesn't disappear completely in the winter. We just choose to let it go unnoticed." She found herself staring off and realized she was rambling. "Sorry," she said, rubbing her nose with her wrist. "I get a little carried away sometimes."

"Why would you apologize? You see things in such a unique way that it gives an entirely different perspective to things we take for granted every day. Never apologize for that. It's who you are," he said. That simple acknowledgement made her happier than he likely knew. No one ever seemed to understand her fascination with the world around her, the way it bewitched her. Not even Paige, although Paige indulged her more than others. Simon made her seem like it was normal.

"Here," she said, taking his hand. She picked up a dahlia and placed it in his hand, roots resting in his palm.

"You're trusting me to plant it?" He gave her a doubtful look, which only had her grinning more.

"Maybe. I want you to understand why I love my job so much. In your hand, you hold power. Plants may not breathe like you and me. They may not have brains or nervous systems, but they are a living part of our world." She fingered a delicate petal. "They live and they die just as we do. You hold the fate of this flower in your hand, the power to let it grow and live its life to its potential or to kill it, stealing away that potential. Plant it, feed it with sunlight, soil and water, and it will live. Crush it, rip its roots, or simply leave it unplanted, and it will die. You hold that power." She stopped and bit her bottom lip, wondering if she should have bitten her tongue instead and not rattled on so. She sounded like she needed to seek therapy.

The brown in his eyes softened to a lush chestnut, and she wondered what he was thinking. Hoping he wasn't contemplating what he'd gotten himself into with her or finding a way to escape without embarrassing her too much.

*Stop it, Violet.*

He glanced down at the plant. "I've never held a life in my hands before. The potential is a little intimidating." Touching the roots, he mused, "Can you imagine truly having that kind of power?"

"What?"

"The power to give or take life that easily. I mean, in terms of a plant, it's an interesting concept and certainly one I've never thought about, but what about the extreme? Imagine having the power course through you to truly decide someone's fate?"

"And I thought I rambled about strange things," she said. "I don't know, Simon. To talk about it on this level is one thing, but on a human level? I don't think I'd want that kind of power. I think it would be frightening."

He placed the flower gently back in her hand. "I think of all the people best suited to have that power, it would be you."

"So, I'll make a good queen one day when my prince comes to take me to his castle?" she joked.

"Ha, I don't have a castle, but we could work on the queen part," he said, giving her a wink that warmed her belly.

Something about being his queen gave her that sense of déjà vu again, but she shook it off. She took the flower and gently placed it in the ground, pushing the dirt around it as he watched.

They spent the rest of the day together and that evening, followed by the next. As the days grew into a week, then into another, they settled into their relationship and let it take them where it wanted, always cognizant of the line they didn't want to risk crossing just yet. Always fighting that desire to do so and wondering when that day would finally arrive.

# CHAPTER 34

T he time is drawing near," Cyric said as Daneele joined him. "They have yet to return, Daneele."

"Have faith, Cyric. They'll come home." Faith. It was all he had left. The ground beneath them shook as the Torathar slammed against the barrier, relentlessly trying to gain access. He could no longer see the magic he knew shimmered from it. It had been a long time since he'd had the power to see it, but he knew it was there, protecting them from Tynan's wrath. For how much longer, though?

Tynan's attack on it had been constant since Keary and Paige had left. Daneele suspected Tynan had sensed the Fates' magic that day, their hand in correcting the mess that had started so many centuries ago, and it drove him mad knowing there might still be power beyond the barrier. As the ground shook again, Daneele prayed Violissa and Sinow would return.

Paige and Keary had left decades ago, and with every passing day, his hope waned a little more. It seemed like forever since he had last seen his daughter. He missed her laugh and her pervasive excitement with life that spilled over to everyone in her presence.

As if she knew what he was thinking, Maggie looked up from

her work across the field and met his eyes. She smiled in the dim light of the torches that stood as the only light during what had once been their daytime. In it, he could see the sadness that never left her eyes and caused her smiles to lack the spirit they'd once had.

Paige's absence had been hard on her. Bedridden with sorrow for the first moon after the Fates had sent their only daughter away, her heart had broken and never fully healed. As the years passed, she had buried her pain in her sewing, never giving up the hope that Paige would return and, with her, their king and queen. Daneele's heart had ached as well, both for Paige and for Maggie.

He had never thought he would have love the way mortals did, but the Fates had made him an exception. He had only loved his queen and the brotherhood of the Council since the day the Fates had deemed him the next Lightbearer. The last time he remembered having those emotions had been as a child, for the parents and a brother he barely remembered. Thousands of years had passed since then, and with them, the memories had faded.

Loving his wife and Paige meant inevitably losing them, just as he had lost his family millennia ago. Mortality would take them both, then his grandchildren, and so on. He shut his eyes to keep the thoughts at bay, preferring to think of the looming loss of their queen and king to the agony the other losses would bring.

If Paige and Keary didn't succeed, it wouldn't matter anyway. They would all be dead the moment Tynan finally broke through the barrier. Paige would remain in the other world, safe and able to live a long, healthy life.

"Time is the enemy," Cyric said, bringing him back from his thoughts.

"But still it remains, old friend," he replied, gently putting a hand on Cyric's shoulder. The eldest of the Lightbearers, he had aged the most since losing their powers. Once strong and proud, the wise sage now looked frail and elderly.

"We have time."

"Less than two moons remain, Daneele."

"It is enough. I choose to keep my faith, Cyric. You would be wise to do the same. The people need hope. The Council's need hope."

"We need a prayer," Cyric replied before turning back to the village and walking away from him.

Daneele sighed, closing his eyes to the endless darkness that greeted him, and prayed, "Please, Violissa, we need you to be strong. Wake up and return to us."

A stir in the air had his eyes flying open. A brief touch of something he hadn't experienced in far too long accompanied it: magic.

"Come home, Violissa. We need you," he prayed one last time before walking away, leaving the scent of lilac that had filled the air behind him.

# CHAPTER 35

Jerking awake, Violet bolted up and held her head against her knees. Bad dreams had plagued her throughout her life, but this dream had been worse than any before. As a child, she'd had night terrors, but they had faded with time so that her nightmares were tolerable. But this one had been different. It seemed so real.

She rubbed her arms against the pervasive darkness and despair it had held. There had been something out there, buried in the darkness. She'd gone toward it, drawn by the glimmer that seemed to surround the space she was in like a shield. As she drew closer to it, the hair rose on her arms, her heart raced, and terror eclipsed her. A shape lay in the darkness, taking form the closer she drew. Horror filled her, making it difficult to breathe.

An endless mass, darker than night, towered just beyond the shield. Frozen in fear, she watched as a massive thick arm smashed against the shield. It shook along with the ground, and she almost stumbled from the impact. Shrieks of frustration pierced her ears, and she brought her hands up to cover them. Her mind screamed for her to run, and she turned, her feet like lead weights that fought her escape. The pounding continued, the ground trembling so much that she weaved back and forth from the force. Darkness eclipsed her, and her terror grew.

But a voice, calm and reassuring, broke through the chaos, and she halted her flight. Listening to the familiar sound.

"Come home, Violissa."

She turned toward the sound to see the outline of a man. His blue eyes, piercing and unique. The same cerulean blue as Paige's. But those eyes held a weariness that broke through the endless night and called to her to understand it. Sadness so heavy it threatened to bring her to her knees drifted from him in waves, and tears sprung behind her eyes.

Only then had she woken, the image of those blue irises ingrained in her mind, the terror of the beast behind the shield still prominent in the chills that shook her body. She rubbed her arms, wishing them away, and looked around her dark room. Sleep would not be returning, and so she reached over and turned on her bedside lamp. Light spilled around her, but the corners of her room remained dark.

She shivered again and thought of Simon. How she wished he were there to hold her. His presence would calm her fear. She felt nothing but safe whenever he was with her.

Her phone read two in the morning, and she considered texting him. It was late, but he had often told her of his trouble sleeping. Her lip twisted between her teeth as she mulled over whether to text him.

Forcing her legs from beneath the sheets, she put her feet tentatively on the ground, then walked over to her door. Opening it, she peered into the darkness. An image of the beast in her dream invaded her consciousness, and she quickly closed the door again. She really was being ridiculous, but as she looked down at her shaking hands, she grabbed her phone and texted Simon.

*You awake?*

She held the phone in anticipation of his answer. Desperation played with anticipation while she watched it, and she sat back down on her bed trying not to stare at the screen. A few seconds later, her phone chimed in answer.

*Yes, I'm always awake at this hour. What are you doing up?*

*Bad dream.* Just knowing he was awake made it better.

*Bad enough to keep you up?*

*Definitely.*

*Need some company?* He knew that was the reason she'd texted him. Just like he seemed to read everything about her.

She exhaled. *Would love some.*

*Be there in 15.*

She put her phone down, her heart swelling with the thought of him. She ran over to her window and curled up on the seat within it. This had always been her favorite spot. She loved looking out the window and watching the world beyond. It overlooked the street, and across from it, she could see into the park. If it were day, fear wouldn't have hijacked her nerves and left her a jumping ball of anxiety, but now only the night looked back at her. At least the half-moon shed its light enough to give her some calm.

A piece of her dream came back to her. There had been a sliver of the moon before the darkness had overtaken it. But no, there hadn't been one moon. There had been two, which seemed odd. She rubbed her eyes and leaned her head on the window, trying to clear the dream from her mind. After what seemed an eternity, she saw the headlights coming up the road.

Jumping from her seat, she ran to the door, only then realizing she'd have to face her sudden fear of the dark. The hallway had a light, but it had blown a few days before, and neither she nor Paige had bothered to change it. She wanted to kick herself for her laziness.

*Stop being silly, Violet, and go down the hall.* The thought made her remember the name the man had spoken in her dream. Violissa. It was an unusual name, but one that held as much familiarity as the man had.

The car door closed outside, and she pushed the thought away.

Taking a deep breath and trying not to look, she ran down the hall, down the stairs, and through to the foyer. Throwing on the light, she yanked the door open. Simon's hand was up as if he were about to knock.

"Well, hello," he said, surprised.

She threw herself in his arms and didn't relax until he wrapped them around her in a tight embrace.

"That must have been some nightmare," he said, running his hand down her hair.

She pulled herself back so she could see his face.

"Mmm hmm," she replied, kissing him.

He drew her in, deepening the kiss. Warmth rushed through her and filled all the spaces the fear had claimed. Her muscles relaxed, and the tension lifted.

Halting the kiss, he brushed the curl from her face.

"That's better," he said, giving her a crooked smile. "Are you going to let me in, or do you want to stay out here the rest of the night?"

She returned his smile but didn't move.

"Do I need to check for monsters?" he joked. A shiver ran down her spine at his words, and sensing her reaction, he said, "That would be a yes."

He took her hand and placed her behind him as he walked into the house. The darkness behind her sat heavy on her back, so she scooted a little closer to him, chastising herself for being so helpless and acting so meek.

"Nothing here," he said as he closed the door behind them. He turned back to her, his eyes going wide before lust darkened them. Only then did she realize she was still in her pajamas—her standard tank top, no bra, and tiny shorts. Not the optimal outfit for a couple trying to remain abstinent. He swallowed ridiculously loud as he took in her exposed skin.

"That's not fair," he said, running his hand through his hair.

"Is that what I have to look forward to once we start sleeping together?"

Her cheeks had to be flaming red by now from the heat that burned within them.

"No, wait. I prefer you with no clothes when the time comes," he said, pulling her in. "Right now, however, I really need you to cover your body from top to bottom, or I may not be able to keep my promise."

She giggled and kissed him, enjoying the safety she experienced when she was with him.

"Not helping, Vi," he responded, kissing her neck and running his hand over her shorts. She pressed against him and laid her head on his chest.

"Sorry, it was a nice distraction," she said, yawning.

"Not used to being up at this hour like I am?"

She shook her head.

"Let's get you back to bed and covered in a blanket. I don't need any more distractions," he continued. "You think you can go back to sleep now?"

Teeth gnawing her lip, she replied, "As long as you stay with me."

"That I can do." He kissed her head. "Lead the way."

She had stayed at his place twice before. Both because she'd fallen asleep while they were watching a movie, and both had included Keary and Paige, of course. This was the first time they would be alone and the first time a bedroom would be involved. They'd taken their pledge to take it slow seriously and had yet to let their hormones control their relationship, even if it was the most difficult thing Violet had ever done. She knew he fought to restrain his need for her just as much, but he remained faithful to their agreement. The fear that this would end if they moved too fast always sat on the periphery.

Tonight would be a challenge for them both. Taking his hand, she led him to the stairs. When she was halfway up, he stopped, and she looked back at him.

"What's wrong?" she asked.

He ran his hand over his face, the light from downstairs creating a halo effect around him.

"Those shorts are deadly," he said.

"Sorry. I didn't even think."

"No, you're fine. I can be patient," he muttered. "Why don't I get that light? I'll be right back."

She put her hand out to stop him, not wanting him to leave her in the dark, but it was too late. He was already jogging back down the stairs in an attempt to take his mind off her bare skin. Once the light went out, darkness drowned her. Her pulse raced as the dream returned to her, fear consuming her until his arm wrapped around her waist and that sensation of safety returned.

"You're shaking. Why didn't you tell me you had a fear of the dark?" he asked.

"Because I normally don't."

"The nightmare?"

She nodded. "I know it's stupid. I feel like a child."

He pushed her hair back from her face. "It's not stupid. You had a really bad one. Sometimes they shake you up a little." He looked toward the light that bled from her doorway. "I take it that's your room?"

"Yes." He'd never been past the first floor of her house.

He looked over his shoulder and nodded toward the door across the hall. "Paige?"

"No, bathroom. Paige is on that side of the hall." She gestured to the back side of the house, where she knew Paige was sound asleep.

"Good to know. Come on, let's get you to bed." He took her hand and walked toward her room, leaving her in the dark. She moved up closer to him.

*Big baby*, she thought to herself.

When they reached her room, he pushed the door closed, then stood and looked around. Vulnerability should have owned her in that moment, standing there raw and exposed while he surveyed the pieces of her life that made up her bedroom. It was the one space that truly revealed who she was. His eyes passed over her bed, the frame with the tall thin banisters, a weaving of fake daisies connecting the four and holding a thin white panel of cloth that hung partway down the banisters. They moved to the darkened closet wall, which held two small closets hidden not by doors but by curtains of light sage on which she had sewn patches of flower patterns one rainy day when she and Paige were in college. He took in the piles of books scattered around the sides of the window seat, then the desk area, where pictures lined the wall along with dried flowers, ticket stubs, and other memories from over the years. The light in her room wasn't bright enough to reveal all the memories, but it sufficed.

She didn't mind that he was seeing into her private world. She wanted this man to know every part of her, to understand who she was and the things she loved.

He smiled. "It's exactly what I thought it would be."

She eyed the small pile of dirty clothes from when she had changed into her PJs earlier.

"Messy and eclectic?"

He stepped closer to her. "No, it's you. Everything I love about you."

Her sharp inhale timed with the expression of surprise on his face.

"I love you, too," she said, pulling his neck down and kissing him.

His hand smoothed over her cheek before he cupped her chin. "I know, just like you already knew."

Self-assurance was something he didn't lack, and it only made him more attractive to her. His kiss was hungry and needy, stirring her desire.

"Let's get you back to sleep and covered up before I get myself in trouble," he murmured.

He was right; they had agreed to wait, and tonight wouldn't be the night they would break that agreement. Although she had a suspicion tonight would test it.

"Okay," she replied, resting her hand on his chest and reveling in the strength below it. She gave him a quick peck on the lips before running over to her bed, hopping into it, and pulling the covers up over her bare skin.

"Better?" she asked.

"No, definitely not better. I much prefer the other look, but this will have to do."

She laughed and patted the empty side of her bed. "Come on, let's test this out."

He groaned and scraped his hand through his hair, making it even messier than he already had the other times he'd done so. Kicking off his shoes, he walked over to the bed and reached for her lamp.

"You sleep in your pants?" she asked, realizing only after she'd asked that there was a reason he was leaving them on.

He lifted his brow. "Seriously? Are you out to test my strength, Vi?"

She crossed her arms and refused to respond, not really having an answer that wouldn't make this situation more challenging. Because every part of her wanted him to take his pants off, even if it would kill her to see him that way and not touch.

"Damn it," he muttered, walking away. "Good thing I wore boxers today."

Butterflies raced through her. The thought of him going without boxers had her lower body in turmoil, and she pulled the blankets closer to her. He met her eyes as he unhooked his belt, then his pants. Her chest burned with the air she couldn't seem to dispel until he dropped and stepped out of them. She eyed his black boxers and watched the muscles of his legs as he walked over and draped his pants on the chair at her desk.

He was gorgeous, like an angel brought to life. Or quite possibly a devil considering how her body was humming. He was almost too tempting. When he turned around, he caught her looking and gave her a coy grin. Her cheeks flared, a sense of extreme bashfulness overcoming her.

Reminding herself that she was a grown woman and a confident one, she released her death-grip on the sheets and said, "What? You can check me out, but I can't do the same?"

He laughed as he sauntered back over to the bed. Hovering over her, he replied, "Any time you want, Vi," before turning out the light.

The darkness filled the void the light had left as he moved into the bed next to her. He pulled her close and, resisting the urge to make out with him again, she laid her head on his chest. He'd left his shirt on, for which she was thankful. As her bare leg draped over his, the spark of intimacy reminded her that as much as she wanted to rub her hands along the muscles of his chest, that temptation would lead to the demise of her attempt at refraining from sex.

He kissed the top of her head and wrapped his arm tighter around her in a protective embrace. She sighed, and the tension drifted away from her completely. Never did she want to leave his arms again. There was a sense of contentment in being there, like this was where she was meant to be.

"Better?" he asked.

"Wonderful," she answered, snuggling her head into his chest a little more.

He rubbed her arm, the sensation lulling her back to sleep. "Want to tell me about the dream?"

The fear that talking about it would make it more real passed over her. She closed her eyes and breathed him in, letting his strength become hers. This was her safe spot, and no matter how real the dream had seemed, he would keep her from its grasp.

As she described the dream and the beast within it, Simon listened quietly. He didn't comment, didn't laugh or question the things she told him, just listened, holding her tight the whole time. When she finished, he remained silent for a few moments. She wondered briefly if she had put him to sleep, but then he kissed her head.

"That's pretty vivid. And you haven't had a dream like this one before?"

"No, I've never had one that seemed so real. And then the end with that man saying to come home, it was like he was talking right to me."

"And you've never seen him before?"

"I don't think so. I couldn't really see him. It was so dark. But he seemed so familiar. And those eyes, I'd remember them anywhere. They were so similar to Paige's."

"Boyfriend from another life?" he asked playfully, but his muscles tensed.

"No, definitely not. I didn't get that idea at all." He relaxed, and she couldn't help but smile that he had been jealous.

Her yawn was loud, and he brought her further into his chest.

"Go to sleep, Violet. Whatever that thing was, it's not here, and it won't hurt you. I'd never let anything hurt you."

And she believed him. He would be her protector, would fight whatever came at her. She understood it on a level that dug far into her core. As sleep tugged at her, she remembered something.

"The dream wasn't here. It was in a different world," she mumbled, sleep slowly overtaking her. "There were two moons. Isn't that strange? What kind of world has two moons?" Before he could answer, sleep took hold and dragged her under, far away from him.

# CHAPTER 36

The steady rise and fall of Violet's chest informed Simon that she had drifted to sleep. He leaned his head down and breathed in her scent. Lilac. She always smelled like a field of lilac. It lingered in his consciousness long after he parted from her, and he hated when it disappeared because it signaled that he'd been away from her for too long.

He'd listened to her description of the dream, his tension growing with each word. Although he hadn't told her, he had dreamed of the same creature and the world with two moons many times. The first time the creature had appeared in his dreams had been a few weeks prior to meeting her. Sweat had drenched him when he'd woken, and it had taken too long to settle the frantic beating of his heart. Few things in life frightened him, but this thing had. The understanding that this beast was one he could never defeat, that he was powerless to destroy it and protect her from it, had bellowed through him, leaving him shaken.

He glanced at Violet, running his hand through her golden locks. In the dream, he'd been certain he needed to protect her and desperate when he realized he couldn't, yet he hadn't met Violet yet. There was no question the woman he'd been concerned with was Violet, but that made no sense.

Pinching his brow, he thought of what she'd suggested so many weeks ago. That they were souls connected from a past life. It seemed improbable, but everything pointed to that conclusion. Maybe she was right. There was certainly a connection neither could explain, a draw that was unavoidable and torture to ignore. If she was right, then in another life she had been his girlfriend, or wife, or even his queen.

His eyes flew open. Queen? A random thought that didn't seem that implausible considering they were dreaming about slimy black beasts and a world with two moons.

He brought her closer and listened to her calm breathing. Taking in the feel of her skin against his, he ran his hand over her cheek. She seemed so peaceful. With strands of hair that appeared more golden with white highlights than typical blonde hair, her thick lashes that surrounded spectacular emerald eyes the likes that rivaled priceless gems, she was the most alluring creature he'd ever seen. And she was his.

Recalling the dreams of blonde hair and shimmering green eyes, he realized she had always belonged to him. All his life he had dreamed of her, and now he no longer had to dream. Closing his eyes, he let the rhythm of her breathing lull him into a sleep that usually evaded him.

***

LIGHT STREAMED across Simon's face, and the absence of Violet's body had him rolling over to discover she was no longer in bed with him. Fear struck him like a deadly bolt of lightning, and a sudden urgency surged through him. A stray thought that the empty bed was something he'd seen before, something he dreaded and that guaranteed intense pain slammed into him, and he bolted out of bed. Panting, he swiveled his head to find the room empty. His hands clenched, and he fought the irrational panic. This was the first time he'd been in bed with her, and she was an early riser, unlike him. It made sense that she would have let him sleep. They were opposites in so many ways, but those ways complemented each other.

Calming some, he stretched and pulled his pants and shoes on. Violet's reaction to his taking his pants off the night before had him chuckling. Her cheeks had been vibrant red, and he'd loved how sweet she looked that way. He wasn't shy about his body, knowing he'd been blessed with extremely good genes. Nor was he cocky about it. So, it didn't embarrass him that she'd been checking him out, wondering what was under his boxers. But it did make him ache for her because he wanted her just as badly.

This agreement to wait was killing him, but he feared the painful reaction, feared losing her too much to risk going too fast. He would be patient until they were ready to test that sensation again. For now, he would relish every day he had with her and take in all the small things that made him love her even more.

Love. An emotion he'd reserved for her. Sure, he loved his family and Keary, who was like a brother to him, but love like this, he'd waited for his entire life. And now he had it. The confession had slipped, but she hadn't hesitated to return it, and with her reaction, his love for her increased.

He shook his head to clear the thought and walked around her room, taking advantage of the time alone in it. Pieces of her life decorated the wall above her desk: ticket stubs, dried flowers, ribbons, and pictures. The pictures varied. In one, she hugged a little girl he thought might be her goddaughter. In another was a group of college-aged kids that included a younger Paige. Another of Keary and Chelsea at the bar. It was a snapshot of her life, and he took it all in, his eyes falling to a selfie of Violet and Paige. In the picture, her eyes, a lush green, sparkled with happiness, and her hair spilled down the arm that held the camera. Paige smiled back next to her, the blue in her eyes a vibrant shade that was so unique it was almost ethereal. Violet had been right; the blue differed from any other.

The rest of the room told him even more about Violet. He soaked in the pieces the dark had masked the night before. A worn copy of *Rebecca* sat on her nightstand. A small bookshelf was next to the worn window seat, the space clearly not enough to encompass her love of reading as books spilled onto the floor. He ran his hand along the purple cushion on the window seat, the faded material telling him this was her favorite spot in the house.

Glancing out of the window, he discovered why the spot was her favorite. The window had a view of the town and looked directly over the park. From here, she could sit and take in the natural world she loved so much.

He lingered there, thinking of Violet and how he adored her more with every new thing he discovered about her. Taking one last glance around the room, he left and found his way to the bathroom across the hall. The water was still cold when he splashed it on his face and washed up. Running a wet hand through his tousled hair, he gave up on taming it and made his way down the stairs.

His feet halted at the last step when he heard Paige ask, "Violet, have you been having nightmares every night again?"

"No...well, yes. But not like the one I had last night." The tremor in her voice informed him that the effects of the dream still lingered. "They returned a few weeks ago and have been getting more vivid. But this one...this one was so real. It was like the thing could see me."

The distinctive clink of a mug landing on a table sounded before Paige responded. "This isn't good. I thought the nightmares stopped years ago."

Nightmares that had plagued her for years. She hadn't

mentioned them, and pieced with so many other things she had in common with him, Simon couldn't help but think of her conclusion that destiny had played a factor in their meeting.

"They didn't, Paige. They slowed down, and I think I just got used to them. I've never had one like this, though." Simon could picture her gnawing on her bottom lip. "There was a man in the dream this time. He seemed so familiar, and his voice...I recognized it but I don't know how and I don't know who he was."

It wasn't right for him to continue eavesdropping, and Simon was about to announce his presence when Paige's reaction stopped him.

"What man?" Her voice rose an octave, the two words strained.

"This older man who told me to come home. He called me a strange name."

That was new. She hadn't mentioned that, and he couldn't help but think back on his dream and the unusual name she had called him in it.

"What did he look like, Violet?" The trepidation in her voice was palpable and his nerves bounded erratically.

"I couldn't really make him out. I think he had a beard, maybe brown hair. But his eyes were so blue, just like yours, exactly like yours."

The sound of a chair moving had Simon tensing, and he moved closer to the kitchen, seeing Paige back from the table. Pale and shaking, she mumbled what sounded like the word *father*.

"Paige?" Violet questioned. Neither of them had noticed him, their eyes locked on each other. Paige's fear was visible.

"Only the Keeper has that connection," she muttered, turning her back to Violet and moving to the sink.

"Paige, what are you talking about, and what's wrong?" Violet stood as Paige leaned against the sink.

"What about the headaches?" she said from where she

remained. "Are you still having them? The dizzy spells, the nausea? Is all that still happening?"

"What? No, no, they've stopped. In fact, I haven't experienced them since...well, since I met Simon."

"Nothing?"

"No, not a single spell, and I told you, like I told the doctors, they aren't dizzy spells. They're something different."

Simon stepped into the room, knowing exactly what they were and too stunned to keep quiet. "No, they're not dizzy spells." Both Violet and Paige spun to look at him. "Everything stops, the world crashes down around you, and there's nothing but this urgent thought that you need to be somewhere else, doing something else, something so important that lives depend on it—"

"And you need to remember that something, but no matter how hard you try, the fog comes up and your head starts to pound," Violet continued for him. "The pain takes over until you can no longer focus on what you need to remember, so you just let the strand go, lost again to the fog." A tear rolled down her cheek.

He stared at her, unable to grasp how she experienced the same thing he had his entire life. Something no doctor could ever explain, and no test could detect.

"Is that really what you've been going through?" Paige asked.

He forced his sight away from Violet and saw how shaken Paige appeared. Sadness sat in her eyes, so strong it seemed to cast a shadow on them.

"Exactly," said Violet. "No one has ever understood what it was like."

But Simon did. He knew all too well. "I've had those spells since I was a kid. It was only as I got older that I understood them better. I don't have any pain though, just that sensation and that damn fog."

Violet brought her hand to her mouth. "Who are we, Simon?"

"I don't know, Violet." He truly didn't, but no matter how he wanted to deny it, he was beginning to think she had been right about them. That she understood long before he had that there was something more to them than just their relentless attraction to one another. His brows scrunched, and he brought his sight to Paige, who stepped back, flinching as he met her eyes. "I may not know, but you do, don't you, Paige?"

Fear slashed her features in answer, and he took a step toward her.

"You and Keary both know, don't you?"

"I don't know anything, Simon," she stuttered. It was a lie. He'd always had a knack for detecting when people were lying. It was a strength that had helped him become a successful negotiator when he was making business deals. And Paige was hiding something.

"Vi, when did you meet Paige?" he asked, not taking his sight from Paige.

Paige's eyes darted between them.

"When we were eight."

"Let me guess, you're an orphan, too, Paige? No memory of a family? Just wandered into the place Violet was playing that day?"

"That's exactly what happened. How did you know that?" Violet asked, and his heart ached at how naïve she sounded. "We haven't talked about that yet."

"Because it's exactly how Keary and I met." He heard the harshness in his words but didn't bother apologizing. Keary and Paige, with their constant chaperoning, calls and texts, questions, and private exchanges, had been aggravating him this entire time, and now he knew there was a reason behind it. "What's going on, Paige?"

Paige's eyes bounced between them again. She almost looked like a cornered animal. Simon's phone vibrated in his back pocket. He didn't have to look at it to know it was Keary. He picked it up, answering, "Speak of the devil."

Keary laid right into him with questions about where he was, further irritating him and only further solidifying his suspicions.

"I spent the night with Violet, and we slept together," he blurted, giving Keary a moment to digest the words. His grip on the phone was so tight, he thought he heard it crack. Paige continued to stare at him, the fear in her eyes making her pupils large.

"Did you, are you...?"

"Jesus, Keary. We had our clothes on, not that it's any of your business. Now, is there a reason you called me, or was it just to parent me more?"

Keary recovered and asked if they wanted to meet for breakfast. Simon gritted his teeth as he looked between Violet and Paige. His mood hadn't simmered, but the confusion etched on Violet's face calmed him some. He hated to see her upset, and his accusations at Paige were doing just that. Rolling his neck and inhaling, he asked, "Did either of you eat breakfast yet?"

There would be another time to press Keary for answers. Paige was too skittish, and from the way her legs looked like they were about to buckle, he knew he needed to ease up on her.

Violet glanced over at Paige, her brows knitted. "We haven't, but I really need to hop in the shower if we're going out," she said.

He checked his watch, knowing he needed to shower and change as well. "We'll meet you at ten."

Disconnecting before Keary could respond, he told Violet, "Why don't you run up and shower. I'll give the two of you a ride if you don't mind a quick stop at my apartment." He gestured to his wrinkled clothes.

Demeanor relaxing, Violet gave him a smile. As if the prior conversation had never happened, she told him, "I'll be right back," before giving him a quick kiss and running up the stairs.

Left alone with Paige, he gestured to an empty chair and asked, "Mind if I sit?"

Her eyes flicked to his, then back down before she nodded. She stooped and grabbed the coffee mug she'd dropped, the one he'd forgotten about, avoiding his eyes. If he hadn't known better, he would have thought she was terrified of him. But that made no sense.

She put the cup in the sink after wiping up her spill.

"I don't bite, Paige. I'm not sure why you dislike me so much, but I'm not a threat to you or to Violet."

She twisted around, surprising him with the speed. "I don't dislike you, Simon. In fact, I think you're perfect for Violet. There's no one I'd rather see her with. You're just what she needs."

He tried not to reel back at the answer he hadn't expected. "Then why the secrecy with Keary? Why chaperone us so closely? Why eye me the way I catch you doing, as if you're afraid of me? I won't hurt her."

She let out a sharp laugh. "No, you won't hurt her, but you'll both wake up, and she'll be confused. She'll think you've hurt her, and it will take all your strength to make her see the truth. By the Fates, her Keeper is calling her. The connection is still strong. It won't be long, and everything will come crashing down." She was rambling, and he had no idea what she was talking about. "No, you won't mean to hurt her, but she's fragile, naïve. She'll end up hurt..." She flopped into the seat across from him. "Keary is going to kill me. I've said too much. Please stop asking questions, Simon. Follow your heart. Love her and let everything else fall in line."

Her phone rang, breaking the tension. Glancing at it, she said, "It's work. I need to take this." He nodded as she rose and answered the call.

With a sigh, he dropped his head to his hands, running the conversation over in his head. She thought he would hurt Violet, that something would happen where Violet would think he hurt her. But he wouldn't. He knew in his gut he would die before he ever let that happen.

And then there was something about a keeper. He rubbed his temples. No, not a keeper. She had specifically said her keeper. It still made no sense, and he sat back, staring at the ceiling as he tried to make sense out of it.

Maybe he did need to drop it and let things play out like Paige had said. But if doing that meant he would lose Violet, he didn't want to.

Paige came back into the kitchen, saying, "I have to run over to the store. Violet and I have off today, but I forgot we have a new client coming by to schedule work and discuss the plans Violet drew up. Kathy is there, but she's still new to this part of the job. I'll meet you both at the diner."

She went to leave the room and hesitated, looking toward the stairs. He didn't have to ask why she'd hesitated.

"Hmm, that would mean you'll have to leave Violet alone with me," he said, hearing the annoyance in his voice. She chewed her fingernail as if debating what to do. "You seriously can't be worried about leaving us alone. We just spent the night together. Besides, we're two adults who do not need chaperones."

She threw her hands up in the air and huffed. "Fine, I'm done worrying about this. Keary can deal with it. I'll meet you there."

She stormed out of the house, leaving him to contemplate her bewildering behavior. He resented their constant presence, that unspoken need to watch him and Violet. As if they were children and not adults. Never had Keary acted that way...not before Violet had come into his life. Granted, there had never been a woman before Violet.

Violet bounded down the stairs a few minutes after he decided he would put a stop to Keary and Paige's meddling.

"Where did Paige go?" she asked, brushing her wayward strand from her eyes.

Dressed in jeans and a T-shirt, she still looked absolutely stunning. The hunter shade of her shirt brought out the spectrum of green in her eyes, making them sparkle. She had clipped her hair up loosely so that wisps of wet curls clung to her neck where they'd gotten wet in the shower. Her shirt was just tight enough to emphasize her chest, which peeked slightly from the V-neck. He averted his eyes, knowing that not doing so would only lead to temptation.

"She said something about running to the store to help Kathy out."

Her lips lifted in a mischievous grin. "You mean we're here alone? Without a chaperone?"

Standing, he closed the gap between them and scooped her into his arms, regretting the move as his body reacted to hers. His mouth found hers, and her lips parted in surprise. When his hands became too greedy and found too much of her skin, he lowered his mouth to her neck and breathed her in. Lilac saturated his senses, and he embraced the calming effect it had on him.

"We're alone," he said, kissing her shoulder. "But we should head out if we want to meet Keary on time."

The sag of her body matched that of his own with the knowledge that they still needed to wait. He stood back, letting his eyes devour her before reaching back and releasing her hair from the clip. It tumbled in waves down her back.

"That's better. I like it down," he said, kissing her pouting lips.

Tipping her head, she studied him before relenting and wrapping her arms around his neck. "Just for that, you owe me one more kiss."

"That is a request I can oblige."

He pulled her back to him, kissing her until her lips were swollen and red. She stumbled out of his hold, breathless, and he couldn't stop his grin.

"That was naughty," she teased, bringing her finger to her lips.

"But it was fun." He took her hand, leading her toward the door. "Come on. I need to get cleaned up. I'm sure our chaperones will hunt us down if we don't get there in time."

She grabbed her house key, and he followed her out of the house. The drive to his apartment was short but should have been long enough for her to question him about the conversation with Paige, yet she didn't. Instead, she talked about miscellaneous things. As much as he loved hearing her voice, he suspected she was avoiding the subject.

When they pulled up to his building, he asked, "Don't you want to talk about earlier, Vi?"

Giving him no answer, she climbed out of the car and walked toward the building. He gaped at her before he left the car and slammed his door shut. Irritation thrummed in his veins. Grabbing her elbow, he twirled her around to face him. "You can't seriously think I'm going to let you walk away without discussing this."

"Discussing what, Simon?" She questioned him with her eyes, almost seeming oblivious to what he was talking about.

"You don't think it's strange how we both met Paige and Keary at the same time and in the same way? Or that they watch us like hawks, determined not to leave us alone long enough to get into any kind of trouble?"

Hand reaching to his cheek, she smoothed her fingers down his jaw. "It's just a coincidence, Simon."

"Really, Vi? Just like everything else is coincidence? You don't believe that any more than I do."

"I don't know what I believe anymore. There is only one thing I know for certain, and that's that I love you. I don't understand how I could fall in love with you so soon because I have been in love with you since the day we ran into each other, but it's a truth I cannot deny. My heart now beats for you, my lungs heave for you, and my mind lives for you. You are all I know now, and I wouldn't trade it for anything." Her hand cupped his cheek, and he leaned into it, moved by her words. "I don't know how I lived before you, Simon, but only pain and sickness that no doctor could explain existed before you came into my life. You freed me of it, and it was almost like my body needed you to survive."

Her words reflected the emotions that had been screeching through him since the day he'd met her. She took his face in her hands and brought it to hers.

"I don't know how to answer the questions you so desperately want answers to. We're different, Simon. You need that control, that black and white answer, but I choose to let things play out as they will. To dance in the gray areas of life. I've always believed in destiny, that each of us has a path we follow and that we need to have faith in our fate because testing it has dire consequences. You are my destiny. I believe that with every fiber of my soul. If Paige and Keary are up to something, it hasn't hurt us..." Her eyes shimmered in the morning sun, entrancing him. "...and I don't think they'll do anything to hurt us. If anything, it's helped us realize that we must take things slowly and build on what we have. If our fate holds something terrible, then there's no way to escape it. Whatever it is, we'll figure it out and get through it."

Yanking him closer, she smashed her mouth to his and gave him a fevered kiss that set his insides blazing. Releasing him, she ran to the front door and beckoned for him to join her. "Come on, they won't wait forever before they track us down again."

Stunned, he stood there, his mind whirling with all she had confessed and the way every part of him had responded like she was summoning him. She had been brilliant, but then, just as suddenly, she had run off as if she didn't realize she'd paralyzed him with her words.

"How do you do that?" he asked, still not moving.

"What?" She glanced back, the sun highlighting the gold in her hair so that it shimmered.

"How do you make everything right, no matter how much I want to fight it? I was ready to battle you, to make you see what I was seeing, and then you go and do that. Upending me so that I'm putty in your hands."

"I guess that's my superpower," she said, her voice dancing in his ears.

"I guess it is. All right. You win." He raised his hands in surrender. "I'll drop it. Let's run with this and deal with our overly uptight chaperones."

Relaxing wasn't something he did well, but with her, it was becoming more frequent. And he certainly never just went with things like she did. He was analytical, calculating, and didn't believe in fate or anything he couldn't support with facts. But Violet didn't think that way. She led her life on instinct, intangibles she couldn't substantiate. Because he loved her, he would have faith in her instincts, no matter how challenging it would be.

# CHAPTER 37

The couch in Simon's apartment was plush gray that complemented the other simple pieces in the room. While Keary had chosen them, Violet knew he had done so with Simon in mind. He was not the kind to have patterns and bright colors, unlike Violet, who reveled in those things. They balanced each other, though. Her free spirit to his rigid need for answers.

She breathed in his scent—woodsy and masculine. Cedar and ash. It was a distinct but familiar smell she could wrap herself in. Resting her head back, she thought about earlier. There was no explanation she could find for why she'd said so much to him, bared her soul, but she'd meant every word. He was her soulmate, and fate be damned if she was going to let anything distract from how amazing that was. Questions continued to stir, but she refused to let them stifle what she and Simon had. It didn't matter to her if there were forces at work, if Keary and Paige were manipulating something behind the scenes for a purpose they couldn't see. All that mattered was that she and Simon loved each other. Everything beyond that could stay in the periphery.

The sound of the shower continued, and she couldn't stop herself from thinking of him in it and wondering what he looked like. Heat flamed her cheeks, and she tucked her legs to her chest, trying to calm her body and her thoughts.

A knock at the door halted any further dirty thoughts, and she jumped from the couch, hoping her cheeks would not reveal them. She didn't have to guess who was on the other side, and she rolled her eyes when it opened to reveal Keary.

Leaning on the side of the door, she gave him an impish grin. "Did you miss me, Keary?"

"What? Of course not," he answered with his usual swagger. "I figured I'd meet you both here rather than wait at the diner."

Shaking her head, she left the door open and returned to her spot on the couch. Leg folding under her, she asked, "Did Paige call you?"

"Maybe." He closed the door and joined her.

"Hmph, of course she did. As you can see, we haven't done anything." She gestured to her clothes. "See, still on."

Simon emerged from his bedroom. With Keary's abrupt appearance, she hadn't noticed the water stop. He was almost too stunning to look at as he stood there, running a towel through his hair. Water dripped down onto his bare chest, and she swallowed as her eyes followed its path. Muscles lined his chest and abs. His arms were equally defined, and she had to chew her lip to keep from gaping at him. What she wouldn't give to trace the path of those water droplets with her tongue. Her next swallow was even louder.

She tried to think of something other than the pervasive thoughts that were making her body tingle and tried to remember when he'd gone to the gym. He looked like someone who spent hours there every day, but not once had he gone since she'd met him.

Forcing her eyes up, she met his, seeing the humor in them. He knew exactly what he was doing, and she had a suspicion it was payback for her revealing pajamas the night before.

"Well, at least one of you is dressed," Keary commented, crossing his arms and giving Simon an icy glare.

"I heard voices out here. Should have figured you'd be here, Keary," Simon retorted.

"Somebody had to keep Violet company. Go put on a shirt. I'm starving."

Simon flashed her a cocky grin that melted her, and she dug her fingers further into the couch, wondering if she could keep up her end of their agreement to remain abstinent for much longer. There wasn't an ounce of insecurity in him, and it made him even sexier. Throwing her a wink, he headed back to his room.

Her eyes followed the movement of his back muscles, but Keary redirected her focus, asking, "Did you talk to him about the festival yet?"

"Hmm?" Her eyes remained on the space where Simon had been moments before. "I don't think so. I mean, he knows it's coming up, and the shop does the flowers for it, but we really haven't talked much about it. Why?"

"Just wondering if he knew you would be singing."

"Singing?" Simon asked, entering the room again, pulling a black T-shirt over his head and covering his exquisite chest. Her fingers twitched to touch it, and she squeezed them into a fist. "You're going to sing again?" Excitement tinged his words.

She didn't think it was such a big deal, but everyone in town acted like it was, and from Simon's reaction, he thought it was.

Keary rose, stretching his arms. "Violet sings at the summer festival every year. Other than on special occasions, it's the only time we get to hear her voice."

Simon leaned over her, caging her in with his arms, and kissed her. The move was an automatic one, like he needed her kiss to bring him back to life. She understood that overpowering need.

Being without touching him for even mere minutes left her hollow, and moments like this refilled her instantly.

"Then I'm definitely going," he said, nuzzling her cheek. "I haven't heard you sing since that night at the theater. Not even a quiet hum. It's like you don't want me to hear it again."

"You two are too much," Keary complained, heading out of the apartment.

Simon pulled her from the couch and wrapped his arms around her waist. Leading her from the apartment, he followed Keary as he took the stairs to exit the building.

"I've always been like that," Violet finally said. "My voice has a weird effect on people, and it makes me uncomfortable."

"You mean they adore you, and you don't like it," Simon nibbled her neck when they reached the bottom of the stairs.

"Something like that." She playfully pulled herself out of his reach, and he yanked back to his side. "It has a weird effect on me, too," she continued, her words souring her mood. "I don't quite know how to explain it, but there's something that stirs deep in my core. It overwhelms me if I sing for too long."

Keary stopped and turned to her, frowning. "You never told me that, Violet."

"It was never something I thought I needed to share. Besides, I never sing long enough for it to be a problem."

It was something she didn't confess because she suspected no one would understand it. She didn't really understand it herself. An uncomfortable sensation would grow as she sang. Like a force that pulsed from within her, almost like another part of her was trying to break out. Music had always been something she experienced deep in her soul, but this was an entirely different experience. Although it had never happened, her instinct told her that if she sang for too long, that force would overwhelm her and take over her body. The thought terrified her.

"Then why do you sing?" Simon asked, with no hint of disbelief in his voice. She loved how he accepted every part of her, no matter how odd.

"Because I love singing. I would sing all the time if it didn't happen. There's a part of me that comes to life when I sing. The music has a way of bringing me peace. The singing strengthens me, and the music changes the world for me—the air slows, the trees sway, and I can hear the buzz of even the smallest insects nearby."

She had put her hand out delicately, as if touching the air current. Her hand snapped back when she noticed how even the thought had her moving like music was coursing through her, and she absently smoothed her shirt with it.

Peeking over at Simon, she waited for his response. As always, he accepted her as she was. Taking her hand, he kissed it before pulling her back into his hold.

"Well, even if you only sing one song, it'll be enough just to watch you with this new perspective you've given me. Although I must admit, your voice is addictive. I need to be careful because I already have a craving for it." He brushed his mouth over her ear and added, "Just like I do for you."

A fire raged through her, and she scrunched her neck to push him away. "You can't say things like that if you want to continue taking things slow," she hissed.

His laugh was a bellow that further stoked the fire. Keary rubbed his face. "You two are going to be the death of me."

"Maybe you should stop following us around," retorted Simon, holding the door to the café open for Violet.

Keary's smile burned into her as he shoved Simon through the door. "Simmer down. You'll hear her sing again in a few weeks. Maybe she'll give you a personal concert to tide you over, but that's not happening right now because we're eating so I can feed my hungry stomach."

Simon kept his hand on her waist, keeping her back against his chest while they waited to be seated. Things were changing between them. She sensed it in the air, like an electric current, and she didn't know how much longer they could resist taking their relationship further. And she knew when it happened, they would be even more inseparable because he already owned her. When he made love to her, he would claim her completely, and she would welcome that claim and never let it fade.

# CHAPTER 38

Throughout breakfast, Violet answered Simon's questions about the festival. She described the celebration that honored both the solstice and the Irish roots that founded the town. Paige joined them not long after the food was served, and she and Violet talked about the costumes and decorations, the music, and other festivities that made the festival so special to everyone.

Sinow's thumb rubbed her palm as he asked, "And you sing?"

She nodded, but Paige answered for her.

"Every year. She's the main event."

"Pfft, and you lie," Violet said, rolling her eyes. "The festival starts early in the morning and ends well after sundown. I take up a few minutes within that span."

"Well, it will be my favorite part of the day."

She couldn't stop the flutter of wings that battered her insides and only intensified when she raised her eyes to his.

Keary changed the subject, throwing in a jab about losing his appetite if they didn't stop making eyes at each other. It didn't stop them, nor did it stop Violet from scooting her chair closer so their legs were touching.

Snagging the bill when it came, Keary hopped up to pay at the counter, leaving them with Paige, who seemed abnormally fidgety. Violet eyed her, thinking about the strange conversation in the kitchen earlier. Keary, who was chatting at the counter with Lisa, their server, disrupted her thoughts when he called over to Paige.

"You need to settle something for us, and you're the only level-headed one of the group now."

"What's that supposed to mean?" Simon asked, raising his hands in the air as Paige jumped up and left them, relief replacing the stress in her posture.

Violet peeked over at Simon, whose eyes trailed Paige, crinkles between them like he'd noticed the same shift in her demeanor. He leaned closer and said, "Now's our chance."

Frowning, she tried to figure out what he meant. He pointed to Keary and Paige, who had their backs to them, then at the door. Heart pounding, she glanced between the two.

"It's the only chance we'll have. Otherwise, one of them will be attached to our hips all day."

A mischievous glint shone in his eyes when she looked back at him. He stood and held his hand out for her to take. She didn't hesitate, slipping hers into his grip. He pulled her through the restaurant, past Mr. McGreary, who threw them a wink as Simon brought his finger up to signal secrecy. Closing the door quietly behind them, they ran down the street and around the corner.

Pulse thrumming, adrenaline rushing, Violet had never been so alive. Especially when Simon gathered her in his arms and spun her around before giving her a kiss.

"Where can we go that they won't find us?"

Pursing her lips, she tilted her head and thought about it before she grabbed his hand and said, "Follow me."

Guiding him toward the park, she embraced the thrill, letting the breeze rush through her hair and relishing the freedom of being alone with Simon. Throwing a look behind them, she was relieved to find Keary and Paige nowhere in sight. When they cleared the open park space, she stopped running and looked for her secret path, never releasing his hand.

She scanned the woods, cursing herself for not going to the other side of the park, but then again she hadn't wanted to risk being caught. She had never come from this side of the park, and it took her a minute to find her way.

Simon released her hand and threw his arms around her waist, nuzzling her neck. "Should I be concerned that you're leading me into the woods now that you finally have me alone?"

She turned around to face him, entirely too comfortable in his arms. "Only if you're worried about being alone with me."

"Hmm, I'll have to think about that."

"Don't take too long," she teased, wiggling out of his hold and moving further into the trees. It took her another minute, and she finally spotted her worn trail.

"Ah, there you are," she mumbled, taking his hand and leading him down a softly trodden path that was barely noticeable from the main trail.

Simon followed silently behind as the path opened to a small clearing filled with wildflowers. A stream bubbled midway through it, continuing into the trees until it eventually reached the pond on the north side of the park.

"Well, well. Have you been keeping a secret from our chaperones?" Simon asked, looking around the space that had become her refuge over the years.

"I come here when I need to be alone." She sat down among the flowers. "I'm at peace here, like I'm home."

She looked up at him, and another wave of déjà vu swept through her, as if she had looked up at him from a grassy seat like this in the past. Considering everything they'd discovered, she risked asking, "Did you feel that?"

His eyes creased, and he studied her for a second before saying, "The déjà vu?"

"This is madness," she said with a nod as he took a seat next to her. "I've never been here with you before, so how can we both have the same reaction?"

Fingers drifting along her arm, he was contemplative. "I've had it several times now, and I don't think it has to do with any specific place. I think it has to do with our movements and our words. It's not often, but when it comes on, it's strong."

"As if you've stood over me like that before."

"Exactly."

"Who are we?" she whispered, exasperation in her tone. There was something they weren't seeing, and as much as she wanted to ignore it and just let things play out, it seemed too important to ignore.

"I thought we weren't worrying about it anymore?"

"I know, I know. I'm not worrying, just wondering." She turned toward him, noting the distinct tones of brown in his irises. "There must be something to it, this connection we have. I mean, it's clear we have a history together, but what is it and how far back does it go?"

He shook his head. "I don't know, Vi, and we may never know."

Chewing her lip, she pulled her legs in and stared off at the stream. "True. And if that's the case, then I can have fun making up our back-story."

His chuckle rumbled over her skin. She leaned back on her elbows and stretched her legs out, looking up at the sky when a thought occurred to her.

"What are you scheming about?" Simon asked her, running his hand through her hair, which had spread around her head like a halo.

"I think we're star-crossed lovers."

"Star-crossed? That's not a very hopeful suggestion. That's what you want to go with?"

"Well, think about it. The pull that seems to control us both, the dizzy spells, the déjà vu..." She sat up. "The guardians."

"Guardians?" He sounded confused.

"Paige and Keary."

"Annoyances is more like it."

"No, I'm serious. What if we've been trying to be with each other, like it's our destiny, but forces keep tearing us apart? And what if Paige and Keary are here to help us find each other so we can get our happy ending this time around?"

"You know you sound certifiable, right? It's cute to me, but I would seriously consider keeping that theory to yourself."

She threw her head back and laughed. "All of this is certifiable!"

"Okay, let's say you're right, leaving Paige and Keary out of the equation, that is. But let's say we are star-crossed lovers, living life after life, trying to find one another. What does that mean for us in this life? If memory serves me, things rarely work out in those stories." He looked at her with worried eyes. "Those stories never have a happy ending."

She didn't want to believe that. Knew it would devastate her if this went wrong. "Maybe some do. Maybe with help, our story does."

He didn't answer her, only turned and looked toward the woods. His brows had furrowed, and his eyes seemed to grow darker, leading her to wonder what was going through his mind.

"Maybe it does," he said after a short time. She leaned on him and rested her head on his chest.

"What do we do now?" she asked as he kissed her head.

"We spend the rest of the day together hiding from our guardians. Then we spend the rest of our lives figuring it all out."

She looked up at him, seeing the love there, the assurance that they would do exactly that. "That sounds nice."

They spent the rest of the day together in her secret grove, as Simon had named it. Violet didn't know how much time had passed until her stomach complained loudly. They had been oblivious to anything but each other, talking, discovering pieces of their pasts they hadn't had a chance to with Keary and Paige always by their sides. And with every passing minute, Violet fell deeper. Every touch Simon gave her, every word he uttered, every kiss that met her lips and her skin solidified that this was a love worth risking everything.

They honored their agreement to wait, curtailing their exploration of their bodies even if it was killing Violet as much as she suspected it was killing him. She was lying on Simon's chest, his one hand wrapped in her hair while the other held her hand. Their shirts were off, the contact of their skin heating her body almost as much as his touches had. Chests still heaving as they calmed down, Simon's hand remained threaded in her hair. She listened to the solid beating of his heart. It was like listening to the rain; there was something about it that brought her peace.

"Hungry?" he joked, clearly having heard her stomach's announcement. He pulled his hand from her hair and looked at his watch. "No wonder you're hungry. It's seven o'clock. We should probably get something to eat before my stomach joins yours."

"Do we have to leave?" she asked, kissing his chest, then looking up at him. Her hair collapsed around her face, and she tried blowing it away with no success. Smiling, he brushed it back for her.

"Probably should," he replied absently, sitting up and forcing her to move with him. His eyes grazed her chest, and she saw the hunger there. It was the same that constantly simmered in her. Handing her shirt to her, he dragged his over his head. She did the same as he continued, "But that doesn't mean we have to go back to our chaperones."

She tilted her head, waiting for an explanation. She could see him devising a plan, his eyes staring ahead, broody like an incoming storm.

"When do you have to work next?" he asked, turning those earthy orbs to her.

"I'm scheduled tomorrow and Saturday, but I have Sunday off."

"Could you get someone to cover those shifts?"

She took a moment to think on it. They weren't working on anything, and Jennie was opening the store both days. An extra person would need to be there, but she had plenty of part-timers who loved taking extra shifts. Grabbing her phone, she texted one, disregarding the tremor in her hand. She never took days off, even as the owner. But there was no reason she couldn't. In fact, Paige had been telling her to take more time off for years.

The reply text came through, and she raised her sight to Simon as anticipation churned through her veins.

"I don't think I've ever skipped work," she said, "and I can't even remember taking a sick day. So, I think it's about time I took a few."

"That's my girl. Now, how do we get back to my car and get you to your house so you can pack a bag?"

"A bag?"

"You didn't think we were going to stay here the entire weekend, did you?"

She laughed, a little embarrassed, but shook it off quickly. "I guess not," she replied, hoping her cheeks hadn't changed a shade. "Let me find out where Paige and Keary are."

She shot a quick text to Chelsea.

*Are Paige and Keary there?*

*Yes, where are you? They've been sulking for hours.*

*Don't say anything! Please, Chelsea. You owe me!*

Bubbles, then nothing, then bubbles again before, *Ok, ok, but Keary will kill me if he finds out.*

*He won't. Can you keep them there for at least half an hour and text me if they leave before then?*

*Yes, what are you up to?*

*Enjoying our freedom.*

Chelsea sent back a winking emoji and replied. *Have fun!*

Seconds later, she sent, *Not too much fun! Please think before you do anything I would do!*

Irritated by that last comment, Violet ignored her and put her phone back in her pocket. She never looked at the ten missed calls from Paige or the chain of unanswered texts, knowing what they contained. This was her time with Simon. And she was a grown adult who did not need a chaperone.

"They're both at the bar, and Chelsea's going to keep them occupied," she said. "We have about thirty minutes."

"That was easy."

"Chelsea owes me. I caught her getting busy with Rick a few years ago on the bar when I was dropping something off for Keary. Keary would have fired her if he'd found out, so I kicked them out and kept her secret. Not to mention Rick was dating someone else at the time, and she would have flipped."

"That was more than I expected," he replied with a laugh. He stood and extended a hand to her. "Let's get moving. Thirty minutes doesn't give us much time to get to my place to grab the car, then back to yours to pack."

"Then you get the car while I run to the house and pack. Pick me up when you're ready." She accepted his hand, and the momentum of his tug sent her into his arms. "You did that on purpose."

"Damn right I did. If I have to let you go again, even for a few minutes, I'm stealing another chance to have you in my arms." His mouth grazed her cheek, and she sighed, her body going limp in his arms.

"I'll only be gone a few minutes, and then I'm yours for the weekend, no interruptions."

He lifted his head. "That seems like a viable trade-off. A few minutes in exchange for a few days." The shimmer of lust that darkened his eyes only made her legs clench more. "I'll pick you up at your place and text you when I'm on my way."

She kissed him once more, hating to leave his side after all the hours they'd been together. When she left his arms, every part of her screamed to go back, but she silenced it, knowing they'd be together all weekend. Smiling one last time at him, she turned and jogged back down the path, praying that Chelsea would keep her word.

# CHAPTER 39

The well of absence hit Simon as soon as Violet left his sight. Leaning on his knees, he waited for the sensation to pass, noting how it worsened every day. When it passed, he straightened and perused her secret grove once more. It suited her. Violet was at home with nature. She'd confessed that and today, like the times he'd helped her at her store, he saw it. She came alive, like the blossoms of her plants.

His mood soured when he thought about his life in the city. Central Park provided an escape from the bustle of the people and traffic, but it wasn't anything like Violet had here. Again, the thought of what would happen when he faced reality jarred his bliss. A return to the city was looming. Only the previous day, his assistant had reminded him of a meeting the following month. The others he had rescheduled, but this was one he couldn't miss. Working remote only went so far, and he had tested the limits. Rubbing his face, he put the dilemma aside.

This weekend was the only thing that mattered right now. He would confront the distance that threatened them when the time came. Glancing at his watch, he realized he'd squandered time. He headed down the path to the main trail, uncertain he remembered the way Violet had led him, but fairly certain his acute sense of direction would lead him to the right place.

Bursting into the open field of the park, he made his way to his apartment, running his plan through his head. A chance to have her alone, just as he had all day, away from everyone and everything, away from reality. Escaping to a world where only the two of them existed. Seeing the grove she'd taken him to had given him the idea, and although he hadn't asked her about his plan, he knew she'd love it.

A few years earlier, he'd purchased a cabin a few hours north of Violet's town. An associate had been paring down his real estate holdings and hadn't wanted to mess with listing it. He hadn't used it in years, and the place needed major repairs. Simon offered to buy it sight unseen, something very unlike him. It was rare that he did anything on a whim, but he'd had an unusual drive to buy it. He'd left it sitting, investing the necessary funds to make repairs and bring it up to date, but not a complete overhaul. Something about the quaint, aged look of the home, along with the untouched, undeveloped land around it, had encouraged him to leave it that way. Since then, he had only visited a handful of times to get away from the noise of the city.

His attorney had asked him why he'd bothered to buy it if he never used it, and he hadn't had an answer. Instinct wasn't a concrete reason, but it was all he could pinpoint. Now, as he hurried back to his place, he realized he hadn't bought it for his pleasure. He'd bought it for Violet. It made no sense, but then again, none of this made sense. He knew without a doubt, however, that she was exactly the reason he had bought it. It was perfect for her. Tucked away in the woods, surrounded by nature, she would be in her element.

Running up to his apartment, he packed a small bag, threw it into his trunk, and drove over to pick up Violet. The sun was just getting ready for its descent. With his back to his car as he waited for her to emerge from her house, he watched the sun lower, anticipation pounding through him. Three days to have her to himself. He didn't care if it rained the entire weekend, as long as he had her with him. His hands clenched nervously in and out as the minutes ticked by.

The front door opened, and she came out, hopping down the stairs full of energy, a small purple bag in her hand. She'd thrown a sweatshirt on that was about three sizes too big, and he couldn't help but smile at how it seemed to engulf her, even with her tall frame.

"What?" she asked, tossing her bag in the trunk he'd left open for her.

"You're cute," he said, closing the trunk and walking over to open her door. "You look a little lost in that big sweatshirt."

She beamed and threw her arms around his neck. "I didn't want to tempt you too much, so I tried to cover as much of my body as possible."

"Ha! Good try, but I wouldn't count on that to work. Besides," he pointed down to her legs, "those are still showing. It wouldn't matter anyway, Vi. Baggy sweats could cover you from head to toe and I would still want you."

She shrugged and pulled the sweatshirt off, revealing a pink tank top underneath. It fit just right on every curve of her and ran down to her hips, where it met a pair of black Capri leggings that hugged her hips and thighs. His eyes followed the curve of the material down to where it ended midway down her calf. He inhaled sharply, wondering why in the hell he thought taking her away for the weekend would do anything but torment him.

"Suit yourself," she said, throwing the sweatshirt in the back-seat. She sat and looked up at him, eyebrow arching.

"You're cruel, Vi," he said, closing the door and walking over to the driver's side. "Very cruel."

"I wasn't sure how long we'd be in the car, so I figured I should be comfy." She reached over and put a hand on his after he got in. Her expression shifted, lips turning downward with worry. "Are you sure we can do this? Maybe it's too tempting? We promised we'd wait, Simon, and maybe this will be too much of a test for that promise?"

He leaned his head on the steering wheel and inhaled before letting out a ragged breath. Lilac consumed his senses, immediately calming him. "No, we can do this, and well..." He sat back in his seat and looked over at her. "...if we don't make it, and we fail the test, so what? Whose test is it anyway, Vi? If we fail, then it's time to move forward, and it's our gain. If we pass," he stopped, moving his hand over to brush her curl back, "then we know we have the strength to make it one more day toward whatever it is we're heading toward. Either way, we win."

Her smile lit her eyes. "That seems fair. Let's go before they find us." She reached back and grabbed her sweatshirt.

"You're just grabbing that for a pillow, right?" he asked.

"I thought you wanted me to cover back up?"

"Ha, no. I like you that way. Just try to warn me next time." He threw her a wink and started the car, trying not to think of the feat that stood before them. This was their ultimate test. And he'd told her exactly how he felt. He wanted her, and if he gave in to that desire and it wasn't time, whatever that sensation was that stopped them each time would flare to life. If it didn't, then he'd explore every inch of her like he'd been imagining for weeks.

***

It was a two and a half hour drive to the cabin. During that time, they talked, Violet's voice and laugh filling the space. They stopped once to grab a snack and some groceries, and he refused every attempt she made to find out where they were going. This was his surprise, and he couldn't wait to see her reaction. As they pulled down the gravel driveway, he knew it had been worth the wait. Her mouth dropped, and she threw the car door open, her eyes wide as she looked around. The moonlight lit the lake so that it appeared to shimmer before them. A slight breeze ran through the trees, their leaves rustling almost in welcome to her.

Simon had never truly appreciated the cabin until he saw it through her eyes. She appeared spellbound. She walked past the cabin and down toward the water, her hand drifting along the tiger lilies that edged the path. When she reached the water's edge, she bent down and ran her fingers through the water, her head tilting up at the sky as if listening for something.

"Do you hear it?" she asked, her voice hushed in reverence.

He had followed her, entranced by her movements.

"Hear what?" he asked, standing behind her.

She peeked up at him, and his breath caught. The moon lit her hair so that she almost glowed like a star. Her eyes were so vibrant they could have easily been exotic gems. She looked like a goddess who had emerged from the lake, and he was so taken aback that he nearly stumbled backward. His lungs burned from the air trapped in them, his mind spiraling as he tried to grasp how she could really be his.

"Nature," she said, the word drifting from her mouth like a chord of music. Her eyes roamed the land. "It's always around us, but we can never hear it." She closed her eyes. "But I can hear it now. It's speaking to me. The trees and the water are calling, the insects answering, the flowers stirring in their sleep. Everything that the noise of our daily lives buries has a voice here, and it's screaming to be heard. Do you hear it, Simon?"

He didn't. The closest he came to what she described was the calm that washed over him when he was here, the same that he experienced whenever he inhaled the lilac that came from her skin. Swallowing, he stuffed his hands into his pockets, struggling to find the words.

When none came, he simply said, "I take it that means you like it?"

Her laugh was a chime in the wind, tingling on his skin. "I love it. It's wonderful." She rose, and her arms embraced him before he could pull his hands from his pockets, the move nearly knocking him over. He steadied them and ran his hand through her hair as she continued, "This is perfect."

Touching his forehead to hers, he replied, "Good, then it'll be worth dealing with the temptation of you all weekend."

Her mouth was on his before he could say more, and he drew her closer.

"I can't say I don't enjoy this, Vi, but if you keep it up, I'm going to ravage you despite whatever rebellion my body or yours might attempt in stopping me."

"That's tempting," she said between kisses, encouraging a groan from him.

Hands explored, mouths tasted, and hearts pounded until the pressure grew, mounting to become the all too familiar squall in his mind. Violet whined, and her stomach tensed like she was in pain when he drew away. Her shirt was on the ground in a ball, his shirt not far, but once again, fate had determined they would go no further this evening.

The look of devastation on her face matched the turmoil in his gut. "Looks like it's not time yet," she said, emotion lacing the words. "Making love out here would have been perfect."

"Do you have to say things like that, Vi?" he asked, swiping his hand down his face and trying to calm his body.

"It doesn't feel good for me either, Simon, but we have no choice." She picked her shirt up and walked back to the car, her fingers draping over his arm as she went by.

Grabbing his shirt, he pulled it over his head. Choice? They didn't seem to have a choice in what was happening to them. The idea of a destiny where they continually sat on the cusp of desire, never fulfilling it, was a brutal punishment for whatever they may have done in a past life. And maybe that was it. This was punishment for some mistake they had made, a price they could never meet to satisfy God or whatever deity they had pissed off. It would have been a ridiculous assumption if there hadn't been so many unexplainable incidents between him and Violet.

He rubbed his face, hating this, hating how weak it made him because he had no control over the situation and how it was hurting Violet when all he wanted to do was keep her safe. If his suspicions were true—that this was atonement for actions neither remembered, that they had been suffering life after life—then he had never been in control.

"Simon?" Violet called to him. He lifted his head toward her. "It'll be fine. You know that, right? Worth it in the end?"

Uncertainty crossed her features, suggesting she felt as powerless as he did and needed reassurance. Needed him to give her a confident answer so she could continue without fear of some unfathomable agony that lingered in their future. Drawing a breath, he pushed his doubts away, questions he could never find answers to, no matter how hard he looked. He had promised her he would stop questioning, and she deserved his faith in what they had.

Moving to her, he tipped her chin up and said, "It will be worth it in the end. This is the life when we break the cycle." The words resounded through him like a declaration.

Her smile returned, lighting every piece of him. "Then let's go enjoy our time alone together."

And they did. They spent every second as if it were their last, soaking in each other's company, avoiding the conversation of destiny, keeping their touches to where they knew they were safe, walking the fine line between their desire and their vow to each other. They spent the first evening outside under the stars, the warmth from the fire pit keeping the cool mountain air at bay. Violet fell asleep in his arms, and although sleep escaped him as it normally did, Simon was content to lie there listening to the soft rhythm of her breathing until he finally drifted off. Contentment. That was the sensation that assuaged him when he woke. It was an emotion he'd never experienced, always on the move, never settling down, always searching.

The weekend meant they were free of interruption, free of company, free to be themselves. His love was twofold by the time he stood by the car waiting for her. He'd left her at the water's edge, giving her space to appreciate the view, while he took the moment to observe her. There was a fullness in his chest, a comfort that sat there along with the knowledge that she was his endgame. The one thing he'd been waiting for. Burying himself with work, distracting himself from the search he could never quench with meetings and acquisitions. Whatever happened from here, he wouldn't question it. He would savor every precious moment and let fate guide their path, handing over control, even though it went against who he was. If it meant waiting lifetimes for her, then he would, because she was worth it.

*If the Fates make me wait that long, I'll hunt them down and show them the meaning of agony*, he thought.

Squeezing his temples, he wondered where the threat had come from and why a violent need to follow through on the threat was rippling through his muscles. Fates. There was that word again. Something in him stirred at the term, but it was gone before he could grasp it.

"Ready?" he asked as Violet came toward him. The wind blew her hair back from her face, and she gave him a radiant smile.

Their long weekend had ended, and there was no way to keep her to himself any longer. She leaned against him and rested her head on his chest. Lilac and a spring day. Those were the scents he associated with Violet, and he breathed them in, letting his cheek fall to her hair as he pulled her into him. The longing that had nagged him since the day they met had lessened to a dull throb that coursed through his body any time she was near. But it was tolerable, and having the weekend with her had made it even more so.

"What are you thinking?" she asked, her eyes a lush green when she looked up at him.

"Just wishing we could stay like this forever."

She turned her cheek and rested it on his chest. "I know and I love you, too, Simon."

Chuckling, a reaction he'd had more in the past weeks than ever in his life, he traced his fingers over her arms. "How do you know that was on my mind as well?"

"Because the two go hand in hand," she said, playfully taking his fingers in hers.

He brought her hand up to his mouth and kissed it. "I do love you, Vi, but those words really don't come close to what I feel."

Her eyes searched his, and she traced his mouth gently with her fingers. "I know. There aren't any words to really describe it," she said, the longing apparent in her voice. A sigh followed her words, and tension knotted his muscles in anticipation of what she was readying herself to say. "We'd better head back. I'm sure they've called the local authorities by now and have called in the FBI."

He lifted her, bringing her to his eye level and kissing her. "I really don't care what they've done. This is about us, not them." Dropping her to her feet, he took her hand and helped her into the car where they'd left their phones, refusing to let Keary and Paige interfere with their getaway. There would be consequences, but it had been worth the risk.

A wave of foreboding passed through him, heaviness sitting in his chest as he drove them back. Glancing at Violet, the sensation grew, and he swallowed back the fear that accompanied it. The thought of losing her tore at him like nails scraping through skin, and he gripped the steering wheel. He had the urge to turn the car around and go back as that fear further increased—one that he recognized had nothing to do with Keary and Paige but something even greater waiting in the periphery.

# CHAPTER 40

Keary heard the elevator open, followed by the key turning in the lock to the apartment door. He waited with anticipation to see who would enter the room, Simon or Sinow.

When they had slipped away, he and Paige had looked everywhere, to no avail. They had texted and called so many times they lost count. The only answer they received was a vague, *we're fine, trust us* from Violet around nine the first night. Forced to sit back and leave things in the hands of the Fates, if they were even watching, they'd waited until he finally left Paige to worry on her own. Her constant jabbering about what might happen had grated on him to the point that he'd finally walked out. He'd been waiting in Simon's apartment since then, knowing they had to come home at some point today. Violet was scheduled to work the next morning, and Paige had confirmed she hadn't changed that shift like she had the others.

One question raked at his mind, sending his nerves into constant overload. Had they woken? There was no way of knowing, although he hoped the Fates would give him some sign if it had happened. Even if they did, he likely wouldn't have recognized it. The Fates were fickle, working in their own ways on their own time, meddling whenever they wanted.

He needed this to be over. For Sinow to walk through that door. He missed his friend, hated this charade he'd been part of for so long. He wanted to talk with him again, hear his voice. Not the voice of Simon, but of Sinow, his king. Seeing Simon every day and pretending he wasn't Sinow was painful, and he often questioned if the Fates were punishing him, too.

Sitting back, he thought back to when he'd first met Sinow. It had been right after he'd been called by the Fates. He'd been very young, merely ten years of age. It had been nearly two thousand years, but he still remembered the day Sinow's father had taken him from his family. Remembered accidentally burning his playmate that day when his powers appeared. He had been so young, so terrified. His mother's cry when she saw the truth, that the Fates had marked her son as a Darkbearer, had faded yet remained.

They had come for him. The entire Council and the king, and terror had gripped him when the king had ordered him to meet his eyes. His parents had taught him never to dare such a thing, yet the king had demanded it.

Keary had expected his death, expected unimaginable pain to ravage his mind and body, but none had come. The true mark of the Fates was to meet the Dark King's eyes with no consequence. Something only his Darkbearers could do. His mother had screamed as they took him, his father holding her down in a kneeling position, afraid for her life if she dared question the Fates' choice.

There had never been a new Darkbearer as young as Keary. Too young to train like a typical Darkbearer, the king had him train with Sinow and Tynan. As Tynan drifted away, Keary and Sinow became closer. Being granted the privilege of spending time to remain a child with Sinow had been the only comfort he'd had while he'd adjusted to his new life. They'd grown up together as brothers, and that bond had remained even after Sinow had assumed the throne. Even now, with his king locked in a prison he couldn't see, the bond remained.

The door opened, pulling him from his thoughts, and Keary jumped. Air constricting in his lungs, he waited to see who entered the room: Simon or his king.

"Seriously, Keary?" Simon asked, entering the room and dropping his bag down.

Keary's shoulders sagged from both relief and defeat. Relief that he didn't have to deal with the pending disaster of Violissa banishing Sinow from her mortal life. Defeat that they were still at this crossroads, waiting for that moment to happen.

"Tell me you haven't been sitting here for days waiting for us to come back. That's really sad. You need a hobby." He walked over and laid his keys and wallet on the counter, then turned and glared at Keary, his arms crossed.

"Have you?"

It sounded ridiculous; he knew that. Hands running down his face, he searched for words that would make him sound like anything but the father figure he constantly portrayed. He was tired of pretending to be someone else, tired of pretending everything was normal.

"Yes, I have. The two of you disappeared and couldn't bother to tell us where you were?"

Simon slammed his hand down on the counter next to him, the anger in his eyes all too similar to Sinow's. "When did I stop being an adult? And when did you become my father? This has gotten out of control. We are two consenting adults. Adults, not children to be chaperoned at every moment. What the hell is going on with you, Keary?"

It was ridiculous, but there was no way for Keary to explain his reasoning. Simon stared him down, waiting for his answer. He wished he could tell him, more than anything, but it couldn't be, so he ignored the question. "Where did you go, Simon?"

"Not that it's any of your business, but I took her to the cabin.

And no, we did not sleep together. I know that's what you want to know."

"I know that," Keary answered honestly.

Simon eyed him, suspicion crossing his face. "What's going on, Keary? What is it you and Paige are so worried about? There's something you're not telling us. Do you really know why we're so drawn to each other? Do you know why that force keeps telling us to wait? Are you really part of all this, whatever all this is?"

*Fates, they know,* Keary thought, scrambling for words.

"You are, aren't you? Just tell me this, is she right? Are we really star-crossed lovers who will never be together?"

The pain that slashed Simon's face was so reminiscent of what Keary had seen on Sinow's for centuries that it broke him. "Not if I can help it this time."

Silence was his answer as Simon cocked his head, evaluating him. "What's happening, Keary?"

"I can't tell you, Simon," he replied truthfully. He had sworn to the Fates that he would not tell him the truth, and he wouldn't cross the Fates. He knew all too well what it cost to do so. "Just know this, trust her. She may sound crazy, but she's not. Trust her and take your time. You'll have her, Simon. Be patient."

Simon stepped toward him. "You told me I had to wait. That if I waited, I would have her for eternity. You were serious, weren't you?"

Keary nodded.

"How is that possible, Keary? Eternity?"

Keary shrugged. "I can't explain it, but the reward is worth your wait. All of this will be worth it one day. I promise."

A need to flee, to escape Simon's penetrating glare, drove him to walk away, intent on leaving. Hand on the doorknob, he paused. It was time for him to trust that the next steps were close. That Simon and Violet had survived the weekend without waking, that their love was strong enough to survive what was coming.

Throwing a look back at Simon, he said, "Get some rest. I hear

Violet doesn't have to work until ten tomorrow morning. Take her out for breakfast. I'm sure she'd like that."

He walked out and closed the door behind him, pausing for a moment in the hall to ponder if this was for the best. They'd made it through several days without consummating their relationship. It was time to leave it in their hands. His part was done. Now, he and Paige would have to trust the power of the prophecy to guide them the rest of the way.

THE WAIT WAS LONGER than Keary had anticipated. Something in Violet and Simon had changed after their retreat. They returned with a comfort in their relationship that spread to Keary and any others who were around them. They acted like lovers who had been together for centuries, how Keary had imagined they would have been if the prophecy had played out the way the Fates had intended. Keary and Paige stepped back to let things play out, let them be alone like they wanted, nervously waiting for the inevitable each night they spent together.

He relaxed more and forced Paige to do the same, although Paige was difficult to tame. Her nervous energy bounded through the air anytime he was with her. Not worrying freed him to watch them develop and appreciate their love with a perspective circumstance had never given him.

What surprised him was how the two continued to honor whatever pact they had made to remain abstinent. Simon hadn't told him directly, but he had hinted at the fact that he and Violet had made some kind of agreement to wait until they thought was the right time.

After all the time he and Paige had waited, living a false life in this world, it had been worth it. The Fates had been right to send them there. The brief break he and Paige had provided gave them time they hadn't had in previous lives. Now Keary only hoped that time was enough to conquer the spell.

Weeks passed, and the day of the festival arrived. Keary woke with agitation in his gut, a nagging notion that something was coming. He wiped his clammy hands on his pants as he approached Simon's door and knocked, the action reminding him of the day he'd knocked on his king's door. That moment was the catalyst for the last thousand years of torment their world and their king had suffered. Raising his hand, he recalled saying goodbye that day and not knowing it would be the last he would see of his king for centuries. There had been no way to see that Sinow's decision that day would set off a series of events that only now were culminating.

He brought his hand down on the door and waited for Simon to answer. Keary wanted this to end, to return to their world, to their life as it had been before that day, before Tynan had cursed Violissa to this fate. But even if this worked out, there was no way they could ever return to those days. They would return to the Banished Realm, to a world Tynan had all but decimated. No matter how he wished to go back to the way things were, he knew only war awaited them.

Simon opened the door, and the melancholy that had settled into Keary was difficult to lift.

"Hey," he said, hearing it in his voice.

"Come on in." Simon gestured him in, not noticing the cloud that hung over Keary. "I'm almost ready, but I need to show you something."

Simon's usual calm, reserved demeanor was off today. Tension sat in his large frame. His hair was slightly disheveled, his motions jerkier, his shirt still untucked. If Keary had to guess, Simon was nervous.

"Something wrong, Simon? This isn't a high-stress event, you know."

Simon ran his hand through his hair, just like Sinow always

had. He pulled something small from his pocket, and Keary moved closer. It was a ring, one that looked distinctly like an engagement ring, even if it bore an emerald in the center and not a diamond.

His eyes flew to Simon.

"You're going to ask her to marry you?"

"Today. I mean, this morning before everything starts. I've been holding onto this for a week, trying to figure out the best time."

"Today?" Keary sat down on the couch. He hadn't even thought of this scenario. Marrying? What if they waited until after the wedding to consummate their relationship? Would Violissa's reaction be any different than it had in the past? Was this why the Fates had wanted them to wait? Or would it make things worse? Would she think Sinow had tricked her into marrying him? Questions riddled his mind.

"Keary?" Simon asked.

Keary jerked his sight to Simon. "Sorry, it's just so sudden. You've only known each other for a short time. Do you think you're moving too fast?"

"No," he stated adamantly. "Violet is it, Keary. There's no doubt in my mind; there hasn't been since the moment I met her."

Keary recognized that look. It was the same look Sinow had when he talked about Violissa. The Fates had done their job better than anyone could ever have fathomed. There would be no one for Sinow except Violissa, no matter the life or the situation, memory or no memory. They were soulmates.

A smile, genuine and hopeful, lifted Keary's frown. "Then I'm happy for you. Violet's exactly the woman you've waited for all these years. She's your one."

Simon fingered the ring.

"She'll love it," Keary said.

"You think so? I had it made especially for her. I hope she likes it."

"You think Violet's the type not to appreciate what you chose?"

Simon shook his head. The stress had fled his body, his motions more fluid now than when Keary had first seen him. "No, she's not."

"Then I can promise you she'll love it." A thought occurred to him. "When did you order the ring?"

Simon palmed his neck and gave him a shrug. "The day after I met her."

Stunned, Keary could only gape at him. He'd known that soon. Of course, he had. He'd told Keary Violet was the one, and the prophecy ensured she was. It only made sense that he'd known that early that he would marry her.

Keary rose and put his hand on Simon's back. "Come on, Prince Charming, let's go so you can claim your princess." He would have laughed at the irony of his words, but Simon would have thought him crazy. There was a shift in the air, and Keary suspected things were about to change. Today was the start, the day that would set everything in motion, and as ready as he was for it to happen, he was terrified of the consequences if it didn't go the way they needed it to go.

# CHAPTER 41

The ring rolled smoothy in Simon's fingers as he headed to the park with Keary. Nerves bounded through him. Maybe Keary was right, and this was too soon. It didn't seem like it was. In fact, it seemed like it should have been years ago, even before Violet had come into his life.

And this day seemed like it was the one to make this move. Keary elbowed him and pointed toward the park. Lights hung throughout it on thin poles in the ground. Flowers of a variety of colors and types filled the space. Violet's work. She continued to astound him with her talents every day. Glancing around the space, he again questioned how he could ask her to marry him when he had no idea how they could live in two places at once. He couldn't take her away from her home. This was where she thrived.

The ring cut into his palm as he clenched it. He'd figure it out. Even if it meant he had to travel, that's what he would do.

Music filled the air with warm-up notes, and Simon noticed the stage set up on the far side of the open park. A few men were tuning instruments, a drummer shifting his set into place. Excitement curled in his veins. He would hear Violet sing again, and the idea had his pulse racing almost as much as when his eyes landed on her.

She was standing with her aunt and a few other women, talking animatedly. Brown shorts and a white tank top hugged her figure, and he fought the instinct to run to her and drag her into his arms. She wore her hair in a loose bun with strands draping over her neck and cheeks. She was every bit as gorgeous as she always was.

She turned, her eyes landing on him. Her lips curved into a wonderful smile as she excused herself and ran toward him. The ring dropped back into his pocket when she jumped into his arms.

"Really Violet? You just saw him last night," Keary groused.

"Shut up, Keary," he replied, kissing her like he hadn't seen her in years. "Let her have her fun." He slowly lowered her to the ground and rubbed his nose on hers. "You're in an especially good mood today."

"It's a great day. It's festival day, the weather is perfect, and you're here," she answered. Her cheeks turned a delicate shade of pink, and he brushed his fingers over one.

"You guys turn my stomach sometimes," Keary complained, walking away. "I'm heading over to hang out with the normal people."

Violet started after him, but Simon snatched her arm to stop her.

"Let him go. It gives us more time to ourselves." He tucked his hand in his pocket, fingering the ring and noticing how sweaty his palms now were.

She frowned, her eyes distant as they trailed Keary. "I'm not sure we'll get much of that today."

"So, I'll have to share you again?" he asked, knowing the answer. It was a given anytime they were with others. A nod led him to tease, "Well then, I may have to rethink this festival thing."

"I don't think you have much of a choice now, Simon. You're committed," she said, her voice playful.

Committed. The word reminded him of the ring in his pocket, its weight suddenly compounded.

"Hey." Violet's voice cut through his thoughts. "Where did you go?"

Pulling her into his arms, he nuzzled her neck. "Nowhere, just thinking about today."

"Well, I need to run home and change. Oh, and I should probably take a quick shower." He couldn't help but cock his brow, the thought of her in the shower too tantalizing not to. "Wanna come with me?" she asked.

And there was the opening to reveal his thoughts. "To take a shower or to sit and wait while I envision what you look like in said shower?"

Her cheeks flamed, and he couldn't halt his laugh. She blushed so easily, and the coloring only added to her beauty. He brushed the back of his fingers over her cheek, noticing the heat in it.

"Should have kept that thought to myself?" he asked, giving her a coy grin.

Bottom lip tucked between her teeth, she gnawed it before resting her hands on his chest and peeking up at him. The morning sun sparkled in her eyes. "No, it's okay. Someday, we'll take that shower together. It won't be much longer."

The thud of his heart was painful, and he plunged his hands into his pockets to avoid demolishing that someday by throwing her over his shoulder and stealing her away to ravage her.

As if she noticed his fight, she backed up, her hand leaving his chest. "We have an hour before the crowd arrives. We should probably go back to my house so we can return when they do."

"Sounds good to me."

She looped her arm through his and leaned against him. This would give them time away. He just hoped it was enough time for him to ask her without everyone around. The schedule was tight, but he didn't want to propose at her house. That wouldn't be special enough, and he knew exactly where he wanted to ask her. The place where she would be happiest: her secret grove.

THE PORCH SWING squeaked below Simon, his nervous fidgeting disturbing it. Violet had been gone too long, the time ticking away, his chest growing tighter with every passing minute. She insisted on changing, although she looked fine to him. But she wanted to dress up like they did every year, and who was he to stop her?

He continued his pattern of pacing and then sitting the longer he waited, all the while thinking of how to make their relationship work with their lives so opposite. He couldn't ask her to move. Knew in his heart he never could, and so he decided he would travel back and forth to the city as needed. If that didn't work out, he had enough money to quit. He didn't need to work, but he enjoyed the negotiations, the intense meetings, the fear when his intended targets saw they had lost to him. Hostile takeovers should not have been easy, but to Simon, they always had been. His targets were the ruthless, the liars, the cheats. The men who dealt with dirty money and needed the experience of losing. Violet didn't know the extent of his work, but he would need to tell her. And he would leave it all behind if it meant she remained his.

He raked his hand through his hair. She hadn't even said yes yet, and he was already two steps ahead.

As if on cue, the front door opened, and Violet walked out. The air froze in his lungs, his mind going numb.

"Don't laugh," she said, biting her bottom lip.

As if he ever would, especially now. She was stunning, and he struggled to find the words. She wore a dress that looked like it belonged centuries in the past. It hugged her curves in every place that called to him, pushing her breasts up and emphasizing her small waist. The bottom half flowed to the ground, loose and ephemeral. With sleeves that followed her slender arms and widened where they reached her hands, it left him with that all too familiar sense of déjà vu. Her hair, still up in its loose bun, now had several small flowers interwoven in it, the loose curl gently swaying in the breeze. The imprint of sage flowers ran the length of the dress and complemented its light purple color, which made her eyes pop. She was breathtaking, but then, he'd always known she was.

"I know, a little dorky, right? I promise I won't be the only one looking like a runaway from the sixteenth century," she said, her words lacking the usual confidence she held. She was worried he wouldn't like it, but she had rendered him speechless because she was breathtaking. "No comment?"

A crease formed on her forehead, and he stood from the swing, closing the gap between them and taking her in his arms. This look on her was so familiar, and the nagging suspicion that he'd seen her dressed like this before returned.

"Simon?"

Like a fool, he continued to stare at her, telling himself he needed to wake up and answer her. Pushing his favorite strand of hair back, he said, "You are ravishing, and part of me doesn't want to share you with anyone when you look like this." He took her hand and held it above her head, twirling her. "You look like you born to wear clothes like this. Like you're a princess."

"A princess?" she asked, beaming at him.

"No," he corrected. "A queen, my queen." He didn't know where the thought had come from, but he knew without a doubt it was the right word. She was his queen in every way.

She leaned into him, the move squishing her breasts up further. Her eyes fluttered, and she breathed, "So, does that make you my king?"

Every part of him wanted to scream a resounding yes, but he silenced it, sending his mouth crashing into hers. Skimming the curves of her body, he fought the desire that was throbbing in him. This wasn't the time or the place. And he had plans. That didn't stop him from pulling her closer, nor did it stop her from kissing him just as greedily. He didn't want to stop, but he needed to because if he didn't, there would be no holding him back. That knowledge soared through him and with it, the sense that there would be no internal warning this time. If they moved forward, abandoned their agreement to leave their needs unsatisfied this time, nothing would stand in their way.

Temptation tormented him, as did the weight of the ring in his pocket. He placed his hands on her arms and gently guided her away from him, resting his head on hers, the swell of her breasts now in clear sight. Fingers draping over them, he listened to her breaths heave. Tempting. Too tempting, and now wasn't the time to test their chastity pack.

*Get a grip*, he chastised himself. Releasing his hold on her, he stepped away, only then seeing the crimson of her face and the gleam in her eyes.

Pinching the bridge of his nose, he tried to calm himself.

"I'm glad I didn't wear this earlier," she said, and he brought his eyes up to meet hers. "I didn't realize it would be so tempting to you."

"You wouldn't think something that covered you almost from head to toe would be more of a turn-on than those pajamas you like to wear." And those pajamas were killers.

"Sorry, I didn't think."

He brought his finger to her lips. "Don't apologize. I love it. You look amazing."

Her face lit and he wanted that happiness to remain forever. The nudging that something sat in the wings waiting to pounce returned, and he shoved it away.

"You think you can make it through the day without trying to get me out of it?"

"I can't guarantee it, but I will try my best."

She took his hand, leading him from the porch. "Let's go, weak man. Maybe if you're preoccupied with the festivities, you'll forget about me."

"You are the only one who makes me weak, Vi." The truth. "And I doubt that could ever happen." Another truth.

They headed back to the park. With each step, he contemplated the notion that things were different today, that not only was it a turning point in their love story, but it was also one in their physical relationship. The voice that had reared its nasty claws each time they'd been physical had been silent lately, and he was ready to test if it was gone.

Once he proposed.

His finger brushed the ring in his pocket, a reminder of his intentions. Violet was talking about the variety of food there would be, her hands gesturing excitedly as she talked. He grabbed her hand and forced her to face him. Emerald orbs, wide with curiosity, met his.

"I need a few more minutes alone with you."

Her lips curved, and she ran her fingers up his chest. "Why, Mr. Black, are you trying to sneak me away and seduce me?"

The tug of a smile fought for recognition. "My intentions are sincere, I promise you."

Her smile turned too quickly, and he regretted his words, even if they had been truthful. Tipping her chin, he ran his thumb over her pouting lip. "For now. But I can't promise they won't stay that way after a day of seeing you in this dress."

Expression lifting, she replied, "I may hold you to that. What did you have in mind for your sincere intentions?"

"Take me to your secret grove again."

Cocking her head to the side, she studied him, and he could see her trying to figure out his plans.

"Don't even try," he told her, motioning toward the park with his head.

"You won't tell me why?"

"Nope. But we need to go now before someone drags you from me and we lose our window to be alone."

She took his hand and led him through the woods and down the path until they came to the small clearing. Lost in her own mind, she dropped his hand and walked to the stream, stooping to run her hand in the water. The sun lit the strands of her hair, making it shimmer, and when she looked back at him, that same sparkle hit her eyes.

Moving to her, Simon helped her stand. "Vi..." The words fled, and he struggled to find them again.

"What is it, Simon? Why do you look so serious?"

There was a way this was supposed to be done. Something about getting on his knee and following tradition, but that seemed wrong. They weren't traditional. Nothing about their romance seemed normal.

"Simon?" she asked, her eyes creasing with concern.

"I can't imagine my life without you, Vi. I don't know how I lived before we met, but I don't think it was truly living. I don't want to be without you again, Violet." The words were tumbling out, and not in the way he had planned.

"Is this about your going home? I know it's coming. I know you must. We've both known it. I'll come with you. I'll move there if I need to."

He stepped back, her words like a punch to the gut. "No. I would never ask that of you."

"Yes. I can leave the business in Paige's hands. It's her baby, too. I can start another business, maybe a small flower shop?"

Her offer only made him love her more, but he would never let her leave the place that made her the happiest.

"No, Violet. I would never ask you to leave everything behind. This is you, all of it." He gestured around the grove. "I could never take you from this, nor would I ever want you to give your life up for me."

"For us, and I would in a heartbeat."

He brought her against him, leaning his forehead on hers. "And I love you even more for that, but what kind of man would that make me? I can't live without you, Vi, but I couldn't live if you weren't happy. We'll figure it out. We can have two places. I can work just about anywhere, so we can spend most of our time here. If I need to, I can stop working."

"No, you love what you do," she blurted.

The conversation had derailed from his purpose, and he needed to bring it back or he would lose his nerve. "We'll figure it out, Vi." He took her hand and kissed the back of it. "But I didn't bring you here to argue about where we'll live, so please let me finish."

She peeked up at him, curiosity back in her eyes. Again, the words faded, and weakness overcame him. He was not a man ever at a loss for words when he wanted to be heard. But now he was like a fumbling boy talking to a pretty girl.

He pinched his brow, telling himself to focus and calming his erratic breathing.

"Vi..." This looked so easy in movies. "I know I'm supposed to do this the proper way, to say everything I want to say in a fancy speech and in the right order...but we're not really your ordinary couple, are we?"

Her smile reassured him. "What are you trying to say, Simon?"

Hand reaching into his pocket, wrapping his fingers around the ring, he gathered his words, which seemed to have scattered somewhere out of reach. Expectant eyes waited for him to explain, and he knew no matter what he said, it wouldn't be enough to fully describe how much he loved and needed her. Romantic efforts cast aside, he pulled his hand from his pocket and held out the ring, saying, "Marry me, Vi."

She drew in a long breath, her eyes glistening, and he knew then what her answer was. Tentatively, she reached her finger out to touch the ring as if it might disappear before she replied. All the while, he stood rigid, waiting for her to speak the word that would guarantee she was his forever.

When she took it from his fingers, she marveled at it, whispering, "It's beautiful."

He was pretty sure the traditional thing would have been for him to do the next part, but as she gingerly turned it and slipped it on her finger, he didn't care about tradition. No answer came from her, but she brought her hand to his cheek. A tear ran down her face, and he wanted to dry it, but her mouth was on his before he could move. It wasn't a needy, longing kiss like they'd had earlier. This kiss was one that exuded her love for him. It reached into the inner crevices of his being and sealed her claim on him. Warmth flushed through him, and he pulled her into his embrace.

This was her answer. Not voiced or loud, but gentle and silent. She was his, just as she always had been, but now it was official. She nipped his lip and pulled away, both hands now holding his face. "I love you."

Voice a mere murmur, he replied, "I take it that's a yes?"

Her laugh rippled through the peaceful glade like water cascading over pebbles. "Yes, absolutely and resoundingly, yes," she answered with an enthusiastic nod. "Did you have reason to believe it would be any other answer?"

He picked her up and kissed her again, letting that answer bounce through his mind. He'd been nervous about asking her, but it was never a thought about her saying no. It had always been about wording it right, making it special. Although with how he'd fumbled to find the right words and forgotten to make all the other expected romantic gestures, he wasn't certain he had accomplished that.

Lowering her back to the ground, he watched as she held her hand out and looked at the ring, which dazzled with the movement of her hand.

"It really is beautiful," she said.

Tracing his fingers along hers, he replied, "It looks even better on you."

"Mrs. Black," she mused. "I suppose I could get used to that."

As could he, because hearing her say it sounded perfect. "Violet Black? It has a little ring to it. If anything, it's colorful."

Her phone chimed, and he stood back, searching for where the sound had come from. "Is that your phone?"

Pulling a few layers of her gown aside, she drew her phone from a pocket.

"It has pockets," she exclaimed, as if it were an unusual occurrence.

"Do dresses not usually have pockets?" He scratched his head in contemplation.

She let out a laugh that skittered delicately through the air. "No, they don't." After a glance at the phone, she asked, "Guess who?"

"Paige or Keary?"

She nodded.

"They really have the worst timing, don't they?" he groaned, making a note to strangle Keary when he saw him next.

Sighing, she put her phone back. "If we're married, they can't possibly keep chaperoning us, can they?"

"Good God, I hope not," he replied, taking her hand and kissing it.

"Married," she said, looking at the engagement ring again. "It seems funny to say after all this time."

He threw her a crooked grin. "After the long month and a half we've dated?"

"Is it too soon?" she asked, concern shadowing her features. It was the same question he had asked himself. The same as Keary had asked.

"Does it seem like it's too soon?" He hoped she would say no because, although it hadn't been long, it didn't seem like it was too soon to spend the rest of his life with her.

"To me, it doesn't. I would have said yes that first day we met, Simon."

And that was exactly the reason it wasn't too soon. "Well, damn, if I'd known that, I would have asked you then." He snatched her waist and pulled her flush against him. "We should probably get you back before you're missed too much." Cheek rubbing over hers, he asked, "Do I really have to share you with everyone the rest of the day?"

Her body sagged. "I'm afraid so, especially once word gets out about this. You know they'll start planning the wedding for us."

Forehead resting against hers, he cringed. Even having her by his side for a few minutes during the day would be challenging. Perhaps he should have waited until after the festival to ask her. "Any way to avoid that?"

"Nope, not in a small town like this. Unless we sneak away to get married."

"Now that I can do." The idea of whisking her away to a secret destination and having her to himself appealed to him.

"We'll see. We need to pick a date first. Would tomorrow be too soon?" she joked.

"I could make that happen." He nipped her neck before letting her go. Against every instinct that told him to keep her there with him for the day, he took her hand and guided her back to the path. As much as he wasn't looking forward to spending the day with the entire town, he was happy knowing she'd be there with him, wearing his ring.

"So, does this mean we're no longer star-crossed lovers?" she asked.

Her words were like a tidal wave that almost drowned him, and he gripped her hand as a shiver scraped down his spine. That sense of foreboding was upon him, its claws sunk deep into his flesh.

Emerald eyes crinkled as they turned to him. "You know what? Don't answer that. It doesn't matter. All that matters is us right now."

A nod from him had her relaxing, but no matter how he tried, he couldn't shake the ominous shadow that had settled over him.

# CHAPTER 42

There was an engagement ring on Violet's finger. Simon's ring. The thought had butterflies whipping through her stomach and giddiness springing in her step. It was beautiful, as beautiful as his proposal had been. She could tell he'd wanted it to have gone differently. The man who embraced control and hated unknowns had stumbled and fought for words, and the woman who loved him had adored him for it. His vulnerability had been endearing and would be a moment she would cherish along with his final question for the rest of their lives.

Maybe it was too soon, but she didn't care. They were more than two people in love. They had a past they didn't remember, but one that defined their relationship. Whatever had happened then, this was their future, and she was looking forward to breaking whatever had separated them in those past lives.

On the walk back to the festival, she noticed a shift within her. The nagging sensation telling her they needed to keep this slow was silent. She'd noticed it earlier on the porch. There had been no underlying grip that pulled at her when she had kissed Simon.

Anticipation tingled through her. Today was a turning point, the beginning of their lives together. She fingered the engagement ring and smiled, looking forward to the end of the festival when she could test that theory out.

Just as they cleared the trees, Paige came running toward them, and Violet winced, knowing this was the start of what the remaining day would be like.

"Here we go," Simon muttered, his hand tense in hers.

The park was full. The band was warming up, people had claimed their spots in the field with blankets and lawn chairs, and their voices carried through the air.

Keary reached them before Paige. There was expectation in his eyes, and Violet could only infer that he knew. Of course, he did. They were best friends.

"So..." Keary started.

She laughed, holding out her hand to give him the answer just as Paige joined them. "Let me see, let me see," she said, yanking Violet's hand toward her.

"You told her?" Simon asked Keary.

"She's not the easiest person to keep a secret from, especially when it involves Violet."

With a frown now replacing her smile, Violet said, "She's also not the best at keeping secrets. How many people did you tell, Paige?"

"Just one or two," she replied guiltily. "I was so excited that they guessed it."

The annoyance rolled from Simon in waves. In the short time they'd been together, she understood how private he was. Being around so many people made him uncomfortable, and she hated that for him. However, she loved that he put up with it for her.

"So much for keeping things quiet for at least a little while," he grumbled.

Paige was bouncing on her toes. She was the worst at keeping secrets; she was too excited to be patient. Violet took her hand back and crossed her arms.

"I'm sorry, Violet, Simon. It was just too exciting. Everyone would have figured it out by the end of the day anyway. I just got it over quickly for you."

"Everyone?" Simon asked, and Violet detected the worry.

"Word travels fast around here, remember?" Paige replied, giving him a shrug.

That's when she noticed all eyes were on them. Simon must have caught it at the same time, because he let out a loud groan. Her stomach plunged, knowing he would hate all the attention. She was the social one, while Simon was the quiet observer, talking when he needed to.

"Paige, go tell everyone to give them some space before they mob them," Keary told Paige.

Paige gave Keary a funny look, then she kissed Violet on the cheek, saying, "I'm so happy for you," before she ran off.

"Really, Keary?" Simon asked, the irritation clear in his voice.

"She's Violet's best friend. I couldn't keep it from her. Besides, she didn't let it slip. She's covering for Chelsea, who overheard me, and told everyone in town."

That sounded like Paige, and Violet couldn't stop the guilt that swirled in her gut for assuming Paige had been the one to spill Simon's surprise.

"Well, then I'll strangle Chelsea when I see her instead of Paige."

Keary slapped a hand on Simon's shoulder. "Simmer down. Paige is right. They'll get the excitement out of their systems early, so you'll be able to enjoy the rest of the day with your fiancée."

Fiancée? That's what she was now, and her heart nearly burst with excitement. Simon caught her eye and winked as they started toward the crowded field.

Just like Paige had said, the first hour had been nothing but talk about the engagement. Hands pulling at her to see the ring and reaching to Simon for handshakes. So many questions about plans they had yet to make. Stressful was an understatement until things returned to normal.

Pulled from Simon's side, Violet floated from family to family, friend to friend, stealing what little time she had to slip away and be in his arms. Those times refueled her so she could carry on with socializing. Simon didn't seem to mind her social butterfly tendencies. Instead, she often caught him watching her as he sat talking with Keary, sipping from a bottle of beer.

As the day turned into evening and the sun began to set, she knew it was time to sing. This was the first year she wasn't looking forward to it. A cloud hung over her every time she thought of singing at the festival. She'd done it since high school, but this year seemed different. She didn't think it had anything to do with Simon being there. This wasn't nerves. This was more of a foreboding, like something would go wrong. It went hand in hand with the sensation she'd had earlier that told her things were different between her and Simon now. That their pact wouldn't need to continue. A premonition that sat dimly in the back of her consciousness, and she worried about what it meant.

As if he sensed something was wrong, Simon came up behind her, wrapping his arm around her stomach.

"Mind if I steal her?" he asked her aunt, who had been cheerfully talking away to her, oblivious to the churning in Violet's stomach.

"Not one bit, my boy. Go have fun before the band steals her," she said, giving them a wink.

Simon took Violet's hand and led her away from the cluster of people who were taking seats on their blankets and lawn chairs, getting ready for the show. He tipped her chin up, forcing her sight to his.

"You all right?" he asked, pushing a strand of hair from her cheek.

"I'm fine. Why?" She couldn't help but lean into his touch.

"You seem a little off."

It was strange that he could already read her moods. Almost

like something more than their love connected them. An intuition that sat in their periphery, seeking notice in times like this.

"Really, I'm fine. Maybe just a little tired from all the excitement today." She couldn't tell him the truth. That some unexplained sixth sense was plaguing her mind, and she was terrified to sing.

His eyes creased, and she knew he heard the lie in her words, but he was too sweet to call her out about it. "Maybe you should take it easy. Sing only one song tonight. Or not sing at all."

Something she wanted to do but couldn't. The people were waiting. It wasn't often that she sang, and they looked forward to moments like this. She covered his hand with hers. "I'll be fine. Besides, everyone waits all year for this. They'd be disappointed if there were no show."

"Then let them be, Vi. You can't always put everyone else above yourself."

Those words bounced in her head, familiar like she'd heard them before. "I need to sing tonight, Simon. Besides, you've been waiting to hear me again. I promise if it gets worse, I'll stop, okay?" He pulled her into his chest and kissed her head. His strength seeped through her, and she breathed in his scent, not wanting to let him go.

"Violet? We hate to take you away from your future husband, but the show's about to start. Get up here and sing!" Flynn, the band's vocalist, called to her. "Besides, I'm ready for a break. It's time to let the ladies sing!" There was a cheer from the field.

"Your fans await," Simon said, pushing her back to look at her. His hands squeezed her arms. "Just remember your promise. You stop if you don't feel right. Promise?"

"I promise," she replied, knowing her smile was a meek one. She leaned up and kissed him, letting his presence assuage the agitation she was experiencing. The music started, and she rolled her eyes as she laughed against his mouth.

"Guess they're tired of waiting for you," he said, releasing her.

Hands encompassing hers, he narrowed his gaze at her. "Keep your promise, Vi."

She hated the worry in his eyes as much as she hated leaving him, but Paige's voice broke the silence, and Violet knew she needed to join her as her smooth alto swept through the air.

"I promise." She let her fingers hang in his before she walked away, knowing she had no choice now that Paige had begun the song.

The set called for four songs that were the usual crowd favorites, followed by Violet's favorite part of the evening, a song request for Tricia. Eight years prior, doctors had diagnosed her with cancer, and they had held the festival in her honor since. Donations collected every year went directly to her medical bills. Whatever difference remained, Violet made sure her family had it, although only Paige knew that fact. When Tricia had been a baby, Violet had babysat for her, so she held a special place in her heart.

The first year of the festival, she had offered Tricia a song request, and every year since, hers was the last song of the night. Usually, they were songs from princess movies, which made it easy since they were songs Violet loved as well. When she'd gone into remission two years earlier, Violet had continued the tradition.

Feeling as she did, she wasn't certain she could make it through five songs. That strange out-of-body experience she had when she sang too long lingered in her consciousness like it was waiting to attack and had her nerves frazzled.

By the end of the first song, she knew she was in trouble. The disturbing sensation increased the more she sang, and she wasn't sure how she would make it to the end. Never had it come on so early. There were usually hints of it after a few songs, but never after the first. But she couldn't stop and didn't want to disappoint the crowd or Tricia. When the first song ended, she teetered and turned away, holding her stomach as it tugged and pulled deep in her midsection.

"Violet?" Paige asked.

"I'm fine," she lied as the band started the next song.

Three songs later, she could barely stand. Her head roared, and it almost seemed like someone else was fighting for control of her body. The thought was terrifying, and her eyes found Simon's. He was off to the side with Keary, his arms crossed, his lips turned downward in a grimace. He knew. She didn't have to say anything. The simple gesture for her to come down, the tightness in his jaw, the worry in his eyes spoke his thoughts. He wanted her to stop, just like she'd promised.

That notion pushed at her again, like an unwanted visitor trying to get in, and she decided she needed to keep her promise. Paige came over to her, with the same concern in her eyes that Simon's held.

"What's wrong?"

"I don't know. I..." Pounding in her head stopped her words, and from her periphery, she saw Simon move toward her.

But Tricia beat him and stepped onto the stage. Clapping compounded the throbbing in her head. The last song. She had forgotten it, and there was no way she could disappoint Tricia.

Putting on a brave smile, she ignored the sensation of someone screaming into her mind and the grip it had on her insides.

Sweat dripping down her back, she said to Tricia, "It's your choice. What song would you like this year?"

Her voice didn't sound like her own, and her hands trembled in fear. She tucked them under her arms and prayed the girl would pick a short, easy song.

"Well, I've chosen something a little different this year," she said, hope in her eyes. She had turned thirteen a few months before and was going through the self-conscious teen stage Violet remembered all too well. "I hope you don't mind, but..." Tricia leaned over and whispered the song title into her ear, and Violet's heart sank.

Reading her reaction, Tricia blurted, "I'm past the princess stage now, so I thought this would be better."

The song choice was not only long, but emotional. A song of angst and heartache that would call on every ounce of her strength to get through. It was one of Violet's favorites, but this was the worst scenario. But she needed to pull herself together for Tricia.

She avoided Simon's eyes when she looked out at the crowd and said, "Apparently, we're going in a different direction this year." Laughter filled the air.

"Did you tell the band about this?" she asked Tricia, who nodded in response. "All right, tell everyone what you've chosen."

"From princess songs to heartbreak. That's a quick jump," she teased, once Tricia announced the song. She was still uncertain if she could pull this off.

"Please, Auntie Violet. I'd love to hear you sing it."

Simon caught her eye, and he shook his head, mouthing the word no. She had promised him, but she'd made a promise to Tricia years earlier, and this was the one gift she had to give her each year. Sending him a mouthed apology, she turned from the frustration on his face and looked back at the band.

"We good?" she asked, receiving affirmative nods.

"Violet," Paige stopped her.

"I'm okay. Go with Tricia. It's one song. What can go wrong?"

That was what every character said right before they died horribly, but she tried not to think about that. Signaling for the band to start, she stood straighter and gestured to her dress. "Definitely not the song I had in mind when I put this on this morning."

The chuckles from the crowd did nothing to erase the turmoil in her gut or the train barreling through her head.

*Please don't let me pass out*, she prayed as the music started.

With each word she sang, she relented to the onslaught from the part of her that demanded entrance each time she sang for too long. Entrance or escape, she wasn't sure because it clawed up from deep in her core. This was the first time it had gotten so close to taking over, but this time, she couldn't stop it. Locked away, she listened as words came from her mouth and her body moved from a volition other than her own. Relegated to the back of her consciousness, images and emotions that were not hers pummeled her. Agony, betrayal, love. A voice inside her told her she had experienced these things just as she saw herself and Simon. Not there, not in that moment, but in a world with two moons. It was the two of them, but it wasn't.

A world witnessed through eyes that were hers but had never truly belonged to her because she was the woman in those images, in another lifetime. The outside world had disappeared as pain and loss drowned her. Suffering, longing, desire overtook her until she could do no more than hold on as the final chords of the song tore from her lungs with the power of every emotion awash in her. The last note reached out and captured the world around her, as the being inside of her tried to make her way to Simon. Fighting to be recognized.

The intensity of passion that riddled Violet's body carried the agony of endless heartache. It coursed through her, battering her until it awakened her to the knowledge that what she'd seen were her memories, her emotions, and this man had been part of her life for much longer than she had fathomed. For eternity.

He was so much more than just Simon; he was everything to her. Her very being depended on him because he was her other half, and a force inside of her screamed to not let him go. She sobbed as she sang, looking out of her eyes from this new perspective and reaching for him with an awareness that their connection was far greater than they'd ever imagined.

# CHAPTER 43

Every instinct had told Simon to keep Violet from getting on that stage. She hadn't said it, but he knew she wasn't well. She was too concerned with pleasing her friends and family, always putting them first. There was a nudging in the back of his mind that he'd thought the same of her in another time. He should have listened to himself and stopped her, but he hadn't.

Watching her up there had mesmerized him, the beauty of her voice enthralling until he'd noticed the signs. Her hand on her stomach. Her fingers trembling. All signs that he should have listened to his gut and stopped her. Paige had whispered to her, and he had hoped she would convince Violet to leave the stage, but damn if she hadn't kept singing.

"She needs to stop singing," he told Keary, his fists bunching at how helpless he was to halt the unraveling he was watching.

"Not a chance, Simon. They wait all year for this. There's no way she'll stop."

"She's not feeling well. Look at her."

Keary's brows knit before he turned from Simon and looked back at the stage. His body was tense when he asked, "What's wrong with her?"

"I don't know. She seemed off earlier and tried to tell me she was just tired."

"Maybe she is. Give her a break, Simon. You asked her to marry you today, and she's been bustling around here since the crack of dawn." Still, Keary's eyes stayed fixed on her movements. "She's just tired, and you're worrying too much about her."

Simon rubbed his jaw. Maybe Keary was right. It had been a really long day for her. But no matter how he tried to relax, his alarms rose. Stepping forward, he heard the change in her voice, the edge to it, the quiver as she strained. If he closed his eyes, it almost seemed there were two voices fighting for dominance: Violet's and a more distant one layered within hers. But that couldn't be, and when she finished the song, relief settled over him. Four songs. That's what Keary had told him.

Then why did it look like she was readying herself to sing another?

"What are they doing?" he asked Keary as Violet and Paige spoke with a girl from town. Tricia. He remembered Violet introducing her to him.

"Violet always sings a request from Tricia. It's a tradition."

"Not this time, it's not."

Keary gripped his elbow. "Trust me, you can't stop her. Tricia is too important to Violet and the town. There's no way she'll skip this."

"Look at her," he argued. Her skin had paled, and he could see the tremble in her limbs. "She can't sing another song, Keary. Something's wrong."

Her eyes met his, and she blatantly ignored his command to stop. He should have known better, but she had promised him, and now she was breaking her promise.

"How do you know something's wrong?" Keary's voice had an edge to it, and Simon looked over to see he'd tensed.

"Call it intuition. She needs to come down now." But it was too late. The music had begun.

Keary's hand gripped his shoulder. "She'll be all right. We'll keep an eye on her, and Paige is right there near the stage. Besides, it's only one song."

But it wasn't a simple song. Emotionally charged, it poured from her with a force that left the hairs on his neck standing. Powerless, he watched Violet sing. The emotions played out on her face, raw and vulnerable. He wanted to strip them from her, to make her whole again, because watching her in torment killed him. The pain of the words and whatever was going on inside of her were palpable as they drowned her. With each note, her voice changed, becoming stronger, more desperate, more familiar to him. Deep within him, something reached for that familiarity. That voice, that pain. He knew them just as he knew their cause.

Pulled by an unseen force, he stepped closer.

"Simon?" Keary's voice was distant.

As the song reached its peak, Violet lost herself to whatever had taken over her. Her voice was powerful, the sound tearing through him. It hit him like a storm, ravaging his mind and his chest.

"Fates, she's waking," he heard Keary mumble as he rushed past him. "She's waking! Paige, stop her!" Keary screamed above the music.

"Waking?" Simon asked, coming to his senses. He grabbed Keary by the shirt and shook him. "What do you mean she's waking?"

"She can't wake without you. She needs to stop singing now." His words baffled Simon, and he struggled to comprehend them as lightning tore through the sky.

Thunder shook the air, the ground buckled, and the lanterns flickered out. The music stopped, but Violet continued to sing, her voice ripping him in two, releasing something in him that funneled back to her. A connection that told him everything she'd surmised was right. That they were something more than simply two people in love. That they shared a past greater than either of them could have fathomed.

Violet's voice shattered the chaos with a note so laced with pain that it drilled its way into every cell of his body. And with it, a call to him. It woke a voice from within that demanded he answer, and he bellowed, "Violissa," a name that came with the knowledge that he knew this name as intimately as he knew every part of its owner. The name tore from him again as he ran to her with a desperate need to save her. Pushing through the crowd, he approached the stage in a full sprint, somehow knowing he had been running to her since the beginning of time.

Sage eyes, the color of a forest on a stormy day, met his, and the tears that spilled from them fractured something in him. Everything slowed as recognition passed through them. They had always known each other, their souls entwined from before they had taken their first breath, and nothing would sever them.

The moment ended, and the world came back into view as Violet fell to the ground just as he reached the stage. His knees crunched when he dropped next to her and gathered her in his arms.

"Vi." She looked so pale and fragile. He smoothed her hair back, worry crushing him. "Vi, come back to me."

He couldn't think and barely registered movement behind him and the hushed words from Keary as he stopped someone from approaching.

"Keary, I need to look at her. If she's hit her head, she may have a concussion," he heard Connor, the local doctor, say.

"Leave them be," Keary commanded, the authority in his voice unusual.

Simon let them bicker about it, continuing to hold Violet to his chest and reassured only when her eyes slowly fluttered open. They met his, their green once again emerald.

The corner of her mouth tugged, and she said, "I kinda broke my promise, didn't I?"

"Broke? Annihilated is more like it. We'll need to talk about your definition of promises, Vi."

Guilt shadowed her eyes.

"You scared me, Vi." Admitting it tugged at the part of him that detested vulnerability.

She chewed her lip before saying, "I'm sorry. If it helps, I scared myself. I saw something. I saw us, memories of us, but not quite us. She loved him so much that it hurt me."

"Who?"

She brought her hand to his face. "The one I was. You experienced it too, didn't you? We were so much more than we are now."

His hands gripped her tighter, her words slashing at the doubt that had resurfaced and the thought that maybe he had imagined it. And as impossible as it sounded, her admission confirmed that what he'd experienced had been real.

"Simon, I really need to look at her. She's talking like she may have hit her head," Connor said again.

But he knew Violet had spoken the truth and that only the two of them understood that.

"I'm fine, really." She sat up, and he helped her stand, holding onto her as she wobbled slightly. "I just got lightheaded and passed out. Likely from not eating enough with all the excitement. Really, Connor, I'm fine."

It was then Simon noticed the crowd that had formed around the stage. Worried faces watched them, and he suddenly wanted her far from their stares.

Keary gave him a look that told him he understood what was going through his mind.

"I'll handle this," he told Simon before turning to the crowd. "She's fine. With all the excitement, she didn't eat enough and got lightheaded. That's all."

A collective sigh went through the crowd.

Connor moved closer to them. "Are you sure you don't want me to check you out? Just as a precaution?"

"No, really, I'm fine. And I'm sure Simon will watch over me tonight and call you if something seems wrong."

"I will," he told Connor before adding, "I promise, and I know how to keep my promises."

Violet gave him a frown. "That was a low blow."

"Call it payback for what you just did to me. I think I lost ten years from my life just now."

She rolled her eyes and reassured Connor once more before he left.

Pulling Simon's head closer to hers, she said, "I know what I felt, Simon." He glanced over to see Paige and Keary talking to the townspeople and encouraging them to go home as lightning sliced the sky again. Violet brought her hands to his face, turning his attention back to her. "Those memories were mine."

It made no sense, and had he not experienced the rush of understanding, that tie that snapped into place between them, he would have called Connor back to have her head checked. But he believed her. They had been something in a past life. Or maybe many past lives.

"So, was I just as handsome in these memories?" he joked, not sure how to respond to her. There was a need to take the time to think through the events and what she had said. That controlled side of him, the one who lived in certainty and not whatever this was, needed time to evaluate the situation.

Her smile calmed every part of him. "Just as handsome."

Finger tracing the wayward curl that hung just along her cheek, he said, "Let's get you home. You need to rest."

"No," she blurted.

"Vi, you don't need to stay here any longer. You need to lie down."

She took his hand, her eyes shifting to an alluring shade of hunter. "I know, but I don't want to go home. I want to stay with you. Take me back to your place."

The suggestive undertone that accompanied that request had

his pulse soaring. He searched her eyes for any doubt and saw none. Chest growing tight with anticipation, he squeezed her hand, imploring the desire that was pumping through his veins to be patient.

"All right, my place it is."

"Why don't we go with you? We should help her. Maybe take Connor with us so he can check her out?" Keary said, and Simon glared at him. He was not about to share this moment with them.

"Let them go, Keary," Paige said, surprising him. Keary shot her a look that could have split ice, but it didn't faze her.

"Let them go. It's going to be all right."

There was something beneath her words, a deeper meaning he couldn't ascertain. Of course, she and Keary had been acting odd since the day he had arrived, so it didn't surprise him. What did, however, was the notion that Violet may have been right. That they were purposely keeping watch over them. Violet touched his arm, and he looked back at her, his thoughts fading away.

"Ready?" she asked.

He was. He had been since the moment he'd seen her, and tonight was the night he would finally have all of her. Nothing would stop them this time. No chaperones, no unexpected jolts in their bodies or heads. It was only the two of them.

He took her hand and led her from the stage. No one stopped them, and a sense that this moment was a stepping-off point to some other juncture in their lives, a path to whatever had led them to each other in the first place, washed through him.

She leaned her head against his shoulder as they walked, and he brought her in closer, not knowing what to expect when they reached the end of that path, but hoping that no matter what it was, she was there with him.

CLOSING the door to his apartment, Simon didn't take his eyes off Violet. Their walk had been quiet, both lost in their heads.

Anticipation had its fangs in him, so when the door shut and she said, "It's time, Simon," he knew there was no turning back.

"It is," he answered, walking to her and pulling the clip from her hair. He watched her blonde curls tumble down before threading his fingers into her hair and tipping her head up to look at him. Her eyes shone a rich green as her lips parted. Vulnerability sat behind them, but it played with the lust that hovered within it.

He lowered his head to hers, the sight of her falling to the stage returning to ruin his mood.

"But you're not well, Vi. It wouldn't be right."

"I'm fine. It's time, Simon. I've known it all day, since we were standing on my porch."

He traced his finger over her lips before he captured her mouth. Lilac and a spring day. The scent rushed through him, along with a feeling of contentment. She pushed at his shirt, her hands frenzied until he broke their kiss and pulled it over his head.

"Slow down, woman," he teased her, nipping at her bottom lip.

"No." And her lips devoured his with kisses that set his fire ablaze.

Done with trying to slow what had been building for too long, he tugged down the zipper on her dress. He pushed her back, letting the dress fall and inhaling sharply when he saw that nothing covered her breasts. His eyes roved every inch of her, from her lithe legs to her lace panties, to the firm breasts he had only touched through her bra.

"You are gorgeous," he breathed, his eyes rising to meet hers.

Color highlighted her cheeks, and he grasped her neck, pulling her back to his mouth and kissing her. Skin to skin, his body heated. Hands skimming her body, he fought the need to ravage her, wanting to take it slow and savor every second of finally having her. He palmed her breast, loving how her head tilted back with her moan. Dragging his mouth down the path of her neck, he licked the swell of her chest before cupping her breast and bringing it to his mouth. His pulse thrummed as his body throbbed, wanting all of her.

His need was like a storm barreling through him, and he picked her up, slamming her into the wall as he kissed his way over every inch of her body. His hands shoved at the lace that kept her warmth from him, and he dropped to his knees, trailing kisses up her leg until he tore a cry from her that had him pulling her further into his face. Her hands tangled in his hair as he licked and sucked, devouring her like she was an aphrodisiac he needed to survive. The trembling of her body had him yanking her closer, and when she fell apart he clung to her, tasting her pleasure until he could resist being inside of her no more.

He traced her curves with his mouth, lingering on the soft swell of her breast as her chest heaved and she moaned his name. He captured her mouth again, desperate for her as she fumbled with his belt, tearing his pants from him with the same frenzied need that was consuming him.

There was no shyness, no hesitation, as if they were rediscovering one another. And when he lifted her, sinking into her depths, the sensation of returning home twisted inside of him. Their bodies moved in tandem, their ragged breaths matching as desperation urged their moves. Legs, long and lean, wrapped around him, shoving him deeper and forcing a groan from him.

Nothing he could have imagined came close to being inside of her, to having their bodies meshed so perfectly. As she trembled, her body tensing, he watched her come undone again, her cry severing any hold he had left. A growl rumbled loud and feral as he lost control and spiraled down the path to follow her release.

The night became a blur of skin and teeth, cries and climaxes, and he lost track of how many times he made love to her. Hours later, lying with her in his arms, their bodies a tangled mess of limbs, he listened to her quiet breathing as sleep overcame her.

She was his. Evry piece of her, every tremble, every cry, every climax. All of her belonged to him, and he knew he would kill anyone who threatened that ownership. Brushing his fingers over the swell of her breasts, he smiled at the moan that slipped from her. As much as he wanted to take her again, she was exhausted. He moved a damp strand of hair from her face and kissed her forehead while looking out at the rain beating on the balcony window. Whatever they had been through in the past, he was certain they had beaten it. They were together, and they were in love, and nothing could take that from them.

He closed his eyes, weariness preying on him. Just as he drifted off, that all too familiar sense of foreboding settled in his subconscious, but sleep had taken him too far away to register it. The rain continued to pound at the window until his breathing settled into a rhythm matching Violet's, and he slept.

# CHAPTER 44

Thunder shook the house, rain slashing against the windows so that it seemed it might crack the glass and make its way inside. Keary wrapped his hand around his beer tightly, his leg shaking as his nerves tried to find an outlet.

At first, he had questioned Paige's insistence to let Violet and Simon go alone. The sexual tension between the two had saturated the air almost as much as the scent of the oncoming storm. But as his eyes had trailed them, Paige had come to his side, saying, "It's time to let them go. Their memories are returning, and I'm tired of waiting. I'm ready to go home, and so are you. So are they."

He had looked at her, seeing the determination in her eyes. She was right. He was tired of this world, tired of the lies. It was time to let things play out.

And so they'd run through the rain, and hunkered down in the kitchen, awaiting the inevitable.

Another streak of lightning had his nerves straining further and Paige jumping.

"The Fates' spell is breaking," he muttered, as the house shook.

He absently wondered if the storm was the work of the Fates or the god of this world, who detested magic. Maybe it was a combination. If the spell was really breaking, then the Fates' inter-ference in this world may have angered him.

He clutched his bottle. With the spell broken, Tynan's spell would take over. If Sinow hadn't been able to break it before, Keary didn't know how they would break it this time.

Thunder rattled the windows. He knew power, and this storm had the feel of an angry god. Paige shivered, and he eyed her. She'd been sitting with him, stoic and brave. He imagined that was why the Fates had chosen her. Although he suspected the part she would play was still to be seen.

"Why don't you try to get some sleep? I don't think we'll know anything until the morning."

She nodded, rubbing her arms, and left the kitchen to camp out on the couch. He looked down at his hands. He felt voyeuristic waiting for his king to consummate his relationship with his queen, and he tried not to imagine what was going on in Simon's apartment. Lightning struck, lighting up the dimly lit kitchen. He'd left the lights off, preferring to wait in the dark where he was most comfortable. Waiting for the inevitable and the real storm to begin.

# CHAPTER 45

Daneele warmed himself by the fire as he sat in contemplation. Without the sun, there was a constant chill to the air. He looked over at Maggie, who was busily humming while she embroidered another flower bloom on the dress she'd made. He had argued that no one would ever wear such a delicate dress, but she had stubbornly insisted it wasn't for anyone here. Rather than argue, he indulged her. Since Paige had left, Maggie had been distant, distracting herself with her sewing.

He sighed and stood, stretching to fend off the weariness that was settling in his bones. The wind blew against the windows, rattling them, giving the sense that someone or something was trying to get in. He halted his movement, quirking his head to the window and listening. The force of the wind seemed unnatural. It had come from nowhere, whipping through the land. An inkling nudged at him, something in the corner of his mind that told him this was important. Slowly, he walked toward the door.

"Daneele?" Maggie asked, lowering her stitching. "Is everything all right?"

He put a hand out to silence her, opened the door, and continued his path. The wind rushed past him, adding resistance to his movement. He heard Maggie step out behind him, but his gaze was on Anwell, who was on guard, watching for any sign of Tynan breaking through the boundary. Someone stood guard in every village throughout the realm. The boundary had been weakening; they could hear the creaks and knew it was only a matter of time before Tynan broke through.

Anwell met his sight, walking toward him, but Daneele continued to listen. He walked out into the open space and stood still, closing his eyes. He could sense it—a change in the air. The wind swept past him, a warm comfort to it. Warmth. There hadn't been warmth like that in the air for centuries. The leaves of the trees, crisp and fragile, rustled with a chaotic frenzy, like they recognized it as well.

Awareness caused his eyes to fly open.

"She's awakening," he said.

Neither Anwell nor Maggie dared question his announcement. The bond between Keeper and his king was stronger than any Council, but the bond between Violissa and her Keeper ran deeper. It was a bond of blood and magic that had raised her from her sleep as an infant. Everyone knew not to question Daneele on matters of the prophecy or Violissa. Nor did they question anything he claimed to sense. Even now, without his powers, he could sense her presence in the air, in the warmth that had touched his face, in the sound of the leaves. She was awakening.

"You've never felt her awaken in any of her other lifetimes," Anwell stated.

"No. I haven't. Whatever Keary and Paige did must have worked. They're coming home, Anwell," he stated.

Anwell backed up a step, his eyes large in wonder.

"Maggie," Daneele said, "sound the alarms, light the torches. Anwell, gather all we can and send the signal that it is time. Their return is on the wind, and the Fates are calling them home."

# PART THREE
# AWAKENING

# CHAPTER 46

Grogginess weighed Sinow's head down, and he struggled to open his eyes. He sat up, groaning at the ache in his head, and wiped his eyes. When the blur was no more, he looked around the room, running his hands through his hair as the pounding subsided in his head.

No, this wasn't his room. This was Simon's. Memories came flooding back. Memories from his time as Simon intertwined with his own. Images from a life he hadn't truly experienced, a life he'd led in someone else's shoes. It was always unsettling to know another version of him had controlled his body while the Fates kept him locked away in his mind.

Images of Violissa drowned him: her hair, her eyes, her skin. Her movements with him the night before. He tore at his hair. The cycle had begun again. But those memories weren't of Violissa. They were Violet, and he had been Simon. Two people who had no idea of the truth hidden within them. The Fates were beyond cruel, letting them touch and experience what could have been, only to rip it from them...from him.

In three days, Violissa would forget he existed, and the Fates would transplant her into a new version of Violet, hiding her somewhere beyond his reach, like they had for centuries. He was certain he was the only one who carried the memory of what had been and all he had lost.

One night of bliss that was not even his own to remember. His touches had never elicited cries from her. Only in the Dream Realm in their youth had that happened. Here it was Simon's memories of her that tormented him every lifetime. Jealousy raged within him, his hands clenching to push away the irrational reaction. He and Simon were the same person. No other man had touched her, but it still didn't make it easier because knowing he hadn't been awake to experience her was a punishment that left gaping wounds in his chest.

Thinking of Violissa had his eyes flying to the empty side of his bed where she'd been when they had fallen asleep. It wasn't a surprise to him that it was empty. It always was. She had fled again, just as she always had. He shouldn't have expected anything different this time.

Warmth from her body lingered like her lilac scent when he moved his hand over the spot. She hadn't been gone long. Hope stirred in him. Hope that would soon be dashed because he knew the outcome. Knowing didn't stop him from shoving the sheets aside and grabbing a pair of boxers. His pants from the night before were still in the other room where Violissa—no, Violet— had removed them. Disregarding the sweep of longing that coursed through him, he ran through the door.

He shouldn't have bothered to run after her, but he did just as he had in every lifetime. Hope was a temptation he couldn't resist. It was a single thought that he could catch her, that by doing so, she would snap out of the spell that kept her running from him. A sliver of prayer that she would listen to him this time when she never had. No matter how she turned from him in every life, he fought for her, facing those who threw him out of town, those who beat him to the edge of death to protect her without ever knowing who they were protecting. Some foolish rationale driving them to think he had hurt her. He was strong, even without his powers, strong enough to take quite a few of them on, but too many, and he'd end up just as he had in other lives.

She'd even had him killed in one life. The cruelty of the Fates became even clearer that day when he'd woken, his body repairing painfully until it was whole again. There would be no dying if Violissa still breathed because the Fates had deemed it so. He had lain there unconscious, unable to move, until the third day, when it no longer mattered. Just like it wouldn't matter in this life. She would barricade herself away from him, oblivious to what was really happening until it was too late.

He ran after her anyway. Subconsciously, he wondered why he had bothered to grab his boxers. A human habit. It still puzzled him that humans were so uncomfortable with nudity. As he adjusted the boxers, he remembered how much he hated wearing the things under his pants. Another ridiculous restriction humans insisted upon.

He ran through the bedroom doorway and across the apartment, pulling the door open before it hit him that something was different this time. Hand dropping from the handle, he turned. Across the room, huddled in a ball on the couch, sat Violissa. She had her knees pulled into her chest, her dress bunched up above them, exposing her calves. A yearning to touch that bare skin passed through him, but he would never again get so close to her.

She stared ahead, arms wrapped so tight around her legs that it seemed she feared loosening them would send her tumbling to the ground. Maybe it would. Her head was down, face hidden in her knees, hair spilling around them in a glorious golden arch.

"Violissa?" he whispered, afraid to startle her. He was stunned she was even there. She never remained. In every life, she had run from him, closing him off with no chance of setting things straight.

"Violissa?" Speaking her name was akin to breathing again. It had been so long since he'd said it, so long since it had rolled off his tongue.

Her hair shifted in a waterfall-like motion as she lifted her head. The sleeve of her dress fell down her shoulder, exposing the top of her breast. But it was her tear-stained cheeks that shredded the caverns of his heart. She appeared so fragile, like she would break if he got too close. Her eyes pleaded for understanding when they met his. For the first time in the centuries that this curse had controlled their lives, those emerald eyes he adored looked at him, truly looked at him. Blood coursed through him as a faint inkling of hope surfaced.

"Vi." He took a step toward her but faltered as she scooted back to the corner of the couch like a frightened stray cat. The action sent his hopes crashing and his shoulders drooping. Nothing had changed. All she saw was what the spell wanted her to see, and nothing he said or did would convince her of the truth.

"Why?" she asked, her voice a faint hiss. "Why would you do this?"

"Vi, you need to listen—"

"Why would you trick me again?" She let out a sob that tore through him like razors. "Did you know? Did you know who we were all this time?"

"No. You must believe me, Vi. I had no memory, just like you. We never have the memories until...until it's too late." He swallowed back the ache that was threatening to unravel him.

Her brow creased, confusion reflected in her eyes until he could see the spell work its magic. The darkness seeped into her eyes, lingering on the fringes and striking. It sank into her irises before infecting her. There was no way for him to fight something so powerful, especially without his magic.

Anger etched in her features, the accusations following too soon. "You did this to me. You took everything." Her voice cracked. "Why? I thought...I thought..."

"Violissa, listen to me. You're not thinking straight." As the words left his mouth, he knew he'd chosen wrong.

She flinched, her eyes narrowing to thin slits. He took a step closer, and she leaped from the couch in fear. She was too frightened, and the spell had her in its grip. With limited choices, he knew nothing would work. He could corner her and force her to listen, but he'd tried that in the past, and it only angered her more when he had. The last time, she had scratched and kicked at him until he'd relented and let her go. There was no way to break through the conviction that he had murdered her Council and tricked her into sleeping with him. It was the same every time.

The more he tried to explain, the more the spell fought. It almost seemed that the more she tried to figure things out, the more the spell twisted itself into her mind and distorted her memories, but he wasn't so sure anymore.

She moved toward the apartment door, giving him a wide berth. "Why do you and your brother want to torment me so?"

His recoil was instantaneous. "Never compare me to my brother," he snarled, as his muscles went rigid. "Wake up, Violissa, because soon it will be too late." He swiped his hand down his face, the ire flaring within him. "You're stronger than this. Open your eyes for once before you damn us both."

Her head snapped back, her face crumbling before she ran from the apartment.

Defeat leeched all remaining energy from him as he stared at the open door. He could have run after her, and likely should have, but he didn't. He was too tired of this fight to do anything more than slam his fist into the wall. The drywall buckled, and he rested his head in the indent, trying to settle down. This was futile. It always had been, and the Fates had known it.

He closed the door and stumbled to the couch, burying his head in his hands. Lilac wafted past his nose, and he sucked it in, preserving it before the inevitable happened. This was his last chance to save her. It would all be over in a few days, and then he would return to Tenebron, and she would live out her eternity in peace. No longer would his presence torment her. Her shattered memories would fade with the reset of her life, and he would haunt her no more. The Fates would send him back to their world powerless and mortal, and he would return his soul to them. There was no living without her. He had done it for too many lifetimes in this world and knew the pain of it.

Sitting back, he rested his head on the couch and stared at the ceiling until a thought came to him. There was something different about this lifetime: Keary.

# CHAPTER 47

Keary sat at the small round table in the kitchen that belonged to Paige and Violet. He stared absently at the flowered print on the curtains that lined the small window over the sink. Paige paced by every few moments, breaking his stare, but he was too lost in thought to be bothered by her constant interruptions. It had been a long night and an even longer morning. He had known just by the hungry look in Simon's eyes that last night was the one to change everything. When he had left with Violet, there was no doubt in Keary's mind that their clock would begin to tick. Not knowing when that countdown would start was what troubled him.

The storm had shrieked and wailed all night, finally intensifying in the early hours. All had been quiet since, but he suspected it was about to turn chaotic.

He had let Paige sleep for a few hours just to get her out of his hair. She was wound way too tight, and her nerves were too on edge for him to handle her. Any minute, he expected a summons from Sinow, and the thought both terrified and excited him.

The front door flew open, and he jumped to his feet, seeing

Violet run into the house. No, this wasn't Violet. This was Violissa. He recognized her when she came to a stop, her brilliant eyes glaring at him from across the open room.

She was a mess. Her hair flowed wildly behind her, tears stained her cheeks, and madness sat in her eyes. Her pained beauty made it difficult for him to look at her. Those emerald orbs flitted around as if she were watching scenes of a movie, and she had been muttering an onslaught of unintelligible thoughts just before she came to a stop.

She stared directly at him, but he didn't look away, even with the accusation and vehemence her eyes held. Paige's gasp came from behind him, and he hoped she wouldn't engage her queen until he had a chance. Not that he even knew where to start.

But it was Violissa who spoke first. "How dare you? Get out, Keary."

"It's nice to see you, too, Violissa."

"Get out and go back to your king." Her eyes softened momentarily as she said the word. Tears welled in her eyes, quickly replaced by a look of confusion and loss. "It won't work. There's nothing you can say that will make any of it better, so you might as well leave."

"Violissa, you need to stop for a moment. You're under a spell, and you need us to—"

"I don't need anything from you or him."

"Oh hell, Violissa, pull yourself together and gather your senses."

"Hell? Hell is what I've been stuck in for the last twenty-eight years. Stuck here without my memories, so he could trick me again!" Her tone and her mood were escalating, giving him insight into why Sinow had never broken through to her.

"Violissa," Paige spoke up from the corner of the kitchen, and Keary ground his teeth in frustration. He had purposely told her to avoid Violissa, and the feral spin of Violissa's head to where

Paige stood assured him this was going to get ugly. "Please, Violissa, listen to him. The Fates..."

There was nothing of the Violissa he remembered in the menacing glare that consumed the room as she advanced on Paige.

"Who are you?" she snarled. Keary shook his head at Paige. The last thing the spellbound queen needed was to hear her Council accused of breaking vows. "You're one of mine," she continued. "How...how could you? You will address me properly. Anyone who betrays me does not have the right to use my name." Her voice cracked, and she brought her hand up before Keary could stop her. The slap landed hard, echoing through the room long after Paige's hand flew to her face in shock.

"Violissa, that's enough!" he commanded. He may not have had his powers, but he wasn't about to let Paige get hurt. Violissa swirled, looked down at her hand momentarily, confusion crossing her face again, then ran from the kitchen toward the stairs.

"I want you out, Keary, and take the traitor with you," she shouted as she ran up the staircase.

An uncomfortable silence remained in the wake of her storm. Keary took a deep breath. This was nothing like he'd expected. It was worse. How were they to untangle her from the spell when she was this far under its influence? He didn't know Violissa other than the few times he'd met her, but he knew enough to know she wasn't herself. Had Sinow recognized the mangled spell was behind all of his failures? He doubted it.

Paige hadn't said a word since her encounter with the queen, nor had she moved. Keary walked over to where she still stood, her hand on her very red cheek. Violissa had hit her hard. He'd watched Paige grow up. She was like a little sister to him, and it hurt to see her in pain and humiliated by the woman she had looked up to for so many years.

"Paige," he said, shaking her shoulders lightly to break her trance.

She blinked, her hand lowering hesitantly.

"Are you all right?" he asked.

"Sure. I mean, yes. Yes, I'm fine." Her answer held little confidence, and she still seemed shaken.

"She's not herself, Paige."

"No, really, it's fine, Keary. I deserved it. She's right. I had no place using her name like that. She's my queen, and I'm not one of you. I'm no one to her." She was justifying Violissa's actions, and it angered the Darkbearer in him.

"You didn't deserve that, Paige. The spell has warped her sense of who she is. From everything I know about Violissa, she would die before she would ever hurt one of her people."

Paige nodded in understanding and gave him a forced smile. But as he went to say more, he heard the chime of a new message from his phone. Sinow. A shiver tingled his spine as he and Paige looked over at the table where his phone rested. Excitement mixed with fear taunted him as he walked over and picked it up. After reading the curt message, he looked back at Paige.

Lifting the phone like she could read the text from where she stood, he said, "My king has summoned me."

"Go, I'll be fine," Paige replied, trying her best to look strong, her shaking hands betraying her words.

"Paige, you can do this. You are the daughter of a Lightbearer and not just any Lightbearer. You are the daughter of the queen's Keeper, the most powerful Council there is. The Fates chose you for this task. Remember who you are and take your strength from it."

His phone chimed again. A brief "Now" was the only word that came through.

He glanced back up at her. "I have to go, Paige. This is it. This is why we're here."

"Go. I'll wait here for her to come down." Her vision slipped to the stairs.

"Don't worry," he said, trying to reassure her. "I can promise she won't kill you, which is more than I can say about what Sinow will do to me."

He left her there, his heart slamming as hard as the door behind him.

# CHAPTER 48

The sound of the door closing told Violissa Keary had left, or maybe they both had, but she couldn't lift her head from the bed. It pounded so viciously every time she tried that she gave up and let it drop back down. Squeezing her eyes shut, she attempted to sort things out, to make sense of anything. But every time she did, images hounded her. The war, her people suffering, her Council torn from her, the betrayal. The tears welled in her eyes, but she squeezed them tightly to keep them at bay.

*Think about something else,* she told herself.

Paige. Why was she here? Why would Sinow use a Cirillian to deceive her? It made no sense. At the thought of his name, pain tore through her chest, and a sob scraped from her throat. She shouldn't have hit Paige. It hurt to even think she'd done such a thing.

*That's it. Focus on something else. Anything else but him.*

There had to be a reason for Paige to be there, but then, she didn't even know why Keary and Sinow were there. That spell had hit her, purposely sending her here, so why would they be there, too? Clarity came the more she concentrated on anything but the past, and she sat up, the pain subsiding. Crossing her legs, she chewed her lip, trying to make sense of it. She had been in a different world, living a life as someone else for twenty-eight years. And she wasn't alone. It made no sense. No power allowed the crossing of worlds like this.

The spell had sent her there. That much she knew, and she kept her focus on who had sent that spell spiraling toward her. Sinow and Tynan. The ache subsided the more she concentrated on that day. He had sent that spell out purposely, cursing her to this world, but as she tried to understand why, she couldn't help but notice how her emotions shifted. Heartbeats raced and butter-flies cascaded. She couldn't ignore the reaction. As Violet, she had loved him, and as Violissa, she had loved him.

She loved him. The thought crossed her subconscious as a thief might sneak through the night, afraid of being caught. Before she could grab hold of it, pain gouged her head. She wrapped her hands around it as the images slammed into her again.

*Love,* the voice in her head said, *he didn't love you. He deceived and tricked you so that Tynan could murder your Council. He cursed you here, tearing you from your world and your people, ripping your heart out as he did.*

He didn't love her. A well of sadness drowned her, a sob threatening to escape even as she attempted to clamp it down. A sob, wretched and broken, scraped at her throat. She was such a fool. She wiped a tear from her cheek, lifting her head. This stopped now. She would no longer play the fool, and no matter what Sinow did or said, she wouldn't let him break her. This room would be her safe space, and if it meant staying in it for the remainder of her life to protect her heart from him, she would.

The agony in her head quieted as her resolve quelled it, but the moment it did, doubt crept in again. Memories of the previous night slipped into her mind, accompanied by butterflies that swarmed in her stomach. His touch, his growls, his taste, his strength. So similar to their time in the Dream Realm. Those had been her memories, but these...these were not hers. They were Violet's.

Had he known? Had he pretended not to remember? But that made no sense. Everything about Simon had been Simon and not Sinow. There were things she saw now that revealed the man below, but the same could be said for her. She gnawed on her lip. No, he hadn't known who he was.

A moment of clarity emerged again. More memories of Sinow's touch and the things he had done to her in the Dream Realm. She had loved him in their world, and the pounding of her heart against its confines assured her of that. An urge to run to him passed through her, quickly overtaken by a wave of stabbing pain. Confusion clouded her mind as images of his betrayal that day in the meeting grove filled her head.

The memories twisted and thrashed until she was certain he had known. That he had tricked her again. The Dream Realm had been a trick. How could she have forgotten? He had taken her there somehow, just to seduce her, just as he had concocted this whole Simon story to fool her again and take advantage of her memory loss. He was likely the one who had taken her memories, knowing she could never love him after his betrayal.

No, that wasn't true. She would always love him, and he knew it. There was no way to escape the prophecy, no matter how hard she tried.

Violissa rested her head on her knees, emotionally exhausted, wanting to pray to the Fates, but unsure if they could hear her any longer.

# CHAPTER 49

A knock at the door informed Sinow that Keary had received his texted summons. He had taken the time to think about the situation and how he would handle it. There was a chance Keary's memory had just returned, but Sinow found that doubtful. His actions over the past few weeks said differently. Which led him to ponder if he would punish Keary for lying to him all these years and for his other transgressions, or if he would simply embrace the fact that he didn't have to suffer alone this time.

"Come," he commanded, ensuring Keary knew his king had returned.

Sinow didn't bother looking up until the door clicked behind Keary. His hesitation was clear in his brown eyes. He was waiting for Sinow to judge him, but Sinow wouldn't. He had made the deal with the Fates, and whatever reason Keary had for being here, Sinow didn't doubt the Fates were involved. Sitting back with a sigh, he let the silence linger.

"Tough night?" Keary eventually asked.

Always the jokester, Sinow should have expected his need to break the tension in the air.

"What are you doing here, Keary?" he asked, knowing Keary's question had dual meaning, including a reference to what was likely his haggard appearance.

"I believe you summoned me," he replied, holding up the cell phone.

Keary waited for a reaction, and Sinow could see him searching for his old friend somewhere below the defeated man he had become. He'd been through too much over the last ten centuries to hide his weariness.

Realizing he was glad to have Keary there after so many lonely lifetimes, he rose and strolled over to him. "I'm sure there's a tale behind why you're here," he said, "but it's really good to see you, my friend." He grasped Keary's right arm up to the inner elbow as Keary grasped his back in the handshake of their people. Clapping his other hand on his shoulder, he added, "By the Fates, you're a sight for sore eyes."

"That's the nicest thing you've said to me in centuries," Keary joked.

Sinow's laugh felt foreign. When was the last time he had laughed? Simon had laughed, but the laughter had disappeared once he woke.

Walking to the kitchen, he grabbed two beers out of the fridge.

"A little early to be hitting the booze, don't you think?" Keary asked, eyeing the empty one on the counter.

"I need something to make it through the day, and this piss-water is all they make in this world. Fates, what I wouldn't give for a mug of our ale. I don't even think our horses would drink this stuff," he replied, taking a long swig of it and sitting.

Keary popped the cap off his beer and sat down across from him. "You know, I've thought that every day since the first time I had one of these. Finally, someone else who realizes how weak the ale here is."

Sinow gave him a sad smile. "You didn't come here to talk

about ale, Keary. What's going on? Why are you here suddenly when you've never been here before?"

Keary's reaction was instant, a slash of worry that settled in the creases between his eyes.

"The Fates sent us to help you. They knew you couldn't break through the spell on Violissa, and they sent us in hopes that we could help."

He couldn't stop his flinch when Keary said Violissa's name. It left a raw, tender spot that he couldn't remove.

"The Fates sent you to help? They created this mess and now they want to help?" He looked up at the ceiling. "We made a mistake, and for that, we've had to endure life after life of torment. I've had to endure..." He stopped, the emotion too powerful, the years of fighting, of rejection, of wandering the world searching for her compounding until he dropped his head back down, the ire washed away with helplessness. "They sent you to clean up their mess?"

"Something like that."

He lifted my head, squinting at Keary. "Wait, you said we. Who else did they send?"

"Paige."

"Violet's friend?" he asked. "A mortal? Why wouldn't they send another Council?"

"Well, that's a rather complicated story." Raising a brow, Sinow waited for the rest. "They thought a female would be better to help Violissa. Paige is mortal, but she's not just any mortal."

Sinow's gaze narrowed as he tried to comprehend.

"Things have changed, Sinow. They've gotten bad, very bad. You need to know the situation before you make any judgment."

"Go on then."

"Your absence left the throne open."

He squeezed the bridge of his nose, his patience thinning. "Of course it did. The throne is waiting for my return with Violissa."

The shake of Keary's head told him he had miscalculated, and trepidation slithered through his veins.

"It was waiting for the call of Dark blood, but it didn't wait long. When you left, Tynan was called to the throne."

He stood nearly dropping his beer. "Tynan ascended?"

Keary shook his head. "No. We don't really know what happened, but he is of king's blood. We think your leaving must have triggered something and called the blood within him. The half that comes from your father and matches yours. He transcended the Banished Realm boundary and seized control of the Council within minutes. He's powerful, Sinow. No one knows why. He never ascended, yet his power is close to yours."

Pacing that had begun with Keary's first words continued as Sinow listened to a nightmare scenario he never imagined.

"He's rained down a terror unseen since your grandfather. His magic is foul, corrupted. He demolished Cirillia, and Tenebron is barely recognizable. Those we could save, we hid in the Banished Realm before he stripped us of our powers. We have no way of saving anyone outside the realm now. We are powerless, aging, and weak."

Sinow gaped at him, unsure how this could have happened. It was some kind of nightmare that didn't seem possible. "How did he become so powerful without an ascension?"

"We don't know. Neither Council knows nor even understands how such a thing was possible. The closest we have is Kanine's assumption that he must have been hiding his power all his life. That he was planning this, planning for the day he could step into your throne."

"Planning for the day he could destroy me." His mind reeled from the truth. The Fates had asked if he was willing to give it all up, but he had never fathomed they had meant immediately. He shoved his hands in his pockets as once again the ragged edges of Tynan's blade sliced him open. His own brother and he had continually betrayed Sinow. Not only that, but he was destroying his world, tearing the realms apart, murdering innocents, and had rendered his Darkbearers and Violissa's Lightbearers powerless. It seemed impossible, and for the life of him, he couldn't understand how Tynan had done it. "You said the people are in the Banished Realm? How did you manage that?"

Scratching his cheek, Keary replied, "With Kanine and Cyric's help. They manipulated the spell the Fates gave to the Light King when he and his Lightbearers raised the boundary between our realms." There was no hiding the drop of Sinow's mouth. "Both Councils joined our powers and created an additional layer of magic over the Banished Realm. Once inside, there is no returning to the other realms, but only those the magic deems worthy can step through the shield. It gave us a sanctuary for those mortals Tynan preyed on and for us when he stole our powers."

"Unbelievable," he muttered, staring at Keary. "And all of you are powerless?"

His nod was a somber one. "Yes, he ripped the magic from everything in the land. He didn't bind our powers; he stole them."

"Something he shouldn't have the power to do." No king had that power. There was something they had missed, something he had missed. Although he had missed many things, considering the man he had trusted most of his life had torn everything from him. "And Paige? Who is she?"

A pause and the clearing of his throat let Sinow know he wouldn't like the answer. "She's Daneele's daughter."

His pacing stopped. "Daneele? Violissa's Keeper? One of her Council broke his vow?" It seemed unimaginable, but then he peered back at Keary, remembering his life with him when he had been Simon. His fists balled, calling for power that was no longer there. "But he's not the only one, is he? As I recall, you bedded many women in this world, Keary."

Keary put his hands up, scrambling for words. "I was only doing my part to protect you. I had to keep all those girls away from you. Somebody had to satisfy them. Besides, you can't blame me. These human bodies are weak."

Sinow's jaw ticked, and Keary slumped into his seat. "I know. You'll punish me when we get home. But I won't be the only one. We're as close to mortal as we can be, and age has hit us all." He rubbed his face, avoiding Sinow's eyes. "The mortal needs are... well, they're hard to ignore. Only the Lightbearers have had the strength to fight them, all but Daneele."

So it was his Council who had strayed. Punishment was in order when he returned. "Are there other children?"

"No, Paige is the only one. Cyric believes she's here by the Fates' design. They chose her to accompany me."

Sinow scraped his hand through his hair. The Fates sent them. The Fates were involved in the birth of a child from a Lightbearer. The Fates had their hands in too many places, and it had done nothing but wreak havoc. Their interference would destroy them all.

"It doesn't matter," he told Keary, sitting across from him. "In the end, none of this will matter. I'm sorry they dragged you into this. I'm sorry so many people had to pay the price for our mistakes."

He dropped his head to his hands, the weight of all Keary had told him doubling what had already been on his shoulders.

"Sinow, you need to go to Violissa. You need to..."

Raising his head, Sinow let out a laugh. "And do what? Have her shut me out again? Run from me, fight me, lock herself away from me? Turn the men of this town on me so that there's a barricade around her? I could take most of them, but I'm still mortal. She knows that. Weapons can still hurt me even if I can't die until she does. Do you know she even had me killed one lifetime?" He shook his head. "No, I won't go to her again, Keary. I will return to our world, return to Tenebron."

Keary was on his feet, his hands bunched before Sinow's last word ended. "Are you mad? Tynan will kill you the instant you return. You gave up everything, just like you said you would. There's no way the Fates would have sent you without some kind of deal." He stalked over to Sinow, but Sinow didn't cower from his temper. If defeat hadn't run through him again, he would have punched Keary. "If you return without winning her back, you will die."

Sinow sat back and rested his hands on the arms of the chair. "Yes. I had thought I would simply return myself to the Fates once I was back, but now it looks as if Tynan will do that for me."

Keary looked at him as if it were his first time seeing him. And perhaps it was, considering he'd never seen Sinow like this. Beaten down and worn out. Giving up. But Keary didn't know what he'd been through. The centuries of hell Violissa and the Fates had put him through. He didn't know that Sinow had accepted his fate the moment Violissa had run from him again.

"You were resigned to die this time."

Sinow reached over and took a swig of warm beer. "Yes."

Keary continued to stare at him, speechless. He dropped back into his chair, rubbing his face. There was nothing he could say or do to sway him. Sinow's fight was gone.

"It's different this time, Sinow." He heard the desperation in Keary's tone, saw it etched in his face. "The Fates sent us this time."

Sinow contemplated that fact, thinking of all the years he'd been unsuccessful in convincing Violissa that he was there to save her. "Maybe you aren't here for me. Maybe you're here for Violissa."

# CHAPTER 50

The house was quiet, leading Violissa to suspect it was empty. Her head was still a blur of images and thoughts that continued to attack her anytime her mind turned to Sinow. She had spent the night balled up in her bed, holding her head to keep from imploding. Her body was so tense, it was difficult to even get air into her lungs. When morning came, she stared out her window until she convinced herself to leave the sanctuary of her room. The only time she left prior was to hurry to the bathroom, relieved she didn't run into anyone. There was no way she could face them, especially Sinow.

Taking slow steps, fearful of the rampant barrage of memories and divisive thoughts, she made her way into the kitchen in search of some water. Paige turned from the window, her coffee mug shattering to the ground when her blue eyes met Violissa's. She gasped, her skin paling, eyes enlarging. Neither of them moved. Her presence reminded Violissa of home, of her people, and tears pricked the back of her eyes.

"My queen," Paige mumbled, dropping to her knees, her hands resting in the liquid and shards of ceramic glass below. She let out a soft *ouch* but didn't move from her spot. A red mark remained where Violissa had slapped her, and guilt gnawed at her. She saw the tremble in Paige's limbs, and it broke her heart.

This wasn't who she was. She wasn't this kind of queen, the kind who demanded obedience and respect. Never had she asked her people to kneel before her. Never had they feared her.

She rushed over and kneeled in front of Paige, tipping her chin up. Familiar. That's what Paige was. And it didn't have to do with her heritage. There was something else that tugged at Violissa's memory, but she didn't want to give it life for fear the terrible thoughts and pain would consume her again.

"You don't have to bow to me. I never demand that of my people." Paige tried to lower her eyes again, but Violissa forced them up. Eyes that reminded her of someone. "And...you don't have to refer to me with any deference. I spoke out of turn yesterday." She touched Paige's cheek. "And I'm sorry I hurt you."

Paige's eyes creased just as the foulness encroached on Violissa's mind, the memories slipping into her periphery, along with words like betrayal and lies. She closed her eyes, taking shallow breaths to stop it from going further. When silence greeted her, she opened them again.

Paige had tipped her head and was studying Violissa, seeing something she didn't, and Violissa wondered what it was. She had known Paige for twenty years. Even if she wasn't who she said she was, Violissa knew her shifts in emotion. Like the one she'd just had. Sadness enveloped her as she took Paige's hand and examined the cut on her finger.

"There was a time I could heal this. Such a small cut, it would have been effortless." She let the words hang in the air between them while she continued to stare at the wound. "Now, I have nothing."

The admission brought forth an agony that wrenched her insides. Her head throbbed, and she threw her hands up to hold it, a whimper escaping her. Doubling over, she tried to fight it, but it was powerful. This time it took her longer to subdue. More calming breaths, more quieting of her mind. But when she opened her eyes again, it hadn't completely left. The pain was a dull thud at her temples, a churning of her stomach. The intrusive thoughts whispering just out of reach.

Paige averted her eyes, as if looking in them hurt her.

"It's fine," she mumbled, picking pieces of the shattered mug from the floor.

Violissa did the same, hoping it would calm her head. It was a mundane task, but the kind she enjoyed. Repetitive and smooth, giving her mind the silence it needed. Paige continued to glance at her while they worked. When they finished, Violissa stood, dropping her pieces in the trash can. Paige remained on the ground, her head lowered. She was one of Violissa's people, but she acted like she was from Tenebron. The observation caused the twisted thoughts to encroach further into Violissa's silenced mind.

"Paige, you don't have to stay down there. I told you that."

Relief splashed across her features, but Paige grimaced when she stood. The fragments of the mug remained in her hand.

"Who are you, Paige? It's clear you're Cirillian. Why would you be here with..." Her voice trailed off and she winced at the sharp sting from even the thought of saying his name. She dropped her eyes to the broken pieces in Paige's hand, focusing on anything that could stop the rebellion brewing in her head.

"The Fates sent us."

That had not been the answer she'd expected, and her eyes jerked to Paige's. "What? Why would they do that?"

"To help you both. It's been a very long time, my queen, longer than I think you realize." She stopped, fear in her eyes.

"It has been a long time. Twenty-eight years is too long to be away from my people." She rubbed her arms, a chill crawling up her spine that she couldn't shake. "But why would the Fates send you to bring me home? And you said us. Are you truly aligned with them?"

Another flicker of fear flashed over Paige's features, and

Violissa narrowed her eyes, her demons lurking, readying to strike. The thudding in her temples had spread, and she didn't think she could stand much longer. As it was, all she wanted to do was crawl back into her bed and pray for the Fates to end this misery. But she needed to understand why one of her people would betray her.

Paige's words came out rushed. "Yes, but it's not what you think. Please listen before you react." The hold Violissa had on her calm snapped, the voices shouting at her, convincing her this woman was nothing but a traitor. "Things aren't as they seem. It's been a lot longer than twenty-eight years. We're here to help you."

Violissa backed away, her eyes growing murky, the room dimming. The storm in her head was raging again. "Who are you really? Why would the Fates send a mortal to help me?" she hissed.

Paige stuttered as she answered. "My name is Paige. My mother is Maggie. Her family hailed from the village of Lonian. And my father...my father is Daneele, Lightbearer and Keeper to the queen."

With each word, she stood taller while Violissa shrank back more. Each was a scalding burn against her skin.

She stumbled away, bumping into a kitchen chair, the screech of the wooden legs against the floor cutting through the sudden silence. Her breathing was shallow, the voices too loud to tune out. Paige was lying, and Sinow had put her up to it to break her more. To lead her to believe Daneele was alive and that he had betrayed his sacred oath.

The mug fragments fell to the ground again as Paige backed away from her, terror in her eyes. Terror because she knew Violissa had caught her in a lie.

Her mind ravaged once again, Violissa pointed at Paige as she backed further away. "Lies. You spew lies. Why? Why would you want to hurt me?" She tore her eyes from Paige's, the pain in her head so severe she could barely hold it up. "I knew it. You've betrayed me. Pretending he didn't murder Daneele. Feeding me this story as if my Keeper would ever betray me. Maybe you're the one under a spell. Maybe he's doing all of this to make me think I've gone mad." She was rambling, the words spewing from her.

"I'm not lying, Violissa. Please believe me. He's not tricking you; I'm not lying. You need to see the truth."

Her head flew up, and she glared at Paige, shades of black and red staining her vision.

"My Council would never break their vow, least of all my Keeper," she hissed. "They are dead, and you play games with me. How dare you!" An ache penetrated her head, sending her crumbling into a crouched position while she waited for the waves to pass. She sobbed, hating the agony, the lies, this situation. She wanted to be home, to have the people she loved alive and around her.

"They're not dead," Paige mumbled. "Sinow saved them. His spell saved them from Tynan's, just as it saved you. Please, Violissa. We need you."

Violissa's chest heaved when she slowly unfurled her body. Every movement was another lance of agony. Paige's words bounded through her head, giving light to the darkness there. She met her eyes, so like Daneele's that it hurt even if she couldn't admit it.

"I loved him," she mumbled, wiping a tear away with her shaking hand, "and he hurt me in the worst possible way."

She turned to leave, her soul fractured even further. Behind her, she heard Paige say, "My father said you wouldn't believe me."

Violissa stopped at the doorway, too shattered to turn back to her. Too fearful of passing out from the violence in her mind and body.

"He said you had too much faith in him and would never doubt his loyalty. He said to tell you to give in and trust in the Fates. That you need to stop fighting them. To know they have their reasons. And to tell you that your power doesn't control your heart. Your heart controls your power. Your heart is what truly defines you as a queen. Trust it as your people do. He said you would know what that meant."

She did, but the possibility that Paige was telling the truth, that Daneele was alive, that she was his daughter was too much to handle, and Violissa fled her presence, running up the stairs and slamming the bedroom door shut. The pain was so intense, her head spun until she collapsed on the bed.

# CHAPTER 51

The chair was one he had sat in often as Simon, and now it had become Sinow's regular spot. He didn't know how long he'd been sitting there, staring at nothing, as he tried to keep his thoughts from turning to Violissa. It hadn't worked. She continually returned to his mind, and he didn't think there was any way to free himself from her.

He peeked over at Keary, who lay sprawled out on the couch. They had spent the prior day and most of the night catching up, telling stories of the past, remembering the good times, long before the prophecy had changed everything, and drinking. Keary had let his frustration over the situation take control of how many beers he had drunk and had finally passed out at about four in the morning. Sleep had been brief for Sinow, fitful and disturbed, and he'd woken a few hours later.

Watching Keary sleep, he questioned if he was doing the right thing. If Keary was right and he needed to give it one last try, and run to Violissa, break down her door, and force her into his arms. He shook the thought away because it wouldn't work. The spell had her too far under its influence.

He rested his head on the chair, wondering what Violissa was doing. If she was as restless as he was and sleep had eluded her. Had thoughts battered at her as they had him? It was romantic to think things were that way, but he didn't believe they were. This was a nightmare he had no way of escaping. Two more days. Then it would end, and she would be left here, oblivious to her past and his existence.

He sat up, a thought occurring that hadn't been there in his prior lives. He was certain the Fates had wiped her memory of him each time, leaving his intact after he failed to convince her of the spell. But would they erase her memory this time or would they be just as cruel to her as they had been to him? Leaving her to spend eternity with the knowledge of what she'd lost. It was a thought that gutted him, and he was glad for the vibration of Keary's phone on the coffee table.

It had been doing so off and on for the last hour, and it was getting on Sinow's nerves. There had been multiple calls as well, but he hadn't cared to look at them. This time, he reached for the phone. Missed calls showed from Paige, and a new text reflected a brief: *Where are you?*

Giving Keary a smack on the back of the head with the phone, he said, "Get up, Keary." Keary groaned and shifted his face further into the couch. "Don't make me throw water on you. Wake up. Paige has been blowing up your phone."

Keary turned his head, his eyes groggy as he squinted at Sinow. "And you didn't bother answering, or at least waking me earlier?" He sat up, rubbing his eyes. "I gotta tell you, as much as I love a good drunken coma, the next morning is a killer. Fates, how I miss my power. We never had this problem when we had magic."

It was true. Their magic burned any alcohol from their systems within minutes, but without it, the hangovers were severe.

"I thought you were used to this? As I recall, you were frequently taking girls home in a drunken stupor and waking up with a bad hangover when we were in college."

"When Simon and I were in college," Keary corrected.

"True. That doesn't mean I don't remember. Be thankful you won't have to face me at home, Keary. Breaking your vow of chastity is grounds for serious punishment. I'm talking the breaking bones kind of punishment." He attempted to hide his laughter at Keary's horrified expression.

"What? No, I told you that was necessary. I was saving you, protecting you from those wenches who were trying to tempt you from Violissa." Sinow couldn't stop the step back as he reeled from the sound of her name. It knocked the wind from him, and he clenched his hands to stabilize himself. Keary blanched. "Sorry. I got carried away. But remember, I'm not the only one. There were several vow breakers at home, and Daneele even has a kid, so don't get started on me."

"It doesn't matter anymore, Keary," he said, wiping his hand over his face. The fun of the moment slipped away as reality set back in. "None of it matters now, does it?" He threw the phone at him. "Call Paige and see what she wants."

Keary didn't comment on his change of demeanor or his words. "I can't believe you didn't answer her. What if she has something important to say about..." He drifted off, not wanting to say the name again, and Sinow gave him a nod of thanks.

"Just call her."

Keary picked up the phone and called Paige back. Sinow could hear her on the other end yelling at Keary for not answering right away. When Keary told her he was sleeping, her voice grew louder.

"Are you sure her mother isn't one of ours? Are you sure she's Cirillian?"

Keary stifled a laugh and, covering the phone, whispered, "She's a spitfire. I blame it on the drinking water in the Banished Realm."

Sinow chuckled, listening to Keary's attempts to focus her.

"Paige. Paige. Okay, stop going on about it and tell me what's so urgent." Keary listened quietly, and Sinow noticed Paige's voice was no longer discernible.

"Wait, what? Hold on." He looked at the phone and hit a button. "Can you hear me?"

Paige's voice came through the speakerphone. "Of course I can hear you. Why wouldn't I..." Her voice lowered to a hush. "Am I on speakerphone?"

"Yes, I put you on speakerphone. Now tell Sinow what you just told me and then tell us both what happened."

"You mean, you both can hear me? I'm talking to the king, too?"

Sinow's patience was wearing thin again. "Just tell me, Paige. I'm not going to bite you. I don't have any powers, remember? Now talk, or I just might figure out a way to kill you through the phone."

A high-pitched squeal came from the other end.

"Really, Sinow?" Keary grumbled. "I mean, it's funny, but not the right time. She's liable to go off the edge if you push her."

"Go on, Paige."

"Okay, well then, I mean... I mean, if you need me to say it all again, I will."

"Yes, I do," he snapped.

Silence, and Keary rolled his eyes at him before she started again. "Violissa came downstairs and talked to me."

"How did she seem?" Keary asked. "Was she in the same state as yesterday? Did she hurt you again?"

"Hurt her?" he asked Keary, his brows pinching. "Violissa would never hurt anyone." He thought about all the times she had lashed out at him. "Anyone except me, that is."

"She was a little distraught yesterday, and she slapped Paige, who should have kept her mouth shut like I told her to," Keary said into the phone.

"I don't need a guilt trip, Keary."

"Continue, Paige." Sinow was done with their banter.

"She was different...at first. She was calm, and her eyes were so bright. They truly are as beautiful as the legends say."

"Legends?" he mouthed to Keary.

Keary nodded. "It's a long story." To Paige, he asked, "Did she say anything to you?"

"I cut my finger, and she said something about being able to heal it in the past. She looked so sad. She's struggling with the spell. I saw it! I saw it in her eyes; it was the freakiest thing."

"You saw it?" Keary asked.

"Yes, it was like this black mist—"

"In the corner of her eyes," Sinow finished for her.

Keary's sight shot to him. "Wait, you saw it too, Sinow?"

"Yes, she was here when I woke. I saw it when she talked to me."

"She talked to you? Is that normal? I thought you said she always runs from you?"

He exhaled, his frustration with the situation growing. "Yes, I said that. But she was here yesterday morning. It was brief though, Keary, and nothing came of it."

"But that shows there's something different going on this lifetime, Sinow. That's a sign."

"It's not a sign, Keary. She still ran off. Drop it and let Paige finish."

Keary eyed him, annoyance at Sinow's response reflected on his face. "Fine, but I'm not dropping it completely. What else, Paige?"

"She started asking me questions, and it all went downhill from there. I told her who I am and told her the Council is alive, but I don't think she believed me. She called me a liar and said... well, she said my father would never break his vow. Then she ran back to her room."

Hope had surfaced, but it smashed once again, leaving him nothing to grasp to stay afloat. There was no way to break the spell, no matter who the Fates sent.

"She hesitated, though," Paige added, her voice introspective.

His head lifting, he looked back at Keary. "Go on."

"Father told me to tell her something that he had always told her as she was growing up. She listened and hesitated before she ran off."

Curiosity piqued, he asked her, "What did you tell her?"

"He said she needed to trust the Fates, and that power doesn't control her heart. Rather, her heart controls her power. Her heart is what truly defines her as a queen, and she should trust it as her people do."

"Your father was always a wise man," he said, thinking about the words. Words had power, and Daneele knew Violissa would understand that better than anyone. She would understand what that message had meant to her back then and now. If he had indeed spoken those words in only her presence, then she would know he was alive.

Paige sniffled before she responded. "I know. I really miss him."

"Has she left her room since?" asked Keary.

"No, there's been nothing from her since."

The spell had Sinow perplexed. It was rare that one could be seen. "Paige, you said you could see the spell?"

"Yes, it moved through her eyes. At first, it was just in the corners. She would close her eyes tight and hold her head like she was trying to make it go away. Once I started challenging what she thought to be true, the black spread so that it changed the color of her eyes. They were so dark they were almost black."

"And they remained that color until she left?"

"Yes."

"She's cursed, isn't she?" he asked Keary, realizing the true impact of what he'd been up against all this time. Understanding now why he had never been able to get through to her.

"Yes," Keary answered, his chestnut eyes carrying the sadness that was currently clawing at Sinow.

Where before the situation had seemed hopeless, now it was impossible. Curses were unbreakable. They ravaged their victim's mind and body from the inside out until eventually the victim died. He held his palm against his forehead, thinking about the circumstances. Keary and Paige were here for a reason, and he didn't think he was that reason.

"Sit tight," he told Paige. "Keary will be there soon."

"I will? Why will I be there soon, Sinow?" he asked as he hung up the phone.

"Because that's where you need to be."

It was the only thing that made sense. If Violissa was indeed fighting a curse, she needed someone to pull her out from under it, if that was even possible. And he wasn't that person. He never had been, which was why he had failed so many times.

"No, I need to be here with you," argued Keary, who stood and crossed his arms.

"Look, Keary, as much as I'm enjoying the company, and trust me, it's nice not to be alone through this for once, the Fates didn't send you here to sit and sulk with me."

"But—"

"No, they didn't. You're here for a reason, and I don't think that reason is me. Like I said earlier, you're here for Violissa." Saying her name was difficult. It left a hollow space in the pit of his stomach. "She needs you more than I do right now. And maybe, just maybe, you and Paige can get through to her this time."

"You're sure?" Keary asked, tugging at his black hair.

Worry marred his features, sadness shadowing his eyes. The pity Sinow saw there was something he didn't want. It reminded him of how weak he'd become, and he needed to stay strong to face what was coming. If Tynan had truly lost his mind, then Sinow would need every bit of strength to face his death at his brother's hands.

"Positive. Now, pull yourself together. You look a mess." He forced a smile but knew Keary saw it for what it was: an attempt to ease Keary's guilt about leaving.

"All right, but you aren't getting rid of me that fast," he said, stretching before heading into the kitchen. "I need some coffee to make it through this day."

Another few hours went by as their goodbye lingered. The coffee wasn't as good as the company, but it was the first thing Sinow had put in his stomach besides beer since Violissa had left. The caffeine provided the adrenaline rush he needed to make it through one more night. This one he would spend alone. As evening drew closer, he could no longer delay the inevitable any more than Keary could.

Keary clasped Sinow's arm before pulling him into a tight hug. "No matter what happens, Sinow, my allegiance has always been with you. You are my king and my brother."

Sinow held back the emotion. "Keep her safe. If the Fates leave you with her, make sure she's happy, and guard her with your life."

"She is my queen because she is yours. My life belongs to her, just as it does to you."

Giving him a nod of thanks, Sinow showed him out, knowing this was likely their last farewell. Keary glanced back at him before he reached the stairs, giving him one last wave before descending into the stairwell.

The door closed softly, and Sinow rested his head against it. He had sent away the only person who understood what he was going through. The only one with whom he could talk. He was alone again.

Taking his spot in his chair, he sent a prayer to the Fates that he'd been right. That Keary and Paige could break through to Violissa. But in his experience, prayers went unanswered, so he silenced his prayers and stored away his hope as he awaited the remaining hours of his existence.

# CHAPTER 52

A heavy fog encompassed Violissa's mind, making her sight blurry and her head heavy. On the floor, with the door behind her, her body in a fetal position, where she'd been since she ran from Paige, she squeezed her eyes against the pressure behind them.

"Please make it stop," she cried, unsure of whom she was asking. There was no one to help.

She didn't know how much time had passed since she'd returned to her room. Time no longer had definition. There was only pain and agonizing memories that left her riven every time they consumed her mind. She needed to move from the floor and at least make it to her window seat. Fighting against her instinct, the one that told her any movement would be brutal, she forced her head up. Slow, deliberate, steady. She brought herself to her feet. Head throbbing, the invasive thoughts and memories continued, causing her to sway. She reached out and caught herself on her banister, waiting for the rolling swell of nausea to pass.

Squeezing her eyes shut, Violissa focused on her breathing, trying to steady each inhale and exhale, concentrating not on the pain or the thoughts but on the motion of each breath as it entered and left her lungs. Each one became deeper until her head quieted and the pain subsided. She stood there, clenching the banister, fearful that moving would bring it flooding back. Her mind was blank, but she knew all too well how quickly that could change. She'd always been a positive person, so the negativity, the viciousness of the words that clustered in her head, drained her each time. Some part of her fought them, believing they were wrong, but it wasn't enough to remain in control once the flood came and turned her thoughts again. If she could just take the time to think about it, to think through everything that had happened, then she could figure out the truth, but there never seemed enough quiet to do this.

As her body calmed, her grip on the banister loosened, and she opened her eyes, savoring the moment of freedom from whatever had hold of her.

*He's cursed you.* The thought came from nowhere, spoiling the quiet.

She shook her head to free her mind again, as if the movement would signal to her subconscious that she didn't want to discuss it. With tentative steps, she walked to the small desk where, as Violet, she had once sat, unaware of her origins, unaware that her entire existence was a façade. She fingered one of the dried flowers on her wall, scanning the pictures of another life, one she remembered but hadn't lived.

It made no sense that she was in this world. That Sinow would have sent her or even known about it any more than she had. Something seemed off with the assumption that he had cursed her there.

*He knew. It was all part of his plan to trick you.* The voice screeched to be heard again, trying to disrupt her peace.

*Stop it.*

Her gaze fell on a picture of Violet and Paige when they were younger. Like so many of the pictures that adorned the wall, it was another memory of her life as Violet. Paige had never hurt her. Nor had Keary. Nothing they had done had been malicious when they'd had years with her locked away in her mind. She pulled one of the flowers down, fingering the dried leaves, only then seeing that pieces of her were evident in so much of the life Violet had led. She and Violet were the same person, even if Violissa hadn't been awake. Burying her memories had not hidden her spirit. No spell could ever change who she was at heart.

Heart. The word made her think of what Paige had told her. Daneele had said those words to Violissa so often as she'd grown up. Encouraging her to rule with an understanding that her power was a gift and used in tandem with her instincts and her heart, her people would thrive. Who else would have overheard him saying that? Only other Council. But if they were all dead, who would have told Paige to say those words?

*Lies, she spouts lies! Treason!* the voice screamed again, and Violissa jumped at its force. Anger gouged its way through her with slashes of red that threatened to overtake her calm.

"Leave me be," she said back, pushing the heel of her palm against her head to quell the voice and the ache that accompanied it. She needed to remain rational. There was an explanation for this, and she would find it, no matter how the voices threatened her sanity.

Her eye caught the picture Violet had taken of Paige with Keary. Touching the corner, she smiled. Now it made sense why he'd always groused about having his picture taken. Again, the thought that he'd never hurt her, had only ever been a friend, returned. If anything, he'd been as protective of her as one of her Lightbearers.

*Open your eyes, Violissa. He tricked you so Sinow could hurt you again.*

But that still made no sense. She allowed herself to think about Sinow, bracing for her body's rebellion. Chest beating rapidly, she thought back to her time as Violet. Even if Sinow had maintained his memory, he hadn't hurt her. He'd loved her just as he had at home. Her breath hitched. If he'd wanted to hurt her, he would have taken advantage of her the first day she'd met him.

*Tricks. Don't be a fool. He lied, played you just like he did in the past, and you fell for it like the fool you are,* the voice said as it slunk through her mind again. Blinding pain pierced the back of her eyes, but it couldn't breach the emotions tied to Sinow. Almost like embracing her love for him offered protection from it.

*But I loved him, I still love him, I will always love him,* she thought, fighting the spell's hold.

A shimmer on her desk made her eyes shift downward. The ring Simon had given Violet. She reached for it but stopped herself, curling her fingers back in. She didn't dare pick it up, or the spell would submerge her again. But she longed to have its weight in her hand and trace the intricacies of the patterns with her fingers.

*It's a symbol of his betrayal. It stands for falsehoods.*

But it wasn't. It was a symbol that he'd been telling the truth. Why propose if he was tricking her? Because Sinow hadn't proposed, Simon had. But it wasn't Simon who had picked this ring. Everything about it spoke of Violissa, not Violet. It was every bit a symbol of Sinow's love for her as it was of Simon's love for Violet. It had been Simon who had bought the ring, but it had been Sinow who had been the driving force behind it. Locked away, just as she had been.

Taking a deep lungful of air, she grabbed the ring, clinging to it as the spell struck back. She crumpled to the ground, the voice screaming again, flooding her mind with the images of everything that had gone wrong in their relationship. Faces of the dead, parentless children, destroyed towns, the cries of her people as they bore the attacks of Sinow and his Council during the war. His hate-filled eyes looked back at her as they fought, the vile touch and taste of his Dark magic invading her senses. She held her hands over her head and prayed to the Fates to make it stop, but she knew they couldn't hear her. There was no one in this world who could answer her prayers.

Violissa's stomach churned as her body bore the pain that was winding its way through it. The bile rose in her throat, and she gagged. With every ounce of strength she had, she ran from her room, down the hall, and into the bathroom, where she threw up what little was in her stomach. She hadn't eaten since the festival, so it didn't surprise her when the dry heaves started.

As her stomach finally settled, she fell into the corner, welcoming the coolness of the bathtub against her skin. She laid her head on her knees, which she'd pulled in tight against her stomach, tears spilling.

She didn't know what was happening to her. This seemed too strong to be a spell. Staring absently at the tile floor, she questioned what kind of spell lingered like this one. She thought back to her magic, the spells she had learned when she was young. There was nothing that stayed in one's system. Even the healing magic she and her Council wielded lasted only as long as it took the body to heal. Nothing she remembered from studying the ways of the Darkbearers led her to believe Sinow's magic was any different.

At the thought of him, she cringed, holding her breath in anticipation of another round of torment from the spell. Was that really what it was? She was beginning to think otherwise. Spells were short and quick in their delivery. This was something very different. More powerful.

When quiet finally returned, she pulled herself to her feet. Reaching to flush the toilet, she took a step back, icy tendrils stretching up her spine. What she'd thrown up hadn't been food or liquid. It was a black substance. Her hand flew to her mouth as the truth rushed to her.

*Curse*, her mind whispered, fearful of waking the wrathful beast inside again.

Her hand trembled when she brought it back down. So, it was true. She had been cursed. It wasn't the same meaning of curse the humans used. She wouldn't shrivel away to nothing like the character in Stephen King's *Thinner*, nor would demons drag her to hell like in the movie Paige had once coerced her into seeing.

Curses were rare. She had learned about them when she was young, but never really understood them until now. The result of a botched spell, curses fed on the mind of the victim, ravaging them until there was nothing left but feral irrationality. Victims faced death and left a trail of murder and devastation behind. There had never been an incident in her realm, but there had been in Tenebron.

But curses were a rarity, which is why she had never been witness to their effects. Spells came in different forms. Most, delivered through the movement of the wielder, formed silently, with no need for vocal delivery. More powerful spells relied on a combination of movement, silent intent, and words. The spell Tynan and Sinow had attacked her with that last day in their world was that type of spell. Maybe something had gone wrong, and the clashing of their spells had misdirected.

Her pulse raced. She was overlooking something, and deep down, she knew that, but she had to stop her thoughts for fear of waking the curse again. If there was indeed a curse thrashing through her body, she needed to keep it at bay or she would lose her mind and her life within days.

Swallowing back her fear, she flushed the toilet, then leaned over the sink and splashed water on her face.

"My queen?" she heard Paige call. "Is everything okay, Violissa?"

She rested her face against the towel she was drying it with. That term of respect was one she'd always hated. She didn't want to be just a ruler to her people and had refused to let them call her that.

"I'm fine. Please leave me be, Paige," she called back. The situation was too dire to speak with Paige, and she didn't have the strength to listen as Paige tried to convince her of things she literally couldn't stomach.

Putting the towel back, she glanced in the mirror. What looked back at her had her jerking away. Her skin was pale from being sick, but that wasn't what concerned her. In the corners of both eyes, the black mist of the curse coiled. Her back hit the wall, and she tore her eyes from the mirror. No wonder she'd vomited. The curse had infected her entire body.

Hands shaking, she opened the bathroom door and walked back to her bedroom, closing the door behind her. She took a seat at the window, leaning back. Fear seized her, and she was at a loss for what to do. She had no one here to talk to, to help her out of this darkness. She was alone. If the curse had nested itself into her that deep, she wouldn't know what was real and what wasn't.

Its power seemed to rest upon her thoughts of anything to do with Sinow or the events that had happened at home. But she didn't know if what had been going through her mind was truth or fiction. Absently, she rubbed her thumb against her other fingers, realizing only then that she still held the ring. She had somehow slipped it onto her finger. At the discovery, her pulse raced and tears sprang to her eyes. She glanced at it, warmth spreading through her. This was real.

She held onto that affirmation, not opening her mind any further to think about Sinow or her emotions or even what the ring symbolized. She focused on that one thought. That the warmth that had spread through her chest and sent her pulse racing was real. Daneele had told her to trust her heart. And while she may not have been able to trust the thoughts in her head, the images that seemed so determined to turn her against Sinow, she could trust the sensation that was currently swirling in her chest. Her heart was the only part of her that the curse didn't seem to control. The curse couldn't lay claim to it because it belonged to Sinow. He had claimed it long ago.

In that moment of introspection, Violissa realized she was in the biggest fight of her life. More deadly than Tynan, more destructive than the Torathar. And she needed to call on all her reserves to break free from it. She savored the determination, letting it settle into her before the curse came careening in to break her again. It attacked with the viciousness of a rabid animal, tearing down her defenses, but she held tight to the sensation in her chest, the one place of peace that still existed in her body as she crumpled against the window.

With tears streaming down her face, Violissa resolved to fight. For herself, for Sinow, for what they had once had and then lost. Time was what she needed. Time to figure out how to beat something she barely understood, and then she would be free. Weariness overtook her, the assault on her head and body too much to bear, and she closed her eyes. She doubted she would find sleep. Her mind was too awake, the pain too present, but she closed them anyway, shutting out the world around her.

Against the black of her closed eyes, the images and angry thoughts held even more power. There was no light to balance them. She concentrated on her breathing, clearing her head as much as she could until the voices quieted and the images grew further apart. She opened her eyes and stared blankly out the window, focusing only on the bench on the far side of the park, knowing anything more would drown her within seconds.

---

THE SUN SET as Violissa continued to stare out at the space where she knew the bench must still be, its outline too dim to make out in the darkness. At some point, she registered a knock on the door downstairs, followed by footfalls and soft talking. Someone had come to the house, but she didn't know who it was and didn't care enough to find out. She wondered if it was Sinow, but then no one came to her door. Why hadn't he come to her? If what he had told her was true, why had he let her leave that morning and not bothered to follow her?

*He doesn't care,* the voice said. *He doesn't love you.*

But he did, didn't he?

*Did he ever tell you?* it answered. *Did he ever say that he loved you?*

No, he hadn't. The words had never crossed his lips. But Simon had.

*It wasn't him; it was all a lie.*

Maybe the voice was right. Maybe everything she was experiencing was really a result of Sinow's magic. Had he really cursed her and now sat waiting for her to crumble? The more she contemplated it, the more real it became, but for the steady pulsing in her heart. It knew better, and it ached painfully as the thoughts took shape.

She shook her head, reminding herself of her resolve to heed her heart and not her mind. That's where her power was. The curse was twisting her thoughts, and that was all. Focus returning to the window, she stared blankly again, silencing her inner demons. It was the only thing she had the strength to do. She would need to figure out how to do something more, but right now, the fight had left her drained, and staring at nothing felt good. This would do for now. She had plenty of time to figure out the curse.

*Plenty of time,* the voice whispered.

# CHAPTER 53

Keary sat at the kitchen table, staring at the pattern of the woodgrains. Leaving his king, his friend, had been the hardest thing he'd ever done. Harder than the day the Fates had blessed him and he'd left his family to live his immortal life among the Darkbearers. He had wanted to stay and fight, to try anything to convince Sinow to go after Violissa, but he knew it would be futile. Sinow had resigned himself to accepting his death. To him, this was his reckoning, the time for him to face his fate, face his punishment for the mistakes he and Violissa made. There would be no changing his mind.

Keary had returned to his own apartment and sat for a long time trying to convince himself to accept his king's decision. He had thought about all that had occurred over the past thousand years and the past twenty since he and Paige had arrived. Thinking about his time with Violissa these past few years, he realized that maybe Sinow was right. Maybe they were here for her and not Sinow. If that were true, then he had no idea what to do to fix things. He had looked up and prayed to the Fates for some kind of direction, forgetting momentarily that another god ruled this world. The Fates probably couldn't even hear him.

After leaving his apartment, he had put off returning to Paige's. He was still contemplating his next move, and with Paige nervously talking at him, he knew he'd get no answer. Finding himself in front of the bar, he had rubbed his hand along the outer wall. He wasn't sure what would happen in a few hours. If the Fates would send him and Paige to their world or leave them here with Violissa. And if they remained in the human world, he had no certainty their memories would remain intact. Left to live out a life of lies with a queen who did not know who she really was. Perhaps the Fates would have mercy on them and take away their memories. It would be a blessing for Paige, who would suffer knowing she would never see her parents again.

He had rubbed his forehead, having no idea how this would work out. None of the options made him hopeful. He had stood there with his hand on the solid foundation of the bar, taking solace in the tangibility in a moment when nothing seemed tangible until he'd finally left to see Paige and wait out his destiny.

Since then, he and Paige had been sitting at the table, neither speaking. He glanced at his phone, which lay on the table next to him. It had been over an hour since he'd arrived, and he and Paige had barely said a word to one another. Neither willing to break the silence, nor to inject the peace with the frightening reality that surrounded them.

He looked over at Paige. She was staring down at her cup of coffee. It was the third he'd seen her drink in the time he'd been there. Her hand shook as she lifted the cup to her lips and took another sip.

"That's it, Paige. Put the coffee down." He stood and took the cup from her hand.

"But—"

"No, you've had enough. For Fates' sake, you've got the jitters from all that caffeine." He pointed to her shaking fingers, which she pulled in against her chest, attempting to hide the evidence. He walked over to the sink and dumped the coffee.

"I don't know what else to do, Keary. She's not moving, and he's not moving. I can't believe he's not coming to save her. It makes no sense. If he loves her, why isn't he here trying to help her?"

Keary had struggled with the same question. Tried to rationalize it until he finally realized he couldn't rationalize something he barely understood.

"We're only seeing this from our perspective, Paige. There's a long history between them in this world that only Sinow remembers. He knows better than all of us what's possible, and apparently, changing her mind isn't. He thinks it's time for him to step back, that we're not here for him."

"We're not here for him," she repeated softly.

"I know. I had the same reaction. It doesn't make sense. We're here for them both. Why else would the Fates have sent us both?"

"No, Keary. I think he might be right."

His brow furrowed in confusion. Maybe the coffee had finally gotten to her.

"You might be here for her, but they sent me to help him, Paige. I don't know Violissa."

She stood and walked over to him, hope blooming in her cerulean eyes. Putting her hand on his arm, she said, "You're exactly the person she needs right now. She won't let Sinow anywhere near her. From what I saw earlier, the spell turns on her anytime she even thinks of him. He's never been able to get through to her because the spell turns her against him."

"So how could I possibly do anything? You haven't been able to get through to her. How would you expect me to?"

"Don't you see? What I told her broke through enough to make her pause. I gave her an alternative to what the curse was giving her. I gave her reality, and if she's anything like my father says she is, she won't dismiss that, regardless of what's happening in her head. The truth has started to open her eyes, and now it's your turn to finish."

She sounded so sure that he began to believe her until he talked himself out of it. "I can't imagine how I could help this situation at all. I'll just be a reminder of Sinow to her."

She shook her head. "You won't. Sinow is right; you're not here for him, Keary. You're here for her. Think about it. Who knows him best? Who is the best person to come to his defense? The best person to be his voice in a time when there's no possible way he could speak for himself? You're the one who needs to talk to her now. Not me. Not Sinow. You."

It was a crazy idea that had him scraping a hand through his hair in a move that reminded him too much of Sinow. But maybe it was worth a shot. He checked the time on his watch. It was now well after one in the morning. They had less than eleven hours to go. At this point, anything was worth trying.

"You're insane, you know that?" he said, smiling at her. He was glad to see that she was no longer letting the situation overwhelm her. When she was like this, she reminded him of her father. Maybe she wasn't Council, but having been raised by them, she had learned their ways.

Placing her hands on her hips, she tilted her head and waited for him to agree.

"All right. It's worth a shot. Hell, it can't hurt." He ran his hand over his face, the growth of stubble that had settled there over the past few days scratching his skin. When this was over, he needed a long, hot shower. He absently wondered if he should have taken one while he had been sitting around, contemplating the meaning of life earlier. If they ended up back in their world, he would kick himself for not taking one. If they ended up back without Violissa, it wouldn't matter.

---

KEARY WALKED up the stairs and over to Violissa's room. Violet's room. Not the room of a queen. Standing outside the door, memory took him back to the day when he'd confronted Sinow about his obsession with finding her. He had pushed his king to take this journey. It may have been unintentional, but it had been his words that had started Sinow on the path. He thought of all the people hidden in the Banished Realm, all those they'd been unable to save, and how much they had lost. The price had been high, and he didn't know if it would be worth it once this was over. He leaned his head against the door, listening to the silence from behind, and prayed it would be. Lifting his head, he brought his hand up and knocked.

"Go away, Paige," Violissa replied, her voice weak.

He turned the doorknob, surprised when the door opened. Walking into her room, he took in the scene that lay before him. Violissa sat huddled in a tight ball in the window seat, her head leaning against the window, eyes vacantly staring out at nothing but the blackness of the outside night. She had pulled her hair back in a loose braid. Strands had freed themselves in the time it had been up, and now they left a scene of beautiful chaos around her face and neck. She was the saddest creature, yet also the most captivating. Everything in him ached to take her pain away, to remove the sadness that seemed to have buried her.

He wondered how long she had been sitting there, wondered if it was the curse that had forced her there or if she had purposely locked herself away to protect herself from its destructive force.

"You know, Violissa, if you want to keep people out, it helps to lock the door."

"Go away, Keary," she replied, never moving her head from the window.

Her arms pulled her legs in tighter, and he noticed the tremble of her hand when she did. The curse had its claws in her, and having this view of its devastation was startling. If the curse had crippled her this much in every lifetime, it was no wonder Sinow hadn't been able to help her. She couldn't even pull herself out from under it. How had the Fates expected Sinow to save her?

"No, I won't go away, Violissa." He closed the door behind him and walked further into the room. It was dark except for the slight glow of the moon from beyond the window. From the looks of it, she had been sitting there for hours.

"Look, I don't know you, Violissa. All I know of you is from your time as Violet and what I've learned from your Council." She flinched at the mention of her Council, reaching her hands up and cradling her head, another internal battle waging in her. He bunched his fists, hating that he couldn't ease her pain. "I do, however, know Sinow."

She buried her head further in her arms. "Please, Keary," she murmured, defeat emphasized in each word.

"I've known him since we were kids. We grew up together, and he's like a brother to me. You see, I know everything there is to know about Sinow. That's why I know he loves you. He's loved you for as long as I can remember."

"He has an odd way of showing it," she snapped, her voice so different from how it had sounded moments ago.

"I can remember him telling me about the princess the Fates had destined him to marry from the time I met him, Violissa. You're the one constant he's always had other than the throne." She lifted her head and met his eyes. He had to keep himself from stepping back as black mist curled in the corner of them, ready to strike if she let herself get too close to the truth. A pained look crossed her features, the brightness in her eyes so dim that he could see it was taking all her effort to fight the war in her mind.

"I can't yet, Keary," she whispered. "I need time. Please leave." She dropped her head back down, hidden once again in the nook of her knees.

"Time is up, Violissa. He has no time left. You have no time left."

Her head shifted, and she rested her cheek on her knees, her face directed to the window. Pity filled him. She was clueless about what had taken place around her all these lifetimes. Left with no understanding that in hours she would forget everything, just as she always did. She and Sinow were pawns in the Fates' hands, and it angered him how they had to endure punishment for a mistake they'd made centuries before. Punishment at the expense of their people and their world.

"We're immortal, Keary. We have all the time in the world. He said he would wait..." Her voice drifted away, and he noticed her hands clench and her arms tighten around her legs. The curse was combatting her attempts to fight it. It would take mere minutes for her to turn, so he decided to be as direct as he could be. Otherwise, he would lose her.

"It's been a thousand years since the spell sent you here, Violissa. Sinow has been trying to find you since that day."

Head lifting, confusion filled her face. "No, it's been twenty-eight years, Keary. I've only been here that long."

He shook his head. "That's all you remember, Violissa. You've been here life after life, and he's been chasing you through each one, never able to break the spell you're under."

"The curse," she murmured.

The mist seeped into the whites of her eyes. It reacted not only to her thoughts but to things she said. He needed to keep her focused.

"You know about the curse?"

"It's inside me, wrapping around every cell, polluting every vein, encasing every organ. It fills my head with thoughts and voices. I see so many things. Pain, death." Her eyes were distant, staring at the floor as she spoke in a hushed tone.

Her sight jumped to him. With terror lacing those dim orbs, she whispered. "It's in my eyes."

Keary shook off the urge to back away more as the black seeped further.

"Why hasn't he come to help me?" The anguish in those words cut him, and he took a step closer, seeing tears well in her eyes just as the ebony spilled into them, leaving no discernible iris. Just as quickly, it retreated from the whites of her eyes, harboring only in her irises. Her eyes were as dark as Sinow's, and it took everything Keary had not to react.

"You lie," she snarled before he could even respond to her question. "This curse is from him. He is the one who did this to me. He is the one who hurt me." It was like another person controlled her. The curse was twisting every part of her.

*Fates, how am I supposed to fight this?* he thought as she crumpled back into her knees.

Fingers bound tight into fists, he fought the overwhelming defeat that threatened to drown him just as he imagined it had done to Sinow so many times. If he could just get through to her, it might give her a chance to fight back. All he needed was an opening. Something he knew would make her pause. Something that would get past the curse and remind her of how she and Sinow loved each other.

He exhaled, loosening his grip and rolling his neck to ease the tension. A small space remained at the end of the window seat, and he walked over to it. Violissa moved, only to squeeze her legs closer to her. Her head remained buried in them.

"Violissa, you know that's not true. Ignore the noise in your head and listen to what your heart is telling you."

"Go away, Keary." Her words were barely a whisper, as if she didn't dare even move her lips.

He leaned his head in his hands. This was futile. She didn't want to hear what he said, and even if she did, the curse would break her resolve in seconds. He looked at the door, considering whether leaving would be best, giving in like Sinow had. There was so much at stake if he did. He was a Darkbearer, not a weakling who tucked his tail between his legs and ran.

Turning back to Violissa, he studied her, remembering her in her former state: strong, bold, confident. A queen who held the power to send this world to its knees, just as his king had once held. It was time for him to remember who he was as well.

Advisor to the Dark King, chosen by the Fates, feared by the mortals.

Sitting taller, he brushed thoughts of acquiescing aside and said, "As the only Council here to advise you, Violissa, I won't leave. It is my job to help you, and you need help. Desperately." She peeked her eyes up at him, fear spilling over them. "All you need to do is sit here and listen to me. I know you're frightened, but it is imperative that you do. Take a few minutes to clear your head, to untangle yourself from the curse so you can hear me, Violissa, because what I have to say is of utmost importance. The fate of our world depends on you hearing this."

She dropped her head back onto her knees, not responding. He gave her the space, the silence, and remained where he was at the end of the seat. However long she needed, he would wait there with her. He was certain there were triggers to the curse. Sinow was a definite, but other parts of their past, her Council even, caused the curse to strike her.

He'd studied curses during his training but had never seen one in action. Botched magic, an error in casting, a spell cast but changed at the last moment, or two Darkbearers casting magic at once, with different intents that clashed. Any of those circumstances could create a curse. If the latter occurred, one spell would typically rebound against the other, but occasionally, they would connect, and their intent would warp. If the target were mortal, the curse would take hold and eventually mangle their minds. Mortals couldn't handle the force of a curse. If left uncontained, the person would attack anyone around them, killing them in unconscionable ways, the curse feeding their strength and their madness. Within days, the person would die, the curse having ravaged their mind, their body no longer functioning.

That Violissa had survived with the curse inside of her was a testament to her strength. Perhaps that was why her memory lay dormant for so long and why the Fates only gave Sinow a finite amount of time to save her. He suspected the Fates knew of the curse because anything past that finite time would surely destroy her completely.

They sat in silence, the minutes ticking by like hours, each one like the lifting of the executioner's axe. Time was not something they had, but it was what Violissa needed. Sweat dripped down his brow as tension lined his body. When he didn't think he could sit any longer, he noted the loosened grip of Violissa's hands. Her breathing calmed, and she shifted her cheek to her knees, eyes trained on the wall across from her.

He took it as a sign. Since the clock on her bedside table read four o'clock in the morning, he had no choice but to talk. There could be no more waiting.

"Violissa, I only need you to hear my words. Try not to move or to show any emotion. That might help." A slight nod of her head told him she understood.

"You've been gone for a thousand years." There was a quiet gasp, but no motion from her. "We tried everything to bring you back until Sinow made a deal with the Fates. He gave everything up to come here. Left it all behind and left it open for Tynan."

Her head lifted, crystal green eyes meeting his. The curse had left them and sat in the corners, coiled and ready to attack.

"Just listen," he said, hoping she could hold on a little longer.

She looked out the window, resting her forehead on it.

"He's been stuck here chasing you life after life, but he can't break the curse. You won't let him close enough."

"It's too strong," she mumbled.

"Yes. But this is his last chance, the last lifetime he has to break through. And if he doesn't, the Fates will send him back to our world and leave you here."

"Then he can take back the kingdoms and live out his life," she muttered, a distinct acidic tone in her voice.

"Really, Violissa? Think about what you just said. Is that really what you want? Think about who you are and everything you stand for. Think about the prophecy."

"I can't. It's better this way."

"Better for whom?" He ran his hands across his face, his frustration mounting. "Both of you are so stubborn," he griped, digging his fingers into the seat cushion. "If he goes back, he won't take back the kingdom, Violissa. Remember, I said he gave everything up for you. Everything. His crown, his power, his immortality."

Her gaze snapped to him. The black had filled her irises again, but there were tiny holes forming in it, small streams of emerald cascading out like the sun on a cloudy day.

*That's it, Violissa, fight.*

"But Tynan—"

"Will kill him. He'll kill him the second he returns to our world."

"No," she cried, bringing her hand to her mouth.

"You saw Tynan for who he was?"

"A snake in the grass of our garden," she whispered, drawing her knees closer.

She looked like a lost child, her sadness reflected for all the world to see. But just as he thought it, confusion creased her eyes. The black of the spell spilled over the pinpricks of green that had emerged. It was terrifying to witness how devastating the curse was, to watch it play out in the quick switches of her emotions.

"Why hasn't he come to me then? Why isn't he here saving me?" she hissed, scalding him with her words. "You lie, Keary. This is just another trick to torment me." She turned her head away from him, but he reached out and grabbed her chin, forcing her vision back.

"You don't believe that, Violissa. It's the curse talking, and you know it is. You recognize it for what it is. Don't let it corrupt all that you know to be true. You are out of time. Fight me all you want. Spit out the thoughts the curse is feeding you, but you will listen to me. Sinow is out of time, and so are you. There are only a few hours left before his chance is over. He won't come to you this time. He won't try to save you, and if you sit and wait for him, then we're all doomed." He released her chin, cringing when he saw how hard he had held it in his aggravation. "You need to fight with all your strength, bring him home, and take back our world. There is no other choice, no other path, but the one that leads to our extinction."

His words were harsh, but they held nothing but the truth. Without her and Sinow, the Councils would slowly die. There would be no heir to inherit the thrones of Cirillia and Tenebron. Tynan would break through the last standing barrier and execute everyone within it for treason. Those were the truths. He knew them as well as Sinow, but it was Violissa who needed to realize the true consequences of not fighting back.

Her eyes, dull green, searched his as if she sought a deeper understanding. To see what he saw. The shade darkened after a few moments, and she banged her head against the wall behind her. Tears welled, but she didn't wince in pain. It was likely a dull ache compared to what the curse was doing to her. Or maybe it helped to focus her clarity for just enough time to make a difference. He hoped it was the latter because his chance was gone. Her hands were now clenched so hard the tendons protruded from the strain as she dropped her head back to the window and closed her eyes.

He laid a hand on her knee and squeezed it gently before rising from the seat and saying, "You have the power to get through this, Violissa. Listen to your heart. Let it speak the truth in the sea of misconstrued images and thoughts you have. Your Council is alive, and they're awaiting your return. Your people wait for you, and the land waits for you. And I'm waiting to call you my queen. We're all waiting. The next move is yours."

He walked to the door, but just as he was about to cross the threshold, she called his name in a soft cry. He halted his steps and turned back to her, finding her in the same position.

"Yes, Violissa?"

"What does *Conimun fates an onumica e bianle limiusil* mean?"

His head snapped back. She remembered, and the hope that had slithered away returned. "It's ancient Tenebron, back from the first generation. It means, Fates protect the one I love."

She made no attempt to move or to respond, and so he let those words hang in the air as he walked out and closed the door behind him. Resting his head against the door, he considered her question. Those had been the words Sinow had yelled when casting his redirection spell that day. Keary had been there. He had shifted the moment he'd noticed the imbalance of power, shifted just in time to see Tynan cast his spell, then Sinow cast his. Violissa had disappeared within seconds. The image was still ingrained in his mind to this day.

She had remembered. Through the noise of the discord and turmoil in her head, she remembered those words.

Perhaps that was all she needed. To hear that Sinow had saved her that day. That those words had caused Tynan's spell to transform and save her. If it was enough, then she would go to Sinow and they would be home soon. He clung to that small glimmer of hope as he started down the stairs to return to his role as watcher, counting the minutes to the end. He would take even the smallest hope and hold tight to it because there was nothing left to hold on to.

# CHAPTER 54

After Keary left, Sinow sat for a long time thinking about all he had experienced and all he was about to lose. He missed home, missed Tenebron, missed everything about it. From the smell of the fresh, unpolluted air to the mountains that ran across the western lands, untouched and pure, to the fields that filled the more southern villages, even to the expanse of the Sacred Groves that bordered Cirillia. He was ready to leave this world and go back.

There was no hiding from what faced him—the damage he'd caused by coming here, the loss of so much life that rested on his shoulders, or the consequences of his decision to go after Violissa.

He rested his elbows on his thighs. Tynan would kill him. That much was assured, especially after what he'd learned about Tynan. The ruthless bastard he'd become. There was no assurance it would be a quick death, but he knew Violissa's face would be the last image he'd see. He prayed the Fates would have mercy on him in death and let his soul be at peace until Violissa returned to them.

Even if they did, there was no certainty he and Violissa would be together after death. Violissa's immortality was still intact. He, however, would die a mortal. His soul would become one with the breeze, just as it was with all mortals. There would be no place among the stars, no offer to take his place with the few immortals whom the Fates blessed to join them in death. So, no, he was unlikely to spend his afterlife with Violissa.

He rested his head in his hands as images of Violissa throughout their lifetimes flooded his mind. Violet, as she was called in every life. Violet and Simon. He remembered the first day of his descent into this hell. His first day as a human boy, the farmer naming him Simon as his memories slipped away so much that even his name escaped him. He had tried to hold on to Violissa's name, her face, her scent, as long as he could, but the Fates had ensured it was not to be. They hadn't taken his dreams, though. She'd filled them each lifetime. There had never been a life where he hadn't searched for her, where she hadn't filled every corner of his subconscious, even without his memories.

The Fates had done their job too well, his soul so entwined with hers that they moved as one, even if Violissa couldn't see that. Even though the spell she was under manipulated every part of her mind, he knew she belonged to him. In every lifetime, her final breath had been her moment of clarity. He had felt her each time, sensed her searching for him as their souls passed by, filling yet another human vessel.

Fingers scraping through his hair, he rose, tired of waiting for what would never come. Tired of waiting for her. The moon shone brightly over the streets as he walked through town, avoiding the street where her house sat, not wanting to give in to the temptation of trying one last time and receiving another gut-wrenching rejection. It was too late for anyone to be on the streets, which left him in solitary, giving him time to think.

His hands squeezed in and out, the reminder of what he had lost a constant in the power that didn't heed his call. Moonlight spilled across the grove where Violet had taken Simon.

Taking a seat where they had once sat, unaware of their identities, and discussing star-crossed love, he mused about how familiar the space seemed. So similar to the meeting grove where their love had blossomed. Thinking of it left a melancholy he couldn't escape, no matter how he rubbed at his chest to remove it.

He gazed up at the sky, watching the stars and wondering if their world was up there somewhere or in another universe. Not that it mattered. If he returned without Violissa, he would never have the chance to seek her out again.

As the night waned, he walked back, resigned to sit and wait for his judgment to arrive. The clock struck six. The morning light slid through his balcony, and he kneaded his fingers, knowing only a few hours remained.

Noon. Such an odd time to always reset their lives. Midnight would have been more menacing and certainly more appropriate. Perhaps the Fates felt it was too cliché. He laughed, laying back on the sofa and throwing his arm over his forehead. Staring at the ceiling, exhaustion crept into his bones, causing his eyes to grow heavy before they finally closed.

*A warm breeze tickled his face, carrying the scent of lilac. Sinow glanced around the field where he stood, brows creasing as he tried to remember how he had gotten there. Patting his chest, he looked down to see the clothes he'd worn when he'd fallen asleep. The Dream Realm? No, it couldn't be. There was no magic in this world to bring him there.*

*The scent of lilac grew stronger, and he shifted his sight to find Violissa sitting with her knees drawn up, her chin resting upon them as she overlooked a ravine. Across from her was a wasteland of flames and smoke.*

*"Where are we?" he asked, taking a seat beside her.*

*"The Dream Realm," she said, her voice like music to his ears. "I think that's home." She pointed across the flames that licked the sky.*

*"Did we do that?" he asked, not sure why when he knew the answer.*

*"I don't think it's done yet. This is my dream, and my fears overshadow it."*

*Silence sat between them. Comfortable as two old friends might sit, the silence a bond between them. He breathed in her scent, relishing the lilac. A calm overcame him and, for the first time in centuries, a sense of peace.*

*"I want to go home, Sinow." The anguish in those words shredded him.*

*His reply was honest. "I've tried to take you home, Vi. You won't let me."*

*She tipped her face to him, a tear slipping down her cheek before she reached over and touched his face. "I can't. The curse is too strong. My mind and body are too weak for it." She traced his jaw, and he leaned into the touch, wishing for more of it. "I need you to guide me home, Sinow."*

*With a heavy sigh, he looked away from her, knowing he couldn't give her what she wanted. Not this time. "I'm tired, Violissa. Tired of the human world, tired of living so many mortal lives, tired of fighting you. I'm tired of losing you. It's time for me to return home."*

*"Without me?" she asked, her voice distant.*

*"If you force me to, then yes."*

*"But you came to rescue me."*

*"I don't know if that's the case anymore, Vi. Maybe that's not why the Fates sent me here. Maybe you're the only one who can rescue you." The power of that statement settled over him, coursing through his cells in affirmation. All this time, he had fought for her when it was really she who needed to fight. She was the only one who could break the curse and escape the prison that held her.*

*He looked at the plumes of black smoke that were now overtaking the flames in the distance. Had their world really come to this, or was she correct that it was only a potential future?*

*"Don't leave me," she whispered, his heart shattering into splinters.*

*Turning back to her, he tilted her face and looked into her eyes. They shone a light jade, tears making them sparkle, but the sadness in them was palpable. She waited for his answer, but it was one he knew she wasn't looking for. Moving her loose curl back, he caressed her cheek with gentle fingers.*

*"You are so much stronger than you think, Violissa. Only you have the power to beat this thing and bring us home. Together."*

*"I'm scared, Sinow, it hurts too much," she said, sounding like a frightened child.*

*"Not as much as it will hurt to lose you one last time, Vi."*

*Black smoke drifted across his hand as the tears fell from her eyes. The smoke swirled around her, and he lowered his hand, knowing the dream was ending. It closed in on her. The curse. Even in her dreams, it held her hostage.*

*"I need you, Sinow," she pleaded, reaching her hand out to his arm and clinging to it.*

*"Then find me, Vi. Find me, and I'll take you home. I promise you."*

*The black smoke totally encased her, and she was gone, the weight of her hand on his arm disappearing along with the smoke. Her absence left a ragged hole in his body that he knew would remain until the moment Tynan took his life. Standing, he gazed across the now smokeless land, the ground charred and black. A glimmer shone beyond the horizon. Light in the darkness. Hope. It was all he had to hold on to as everything went dark.*

The ceiling of Simon's apartment came into focus when Sinow opened his eyes. He blinked against the light, memories of his dream returning to him. Sitting up, he rubbed his eyes and stretched, wondering when he'd fallen asleep.

The scent of lilac lingered on his skin. Had it been a shared dream? Or had she somehow pulled him into hers? It didn't really matter at this point. She had been there, devastatingly beautiful and heartbreaking at once. The sensation of her touch on his cheek remained, and he brought his hand to it, savoring it. The clock across the room clicked, and he glanced up to find that it was now eleven. One hour until this was over.

He had expected to have more emotion about it, but he was numb. The dream with Violissa had given him insight into her situation, and he didn't know if she had the strength to fight the curse. She'd looked so broken.

Running his hand down his face, he rose, noticing the lilac had faded. The last tie he had to her was gone. He made his way into the bedroom, knowing he needed to wake and clear his head. If Tynan truly was as insane as Keary said, then he would need his wits about him when he finally returned to Tenebron.

Reaching into the shower, he started the water. Thoughts of Violissa needed to be far from him when he faced Tynan. Only in his last moments would he indulge in thinking about her.

With only an hour left, there was no chance of her coming to him. The dream had given him hope, but hope had failed him once again.

As the water warmed, he pondered if he would miss this world. He doubted he would have time to contemplate it again before Tynan killed him, but if he did, there wasn't much to miss. It was so different from home. Too busy, too hectic, too overpopulated. Backwards in many ways from this world, Tenebron had more to offer with its untouched countrysides, unclimbed mountains, and unpolluted oceans. It held freshness he suspected this world had once held before technology and greed took command.

He stepped into the shower and held his head under the water, letting it cascade down his face. Showers were certainly something he would miss. Why hadn't they created showers in their world? It was such a difference from the baths they used at home.

Closing his eyes, he tried to push aside the thoughts of what he would face when the Fates returned him to Tenebron. Instead, his mind flooded with images of Violissa. Even after all this time, he loved her. If anything, through all his strife, that love had grown. It went beyond the lust he had experienced when he first met her and far past the love he'd recognized the day she brought him from under the Darkness. Now it was an endless well of emotion that set his body on fire and had his heart pushing against the confines of his chest to meet its other half. A half it would never bond with after today.

A stabbing sensation throbbed in his core, a recognition that he was losing everything, including the most important part of his life.

It would be over soon, and he would finally be at peace. As long as Tynan granted him a quick death. Nothing his brother did to him could compare to the agony of losing Violissa again. He knew pain, and nothing matched it.

Sinow leaned his head against the shower tile and let the water hit his back. His brother held their world hostage, and he could do nothing to stop him. Nothing but offer himself up for slaughter, an offer Tynan would gladly accept and kill him the minute he returned.

A muted sound caught his attention, and he opened his eyes, listening for it. Nothing but the sound of the water filled the room. Perhaps it had been his imagination, the stress making its way into his subconscious. He turned the water off and grabbed a towel. As he toweled his wet hair, he heard it again. This time, it was a soft knock on his door. One, two, three knocks, light and barely audible, as if the hand making the sound wasn't sure it even wanted to knock.

Keary? No, he and Keary had said their goodbyes the prior night after Keary had made his final pleas to change Sinow's mind.

He had the temptation to ignore the knock, but something nagged at him to answer. Pulling on a pair of pants and grabbing a shirt, he walked toward the door. His shirt still in hand, he paused momentarily to consider walking away before turning the knob and pulling the door open.

# CHAPTER 55

Violissa woke with a start, her eyes darting around the room. She was back in Violet's bedroom. The sun shone through the window, hurting her eyes with its brightness. She had sat fighting the curse for a long while after Keary left. His words had repeated in her mind, stirring the curse so that a battle had ensued each time she considered them.

At some point she must have drifted off, still curled in the same corner of the window seat.

The dream. Had it been a dream? Sinow had been there. Excitement flittered in her stomach, her heart sputtering back to life until the spell slammed back into her. She held her head in agony, fighting the pain. The negative thoughts and memories flooded her mind as she tried to hold on to the sensation of his touch. But the spell dug its claws into her, and she whimpered, rolling into a ball.

She had asked Sinow to save her from this, but he had told her he couldn't. Had said she needed to free herself, but that seemed impossible. Even the thought sent a jarring bolt of pain through her temple. She had to quiet her mind again; it was the only time she had peace.

Starting with thoughts of Sinow and the dream, she strategically shut her mind down. Clamping it closed like a vault. The dark thoughts quieted, taking the pain with them. Eyes opening, she stayed within the calm, avoiding setting the chaos free. That was the trick. To lock the emotions and thoughts of Sinow behind a wall and leave nothing for the curse to feed upon. As long as it stayed dormant, she had control.

Gingerly, she stood, slipping her feet into a pair of shoes before leaving the room in minuscule steps, too frightened of waking the spell to move too fast. This was risky, going beyond the sanctuary she had defined that first day. But after her dream, she had no choice. Their world was crumbling, and Sinow was waiting for her.

A snap of awareness had the curse encroaching, and she chastised herself for thinking of Sinow. She cleared her mind again, donning a neutral face and continuing to take small steps. When she came to the bottom of the stairs, she heard a gasp. Stepping toward the kitchen, she spied Keary and Paige. Keary shot to his feet, his chair tumbling behind him. Paige, who had been pacing, froze in place. Both stared slack-jawed at her.

"Violissa?" he asked, his earthy eyes wide with disbelief.

"If I don't think about it, I can move," she mumbled. Her eyes flicked to the microwave clock. "How much time do I have?"

Keary shook his head. "Very little, maybe forty minutes."

She let out a ragged cry before clamping her teeth down. Gathering herself, she said. "I need...I need to go."

Knowing she had no choice but to run, she turned and fled, keeping her mind empty of her task and her destination. Trying to trick the curse and buy herself the time she needed to make it to Sinow. Tremors of anticipation skittered through her, and she could sense the spell unfurling with each one. Her mind needed to stay empty, and so she repeated the word 'empty' over and over, focusing only on it until she reached the apartment.

Taking the steps two by two, she raced to his door, raised her hand, and knocked. Her heart pounded erratically, and her breathing had become shallow tugs of air that didn't seem to reach her lungs. The curse inched closer, whispering in the distance, and it tempted her to walk away when there was no answer. But he had to be home, and if what Keary said was true, then he was inside waiting for death.

A scrape of pain knotted in her stomach, but she wouldn't let the curse win. It dug into her mind, sending its whispers with more fury, and she knew her time was running out just as quickly as Sinow's. Distraught, she brought her quaking hand back up and rapped on the door one last time.

# CHAPTER 56

Hesitation left his hand lingering just above the doorknob, and Simon wasn't sure he wanted to deal with whatever awaited him on the other side of the door. An inkling pestered him, urging him to open it, going against his rational thought to ignore the knock. A third one had not come, so perhaps it wasn't important. He dropped his hand and turned around, intent on spending his last minutes with a watered-down beer and a spot in his chair. That nudging in the back of his mind grew, and he swiveled back to the door. If there was anything he had learned over the years, it was to trust his instincts even if he lived in facts and proof. Instinct was Violissa's dependency, but he was starting to appreciate it.

He reached back to the door and opened it, spotting Violissa walking away. Pulse racing, he watched as she stopped and turned toward him. She was breathtaking with her golden hair in a loose braid, strands scattered wildly about her cheeks and neck. The one curl he loved so much brushed her eye, and she absently pushed it aside. Her green eyes were bright, but lacked the true brilliance that came with her power. Within them sat the black shadow of the curse. It had leaked into the white of her eyes in branches that looked ready to take root in her irises.

It struck him that it had been there in every lifetime, but he'd never truly understood what it was and how it had been polluting her mind all these centuries. With her hands fisted in tight balls, her eyes searched his in desperation. A flicker of pain passed through her features. She was fighting the curse, and he had every desire to run to her and sweep her into his arms to protect her. But that would only send the curse into a frenzy and her running. She already looked like a cornered mouse ready to flee its predator.

Never had she come to him, but there she was.

"Vi?" he said, as softly as possible so as not to frighten her.

She rubbed her nose with the back of her hand, nervously shuffling her feet. "I...I thought you might not be home."

Home? She'd been human too long if she considered this his home.

"I was in the shower. I didn't hear you," he returned, wondering where his senses had fled to. He sounded like a bumbling idiot, not a king who had mere minutes to convince his queen that he loved her.

Her eyes flicked to his chest, and he realized he was still holding the shirt he'd grabbed. When they met his gaze, her heartbeat stopped for those few precious beats as it did every time she looked at him.

"Did you come for a reason, Violissa?" he asked, needing to hear that she had come for him.

She sucked in a breath and nodded. The branches of ebony spread closer to her green irises, and she closed her eyes, placing the heel of her hand against her forehead.

"Stop," she muttered, almost crying the word.

If this was what she'd been fighting all these lifetimes, if the torment had been this bad every time they'd awakened, then it was no wonder she had run from him. He loathed the idea that he was the cause of her pain and fought the need to step closer to her. This was her battle, and he would only ruin things if he did.

Her hand lowered, but the shaking was clear. She met his gaze again, a look of determination crossing her eyes. "I need to ask you something."

"Anything," he blurted. Anything she wanted, as long as it meant she wouldn't leave him again.

The intensity of her emerald orbs burned deep into his core. Nervously chewing her lip, she hesitated, silence hanging like a thick fog between them until she finally asked, "Do you love me?"

He reeled back, ire stirring in his belly. The insinuation that she doubted his love for her slashed him, fracturing what remained of the heart she'd done nothing but destroy life after life. Maybe he should have replied with an immediate yes and told her the words she wanted to hear, confessing his love for her, but what he should have done was not what he did.

"How can you even ask that? After all this time?" he spat. The words tumbled out, encouraged by the agony he'd suffered with each rejection and the centuries of living with that rejection. He'd lived life after life of her turning him away, of quietly suffering, then starting over to experience it again and again. The one question she shouldn't have dared ask him was the one question she asked.

She backed away, the streaks of ebony lurching into the rest of her eyes.

"I shouldn't have come," she muttered. "This was wrong. I knew the answer, and I shouldn't have come." She turned and ran from him.

"Violissa!" he shouted after her, only then seeing what he'd done. But she was gone, the door to the stairwell slamming closed behind her fleeing form. He punched the wall, roaring. Paint and drywall flew around him, leaving a gaping hole where his fist had gone.

It was only then that he noticed Keary and Paige in his periphery, standing near the elevator. Paige's mouth hung open in shock. Keary simply looked pissed.

"What in the Fates are you thinking? Have you gone mad?" Keary bellowed.

He wasn't in the mood, so he growled, "Leave it be, Keary. She shouldn't have asked. She knows the answer, and it's insulting that she even asked." He doubted the words as they spilled out, but the damage was done.

"Are you kidding me? Did you ever tell her?" Paige stepped forward, stopping when he met her eyes. He sensed the fear pass through her, but she held her ground. She was either brave or stupid for daring to question him.

"You don't know us, so stay out of this. You don't know anything about this," he spat, expecting her to back away. She didn't even flinch.

"You're right. I don't know either of you," she said, holding her head high as she confronted him. "But I know enough to see that it took every ounce of strength she had left to come to you. An unseen enemy has taken over her, morphing everything she knows and ravaging her mind and body. She didn't come here to insult your pride. What she wanted was an affirmation from you that the memories and emotions she's fighting to hold on to are real. She came here for you to tell her you love her and that you'll be by her side while she fights the beast inside of her that is telling her you used and lied to her."

So, Paige was braver than she looked. And she was right. This moment was the one he'd waited for all these centuries, and he'd thrown it back in Violissa's face when she had finally given it to him. He tore his hands through his hair, seeing what a fool he'd been for letting his emotions get the best of him.

"Go after her," Keary said.

Sinow locked eyes with him and gave him a nod before tearing through the hall and down the stairs. Searching for Violissa and praying he wasn't too late.

# CHAPTER 57

Her feet pounded on the pavement as Violissa ran as hard as she could. Ran past people she'd known as Violet for years who tried to stop her out of concern. Ran past the places she'd gone as Violet, down the streets she'd walked. All the while, tears streamed down her face. She didn't know where she was heading; all she knew was that if she stopped, everything would come crumbling down on her. She was running from the curse that was tearing through her head as much as she was running from Sinow.

She'd been so sure that the curse had distorted her memories. But now, doubt had crept back in. It had been foolish to approach him, foolish to ask. His answer hadn't been the one she expected, but then maybe Keary had lied to her as well. Both working to tear her apart again. An emotional game to drive her to madness until they put her out of her misery. Getting off on seeing her suffer. It sounded just like something a Dark King would do.

The voices battered her mind as she ran, convincing her she'd been nothing more than a pawn they were playing with.

She wanted to stop running, to have the voices stop screaming in her head, the pain to stop slashing its talons through her, the memories to stop flashing through her vision. Exhausted and defeated, she continued to run, even when all she desired was to drop to the ground and crawl into a ball and cry for days.

"Violissa!" Her name was a faint call, but she recognized Sinow's voice. She hesitated, slowing down. Had he come after her? No, he was still toying with her. She picked up her pace again.

"Violissa, please stop running and listen to me." The tone of his voice was demanding, which should have irked her, but for the hint of desperation below it. She stopped and rested her hands on her knees to catch her breath before turning back to face him. The curse battered her body, and she stumbled before catching her balance. Sinow was jogging toward her. Fates, he was beautiful. His shirt was on, but that didn't make him any less attractive, especially with the ripple of muscle below it. His thick ebony hair had slipped further onto his forehead, and she wanted so badly to walk up to him and run her hand through it.

The warped memories rushed forward, drowning out her thoughts, and she closed her eyes, trying to fight them away. Since she'd knocked on his door, the curse had only grown worse. It took all her effort not to collapse.

Eyes opening, she saw him pull up short, keeping a distance between them. Concern creased his brow.

"By the Fates, you run fast," he complained before he scraped his hand through his hair. His brown eyes evaluated her, drawing her into their darkness. "You asked me a question I refused to answer. I should have answered you, but I couldn't."

Not needing to hear any more, she turned from him. His hand wrapped around her arm, forcing her back, and her body became a war zone. Between the sharp currents that warmed her body and the barrage of angry stings from the curse, she could barely catch her breath.

Too keen on her emotions, he dropped her arm and took a step back from her. "Would you wait just a second and let me finish for once?"

His eyes held a plea she couldn't deny, so she gave him a nod. Wrapping her arms around her middle for support, she listened.

"This is going to make me sound like one of your Lightbearers, but since you insist on asking me something I thought you already knew, I will tolerate it." She wanted to tell him those words didn't make her care to listen more, but she bit her tongue. Her body began to shake, starting in her toes and making its way to her head, and an icy chill settled in her bones. The curse was changing tactics, and she feared what would come next.

He palmed his neck and dropped his eyes. "I guess I've never said those words to you. Simon told Violet, but I never did. There was so much that kept me from those words when we were young, and since then, well..."

He peeked back up at her, his eyes the soft shade of tilled ground. "Those words don't come close to expressing the emotions I carry for you. You asked if I love you. And I do. I always have. There isn't a thing about you I don't love. I love the way your brow creases when you're confused and how you chew on your bottom lip when you're nervous. That you have one curl that refuses to conform to the rest of your hair and instead hangs free as if it's waiting for me to wrap my finger around it."

He took a step closer, and the curse lunged, forcing its way through her limbs. "I love how your eyes are the deepest green of any ocean when you're angry, so dark they could almost match mine, but when you're happy," he paused and smiled at her, "they're a brighter green than any emerald this land has ever seen. I love that when you sing, your voice wraps itself around me as if there's no one else but me who's hearing it, and I hate how when you stop, there's an emptiness that wasn't there before. And that even after all this time, your heart stops and skips three beats every time our eyes meet and that I count each lost beat. I love that the room fills with the scent of lilac even as you approach it, and how that scent clings to the room, my clothes, my skin long after you've left."

He dropped his arm, his throat bobbing. "You see, Violissa, I love everything about you, from your stubborn side to your overly emotional side. I have chased you through lifetimes, and I will continue to chase you if that's what you need to see that I've loved you since the moment I was born, and I will love you long after I've returned to the Fates."

Her chest burned from the breath she was holding, and she exhaled. Tears spilled over her eyes, and she couldn't grasp the words to respond. He loved her, loved her more than she could ever have imagined. Her mouth wouldn't open; her mind couldn't focus. The curse had struck while she'd listened, slinking further in so that it now controlled her functioning.

Sighing, he said, "Now you know." And she saw then that he was reading her silence wrong, but the curse held her prisoner in a cage she couldn't break open. "The only solace in this is that soon, you'll forget it all. I'll be gone, and I'll no longer be here to torment you as I have all these lifetimes." Hurt shadowed his eyes, but he forced a sad smile. "You'll never have to suffer again. Goodbye, Violissa."

Before she could respond, he was walking away. She screamed inside her head for him to come back. He loved her as deeply as she loved him. And she loved him. She knew that with every fiber of her being. None of the memories were true. Opening herself to the truth awakened memories and emotions that had remained hidden. But the revelation only caused the curse to make its final stand. Paralyzed by pain, she watched him walk away, knowing this would be the last time she would ever see him, their last chance.

Dark images and thoughts crashed through the awakened memories, invading them and warping them to fit the curse's agenda. She remained frozen, an internal battle raging inside of her that no one could see. The harder she fought, the worse it became. She was so tired of fighting it. A tear rolled down her cheek, but she couldn't move to wipe it away. Sinow was leaving her, not understanding how badly she needed his help as she fought to stay afloat.

But he had told her he wouldn't help her. That this wasn't his fight. It was hers, and she alone had to break the curse. But how? Keary had said it had been a thousand years since the spell had sent her there. A thousand years of trying to fight her way out from under its grip. Maybe that was why she'd always failed. She needed to stop fighting, just as Sinow had to embrace the darkest side of his powers to finally be at peace. Maybe she needed to accept the spell, let it overtake her, and stop fighting this one time.

Trepidation had her questioning herself. If she was wrong, she would drown beneath the weight of the curse, and Sinow would never realize what had happened. And she was certain that if she did drown, he was the only one who could save her.

Urgency driving her to fight back once more, she rasped, "Will you pull me back out if I drown?"

She didn't hear his answer, didn't know if he'd heard her. The force of the curse was too strong, and for the first time in centuries, she stopped fighting the unseen beast that was so intent on destroying her. It weaved itself around every cell, slashed into every vein. It seized her lungs, infected mind, stymied the rush of her blood, and slunk through the chambers of her heart. Darkness swallowed her, and she was falling, submerged in a sea of black. She'd been wrong. There was no battling this. It had control of her, and this time she would lose.

***

*THEY WERE IN THE MEADOW, her Council on their knees. The day was overcast with ominous clouds that reached down to blanket the land in night. Powers bound, she watched helplessly as Tynan's spell hurled toward them. Laughter that didn't fit such a dark moment came from him and Sinow. She looked back to meet Sinow's black eyes. His laughter ceased as his face turned to a scowl.*

*"I've always hated you,"* he snarled, lifting his hand, his magic coiling around his fingers like black snakes.

*"Then get rid of her." Tynan's sneer made her step back.*

*Sinow let his magic roll between his fingers before he cast it at her. She reached her hands up in defense, but it was too late. Fire burned through her, and she gasped for air before everything went dark.*

Hard ground and murmuring. Violissa blinked away the memory, her body now in a ball on the ground, dampness on her cheeks. The memory was so raw, like it had just happened, and a cry rattled from her right before the curse tugged her under again.

*Her dress dragged behind her, soaking in the bloody field. Bodies surrounded her, their lifeless eyes staring at her. Condemning her.*

*"You let him do this to us," they seemed to say.*

*Tears streamed down her face. With each step, she sank further into the blood.*

*A child's body, his mother's arms holding him in a futile attempt to save him. A young man, not over twenty years, his eyes open in horror, his hand still outstretched as he pleaded for mercy. Body after body brought anguish that fragmented her heart. She let out a ragged scream, dropping to her knees. Across from her, Sinow pulled his hood down, his lethal eyes so black they were endless voids.*

Another gasp and Violissa sensed Sinow's presence. Not like it had been in the memory, but gentle. She stared ahead, fighting for survival and clinging to the scent of ash and home. His voice. She could hear it in the distance, too low as the curse enveloped her vision, submerging her into another memory. Barely holding on, she whimpered, the strands of her sanity unraveling the further into her past it plunged her.

# CHAPTER 58

The lack of reaction to his confession had been like a smack of dull magic mutilating Sinow's insides. He had given Violissa everything, and in return, she had stayed silent. Hope dashed, he had walked away with every intention of passing the next few minutes alone until he faced his death.

But he'd been wrong in assuming her silence was her refusal. Now as he held her, watching her flutter in and out of consciousness, seeing the full force of the curse spreading in lines through her body after turning her eyes black, he understood that she'd been unable to respond. The curse had taken control. Its final attack too devastating for her to stop.

"Will you pull me back if I drown?" she had said before collapsing.

He would. Every time, no matter what had happened between them. But he didn't know how to bring her out of this and didn't think it was his battle to win. She whimpered, tears sliding down her cheeks, and a sense of utter helplessness overcame him. She was so pale, and blood trickled through her fingers where she had gouged her nails into her palms when she'd listened to him. All the while fighting an unseen monster. He'd been so blind to it, making assumptions and walking away from her.

He had turned back at her words and only then had he seen the truth and understood what she was doing. Inviting the beast in fully and trusting that he would bring her out from under its hold. He had screamed her name as he'd run to her, catching her just before her body landed on the sidewalk.

"What's happening?" Paige asked.

He sensed her and Keary behind him as he brushed the hair from Violissa's face, hating the anguish that hazed her features, the ebony tendrils that lined her delicate skin.

"Sinow?" Keary asked when he didn't answer. He moved across from Sinow and stooped, his eyes creased with worry.

"She's trying to break the curse by letting it overtake her."

Keary's eyes jumped to his. "Is she mad? It will kill her. Two spells from powerful wielders formed that curse. Tynan's spell was Dark magic that we don't even understand. The only reason she's still alive is because your spell collided with it."

Sinow leaned over her, close enough to hear her strained breathing. "I know, but I don't know how to fight magic I don't recognize." Tynan's spell continued to confound him. It was old magic, the kind Sinow had never seen. "I don't know that there's anything we can do now that she's stopped fighting it."

"But if we do nothing?" Paige asked, coming beside Keary.

Violissa's eyes flickered open, her hand clutching his shirt just before she went under again. "It will drown her piece by piece until it has devoured every part of her and nothing remains."

"Unless the clock strikes noon?"

His eyes shot to her. He had forgotten the time, forgotten the fate that awaited him. Caressing his fingers over Violissa's cheek, he watched her eyes flutter below their lids. Strain emphasized the circles under her eyes, and he wondered how long it had been since she'd slept more than the few minutes she had dreamed.

There was no way he was leaving her like this. The Fates would have to pry his fingers from her before he left her suffering. He leaned close to her ear. "Vi, if you can hear me, you need to fight back again. What you're doing won't work. The magic that formed the curse is too strong. Tynan's magic has an unknown source, and my spell came from the depths of my core."

His spell. He remembered casting it, not knowing what he was doing but desperate to stop Tynan's spell. The words had come to him as if they'd always been there, but it was a spell he had never known before that day. Mixed with panic and the fear of losing her, his love for her had encased it.

"This isn't good, this isn't good," Paige mumbled, disrupting his thoughts. "We have no time left. Oh God, what are we going to do?"

"Keary, keep her quiet before I'm forced to, and remind her who it is we worship in our world," he snarled.

His focus returned to Violissa, who was trembling in his arms. What had he been thinking about? His counterspell and how it had woven around Tynan's? That was it, and that was the key. He pulled Violissa into his chest, burying his face in her hair. Lilac infused with a summer storm.

"Listen to me, Vi. Find the edge of my redirection spell. Find it and grab it. Let it help pull you back. Find it, Vi. My magic was protection. Use it to break through the curse. Separate it from Tynan's spell. The two connected to send you here, and the curse formed when they did, but you should still be able to detect the two layers of magic that created it. Find my piece and let it bring you back to me."

It was the only hope he had left, and he would cling to it until his time was up.

# CHAPTER 59

Something caused Violissa to wake. Alarms and a sense of danger. Sinow was there in her room. She sat up and scooted back in her bed. Anger twisted his features and pulsed through the room, coating her skin with singeing heat. She pulled the blanket up to her chin, defenseless to stop him.

"My, my, Violissa. What a convenient position I've found you in."

"Get out of my room." Fear held her captive, but something gnawed at her. Fear? She had never feared him.

An agonizing, scalding flame came from his hands, burning her skin, and the fear returned.

"What do you want?" she asked, her voice unsteady.

"You. But since you won't appease me, I'll start with war. I will tear the boundary down and slaughter your people as revenge for refusing my hand."

Hand? That didn't sound right. She tilted her head. Prophecy. That's what drove them, not a negated marriage proposal. Before she could think more, he grabbed her by the shoulders and ripped her from the bed. Terror consumed her as black tendrils escaped his body and surrounded her.

*"The spell...two layers...find my piece." Sinow's voice, but the words hadn't come from him. It came from somewhere outside, but outside of what? The pressure of his hands dimmed, his body flickering.*

*The curse. This was another memory, but it wasn't right. None of them were.*

*He smacked her so hard she fell from his hold, and she crawled away. The spell...two layers...find my piece. What had that meant, and where had it come from?*

*"You will suffer, Violissa, for all you have done." He grabbed her by the hair and threw her across the room.*

A solid hold on her body, the scent of ash and oak, calming yet determined words.

"Violissa, fight your way out."

It had only been another twisted memory. Her Sinow would never hurt her like that, even under the influence of his Darkness.

Another memory slammed into her like a wave crashing down over her head.

*They were in the meadow again, her Council gone. Tynan laughing. She knew what the curse would show her. Exactly what it had the last time and all the times before. This time, she had Sinow's words to cling to. Find his piece.*

*Tynan said something about hurting her, but she ignored him this time, instead focusing on other parts of the memory. Two pieces. The curse contained two spells. She saw Tynan raise his hand as Sinow did, drawing his magic.*

*Sinow. He was the key to the memory. She studied him, seeing his expression flicker from anger to panic. Concentrating on the panic, she saw his features shift. His eyes were wide with fear, confusion reflected in his pinched eyes. Emotions the curse could no longer hide from her now that she'd uncovered them.*

*She glanced at Tynan but saw nothing of the same. Only excitement that glimmered in his eyes. His spell left his hands, and she looked over at Sinow. Everything slowed, and she saw it then, the terror in his eyes, the way his hand reached toward the spell right before he threw his own after it. Heard the words he had said. He had been trying to redirect Tynan's spell. She saw that now.*

*The two spells clashed, and she watched as they sparred, spying the two unique magic patterns. Tynan's was menacingly black with angry red lines flickering through it. Sinow's was gray, safe and protective. She could almost see the love it held, the determination to save her. It wrapped around Tynan's spell, but there had not been enough time to stop it completely. That was why the spell had sent her there. It had been a mix of two incomplete spells, warped with two distinctly different intents. Sinow's spell had protected her, had saved her life, but then life after life it had helped her stay sane, helped her fight Tynan's spell, fight the curse it had become. The combined spell hit her, and the curse shoved her into another memory.*

This time, she went in prepared. She invited each memory, the curse all too happy to provide them, but in each, she saw the hues that defined fact from reality. Spotted the subtle shifts of gray in each vision and clung to them, changing the narrative to the true one.

The curse was losing its force with each memory she reconstructed. And as it submerged her back into the field with Tynan and Sinow, she found the undertones in Sinow's spell, latching onto the gray and transforming the memory completely. As it faded, a small shaft of light appeared in its place. She was breaking through.

The memories continued, round and round, repeating as she pieced each together with the hue of Sinow's magic, weaving the gray as she slowly surfaced. Between the pain that immobilized her, the voices that continued their assault, and the memories, she didn't think she would make it out in time. Reworking another memory, she prepared for another fight and prayed she could find her way back to Sinow before their time was up.

# CHAPTER 60

Through lifetimes, Sinow had wished for time to move faster so he could begin his next life. This was the first time he wanted it to slow down. They were almost out of time, and with every passing minute Violissa lay unresponsive in his arms, he could do nothing to stop it from passing by.

Paige had gone quiet, her body slumping against Keary's as they looked down on Sinow. No one disturbed them, a blessing he didn't question but for which he was thankful. Having to deal with nosy townspeople would have put him even further over the edge. He was barely hanging on as it stood.

Violissa's skin had grown pallid, and he worried she wouldn't make it. That he would lose her after all this time, when he was so close to finally having her. He dropped his head to her chest, clinging to the faint rise and fall of her breath and knowing she was in there, finding her way back.

"Please, Vi." His voice cracked, the emotion taking its toll, wearing down his defenses, breaking him.

She drew in a loud gulp of air, and his head flew up. Color returned to her face as the ebony strands receded from under her skin. Her breathing calmed. Bright emerald eyes blinked back at him. Relief swelled in him, and he brought his hand to her cheek, stroking it with the back of his fingers. She was back, and as the last of the curse fled her eyes, he knew she had won the battle.

Her hand rose, the trembling gone as it rested on his jaw. A smile tugged at her lips as she said, "I remember you." The words came out softly, like she feared the curse would return if spoken too loud. "I remember everything. The good and the bad. All of it. Every lifetime, every death." She paused, her smile dimming. "I remember everything I said and did to you."

Tears filled her eyes, and she pushed herself up to a sitting position, forcing him to let her go, something he didn't want to ever do again. Panic tinged her eyes. "Fates, what have I done? I'm so sorry, Sinow. We lost a thousand years. Our people, our lands. All of them suffered because of me." She scrambled to her feet, rambling on as the blank spaces he imagined had been in her mind slowly filled. "If only I'd stopped to listen to you."

She was distraught. Of all the ways he had imagined this moment, this had not been one. And they had mere minutes left before it ended.

Frantically wringing her hands, she said, "I couldn't find my way out. No matter how hard I tried, I couldn't find my way back to you. What have I done, Sinow?"

He stopped her motion, grabbing her by the arms and pulling her closer. As her eyes lifted, he sensed the familiar skip of heartbeats.

"Shh. Neither of us is to blame for this, Violissa. This is Tynan's doing. We may have foolishly set it in motion, but we did not do this, and I won't stand here listening to you blame yourself."

Her tension eased, but his remained.

Tears spilled down her cheeks. "I pushed you away in every lifetime, but you came back over and over." She sniffed, wiping the tears. "There were lives when I fought back, trying to untangle the memories, thinking I could find my way out. Thinking I had time to do that, but I never did." Green, the color of the fields at home, overtook her eyes as they widened. "I made you suffer all those lives, but I never forgot you. I searched for you." Heartbeats racing, he smoothed his hands up her arms while he listened. "When I would wake again, the memory was still there, tucked away but calling to me. I looked around every corner for you, dreamed of you, went through life never understanding why my heart ached so badly."

Her voice broke as she continued, "Knowing I'd lost something and feeling so empty from the loss, but never knowing I was the one who ran from it."

More tears fell, and this time, he reached up and caught one. He'd waited so long to hear her say these words. To know that she had been fighting silently in the only way she could. To know that he had never really been alone because she was searching for him like he had been for her. Endless centuries of waiting and their struggle was coming to an end.

"I love you, Sinow. I've always loved you. I've loved you since the Fates created us, loved you through every lifetime, and I, too, will love you long after we've returned to the Fates. There has never been anyone but you. I'm yours. For eternity."

She stopped, meeting his eyes, her heart skipping three beats as her breath caught. He twisted his finger in her wayward curl before pushing it around her ear. She had spoken the words he'd longed to hear. An exchange of affirmation: his love for her and hers for him. His fingers draped over her cheek and down her neck, her lips parting perfectly in reaction as his hand encased the back of her neck and drew her to him.

Mouth lowering to hers, he breathed in her scent before capturing her lips and kissing her. His body came alive, sparks bounding through him and igniting a fury within him that only she could calm. Soft lips, the taste of sun rays, lilacs and a summer breeze. Those were the things he would remember about that kiss as it wound through him, lighting the deepest recesses of his soul.

Fingers gripping her waist, he drew her closer. Her fingers played in his hair, the sensation only encouraging him to deepen the kiss.

For a thousand years he had waited for this moment, and he savored it like he would lose it again. A rumble shook the ground, and a whoosh of power swept over his skin as the Fates' spell lifted. The force caused him to release her mouth. And although the urge was there to take more, he kept the desire at bay, something he never would have had the strength to do in the past.

Her eyes shimmered as she dragged his mouth back to her. The knowledge that she was his, that nothing could break them apart now, crashed through him with the emotion exchanged in their kiss.

"All right, you two. Point made, spell broken. And as much as I've been waiting for you two pains in my asses to do this, we really need to go."

He ignored Keary, pushing his hand over Violissa's hip and pulling her into him. She let out a gasp against his mouth, and he gave her a smirk, knowing she had noticed how hungry he was for her.

He heard Paige mumble but didn't bother to pull his sight or his hands from Violissa. He kissed her again, needing more.

"I'm serious, Sinow, Violissa," Keary said, placing his hand on Sinow's shoulder and separating them. A growl sounded from Sinow that came with an instinctual need to punish him for the interruption. And alongside it was something he hadn't felt in centuries. Faint but growing, as if it was funneling back into him through a fracture that was about to break. Power.

# CHAPTER 61

The growl clawed at Violissa, stirring something deep within her. The sound had been one of ownership and lethal threat. A sign that no one would separate them again. And if they tried, Sinow would tear them apart piece by piece. He had already given everything up to protect her. She did not doubt he would kill for her if necessary.

Keary stepped back, but neither she nor Sinow moved.

Her battle with the curse had left her shaken and exhausted. Their admission of love had left her reeling. And that kiss. Fates, that kiss had been one she would never forget. A claim and a reunion, a reawakening of something that circumstance had never given time to develop. Love. Their love. And it was unbreakable. Even after all they'd been through, it remained.

Sinow had stopped their first kiss, and the strength it had taken him to do so was one she understood. The spell may have broken, but the prophecy still controlled them, and she suspected it always would. It had formed the seeds of their love and would continue to play a part in what they had. While that thought had bothered her in the past, it no longer did. Prophecy had gifted her the love she shared with Sinow, and for that, she would never question it again.

Sinow's sight dropped to his hands, and she followed the movement, seeing him close and open them. When she looked back up into his eyes, they were a shade darker, reminding her of how they had been at home. Always on the cusp of ebony. And within them sat something familiar. Something she hadn't seen in far too long. Power. His power was returning. An unexpected chill seeped into her, but before she could think about it more, Keary interrupted again.

"Our ride is here. Look." He turned Sinow's head and pointed toward the park.

"You know, if you were anyone else, Keary, I would have killed you by now, right?" Sinow's voice was rich and authoritative. The king had returned, and Violissa's pulse quickened.

"Trust me, I know. That's why being best friends with the king comes with benefits." To her surprise, Sinow laughed. It amazed her how Keary bantered with Sinow, something she would have thought was only part of their human relationship.

Sinow gave Keary a sideways look, then smiled and slapped him on the back. "Annoying and as assumptive as always, Keary."

Violissa looked toward where Keary had directed them and saw why he was so insistent.

"That's the way home?" she asked.

The humor stopped, a serious heaviness falling over them. Sinow's hand came around her waist and moved her to his side. His muscles strained against his shirt with tension. All eyes were on the funnel of light over the park. It stretched far into the sky, brilliant white with shades of gold swirling through it.

"It's like a beacon," she said.

Sinow peered down at her. "A beacon home."

"Home," she repeated.

"Uh, guys," Paige said quietly behind them.

Violissa had forgotten she was there.

"It's okay, Paige. The Fate told me there would be a portal," Keary answered, not bothering to turn around.

Violissa wanted to ask what Fate and why he knew there would be a portal, but this wasn't the time. He had told her the Fates had sent him and Paige here, so she assumed it was part of that story. One that could wait until they returned home.

"Then what does this mean?"

Violissa turned at the concern in Paige's voice. She was pointing to the necklace she had worn since the day they'd met as children. Violissa didn't remember her ever taking it off. For all those years, it had been a dull green color, but now it glowed a brilliant golden white that matched the beacon in the park.

"Fates' magic," Violissa said, walking toward Paige. She gently picked up the stone, noting the warmth beneath her fingers. She sensed Sinow behind her.

"A key?" he asked.

She looked back at him. "Key?"

"It's a key to what's in the park, isn't it, Keary?" he asked, never taking his eyes from hers.

"Yes, but not to open it. It's the key that takes us to the Banished Realm." Sinow and Violissa both looked at him as he continued, "Once it's opened, the portal will return us to the spot where all of this started, the spot where Tynan cursed Violissa. There's a stream of light, the sister to this one, that will have emerged there. The Fates knew Tynan would see the beacon and lie in wait for us to return. If he strikes first, well, we can all imagine what happens since neither of you seems to have your full power back. The key will create a second portal that Tynan can't detect."

"One that lands us in the Banished Realm instead," Sinow continued for him.

"Why would we want to go to the Banished Realm?" Violissa asked, not really wanting to know the answer. Confusion already muddied her brain with thoughts that the Fates were anticipating Tynan's moves. Why not just end him if he was that much of a threat? But the Fates acted in their own ways and had a purpose to everything. One she would never question again for fear of the repercussions.

"Because that's where what remains of our free people live. That's where our Councils have hidden them," Sinow answered, looking down at her as if gauging her reaction.

She inhaled sharply at the impact of his words. This was worse than she had imagined.

She looked at Keary. "You didn't—"

"It would have been too much for you to handle, Violissa. We can fill you in once we get back. But now, we need to get to that beacon and open the portal."

"How much time do we have?" asked Sinow.

"I didn't really have time to get a lot of details, Sinow. We're going in blind on that one."

"Then we shouldn't waste any more time," Paige said, the determination clear in her voice. "The beacon is in the park. It looks like it's over the lake." She glanced around. "And it's attracting attention."

Violissa could see the park in the distance. People were emerging further up the road, crossing over into it.

"That's not good," Sinow said. "We need to get moving before a crowd forms. That's the last thing we need. What's the quickest way to get over there?"

"We can run there, but I doubt we'd beat many of them," Violissa said.

Sinow cocked his brow at her. "Darkbearers don't run, Vi."

"Just like they don't walk, right?" she replied playfully, recalling their conversation so long ago walking through her castle.

He gave her a crooked grin, but before he could respond, Keary asked, "Has enough of your power returned to shift us there?"

"Some of it has, but not enough to shift more than myself. No, we'll need another way." He put his hand in his pocket, and she knew he was thinking about the car keys he would keep there. No, that Simon kept there. "And I have the way," he said.

He raised his hand toward Simon's car, a mist of black floating toward it. Not enough power to fight Tynan, but enough to start a car. A rush ran through her when the car roared to life.

"Let's go," he said, his voice that of a man who had no doubt of the power he held.

"That...that was magic," Paige mumbled, rubbing her arms.

Keary pushed her to move. "You'll get used to it. Just remember not to look him in the eyes."

"Move, Paige," Sinow commanded, and she jumped before she ran toward the car, Keary following.

About to run after them, Violissa eyed Simon, who was strolling toward the car. Warmth settled in her belly with the look he gave her.

"I'm a Dark King, Violissa. I don't run," he said, walking past her.

She shook her head, confounded by the things that made them so different. "Ever?" she asked when they reached the car.

He only chuckled and climbed in. As she climbed into the passenger seat, she considered it odd that they were sitting in a car together. Such a mundane thing in their human lives, but so different now.

"Think we can take this car with us, Sinow?" Keary asked from the back seat. "It really is a beauty."

"This over one of my stallions? Not likely," he answered.

"Would this be a bad time to mention Tynan destroyed the stables and killed all of your horses right after you left?" Keary responded.

Violissa didn't think it was a good time as she watched Sinow's grip on the steering wheel tighten, the whites around his knuckles showing. "No, not a good time, Keary," he replied, pulling out and racing down the road.

"Well, it was centuries ago. They would all be dead by now anyway," said Keary, trying to soothe his king's temper.

"Does anyone else think this is completely surreal?" Paige asked, oblivious to the tense situation around her. "I mean, the Dark King driving a car with the Light Queen in the front seat?"

No one answered her as the car passed the last storefront. Sinow turned them toward the park, running over the pathway and tearing through the grass, sending people jumping out of the way as he barreled toward the lake. He brought the car to a hard stop, spinning it into a parked position next to the lake where the beacon shone brightly. Violissa said a silent prayer of thanks that he had run no one over as Sinow got out, slamming the door behind him. She turned back and shot Keary a look.

"It's my job to irritate him, Violissa. You'll find out quickly that I'm the only one he lets push his buttons."

Paige looked like she was going to throw up, her fingers fumbling with the door handle. Sinow thumped his fist on the hood after walking over to Violissa's door and opening it for her.

"Out of the car, Keary, now. There are too many curious people gathering."

A crowd was forming. They hadn't reached the lake yet, but they were approaching. Dark power slinked across her skin, and she glanced at Sinow. He was standing so close to her that she had to cross her arms to keep from touching him.

When was the last time they had been this close? Only as Simon and Violet, except for the day that had started this mess. She didn't want to deal with going home or mortals crowding to ask questions. She wanted to be alone with Sinow, to continue where their kiss had been leading. To have him make love to her. Not as Simon, but as himself. His chestnut eyes flicked to hers, and heat filled her cheeks. He quirked his brow, his lip tugging upward like he knew exactly what she was thinking.

Jerking her to him, he leaned toward her, running his cheek

against hers and saying, "When we get home, Vi, I will devour every inch of you for eternity."

Her knees turned to mush, and if he hadn't been holding her waist, she would have toppled. His mouth dragged back over her cheek until he reached her lips. She melted then, closing her eyes and forgetting anything else existed.

Keary cleared his throat. "I hate to do this again, but you two need to focus. This is as bad as when you were under the spell. Save that for later."

She heard Paige laugh as Sinow released her from his hold. He brushed his thumb over her bottom lip before taking her hand and turning back to Keary and Paige. Holding hands was not something they'd ever done, but she embraced it, loving how his large hand encompassed hers like a protective layer.

Comfortable. That was the sensation she associated with Sinow now. Comfort. Like slipping into a fuzzy sweater on a chilly day. It wrapped around her, securing her, providing a calming sense of peace. They'd barely had any time together as themselves in all these years, yet the comfort that now existed made it seem as if they had spent the last few centuries together day upon day.

She leaned into him and listened as he asked, "So, how do we get home, Keary? Is it as simple as using the stone Paige has, or is there more to it?"

"There's more to it. You and Violissa must use your powers together. Throw the stone into the beacon with your magic focused on it, and that combination will unlock the portal."

"Together?" Violissa asked, flexing her hands in and out. Missing what had yet to return to her.

"Even after all this, they don't trust me to bring you back," Sinow answered. His irritation simmered in the air like a building storm.

Paige, who had been surprisingly quiet all this time, rubbed her arms and took a step back. And it struck Violissa that Paige had never been around magic. A rush of sadness washed through her at all her people had lost.

"Regardless of the reason, that's what you need to do," Keary replied. "So get moving. Those gathering fools won't stay back much longer. Look at them. They've already got their phones out."

"That's the least of our problems, Keary," Violissa said, dreading this confession. She'd been waiting for her power to return, hating how empty she was without it.

Piercing dark eyes evaluated her, and she gnawed at her bottom lip.

"Your powers haven't returned, have they, Vi?" Sinow asked, running his hand through his hair. "Please tell me I'm wrong."

She shook her head. There was nothing there. She'd been searching for it since the moment she'd noticed the change in him, and all she'd found was a hollow sensation. All the time in this world had turned her mortal.

# CHAPTER 62

Elation turned to horror as Sinow stared at Violissa. He hadn't detected power from her, but Light magic didn't have the same aura as his, and since only his innate powers had returned to him, he had thought nothing of it. The trickle of power was still building in him, and he could sense the full spark of it below, waiting to break free. But Violissa had nothing.

"Nothing?" he asked.

Her eyes dimmed as she shook her head again. "No. I've been waiting for it, but there's not even the sensation of it." Tears brimmed in the corners of her eyes. He'd forgotten her emotions were so volatile, triggered too easily. The Elvin side of her ruled them.

"You won't have all your power back, Violissa. Sinow certainly doesn't, or Paige wouldn't be this comfortable standing here," Keary said.

"I'm a little uncomfortable," Paige said, still rubbing her arms.

"Keary's right. I have only my innate powers. I'm still weak, and I'm still mortal."

Violissa opened her mouth to ask something when Chelsea

came running up to them. "What are you guys doing up here so close to that thing?"

"Not the right time, Chelsea," Keary snapped.

"Get her out of here," Sinow commanded. Mortals were the last thing they needed to deal with right now. His hands clenched, the ire building in him and threatening to spill over. This situation was out of control. His magic was weak, Violissa didn't have hers, and the Fates had some scheme to get them home that needed power neither of them had. Add in the mortals and he was one word away from losing it.

"Oh my God, you are really scary right now, Simon," Chelsea said, backing up slowly.

"Not as scary as I should be," he replied, narrowing his eyes at her and wishing he had the power to throw her and all the other mortals far from them.

Her hand flew to her mouth. "You woke up! They woke up and...and you're trying to go home!"

Sinow whipped his head to Keary, lifting him from the ground with his power. With his hand raised, he squeezed his fingers together, welcoming the magic that surged in his veins. The skin around Keary's neck buckled as an unseen hand tightened around it. He heard Paige gasp in fear and Chelsea scream, giving neither a glance.

"You told her? Couldn't keep your mouth shut enough to protect our secrets? Or were your pants down too far to worry about keeping your mouth closed?"

"That's a low blow, Sinow," Keary croaked out, not fighting because Sinow would have punished him more. "If you're going to punish me for that, can you at least wait until my powers are back? This is not a fair fight."

Sinow released him, and he fell to his knees, coughing.

"That punishment is going to hurt, isn't it?" Keary rasped through a cough. "Damn human body."

Keary was the only one who wasn't terrified of his king, which made him the one to whom Sinow had always been closest. It also made it frustrating when he needed to be serious.

"Sinow?" Violissa asked from behind him. "Is this really the place and the time?" She sounded amused, but there was a hint of annoyance in her voice.

He cast a glance over his shoulder, noting the crossing of her arms over her chest and the frown.

"I'm not in Cirillia, Violissa. So yes, it's a fine place."

"I told Chelsea about us," Paige said, lowering her eyes and keeping her head dropped in deference to him.

Of course, Paige had been the one. She was weak and mortal. If they were in Tenebron, he would have punished her and likely killed her for the transgression, but they weren't in Tenebron and things had been different then. He had forgotten how different he and Violissa were, and from her keen eyes that were watching for his reaction, he had a distinct notion the difference would take some adjustment.

His jaw ticked as Violissa walked over to Paige and lifted her chin. "It's all right, Paige. You were under so much pressure, and you held onto our secret for so many years." She paused, touching the glowing necklace. "All this time, you've been my Keeper here in this world. Filling in for your father and protecting the stone." Paige's eyes filled with tears as Violissa brought her to a standing position, took her hand, and kissed her cheek. "He would be so proud."

"That will take some getting used to," Keary said, moving next to him. Sinow glared at him. "Don't take your need for punishment out on me." He rubbed his neck, and Sinow saw the bruises forming. Mortal. Keary was still mortal here.

His mood softened. "We'll figure it out," he replied, gripping his hands to dull the Darkness that swirled with its rising presence. "But right now, we need to deal with the mortals, and we need to get home."

So far, they'd stayed back, and he wondered if they had sent

Chelsea as a sacrifice, unsure if the beam of magic would harm them.

Violissa met his eyes. "They're venturing closer. Can you push them back with your power?"

"Not without hurting them," he admitted. "And I don't want to take the chance of hurting any of them."

He heard a sigh of relief from Paige, who had clearly convinced herself he was a danger. Good, let her think that. Dark Kings ruled with fear. It kept the mortals safe and respectful of the crown.

"And you won't hurt them," Violissa said, nodding in agreement.

"Why?" Chelsea asked, seeming to wake up. "You just strangled Keary."

"I deserved it. That's nothing compared to what he'll do to my ass when we get back," said Keary with a laugh.

"He can't because it goes against the code of a true Dark King to hurt an innocent," Paige answered. "I remember learning that only the corrupt kings hurt innocents. True kings protect them."

She smiled at Sinow apologetically, and he nodded in response. At least they had taught her properly. Now she just needed to remember to keep her eyes off him. If they were home, she'd be clawing her eyes out with madness since he hadn't given anyone permission to look at him. He pressed his palm to his forehead, adding one more worry to his growing list.

Violissa took the lead, and he was grateful because he was one question away from losing control, especially with the burning of his full power in his core still unreachable but there, waiting to break free from its prison. It would be best if it broke free soon because it was like an itch he couldn't reach, and with that and the current situation, he was about to take his frustration out on everyone there. Doing so would break his code, so Keary would suffer the brunt of Sinow's ire for now—as much as his mortal form could withstand.

"We need your help, Chelsea," said Violissa. "We need time to figure out how to get home, and we can't take a chance of anyone getting too close to that light or to us. Can you get everyone back toward the trees and away from us?"

"How am I supposed to do that? And here comes Rich now," Chelsea said, pointing behind them to the local sheriff.

"Chelsea, use your charm. Besides, he likes you. That's why he always follows you around like a puppy. Please, Chelse, if we can't be alone here, we won't get home."

"Okay, okay. I'll buy you some time."

Violissa pulled her in for a hug and kissed her cheek. "Thank you."

"Hmm, there's something different about you, too, Violet," she said, walking backwards. "King and queen? You both better give me a good show for all the work I'm gonna have to do. I'm expecting something amazing."

Sinow watched her run toward Rich. His fingers flexed as he reached for his innate power. "If she gets them far enough back so the stragglers are closer to the others, I can throw out a shield that should keep them at bay."

"And that's an innate power?" Paige asked.

"One of them," he responded.

"What's the rest?" Paige asked.

"You don't want to know, and we don't have time to educate you. Let's just say I could easily kill everyone in this park without batting an eye." He had been terse, but he wasn't one for pleasantries or softening his words like Violissa was.

A look of terror crossed her face, and she swallowed loud enough for him to hear. The reaction tugged at his power, the Darkness reveling in it.

"All right, let's stop wasting time. Violissa, Sinow, get us home. Violissa, your innate powers should be enough," Keary said anxiously.

Sinow looked over at her, but she still appeared as perplexed as she had been before Chelsea had interrupted.

"What are innate powers?" she asked, brows knitted.

Eyes narrowing, he studied her, looking for any sign that she wasn't serious. It made no sense that she wouldn't know something as basic as innate powers. Every ruler had them as children.

"This is not the time to play, Violissa," Keary said.

But from the confusion on her face, she wasn't playing.

"I don't think she's joking, Keary. How can you not know, Violissa? Every king explains innate powers to his son..." He trailed off, noting the flash of sadness that quickly crossed her expression. "But you wouldn't have had that conversation," he continued. "I'm sorry, I forgot."

"And your Council wouldn't have known to teach you," Keary continued. "Cyric is the only one left from the last king's time, and he was too young to have witnessed it."

"Damn, this is a problem." He rolled his neck, wondering if this was more punishment from the Fates. It never seemed to end. "Every king is born with a certain set of powers. It's what makes our magic unique from the prior king. They show when we're very young and then develop from there. In my case, and I'm guessing yours, mine were active at birth. That's how my father knew I was the chosen child. It's how he knew to signal your Council. Those abilities are at the core of our magic, and they grow as we age. The power that develops as we age weaves around those innate ones, strengthening our overall abilities. At ascension, the Fate given power then fuses with that core, and we yield magic to our full potential. If you strip it all away, that core, those innate powers, define who we will become as rulers."

"I don't know what those are, Sinow."

"Remember back to when you were young, Vi. There must be something that stood out." He could almost hear the minutes ticking by. The beacon pulsed steadily, and he didn't know if it would disappear before they reached home. Every muscle in his body was taut with tension, and he was nearing the end of his patience.

"I don't know, Sinow. All my powers have always been there."

"That can't be, Violissa." Maybe it was lost in the memories that were still returning to her.

Keary seemed just as frustrated. He had his arms crossed, his jaw squared. "Paige, I'm sure your father taught you everything he knew about your queen. Do you remember anything?"

"No, Keary. I don't. I'm sorry."

Any inkling that there was a way home vanished with that answer.

"What do I do, Sinow? We're going to run out of time."

There was desperation in her question, and fear darkened her eyes. But he had no solution, no way to ease the fear and carry her burden. No way to save them.

# CHAPTER 63

With no answer to provide her, Sinow observed Violissa. She was a mess of emotions he attributed to her Elvin side, the human in her escalating them. Thinking of her Elvin half, he thought of the books he'd once scoured in the lower library when he'd been hunting for information on Violissa's mother.

Pacing, he held his hands behind his back and mumbled, "There was something long ago that I read. Something about the Elvin that made them different from the other races." As he said it, the passage came to him. "The Elvin didn't ascend. They were born with their powers. Their powers grew over time like ours, but they never had an ascension. That's why they were no match against the Darkbearers and why they befriended the Lightbearers for protection. Your nature abilities are your innate powers."

Violissa gnashed her lip before saying, "But I had two ascensions, Sinow. The Fates granted me an Elvin ascension."

"You and I are different, Vi. You are the first to be born of two powers, and you're a child of the prophecy."

"Of course, the Fates would treat you differently," Keary

continued for him. "You would have needed both ascensions to bring you to equal power with Sinow."

"I remember something," Paige blurted, bouncing on her toes. "They're right, Violissa. Father once told me a story from your childhood. You would run away from the Council, but you would leave a trail of flowers in your path. You would sing while you hid from them, and they would follow your voice to find you in a newly sprouted tree grove or surrounded by a tangle of vines. Father said it was frustrating because you would laugh while they cleared a path to get you out, and when they were close, you would start singing and encase yourself again."

Her voice. He should have known it was innate. "Your voice holds power, Vi. That's why you couldn't sing very long as Violet. It would awaken your memories and your powers," he said.

"That's what happened at the festival," she replied, her eyes lighting up. "I woke. I remember feeling like two people were in my body."

He remembered the experience and how it had called to him. "Your voice is innate from your Light side, and your nature powers come from your mother's side."

"Wait, so that means I need to sing and somehow use all this," she gestured to the park, "to get us home?"

"That's exactly what I mean," he said, looking over at the crowd. Chelsea had them corralled close to the tree line. He raised a hand and sent a wave of magic to gently urge them further back as he created a barrier to keep them away.

"Why can't my innate powers be easy like yours?" Violissa huffed. "Doesn't seem quite fair."

Turning his attention back to her, he shrugged. "Because Dark powers are superior."

Her down-turned lips let him know she hadn't appreciated his teasing. It had given him a moment of relief from the stress that was mounting in his body.

Behind her, the funnel of magic pulsed, and he frowned, concerned it would fade and leave them stranded there forever.

Fingers scratching at her ear, she followed his line of sight. "I don't know, Sinow..."

He peered back at her as she trailed off. Doubt shone in her eyes, dimming the green, and it puzzled him. Never had doubt surfaced in her at home. It was almost like she didn't fully remember who she was or how powerful she was.

Taking her shoulders, he turned her to him and said, "Listen to me, Violissa. You need to remember who you are. Not a human. Not a mortal. And this is not your world. You are a queen. The most powerful ruler Cirillia has ever had. I have seen you sing life back to groves once stripped bare. Suffered your wrath as you brought a torrent of rain down upon my realm that lasted for moons." He hated going back to that time, thinking of the mistakes they had both made that had brought them to this point. "This is nothing compared to what you can do. Remember who you are and become that person again." He looped his finger through her wayward strand. "Be the queen I know you are."

"Your queen," she breathed.

"My queen," he replied, warmth flowing through him at the thought.

"But I've been human for so long."

"I know." He, of all people, understood how easy it was to lose oneself in this world, and that was with his memories intact. She'd been asleep for centuries, wandering the world as Violet, a mortal with no understanding of how special she was.

"Find yourself again, Vi. For your people, for your Council, for me."

She looked back at the funnel of magic, her lips pursed. Her chest rose as she took a deep breath, then exhaled, her spine straightening, the doubt falling away. Hand draping over his, she walked away, not to where Paige was standing like he assumed since

Paige still held the stone, but into the open field of the park where she kneeled.

"What's she doing?" he asked, concerned that something was wrong. Didn't she know how crucial every second was? They'd already wasted too much time. "I thought she was going to sing?"

"I don't know. You've seen her sing more than I have," Keary replied.

"Twice, Keary. That doesn't make me an expert."

"She's praying," Paige said.

He swiveled toward her. "Praying? Why would she need to pray? The Fates sent the beacon, and you have the key."

A look of awe shone on Paige's face. "I don't think she's praying to the Fates."

"She's lost her mind," said Keary, kicking a tuft of grass. "We'll never get home."

In the past, he would have agreed with Keary, but after being trapped in this world, he'd had countless time to replay scenes from their past and analyze her actions. Especially in this lifetime. She may not have known who she was in this world, but her personality traits remained constant. Small things like the dried flowers in her room, the wistful way she'd decorated it, her volunteer work at the children's hospital in town, the way she'd weaved herself into the hearts of everyone she met, the way she danced in the raindrops the day it had poured on them. These were not just Violet. They were Violissa. These things spoke of who she truly was as a ruler and a person. An imprint of her the Fates couldn't remove.

So, as he watched her praying in the field, he understood there was a purpose to it. A reason she needed to be out there, and only she needed to know that reason. It was up to him to trust her.

The weight of Keary's stare didn't dissuade him from saying, "Let her be, Keary. Trust her."

Keary's eyes sharpened on him. "Trust her? Trust that kneeling in a field will somehow get us home?"

"It's Violissa's way," Paige said.

Sinow studied Paige. She'd been quietly observing them for most of the interaction. Her cerulean eyes flitted to his before dropping, but it was long enough to remind him of Daneele. Thoughtful, observant. A mortal with a heritage that shouldn't have been, but the Fates had allowed. And knowing that, Sinow thought she just might be there for more than this.

"Look, she's returning," Paige said, her focus back on Violissa.

A look of determination veiled Violissa's face, her confident eyes sparkling in the sunlight as she walked back to them. She gave him a mischievous smile.

"Should I ask?" he said, wondering at the comfort they seemed to have with each other now.

"I needed to ask permission to use our powers. Their god doesn't like magic," she stated, brushing her hands off.

Her statement didn't surprise him, but Keary's face contorted with confusion. "How do you know that, Violissa?"

"I don't know. I just do," she replied as she slipped her feet out of her shoes.

Sinow's brow quirked.

"I forgot. I don't like wearing shoes."

She wiggled her bare toes in the grass, then walked over to Paige, extending her hand. Paige placed the necklace in it, and Violissa slid the stone from the chain, which she then handed back to Paige.

Slipping it into the pocket of her dress, she walked back toward where she'd just been, saying, "Sinow, please lower the barrier."

Now she was confounding him. The praying and wistful things she did, he could handle, but he wasn't about to deal with mortals. "No. We need to keep them back, Vi. It's safer that way."

Swirling around to face him, she explained, "I need to feel the trees, the land beyond, and I can't do it through your magic."

She pulled her braid and began unraveling it as she continued on her backward path. Loving her was going to take patience, and he didn't know how his Dark magic would deal with the unique nuances that were Violissa, no matter how much he adored them.

"I forgot, I also prefer my hair down," she said, likely reading the perplexed expression he was now wearing.

"You're going to constantly test me, aren't you?" he asked, his smile tugging for him to set it free.

"All of us," Keary muttered.

She shook her head to loosen the final golden strands and turned toward the beacon, walking with such grace she appeared to glide. "I'm certain I will."

He watched her long, loose curls bounce along her back, remembering how he preferred them down. Wild and free, like she was. Halting her steps so she stood across from the lake where the beacon shone, she closed her eyes. The wind lifted her skirt to take it further up her thighs, and desire hummed through him.

It wasn't the time to think about her long legs or the curve of her hips where her dress hugged before cascading down. Nor was it time to think about how he had touched those legs as Simon. Always as Simon, with one exception: the Dream Realm. But even that had been nothing more than another manipulation by the Fates. He was ready to claim her the right way this time, to claim every inch of her as she did the same to him. To truly have her skin beneath his, to taste her kisses, to touch her until she was trembling, to hear her cries. To hold her close and have her fall asleep in his arms, only to wake this time with her still there.

But this was not the time to dwell on such things, so he cleared them from his mind and concentrated on what Violissa was doing. She had moved closer to the lake and stood about ten feet back from it. The stone was now in her hand, held in her outstretched palm. A hush fell around them.

"What's it like to hear her sing?" Paige whispered.

In another lifetime, he would have punished her for the question. But time had changed him, and he understood her curiosity.

"It's magical. Not like her voice as Violet. Violissa's voice is power. It touches the deepest recesses of your being, weaving itself through it like a spell. It will leave you filled yet longing for more for the rest of your existence."

Head turning their way, Violissa smiled as if she had heard him. It lit her face just as the glow from the stone danced in her eyes, illuminating their green.

Turning back to the lake, her voice shattered the silence. Delicate, ethereal. As if it were part of the wind, the sound caressed him, weaving its way through every part of him. There was strength in it that hadn't been there when she'd been Violet. It held power that cascaded through the air, holding everything in its command, including him.

Keary moved beside him. "I forgot what that sounded like."

"I didn't," he replied, eyes still fixed on her.

The stone lifted with her notes. Dancelike steps led her further from the stone, her moves graceful. Her arms reached out as her back bent, her fingers drifting in an arc through the grass that stretched tall to reach them. Flowers sprouted in their wake, and the field became awash in color. Posture straightened, she continued her song, the wind carrying her voice as it rose and fell.

He saw then what power her voice truly held. Command over nature. She enchanted the land, and it responded. Wind whipped through her hair, the ground rumbled beneath his feet, and leaves rustled as they answered her call. Waiting for her instruction to do her bidding. She stopped moving, but continued singing, her voice growing in power as she seemed to command the trees.

Her voice increased in strength, building to a crescendo that called to him. Like a summons that told him it was time to join her. The stone needed both their powers to open the portal, and she was doing her part. Now it was his turn. Shaking off the trance-like state that had kept him enthralled, he moved closer to the beacon. Rolling his shoulders and flexing his hands, he reached inward, drawing on what magic he had, sensing the lock that held most of it prisoner still.

Violissa belted a note that shook the ground and pushed her hand out toward where the stone spun in the air. A wave of power hit it, her voice creating and focusing the magic. Hands balled, he waited, knowing it wasn't time, that he would sense through their connection when it was. The stone tore through the air with the force of her magic and penetrated the beacon. Large droplets of water lifted from the lake, slow at first, then steady like an upside-down rainstorm.

Energy buzzed in the air, and his skin prickled. It was time. The note she was holding ended abruptly, and the water froze, the stone hanging in stasis. Raising his hand toward the beacon, he poured every ounce of power he could access toward it. As it met the stone, Violissa leaped into the air, landing with an intensity that sent roots lurching from the dry lakebed and climbing toward the stone. As her song began again, the roots tangled through the beacon, wrapping around his power and weaving through the light. His magic collided with hers, the two becoming one, and he stopped, stepping back to witness the power of their combined magic.

The trees pounded a rhythm to her song, thunder rolled, and clouds overtook the sky. The funnel of light flashed a myriad of colors as water and root meshed to form a portal. An opening to their word. Gray and black, his magic blended with the golden light of the Fates' beacon and the bright green of Violissa's nature magic to create a purple haze with accents of black.

The portal took form as Violissa continued to sing, dancing between the roots that had sprouted outside the lake, moving her body between them as she rose to her full height, then dropped back to the ground. The lake water fell, splashing down in rhythm to nature's song. Another crescendo in her song caused the wind to pick up and the ground to roll. As if in answer, the flickering light of the portal stalled, and the opening solidified to a brilliant golden hue, pulsating to the rhythm of the trees.

Violissa released one final note, powerful and commanding, her arms thrown out as the natural world bellowed one last chaotic symphony to her. At the halt of her voice, the world stilled. Roots slinked back below ground, the earth and grass healing from the damage they had caused, and the water in the lake rippled calmly until it stilled once again. The wind swept away the clouds that had gathered. A peace fell across the land, and Sinow released the air locked in his lungs.

Violissa's arms came down, and she twirled around, laughing. He sensed Keary move next to him, and they both continued to stare at her. "If those are her innate powers, you're in trouble."

He cast a sideways glance at Keary. "I am not in trouble. And you'd better be glad your powers haven't returned, or you'd be across that field on your ass by now."

"Like I said, you're in trouble."

Sinow ignored him and made his way toward Violissa.

"Keep up, Paige," Keary shouted.

Sinow looked back to see her still standing there, mouth agape, staring at the portal. Mortals didn't comprehend the amount of power the immortals had. No description Daneele could have provided her would ever have let her come close to imagining the sheer force of what they could do. He'd seen that reaction several times, and each time it reminded him of how fragile mortals were, reminded him of just why the king and his Council needed to protect them.

Sinow kept walking, unconcerned about Paige's inability to move. She'd catch up if she really wanted to go home.

Home. They were so close, he could feel it. When he reached Violissa, he crossed his arms and cocked a brow at her.

"I did it," she cried, jumping into his arms. The unexpected action had him throwing his arms around her to avoid them both crashing to the ground. "I had forgotten how good it felt to wield magic," she said, kissing him.

She froze mid-kiss and jerked back, her eyes scrunching. This was human behavior, not theirs, and they both knew it. She looked like she wanted to pull away, but he held her tight, nudging her nose with his.

"I don't like public displays of affection. It goes against my Dark nature." Her smile faltered more. "But we're not home yet, and I really don't want to let you go." The smile returned.

"I don't usually do this," she said.

"I hope not, because I'd have to kill anyone who touched you like this."

"Save it for when we get back," Keary said. "We have a portal waiting for us, and that crowd is no longer shocked, but curious."

Sinow released Violissa and sent another wave of magic toward the crowd, fortifying his shield to keep them back. He jerked her closer and leaned near her ear. "We'll resume that position when we're alone. I like watching you crumble when you're pinned to the wall, but this time I want to experience it myself."

She stumbled, her cheeks flaring a brilliant red, which he kissed before letting her go. He enjoyed how her delicate countenance contradicted his darker one and was looking forward to unraveling her further with his words and his actions when they returned home.

"You two are just as annoying now as you were as Violet and Simon," grumbled Keary. "Come on. You're making Paige uncomfortable, and I don't know what to think about this. All I know is you can keep it behind closed doors, so I don't have to contemplate gouging my eyes out all the time."

"I'd happily do it for you, so there's no contemplation involved," Sinow replied, giving Violissa another peck as he took her hand and walked toward the portal.

"I'll pass. It took a painfully long time for my vision to return the last time you did that."

Violissa's fingers tightened around his, and he peered down at her, giving her a shrug.

"You'll get used to it."

"No, I don't think I will."

"Too bad," Keary quipped when they stood before the portal. "That's who we are, Violissa."

"Can we just focus on the portal?" asked Paige, who looked deathly pale. Perhaps talk of torture wasn't the ideal topic around her, or even Violissa, for that matter.

"Agreed." Violissa moved closer to the portal, but he yanked her back to his side. The withering glare she gave him reminded him that she wasn't as delicate as he remembered.

"Keary, did the Fates say anything about how we should enter the portal?"

"No, just about using the stone to redirect the portal, so we're hidden from Tynan."

Tynan. He hadn't thought about him, but as he contemplated what lay on the other side, he had a concern, and that meant not letting Violissa through that portal first.

"What are you thinking?" Keary asked him, knowing too well how his mind worked.

"Keary, how long have you been here?"

"About twenty years. Not that long, why?"

"Not long, but long enough for things to change. Long enough for Tynan to change things."

"You're worried about what's on the other side of the portal," Violissa said, as if she knew exactly what he was thinking.

"What if Tynan broke through to the Banished Realm? What if he's waiting on the other side right now?" he said, each word further raising his alarms. "Tynan's always been a step ahead of me. He's always been calculating. There's no way he didn't sense the Fates open that portal for you and Paige, Keary. Magic that powerful doesn't go unnoticed. So what if he's lying in wait for our return? He's had years to ponder the magic that brought you here and has now had time to study the portal that undoubtedly stands in our world as sister to this beacon. What if he's smart enough to realize the one he sees in that field is a decoy?"

"That's a lot of ifs," Paige said, wringing her hands.

"Too many," he answered. He looked at Violissa. "I'll not let Tynan burn me again by not considering them."

She searched his eyes, and he knew she saw into his thoughts, anticipating what he was planning. "You want to go through first."

"Yes."

"But you both have powers," Paige said. "Wouldn't it be better for both of you to go?"

"No," Keary answered, "he's right. Tynan's strong. His power is tainted, and he's lost his mind. That makes him even more dangerous. If Sinow is right, he could kill some of us or all of us the minute we return."

"But we'll be immortal again, right?" Violissa asked.

"We don't know that. If our powers don't return right away, if there's any delay, we're dead. I can fight Tynan. I know his magic, I know where it comes from, and can hold him off long enough for my powers to return in full. What I can't do is fight him and protect all of you at the same time if there is any delay."

"But Violissa has power now," Paige said. She had such faith in her queen, and he had to imagine it came from her father. But that faith could get Violissa killed this time.

Violissa gave her a sad smile. "Trees and thunder do little harm against a Dark King, false or true, Paige. He's right." Sinow knew she had downplayed her powers, for he was sure she could do plenty of damage with what she currently held.

"I won't take the chance. I need to go through first." He looked over at Keary. "Keary, you set your watch for say, five minutes. Then all three of you come through. That should give me enough time to occupy Tynan if he's waiting for me, and hopefully, my powers will have completely returned by then. If anything goes wrong, you protect her, Keary. Protect your queen."

Keary nodded his understanding.

Violissa bit her bottom lip for a moment, then said, "Are you sure it's good to be apart again?" She hadn't said leave me, instead she'd said to be apart. She didn't want to be without him as much as he didn't want to be without her again. Hand embracing her waist, he drew her to him.

"It won't be long, and it'll be worth the wait." He didn't want to leave her, but he couldn't stand the thought of seeing her hurt.

She smoothed her fingers over his jaw. "That should be our motto."

"I can't fathom the thought of losing you again, Vi. If it means we're apart a few minutes longer, then I'm willing to deal with it."

She pulled his mouth to hers in a kiss that spoke of her emotions. The need, the frustration, the fear, the impatience, the love all rolled into one kiss. Her fingers touched her lips when the kiss ended, like it would keep the kiss from fading.

"Would it be wrong for me to tell a Dark King to be careful?"

"Yes, it would," he replied with a laugh. "Keary, are you ready?"

Keary held his watch out. "Ready."

He backed away from Violissa, hating every step that kept them separated. Giving her one last look, he turned and stepped into the portal.

# CHAPTER 64

The beam of light penetrated the field, casting a golden-white hue that lit the surrounding area. Tynan studied the field, too keen not to notice it was in the same spot where he had cursed Violissa that fateful day. The event that had led him to this point. A king feared above all others. Power unmatched. Everything he had desired. Yet here he was alone, just as he always was. No Council, no friends, no family, no lovers or at least no women who chose to be his lovers. He took what he wanted and whom he wanted, with no regard to the devastation he left in his wake. Nothing mattered but the power. That was all he lived for now.

The pulse of power that had disturbed the air had led him to this field. The air hummed, the light spilling out and irritating his eyes. It shone for miles against the backdrop of constant night. A sign that could only mean one thing: Sinow had found Violissa and was bringing her home.

His fingers curled into his palms, ripping the flesh. Excitement and anger slithered through him like a beast hunting its prey. He relished the thought of fighting Sinow. Of crushing his brother and stripping him down to the weak man he was.

Ending him only after he had suffered for taking everything from Tynan.

He moved closer to the light, studying its features. It gave off the warmth of magic, but there was something lacking in it. The source was weak, not powerful enough to move someone between worlds. And he knew beyond a doubt they were in a different world. There was no other explanation for how he had gained control of the realms.

The light pulsed, its shape morphing. The colors changed rapidly, shifting from green tones to shades of black and gray. They seemed to dance within it until they merged into a light purple hue. Nature and Dark powers merging. The beacon took shape, stretching and thickening as the purple faded, and bright gold flared from it. Tynan took a step back. A portal. They had opened a portal using their magic.

Moving closer to it, he absently wondered why there had been no Light magic present, but the thought didn't settle as he contemplated the sight before him. Anticipation shivered through him. The time was drawing near.

As he prepared to face his brother, Tynan again had the sensation that something still wasn't right. The magic had held strength, but only temporarily. Now that the beacon was before him, the power had dimmed. Like it wasn't the true source of power, but a replica. He swung his head to the east in the direction of the Banished Realm and sent his power out, searching for anything that could solidify his suspicions. At first, there was only the magic of that confounding barrier that surrounded the realm. But then he detected a faint thrum of magic that didn't match the pattern of the barrier. He had yet to break through the barrier, but he sensed the differing magic.

Turning back to the portal, he pondered the difference. The magic he sensed from it was weak, while whatever was happening in the Banished Realm was strong enough for him to notice. His lips curved to a devious grin. So the Fates were trying to fool him with a decoy. He threw his head back and laughed, the sound echoing through the field. Always underestimating him, just as everyone always had.

The portal pulsed before him as if reveling in its deception, but a change caught his attention. The colors darkened slightly, and the pulsing turned to more of a circular motion. Someone was coming through. The motion froze, then returned to a pulse. Sinow. He noted the stir of power, the pull of his Dark magic to his brother's the moment Sinow stepped into their world. He'd always been able to sense his brother. Sinow was back but hidden with the rest of them in the Banished Realm. And now there were now two Dark Kings.

The last thread of dark color twisted away, and Tynan reached into the portal and latched onto it. There was no pull to the portal as if it would give him access to the other side. It provided access only in one direction—to their world. But if he could manipulate the Dark magic in the thread, he could change that. Sweat beaded on his skin as he struggled to force the ebony thread back toward him. It bucked and rebelled, but he held tight, letting his power pour into it. His magic infected the thread, then spilled over into the golden light of the portal.

Intent on forcing his way to the other opening in the Banished Realm, he sent another surge of power into the thread that was growing larger. It was working, and he would soon be face to face with Sinow. Finally kill him and the traitors who claimed loyalty to him, fleeing like cowards from Tynan's grasp. The thread burst to fill the entire portal, his magic turning the golden hue darker. It was working. All he needed to do was transform it enough to reach through to the other opening in the Banished Realm.

The magic of the portal twisted, fighting his attempt. Flickers of crimson and black told him he was winning the battle. He sent another wave of power into it, grunting from the exertion. His muscles were shaking, seizing up as the portal yielded to him. Ebony climbed into its borders, the inner layers clouding in crimson tones as it gave over to his control. It swirled, yielding completely to the invasion, and he stopped his attack when he detected a pulling sensation.

Tynan leaned on his legs, which were shaking from the energy he had expelled. He took mere seconds to recover and let out a deep, throaty laugh that cut the silence.

"Time to say goodbye, brother," he said, straightening himself up to full height.

As he stepped into the ominous sphere, darkness eclipsing him, he had only one thing on his mind: destroying Sinow.

# CHAPTER 65

The portal cast a soft golden hue over Violissa as she watched Sinow disappear through it. His absence left an emptiness that rushed through her, leaving her wounded like the action had severed half of her being. It was the same hollowness that had shadowed her existence in each lifetime. One she could never explain, but that followed her like a ghost haunting her every move. Now that her memories had returned, she recognized how it had continued through every life.

A sob clawed from her throat at the distance that now separated them.

"Are you all right, my queen?" Paige asked. Violissa could tell she still didn't know how to address her, but she didn't have the energy to talk to her about it now. Her nerves were too high, the pain of Sinow's absence too overwhelming.

"Violissa?" Keary asked, not concerned about formality.

She waved them both off. "I'm fine. I didn't realize how much I'd miss him."

Keary rolled his eyes, and she frowned at him. He reminded her of her Council. There was a lightheartedness about him that didn't fit the Darkbearer reputation.

"Violet! That was amazing! Oh my God, you both used magic!"

Violissa's head jerked behind her to find Chelsea running toward them, with the others following.

"Sinow's magic didn't hold," Keary grumbled. "This is a disaster."

"It must have faded when he left," she said, cringing as Chelsea continued her path.

"We need to get them out of here. We have four minutes left, and I don't need to deal with this mess while I'm worrying about Sinow."

"I'll go," Paige volunteered, running to meet Chelsea and Rich, who wasn't far behind.

Keary bunched his hands and looked at Violissa. "We need to stay together."

"Let me handle this. Just watch the time."

She jogged away, hearing Keary complain. He had every right to. Having mortals anywhere near the portal, or even them right now, was a risk.

"Where did he go?" Rich asked as others joined him and Chelsea. Paige was trying to diffuse the situation but was failing. "He disappeared. Where did Simon go, Violet?"

"Is that dangerous, Violet?" Aunt Emma asked. Violet's aunt, not hers, and something in her churned. An ache that told her she would miss the people she'd loved in this world.

"What did you do? Was that magic?"

The questions fell from every direction. There was no time to answer them. If only the barrier had remained, but she supposed it was for the best. They couldn't leave traces of their magic in this world, plus it wouldn't do to have the people blocked off from a part of their town forever.

Chelsea's frightened voice pitched higher than the others as she pointed to the portal. "Is that supposed to happen?"

Violissa whipped around.

"Oh God," Paige muttered.

"Fates, Paige," she corrected absently as she stared at the portal, which looked like a surging storm of violent crimson and black.

"Violissa, that doesn't look right," Keary yelled.

Blood pounded in her veins. "Sinow."

Keary ran over to her. "Do you still feel him? Is he still alive?"

She closed her eyes, pushing aside her fear and sensing the connection they had. "He's alive, that much I know, but I can't sense him. I haven't been able to since he left."

"What is that?" Paige pointed to where the portal stretched and writhed.

"Tynan," Keary replied.

Violissa shivered as a chill crawled up her spine. The portal had changed to a viscous hue with black around its ring. Red and black tendrils of smoke poured from it. Fates, if it was Tynan, they were all doomed.

Turning to the crowd, she bellowed, "Run!"

Like frightened deer, they froze, panic blanching their faces.

"Run now!" Keary yelled. "Get as far away as you can!"

Chaos ensued, with people running in every direction. Violissa grabbed Chelsea by the shoulders. "Tell them not to look in his eyes. Do you understand me?"

"What if they do?" she asked, her lips trembling.

"He will kill them if they do. Go Chelsea. It's imperative that everyone stays as far away as you can get them and do not meet his eyes."

"Violet?"

"I'll be fine. Please go."

Chelsea ran off, and Violissa hoped she and the others would heed the warning.

Violissa turned to Paige. "Run to the side of the portal, Paige, as far away as you can, but close enough to go through. When he's not looking, you jump in."

"But Violissa—"

"No, she's right, Paige," barked Keary. "He will not hesitate to kill you. You must go in. Save yourself and find Sinow."

"Go Paige. That's a command from your queen," Violissa said, knowing Paige wouldn't defy her. As much as she hated doing it, she wanted Paige safe. She'd been by Violissa's side for twenty years, and even if she had been Violet's friend, she was also Violissa's. Once they were home, she would sort through their convoluted relationship and hopefully salvage it. The thought of not having Paige to talk to was too difficult to fathom.

Paige looked between them before she hurried off. She made it to the far side of the portal just as a thunderous scream erupted from it. The portal swelled and shook as Tynan forced his way through.

Keary hurried toward it, leaving a distance between them and clearly placing himself in front of Violissa.

She rushed to him, the violence of the portal heating her skin. "Keary, what are you doing?"

"Protecting you. Now get back."

"You have no power. Let me handle this."

Keary looked over at her. Even without his magic, his brown eyes were lethal. "My king gave me an order. I will protect my queen as I promised. With my life." He turned his back to her, signaling that he was done with the conversation and ready to face Tynan.

There was no arguing. She'd heard Sinow's command, and Keary was too loyal and brave to break it. He rolled his shoulders and stood proud. Built like all the immortals, he was a solid wall of muscle, a formidable opponent. However, with no power, to a full-powered Tynan, he would be no more than a gnat to swat away.

Although she feared for his safety, there was no dissuading him, and their time was up. Tynan was coming. Tendrils of ebony poured forth as dark matter flew from the opening. Within it came Tynan, who landed on his feet with a force that shook the ground. Violissa held her breath, trying to keep her limbs steady but failing as her knees quaked. He straightened, rolling his neck, and she dug her nails into her palms to keep from collapsing in fear. Without her power, she was vulnerable to the Dark magic but still immune to its deadlier effects.

He wore no robe to shield innocents from his power like any other Darkbearer would, and Violissa prayed everyone had heeded her warning. His black eyes perused the area, landing on Keary before flicking to her. He had changed. No longer did he seem a harmless mistake, fumbling around and distracting them. Now she saw him for who he was: a terrifying madman.

He stood almost to Sinow's height; he was just as massive now. His hair, long and unkempt, hung to his shoulders. Black tendrils seeped from him as if he had so much power he couldn't contain it. But it was the eyes that belied the true extent of his mental state. They were as black as an endless night, penetrating and so terrifying she wanted to look away.

"Well, well. This was not what I expected," he said, rubbing his hands together. His voice was like a thousand insect legs scurrying over her skin. "This is even better."

"Stay back, Tynan," Keary ordered with the authority of a man with power.

"Keary, so you were the disturbance all those years ago. You came after Sinow, didn't you? Speaking of my brother, where is he?" Tynan's head swiveled around, and Violissa let out a sigh of relief that he hadn't noticed Paige.

"It doesn't matter, Tynan. We're going home," Keary replied.

Tynan walked closer, sniffing the air. "I smell mortality, and it's not a good scent for you, Keary." With the flick of his hand, he sent Keary through the air. Landing with a thud on the side of the car, his body left an indent after it slid to the ground.

"No!" Violissa yelled, running toward Keary. Tynan gripped her with his magic, holding her in a vice-like position. The pressure was almost unbearable, but she refused to show him any weakness. Her innate powers wouldn't heed her call, yet she kept her head up even with his magic digging into her skin. She took small, shallow breaths as Tynan sauntered over to her. The hold on her released, but his hand replaced it, encircling her neck and cutting off her airway.

In her periphery, she spied Paige running through the portal. She prayed to the Fates that Paige would survive the Dark power that had overtaken the portal and that she would find Sinow.

Pulling her closer, Tynan stared into her eyes. Pure terror gripped her, and his lips curved into a devilish grin, as if he sensed it.

"Violissa." Her name peeled from his tongue in that slimy, corrupt way it always had when he said it. "My brother went to all that trouble to find you. He left everything behind, left our world vulnerable, and what does he do to his precious prize when he finds you? He leaves you behind?"

"He'll be back, Tynan, and when he does—"

He squeezed her neck tighter, stopping her words. Fear blindsided her, and she ceased her attempt to reach her innate power and grabbed at his hands instead. He ran his nose over her cheek and down her neck. Her skin crawled at the contact, which only made her struggle more.

"Do you know what I smell? I smell fear and something else. What is that smell?" He sniffed again. "Ah, yes, mortality."

Instinctively she whimpered, all those years as a human taking over.

*Remember who you are,* she told herself, Sinow's words coming back to her.

"Release her," Keary ordered, rushing toward them in one last attempt to protect her.

A useless attempt. Tynan didn't bother to look at him. He raised his hand and slammed Keary back down onto the ground, all the while keeping his grip on Violissa's neck. Keary emitted a grunt when he landed. He fought against the restraint of Tynan's power, but there was no fighting it. Violissa squirmed, digging her nails into Tynan's hands, ripping the skin, which constantly healed as quickly as she inflicted the damage.

"Stop struggling, Violissa," Tynan sneered. "It's unbecoming of a queen."

She stopped and looked him defiantly in the eyes, reaching out again for her powers.

"That's better. Now, what do I do with you? Let's see, I could kill you now. Go home and kill Sinow as he crumbles once again from losing you." Black eyes turning upward, he pretended to ponder his dilemma. "Or maybe he'll do me a favor and return himself to the Fates because he's so miserable." He lifted her off the ground. Feet dangling, she reached for air that wouldn't come. "But what's the fun in that?"

He smashed her body against his chest, and bile rose in her throat, constricting her airway further. She needed to gain control of the situation quickly and find her power before he killed her.

"Or," he said, rubbing his mouth over her cheek. The bile surged, and she struggled for air as it burned her airway. "I could keep you for myself. Find out what it is about you that my brother finds so irresistible." His hand pawed at her breast, and another whimper escaped her. "I've found Cirillian girls to be quite tasty while they last." His fingers loosened around her neck, and she choked back the vomit while she gasped for air. "What's that, Violissa? You'd like me to show you how a real man treats his woman?" Fingers gripped tighter, his grin turned maniacal as her body flayed with her attempts to find even the slightest hint of air.

It couldn't end like this. Not when they'd been so close. Not after all they'd been through. Perhaps it was yet another price she had to pay for straying from the prophecy's path. But it seemed a harsh punishment after what the Fates had already done to her.

If only she could distract him, get him to loosen his hold on her long enough for her to focus more on connecting with her innate powers. Then she might stand a chance. As he waited for her response, she promised she would never again question the Fates if she survived.

# CHAPTER 66

The trip through the portal was just as it had been the first time Sinow traveled through it, but now the anticipation of finding Violissa was gone, replaced with the trepidation of leaving her behind. There was no guarantee that he had made the right decision. Too many centuries of searching for her had influenced his decision. He wouldn't take the chance of something happening to her if a trap lay on the other side.

That hollow sensation deep within him that had begun the day Tynan had ripped her from him and continued through each life the Fates had taken her, returned and with it an ache that wouldn't subside. Ignoring it, he focused on the gateway that came slamming toward him. Magic pulled him through, and he landed on his feet in a crouched position, ready to fight if Tynan was indeed lying in wait for him.

Only night greeted him, but it was far from his mind as the tide of his power surged through him. It settled over him, racing across his skin, through his veins, and filling every cell. Breathing in, he let the power course through him, embracing it like an old friend. Crouched still, he awaited Tynan's attack, ready to meet it head on and crush him until he was begging for mercy.

But no attack came. Body stretching, he stood and breathed in the scent of home, letting it wake his senses.

"My liege?" A voice said.

He blinked his eyes, still adjusting to the dim light ahead of him that sprayed down from a few torches in the distance. The light from the portal fanned out behind him to show figures slowly approaching.

His magic sat ready to be drawn, but he detected no threat from the figures. That voice had been so familiar.

An old man approached him, and Sinow lowered his defenses as others joined him. Ten, then more, adding up to nineteen. All aged, all wearing expressions of shock and wonder.

Nineteen. The number of Council left in their world. Ten Lightbearers and the remaining nine Darkbearers.

"My liege?" the man asked again.

Sinow studied the weathered face and the bold brown eyes alive with youth. The eyes of a younger man. Ones with eternal sadness that came only from missing the youth, power, and immortality they had once held.

"Kanine?" Sinow asked, and the old man returned his question with a smile.

"Welcome home, my king."

"It's him. He has returned. Throw up the torches, give us light!" another voice called as the men moved closer to him.

Sinow grabbed Kanine's arm, squeezing tight. "You look a little worn, old man," he said, chuckling as a rush of relief nearly strangled him. He recognized the aged faces of his Council as they jubilantly welcomed him back.

"Your Highness, where is Violissa?" a voice to his right asked. "Where is our queen?"

Sight turning to him, Sinow peered into the blue eyes that no longer held the vibrance that came with the Light power they had once contained. Youth remained in them, however, contrasting the withered face to which they belonged.

"Cyric?"

Cyric nodded. "Yes, a little more weathered than I should be, but it is I."

Both Councils were still alive, and he greeted them each with a joy that nearly burst from him. Violissa would be so relieved to see her Council after thinking them dead.

"Where is Violissa, Sinow?" Cyric repeated.

"She's fine. She's coming through behind me. We didn't know what awaited us, and I didn't want to take the chance of letting her through first."

A collective sigh and some chatter came from the men before endless questions bombarded him. He raised his hand to silence them.

"And Paige and Keary?" He heard a familiar voice ask.

"Daneele?" Sinow asked. The man nodded. "You had some fun while we were away."

Daneele's face crumpled. No one had ever broken the rule of chastity. Nor had anyone ever questioned it. The magic the Council received from the Fates diminished all cravings for the flesh. Until that magic had faded.

Awkward silence came from where his Council stood. So, there'd been fault on both sides, Keary included, since he had indulged repeatedly during his time in the human world. There was no easy way to handle the situation, since it was so complex. It was something he would need to ponder before he decided.

Resting a hand on Daneele's shoulder, he gave him a reassuring smile. "You can stand in line with the others," he said, glaring at his Council, "and well behind Keary, who enjoyed his years away too much."

The tension fled Daneele's shoulders and would have eased from Sinow's body save for the alarm that signaled five minutes had passed.

"Amazing, it works even in another world. The three of them should be..." Attention now on the portal, his words drifted off.

Something was wrong. Where it had once been a golden light, it was now a deep ebony, the inside of the portal swirling violently with crimson sparks.

"What's happening, Sinow?" Kanine asked.

He had miscalculated. Once again, Tynan was a step ahead. He hadn't been lying in wait for Sinow to arrive; he'd been lying in wait for Sinow to leave. Violissa was defenseless. Keary couldn't protect her. Her trees and flowers couldn't protect her. Not against Tynan.

The portal groaned, black mist spilling from it right before Paige came tumbling out. She scooted back like a frightened child, looking around wildly.

"Paige," Daneele said, but Cyric brought his hand out to stay the man as Sinow ran over to her. She was shaking. The Dark power that engulfed the portal had left her terrified. It amazed him that she'd even survived.

Just as he stooped down to check on her, someone yelled, "Sinow, your powers!"

Quickly granting her silent permission to look at him, he quelled the Darkness that fought to escape. It had been too long since power had filled his veins, and he'd need to adjust to controlling it again.

Grabbing Paige's arms, he forced her to look at him. She cringed, squeezing her eyes shut. "Paige, you have permission. What happened, and where is Violissa?"

She peeked her eyes open, and he saw the fear that remained. Even with permission, mortals had a difficult time looking into a Darkbearer's eyes. Few ever had permission to face the king.

"Ty…Ty…Ty." Her stammering pushed his patience, and he shook her. If Tynan had gone through the portal, he had no time to deal with her emotions.

"Get a hold of yourself, Paige. You're safe now. I need you to focus. Where is Violissa?"

She swallowed, her eyes meeting his again without reacting.

"Tynan. Tynan came through the portal. He knocked Keary out. He has Violissa."

That was all he needed to hear for every nerve in his body to strain. He dropped her arms and backed away from her, running his hands through his hair.

"Damn it." Stalking to the portal, he placed his hands on it, feeling only resistance that told him it didn't allow travel both ways. But Tynan had done it.

"Someone tell me how to turn this portal so I can go back through." His command echoed through the night, a bellowing demand.

"We don't know," Cyric responded, moving toward him. He detected movement where he'd left Paige and assumed Daneele had gone to her. "Keary said it would only go one way. I don't know how to turn it outward."

Tynan figured it out. He had always bragged that he was smarter than Sinow. Always used it as his defense for being so weak. He'd been wrong. Sinow had been wrong in seeing him as weak, and Tynan had been wrong in underestimating Sinow's intelligence.

Within the portal swam dark colors where before had only been light. Dark power. Tynan had infected the portal. That's how he had gone through.

Drawing his magic, Sinow shoved against the resistance of the portal, breaking through enough to grab a strand of black power. The foulness of it burned his skin, the tainted touch of Tynan's magic biting back at him. Releasing it, he searched the hues, seeing only crimson and black at first. With a more discerning look, he saw flickers of gray streaming through the black. His magic always had a shade of gray within the ebony. The portal must have retained some residual of it when he passed through.

Grabbing a stream, his power responded, primed for release. He let it flow from his other hand, keeping his hold on the stream of magic. The portal quivered, fighting his invasion, and he gritted his teeth as he poured more power into it.

"Come on," he said, seeing the gray strand increase in size. Still, the portal fought the invasion, intent on maintaining its purpose. Grinding both heels into the ground, he willed the portal to open. It bellowed in response to the command until a roaring burst of sound came from it and it yielded. The gray spilled over his hand, filling the portal until it had overtaken the ebony. With the change, he didn't hesitate. He threw himself into the portal, intent on saving Violissa before Tynan did something no amount of praying to the Fates could undo.

# CHAPTER 67

All attempts to draw on her magic had failed Violissa. Tynan's hold on her neck left her too incapacitated to do more than scratch at his hand.

The air stirred. Familiar warmth flooded her as the hollow void in her core filled. Sinow. The ground trembled. Over Tynan's shoulder, she saw him emerge from the portal.

"Let her go, Tynan. It's over." His smooth baritone washed over her skin.

His power tinged the air, and Tynan flipped her around quickly. Her back slammed into his chest, sending what little air remained through her narrowed throat. His hold on her neck didn't lessen, and he put his other hand around her stomach, forcing her flush against his body. Chills coursed through her as more bile searched for a way to escape.

"I wouldn't try it, brother. I'll kill her before you even reach me, and you know I'm right. Test me if you don't believe me."

Sinow hesitated, his black eyes surveying the situation. She'd forgotten how terrifyingly beautiful he was when he was at full power. His eyes, rich black, surveyed the situation. Lowering his power, his eyes fixed on her, creasing as they jumped to the hand around her neck. The sharp lines of his face and the bulging muscles in his arms revealed his mood.

"I've waited a long time for my revenge, Sinow. I had hoped you'd be stuck in this world for eternity, and I wouldn't need to bother, but this will be more rewarding."

Sinow remained silent but took a step forward. The flexing of Tynan's fingers on her throat as they tightened stopped his motion. Violissa squirmed, fighting to stay conscious as her sight turned hazy. Power rippled through Sinow's muscles, anger flashing in his eyes. Safety, security. That's what she experienced when she looked at him. She wanted to be safe, to be out of Tynan's grip and back in Sinow's arms.

They'd been so close to having their happy ending, but now Tynan was stealing it again. Just like he had when they were younger. Fury surfaced in her, spreading to encompass the fear so that only her rage at Tynan remained. And with the emotion, she sensed the magic that was an intrinsic part of her. It leaped from deep within her, ready to strike back at the man who continued to ruin everything. Latching onto it, she dropped her hand to her side and reached out again to the natural world.

"You see," Tynan continued as Sinow's sight flicked to her. "I had intended to kill her and be done with her." He ran his finger down her cheek, cutting the skin with magic. She winced but refused to give him the satisfaction of hearing her cry out. Instead, she held onto the pain and let it feed the angst. He caught the blood that dripped from the fresh wound and held it up for Sinow to see. "She is mortal, after all."

Power swirled around Sinow, spilling out to the ground in stormy tendrils waiting to be used, but Tynan had him trapped. Violissa knew he could do nothing without hurting or even killing her. With the grip on her neck, Tynan would break it before Sinow's magic even reached him. And he wouldn't risk hurting her. His eyes reflected the conflicted emotions going through his mind.

"You don't want her, Tynan. It's me you want to fight. I'm the one you hate. Let her go and fight me. Brother to brother," Sinow said, taking a step closer.

"Tempting offer. I could kill you now and keep her for myself." He ran his hand down the front of her dress, and she almost lost her concentration with the unpleasant sensation. Sinow shifted his weight. His piercing orbs were so narrowed, there was no doubt in that look that he would tear Tynan to pieces if given the chance. "I've taken a liking to Cirillian women. They squirm much less, and they're softer than our women. Pity they all die, though. I'd sure like to keep one as a pet. You won't fight me, will you, Violissa?"

A growl, feral and protective, came from Sinow, and his power snapped in angry tendrils along the ground.

The connection to Violissa's power dimmed as she bucked in Tynan's arms.

"I will fight you if I don't kill you first." The words were a hoarse rasp, and she doubted he could even understand them, but she'd made her point.

"Ah, ah, ah," Tynan said in response to Sinow's more effective show of emotion. "We seem to be at a standstill, brother."

"Then let her go," replied Sinow through bared teeth.

Violissa dug back into her magic. She'd been so close to finding it before Tynan had touched her. Reaching back out, she pushed further, sensing the tie to the land. She closed her eyes, tuning out their argument, and let her innate powers flow outward. The sensation of tree roots waking let her know they were there to do her bidding.

Her eyes flashed open and met Sinow's. Understanding passed through them, and she imagined her irises had turned another shade of green as what little power she had listened for her command. His power drew closer to him, circling like a predator awaiting her signal.

Tynan continued to talk, oblivious to their exchange and the nature magic poised below his feet. "No, I think I'll just kill her and be done with it."

He moved his fist, tightening his grip, and crushing her windpipe. He wasn't opting for a quick kill. He wanted Sinow to watch her death. To revel in breaking his brother with the sight. Horror sank into Violissa at the thought.

Taking her pain and anger, she folded it around her magic and sent her command through it. Nature reacted. The ground under them reared up, throwing them off balance. Tynan's grip loosened, and she gasped for breath while ordering the ground to continue its attack on him. Roots tore from below and encased Tynan, who released her in his surprise. The roots dragged him down just as the ground opened behind them. Sinow raised his hand to attack, and she leaped out of the way. A bolt of magic hit Tynan in the chest and sent him flying into the opening, which Violissa sealed, instructing the roots to keep him restrained.

Power, familiar and safe, curled around her and brought her to Sinow. His arm curved around her waist as he sent his magic at Keary and released him from Tynan's spell.

Keary scrambled over to him. "Nice to see you back," he said with a grunt.

"We don't have time for greetings. Get in the damned portal," Sinow snarled.

He scooped Violissa into his arms, and she didn't argue. Not when the ground bucked below their feet. She clung to his neck, embracing the strength of his arms around her. Pressing her head against him as the darkness of the portal swallowed them, she breathed in the scent of Dark power. Ash and thunderstorms. It calmed her as they fell through the portal.

A disturbance shook the portal, the air growing heavy in the void that surrounded them. Tynan had escaped his temporary prison and had entered behind them. Sinow must have sensed it as well, for he held her tighter as they slammed through the portal gateway into their world. He landed on his feet, knees bent from the force, then straightened and let her legs down, never fully letting go of her body as he pushed her behind him and swiveled to face the portal.

It pulsated rapidly, swelling out until something smashed into it. Fractures formed, but the portal didn't give. Sinow's hand gripped her body, keeping her behind his wall of muscle as they stared at the portal. The gateway warped, twisting and churning. Tynan's face pressed against it, stretching the magic, straining in a mask of black and red, but the portal refused to grant him access. Sinow's power flared in defense of what was coming at them, but something tugged Tynan back.

The portal began swirling again, the colors bleeding softer until they returned to a bright golden color. A howl of anger broke from the portal, but Tynan never emerged. The swirling hastened, drawing the light in until, with an explosion of color, the portal disappeared. Sparkles of gold drifted down around them as the Fates' magic dissipated.

The tension sagged from Sinow, and he spun Violissa around, touching her face and neck. "Are you hurt?" he asked, searching for wounds.

"No, I'm fine," she answered, taking his face in her hands. "That's twice you've returned for me."

"I will always come for you, Violissa."

She reached up and kissed him, leaning against his body, her knees still weak. His hand ran along her face but stopped when he reached the wound on her cheek. Drawing his lips from hers, he pulled his hand back. Even in the darkness, she could see the drop of blood resting on his fingertip. Bringing her hand up to her cheek, she touched the cut Tynan had given her. Sinow tilted her neck and looked more closely at it. His fingers draped over the place where Tynan had held her, and she winced at the tenderness on her skin.

"Bruised," he stated, crinkles forming around his eyes. He lifted them, understanding passing through them.

They left the words unspoken. The truth her bruises revealed. The marks on her flesh that should have healed the moment she returned to their world. And the emptiness that sat in her core, reminding her of the power she'd once held.

She gave him a small smile, the most she could form with the reality that now hung over her. "Maybe it will take me longer?"

"Maybe," he said, the sadness in his eyes causing her chest to ache.

She pulled him close and kissed him again, only this time he held her tighter, as if every kiss they had going forward needed to be cherished. And she thought maybe they should, whether they had all of eternity or only a few decades. They had been through so much to get to this point—the journey painful and heartbreaking —so they would cherish every kiss, every touch, every look, every moment.

In his kiss, she tasted his fear, his relief, his sadness, his hope, his need for her. All of it poured through, and she soaked it in, letting it spill through into her soul. She never wanted to let him go, but as a booming shook the air, she pulled back and looked up. She could see nothing, but if they were in the Banished Realm, the barrier protected them.

"The barrier?" she whispered.

"Tynan. He made it back through." He leaned his forehead on hers momentarily, and she brought her hands up to hold his face, knowing their battle was only beginning.

A cough behind them caused her to drop her hands.

"We're not alone, are we?" she asked him, looking into those expressive black-brown eyes she loved so much.

He chuckled and took her hand. "No, we're not." Leaning closer, he kissed her ear and whispered, "Welcome home, my queen."

Home. Centuries before, a spell had torn her from her home. Now she was back, but she feared what awaited her, knowing their world was no longer what they'd left behind.

Violissa turned around, staying close to Sinow as she clutched his hand. Torches lit the surrounding area, the moons above peeking out as the clouds shifted over them. It took her eyes a moment to adjust before she could truly see what lay before them.

Closest to them stood two groups of old men, a familiarity about them. Paige stood on one side, Keary on the other. Heart racing, she took in the crowd of people in the distance, their people, Tenebron and Cirillian, standing together behind them, spread as far as the eye could see. She brought her hand to her chest as she watched them move to their knees, heads bowed in deference.

"We're home," she said, tears welling.

Sinow squeezed her hand in silent agreement. It wasn't the same home they had left when this journey had begun centuries before, but they were one step closer to taking their lives back. This was only the beginning. The Fates still had plans for them. The path back to their happy ending was still far from where the prophecy would have led them if a whimsical princess hadn't made a foolish decision and a cocky prince hadn't let her. If the next part of their journey was just as long and heartbreaking as the last, she knew they would endure.

They had each other now. Their love had endured a thousand years of misery. It could face a thousand more. It had to. Otherwise, she didn't know how she would survive what waited around the bend, poised to crush her once again.

Violissa and Sinow's path continues in Surfacing, where the Fates will test their love once again. Coming January 2026.

---

Thank you for reading Descent. If you enjoyed the story, please consider leaving a review. Reviews are like rare gems to authors like me.

# ABOUT THE AUTHOR

J. L. Jackola is a writer of love stories with fantasy, darkness, feisty women, and morally gray men. She's an admitted sugar addict with a penchant for anything with salted caramel. When she's not weaving tales, snacking on sweets, or downing her morning cup of tea, you can find her logging miles in her running shoes, watching movies with her family, or curled up with a book.

She resides in Delaware with her husband and three children.

Visit her at www.jljackola.com and be sure to sign up for J L's newsletter to keep up with all the latest release news.